Acclaim for *Kingdom of the Blind* by Louise Penny

"Penny pulls together an insightful plot that weaves in family feuds, clandestine investigations, undercover cops, and a loving look at Three Pines." —Oline Cogdill, *South Florida Sun Sentinel*

"Louise Penny's novels are unique for how seamlessly they straddle the line between charmingly small-town mysteries and big-city police procedurals. . . . It's not to be missed!" —*BookPage* (Top Pick)

"It's hard to see how Louise Penny can raise the stakes any further for her iconic, fatherly good guy, Chief Inspector Armand Gamache, but somehow in each book she does." —*The News & Observer* (Raleigh)

"Brain-teasing puzzles, life-and-death stakes, and lots of Three Pines, a magical place where the warmth in the villagers' hearts thaws the ice on their eyelashes." —*St. Louis Post-Dispatch*

"Complex ongoing saga . . . Wait anxiously for the next installment." —*Pittsburgh Post-Gazette*

"Penny does a splendid job of interweaving those three main plot lines, studding them with several life-threatening scenes that had me holding my breath, and building to a wild finale." —*Tampa Bay Times*

"Nimble sleight-of-hand plotting, strong characters, profound compassion, and luminous prose are hallmarks of Penny's novels. Although darker than previous books, this new entry is no exception." —Adam Woog, *The Seattle Times*

LOUISE PENNY

~

KINGDOM
OF THE
BLIND

MINOTAUR BOOKS
NEW YORK

KINGDOM OF THE BLIND. Copyright © 2018 by Three Pines Creations, Inc. All rights reserved. Printed in the United States of America. For information, address St. Martin's Press, 175 Fifth Avenue, New York, N.Y. 10010.

www.minotaurbooks.com

The Library of Congress has cataloged the hardcover edition as follows:

Names: Penny, Louise, author.
Title: Kingdom of the blind / Louise Penny.
Description: First U.S. Edition. First international edition. | New York : Minotaur Books, 2018. | Series: A Chief Inspector Gamache novel
Identifiers: LCCN 2018022773 | ISBN 9781250066206 (hardcover) | ISBN 9781250313522 (international, sold outside the U.S., subject to rights availability) | ISBN 9781466873698 (ebook)
Subjects: LCSH: Gamache, Armand (Fictitious character)—Fiction. | GSAFD: Mystery fiction.
Classification: LCC PR9199. 4. P464 K56 2018 | DDC 813/.6—dc23
LC record available at https://lccn.loc.gov/2018022773

ISBN 978-1-250-06630-5 (trade paperback)

Our books may be purchased in bulk for promotional, educational, or business use. Please contact your local bookseller or the Macmillan Corporate and Premium Sales Department at 1-800-221-7945, extension 5442, or by email at MacmillanSpecialMarkets@macmillan.com.

First Minotaur Books Paperback Edition: June 2019

10 9 8 7 6 5 4 3 2 1

For Hope Dellon, my editor and friend.
Whale oil beef hooked.

CHAPTER 1

—

Armand Gamache slowed his car to a crawl, then stopped on the snow-covered secondary road.

This was it, he supposed. Pulling in, he drove between the tall pine trees until he reached the clearing.

There he parked the car and sat in the warm vehicle looking out at the cold day. Snow flurries were hitting the windshield and dissolving. They were coming down with more force now, slightly obscuring what he saw outside. Turning away, he stared at the letter he'd received the day before, lying open on the passenger seat.

Putting on his reading glasses, he rubbed his face. And read it again. It was an invitation of sorts, to this desolate place.

He turned off the car. But didn't get out.

There was no particular anxiety. It was more puzzling than worrisome.

But still, it was just odd enough to raise a small alarm. Not a siren, yet. But he was alert.

Armand Gamache was not by nature timid, but he was a cautious man. How else could he have survived in the top echelons of the Sûreté du Québec? Though it was far from certain that he had survived.

He relied on, and trusted, both his rational mind and his instincts.

And what were they telling him now?

They were certainly telling him this was strange. But then, he thought with a grin, his grandchildren could have told him that.

Bringing out his cell phone, he listened as the number he called rang once, twice, and then was answered.

"*Salut, ma belle*. I'm here," he said.

It was an agreement between Armand and his wife, Reine-Marie, that in winter, in snow, they called each other when they'd arrived at a destination.

"How was the drive? The snow seems to be getting worse in Three Pines."

"Here too. Drive was easy."

"So where are you? What is the place, Armand?"

"It's sort of hard to describe."

But he tried.

What he saw had once been a home. Then a house. And was now simply a building. And not even that for much longer.

"It's an old farmhouse," he said. "But it looks abandoned."

"Are you sure you're at the right place? Remember when you came to get me at my brother's home and you went to the wrong brother? Insisting I was there."

"That was years ago," he said. "And all the houses look alike in Ste.-Angélique, and, honestly, all your hundred and fifty-seven brothers look alike. Besides, he didn't like me, and I was fairly sure he just wanted me to go away and leave you alone."

"Can you blame him? You were at the wrong house. Some detective."

Armand laughed. That had been decades ago, when they were first courting. Her family had since warmed to him, once they saw how much she loved him and, more important to them, how much he loved Reine-Marie.

"I'm at the right place. There's another car here."

Light snow covered the other vehicle. It had been there, he guessed, for about half an hour. Not more. Then his eyes returned to the farmhouse.

"It's been a while since anyone lived here."

It took a long time to fall into such a state. Lack of care, over the years, would do that.

It was now little more than a collection of materials.

The shutters were askew, the wooden handrail had rotted and gone its separate way from the sloping steps. One of the upper windows was boarded up, so that it looked like the place was winking at him. As though it knew something he did not.

2

He cocked his head. Was there a slight lean to the house? Or was his imagination turning this into one of Honoré's nursery rhymes?

> *There was a crooked man, and he walked a crooked mile,*
> *He found a crooked sixpence against a crooked stile;*
> *He bought a crooked cat, which caught a crooked mouse,*
> *And they all lived together in a little crooked house.*

This was a crooked house. And Armand Gamache wondered if, inside, he'd find a crooked man.

After saying goodbye to Reine-Marie, he looked again at the other car in the yard, and the license plate with the motto of Québec stamped on it: JE ME SOUVIENS.

I remember.

When he closed his eyes, as he did now, images appeared uninvited. As vivid, as intense as the moment they'd happened. And not only the day last summer, with the slanting shafts of cheerful sunlight hitting the blood on his hands.

He saw all the days. All the nights. All the blood. His own, and others'. People whose lives he'd saved. And those he'd taken.

But to keep his sanity, his humanity, his equilibrium, he needed to recall the wonderful events as well.

Finding Reine-Marie. Having their son and daughter. Now grandchildren.

Finding their refuge in Three Pines. The quiet moments with friends. The joyful celebrations.

The father of a good friend had developed dementia and died recently. For the last year or so of his life, he no longer recognized family and friends. He was kindly to all, but he beamed at some. They were the ones he loved. He knew them instinctively and kept them safe, not in his wounded head but in his heart.

The memory of the heart was far stronger than whatever was kept in the mind. The question was, what did people keep in their heart?

Chief Superintendent Gamache had known more than a few people whose heart had been consumed by hate.

He looked at the crooked house in front of him and wondered what memory was consuming it.

3

After instinctively committing the license-plate number to memory, he scanned the yard.

It was dotted with large mounds of snow, under which, Gamache guessed, were rusted vehicles. A pickup picked apart. An old tractor now scrap. And something that looked like a tank but was probably an old oil tank and not a tank tank.

He hoped.

Gamache put on his tuque and was about to put on gloves when he hesitated and picked up the letter yet again. There wasn't much to it. Just a couple of clipped sentences.

Far from being threatening, they were almost comical and would've been had they not been written by a dead man.

It was from a notary, asking, almost demanding, that Gamache present himself at this remote farmhouse at 10:00 a.m. Sharp. Please. Don't be late. *Merci.*

He'd looked up the notary in the Chambre des Notaires du Québec.

Maître Laurence Mercier.

He'd died of cancer six months earlier.

And yet— Here was a letter from him.

There was no email or return address, but there was a phone number, which Armand had called but no one had answered.

He'd been tempted to look up Maître Mercier in the Sûreté database but decided against it. It wasn't that Gamache was persona non grata at the Sûreté du Québec. Not exactly, anyway. Now on suspension pending the outcome of an investigation into events last summer, he felt he needed to be judicious in the favors he asked of colleagues. Even Jean-Guy Beauvoir. His second-in-command. His son-in-law.

Gamache looked again at the once-strong house and smiled. Feeling a kinship toward it.

Things sometimes fell apart unexpectedly. It was not necessarily a reflection of how much they were valued.

He folded the letter and placed it in his breast pocket. Just as he was leaving the car, his cell phone rang.

Gamache looked at the number. Stared at the number. Any sign of amusement wiped from his face.

Dare he take it?

Dare he not?

As the ringing continued, he stared out the windshield, his view obscured by the now-heavy snow, so that he saw the world imperfectly.

He wondered if, in future, whenever he saw an old farmhouse, or heard the soft tapping of snowflakes, or smelled damp wool, this moment would be conjured and, if so, would it be with a sense of relief or horror?

"*Oui, allô?*"

The man stood by the window, straining to see out.

It was distorted by frost, but he had seen the car arrive and had watched, with impatience, as the man parked, then just sat there.

After a minute or so, the new arrival got out but didn't come toward the house. He was standing beside his car, a cell phone to his ear.

This was the first of *les invités*.

The man recognized this first guest, of course. Who wouldn't? He'd seen him often enough, but only in news reports. Never in person.

And he'd been far from convinced this guest would show up.

Armand Gamache. The former head of homicide. The current Chief Superintendent of the Sûreté du Québec, on suspension.

He felt a slight frisson of excitement. Here was a celebrity of sorts. A man both highly respected and reviled. Some in the press held him up as a hero. Others as a villain. Representing the worst aspects of policing. Or the best. The abuse of power. Or a daring leader, willing to sacrifice his own reputation, and perhaps more, for the greater good.

To do what no one else wanted to do. Or could do.

Through the distorted glass, through the snow, he saw a man in his late fifties. Tall, six feet at least. And substantial. The parka made him look heavy, but parkas made everyone look heavy. The face, not pudgy, was, however, worn. With lines from his eyes, and, as he watched, two deep furrows formed between Gamache's brows.

He was not good at understanding the faces faces made. He saw the lines but couldn't read them. He thought Gamache was angry, but it could have been simply concentration. Or surprise. He supposed it could even have been joy.

But he doubted that.

It was snowing more heavily now, but Gamache had not put on his gloves. They'd fallen to the ground when he'd gotten out of the car. It was how most Québécois lost mitts and gloves and even hats. They rested on laps in the car and were forgotten when it came time to get out. In spring the land was littered with dog shit, worms, and sodden mitts and gloves and tuques.

Armand Gamache stood in the falling snow, his bare hand to his ear. Gripping a phone and listening.

And when it was his turn to talk, Gamache bowed his head, his knuckles white as he tightened his hold on the phone, or from incipient frostbite. Then, taking a few steps away from his car, he turned his back to the wind and snow, and he spoke.

The man couldn't hear what was being said, but then one phrase caught a gust and made its way across the snowy yard, past possessions once prized. And into the house. Once prized.

"You'll regret this."

And then some other movement caught his attention. Another car was pulling in to the yard.

The second of *les invités*.

CHAPTER 2

———

"Armand?"

The smile of recognition and slight relief froze on her face as she took in his expression.

His movement as he'd turned to face her had been almost violent. His body tense, prepared. As though bracing for a possible attack.

While she was adept at reading faces and understood body language, she could not quite get the expression on his face. Except for the most obvious.

Surprise.

But there was more there. Far more.

And then it was gone. His body relaxed, and as she watched, Armand spoke a single word into his phone, tapped on it, then put it into his pocket.

The last expression to leave that familiar face, before the veneer of civility covered it completely, was something that surprised her even more.

Guilt.

And then the smile appeared.

"For God's sake, Myrna. What're you doing here?"

Armand tried to modulate his smile, though it was difficult. His face was numb, almost frozen.

He didn't want to look like a grinning fool, overdoing it. Giving himself away to this very astute woman. Who was also a neighbor.

A retired psychologist, Myrna Landers owned the bookstore in Three Pines and had become good friends with Reine-Marie and Armand.

He suspected she'd seen, and understood, his initial reaction. Though he also suspected she would not grasp the depth of it. Or ever guess who he'd been speaking with.

He had been so engrossed in his conversation. In choosing his words. In listening so closely to the words being spoken to him. And the tone. And modulating his own tone. That he'd allowed someone to sneak up on him.

Granted, it was a friend. But it could just as easily have not been a friend.

As a cadet, as a Sûreté agent. As an inspector. As head of homicide, then head of the whole force, he'd had to be alert. Trained himself to be alert, so that it became second nature. First nature.

It's not that he walked through life expecting something bad to happen. His vigilance had simply become part of who he was, like his eye color. Like his scars.

Part DNA, part a consequence of his life.

Armand knew that the problem wasn't that he'd let his guard down just now. Just the opposite. It had been up so high, so thick, that for a few crucial minutes nothing else penetrated. He'd missed hearing the car approach. He'd missed the soft tread of boots on snow.

Gamache, not a fearful man, felt a small lick of concern. This time the consequences were benign. But next?

The threat didn't have to be monumental. If it were, it wouldn't be missed. It was almost always something tiny.

A signal missed or misunderstood. A blind spot. A moment of distraction. A focus so sharp that everything around it blurred. A false assumption mistaken for fact.

And then—

"You okay?" Myrna Landers asked as Armand approached and kissed her on both cheeks.

"I'm fine."

She could feel the cold on his face and the damp from the snow that had hit and melted. And she could feel the tension in the man, rumbling below the cheerful surface.

His smile created deep lines from the corners of his eyes. But it did not actually reach those brown eyes. They remained sharp, wary. Watchful. Though the warmth was still there.

"Fine," he'd said, and despite her disquiet she smiled.

They both understood that code. It was a reference to their neighbor in the village of Three Pines. Ruth Zardo. A gifted poet. One of the most distinguished in the nation. But that gift had come wrapped in more than a dollop of crazy. The name Ruth Zardo was uttered with equal parts admiration and dread. Like conjuring a magical creature that was both creative and destructive.

Ruth's last book of poetry was called *I'm FINE*. Which sounded good until you realized, often too late, that "F.I.N.E." stood for "Fucked-Up, Insecure, Neurotic, and Egotistical."

Yes, Ruth Zardo was many things. Fortunately for them, one of the things she was not was there.

Armand stooped and picked up the mitts that had fallen off Myrna's substantial lap, into the snow. He whacked them against his parka before handing them back to her. Then, realizing he was also missing his own, he went to his car and found them almost buried in the new snow.

The man watched all this from the questionable protection of the house.

He'd never met the woman who'd just arrived, but already he didn't like her. She was large and black and a "she." None of those things he found attractive. But worse still, Myrna Landers had arrived five minutes late, and instead of hurrying inside, spouting apologies, she was standing around chatting. As though he weren't waiting for them. As though he hadn't been clear about the time of the appointment.

Which he had.

Though his annoyance was slightly mitigated by relief that she'd shown up at all.

He watched the two of them closely. It was a game he played. Watching. Trying to guess what people might do next.

He was almost always wrong.

9

Both Myrna and Armand pulled the letters from their pockets.

They compared them. Exactly the same.

"This is"—she looked around—"a bit odd, don't you think?"

He nodded and followed her eyes to the ramshackle house.

"Do you know these people?" he asked.

"What people?"

"Well, whoever lives here. Lived here."

"No. You?"

"*Non*. I haven't a clue who they are or why we're here."

"I called the number," said Myrna. "But there was no answer. No way to get in touch with this Laurence Mercier. He's a notary. Do you know him?"

"*Non*. But I do know one thing."

"What?" Myrna could tell that something unpleasant was about to come her way.

"He died six months ago. Cancer."

"Then what—"

She had no idea how to continue, and so stopped. She looked over at the house, then turned to Armand. She was almost his height, and while her parka made her look heavy, in her case it was no illusion.

"You knew that the guy who sent you the letter died months ago, and still you came," she said. "Why?"

"Curiosity," he said. "You?"

"Well, I didn't know he was dead."

"But you did know it was strange. So why did you come?"

"Same. Curiosity. What's the worst that could happen?"

It was, even Myrna recognized, a fairly stupid thing to say.

"If we start hearing organ music, Armand, we run. Right?"

He laughed. He, of course, knew the worst that could happen. He'd knelt beside it hundreds of times.

Myrna tipped her head back to stare at the roof, sagging under the weight of months of snow. She saw the cracked and missing windows and blinked as snowflakes, large and gentle and relentless, landed on her face and fell into her eyes.

"It's not really dangerous, is it?" she asked.

"I doubt it."

"Doubt?" Her eyes widened slightly. "There is a chance?"

"I think the only danger will come from the building itself," he nodded to the slumping roof and sloping walls, "and not from whoever is inside."

They'd walked over, and now he put his foot on the first step and it broke. He raised his brows at her, and she smiled.

"I think that's more the amount of croissants than the amount of wood rot," she said, and he laughed.

"I agree."

He paused for a moment, looking at the steps, then the house.

"You're not sure if it's dangerous, are you?" she said. "Either the house or whoever's inside."

"*Non*," he admitted. "I'm not sure. Would you prefer to wait out here?"

Yes, she thought.

"No," she said, and followed him in.

"Maître Mercier." The man introduced himself, walking forward, his hand extended.

"*Bonjour*," said Gamache, who'd gone in first. "Armand Gamache."

He swiftly took in his surroundings, beginning with the man.

Short, slight, white. In his mid-forties.

Alive.

The electricity had been turned off in the house and with it the heat, leaving the air cold and stale. Like a walk-in freezer.

The notary had kept his coat on, and Armand could see it was smudged with dirt. Though Armand's was too. It was near impossible to get into and out of a vehicle in a Québec winter without getting smeared by dirt and salt.

But Maître Mercier's coat wasn't just dirty, it was stained. And worn.

There was an air of neglect about him. The man, like his clothing, appeared threadbare. But there was also a dignity there, bordering on haughtiness.

"Myrna Landers," said Myrna, stepping forward and offering her hand.

Maître Mercier took it but dropped it quickly. More a touch than a handshake.

Gamache noticed that Myrna's attitude had changed slightly. No longer fearful, she looked at their host with what appeared to be pity.

There were some creatures who naturally evoked that reaction. Not given armor, or a poison bite, or the ability to fly or even run, what they had was equally powerful.

The ability to look so helpless, so pathetic, that they could not possibly be a threat. Some even adopted them. Protected them. Nurtured them. Took them in.

And almost always regretted it.

It was far too early to tell if Maître Mercier was just such a creature, but he did have that immediate effect, even on someone as experienced and astute as Myrna Landers.

Even on himself, Gamache realized. He could feel his defenses lowering in the presence of this sad little man.

Though they did not drop completely.

Gamache took off his tuque and, smoothing his graying hair, he looked around.

The outside door opened directly into the kitchen, as they often did in farmhouses. It looked unchanged since the sixties. Maybe even fifties. The cabinets were made of plywood painted a cheery blue the color of cornflowers, the counters of chipped yellow laminate and the floors of scuffed linoleum.

Anything of value had been taken. The appliances were gone, the walls were stripped clean except for a mint-green clock above the sink, that had long since stopped.

For a moment he imagined the room as it might once have been. Shiny, not new but clean and cared for. People moving about, preparing a Thanksgiving or Christmas dinner. Children chasing one another around like wild colts, with parents trying to tame them. Then giving up.

He noticed lines on the doorjamb. Marking heights. Before time had stopped.

Yes, he thought, this room, this home, was happy once. Cheerful once.

He looked again at their host. The notary who did and did not exist.

Had this been his home? Had he been happy, cheerful, once? If so, there was no sign of it. It had all been stripped away.

Maître Mercier motioned to the kitchen table, inviting them to sit. Which they did.

"Before we begin, I'd like you to sign this."

Mercier pushed a piece of paper toward Gamache.

Armand leaned back in his chair, away from the paper. "Before we begin," he said, "I'd like to know who you are and why we're here."

"So would I," said Myrna.

"In due course," said Mercier.

It was such a strange thing to say, both as a formal and dated turn of phrase and in its complete dismissal of their request. A not-unreasonable request either, from people who didn't have to be there.

Mercier looked and sounded like a character from Dickens. And not the hero. Gamache wondered if Myrna felt the same way.

The notary placed a pen on the paper and nodded to Gamache, who did not pick it up.

"Listen," said Myrna, laying a large hand on Mercier's and feeling him spasm. "Dear." Her voice was calm, warm, clear. "You tell us now or I'm leaving. And I'm assuming you don't want that."

Gamache pushed the paper back across the table toward the notary.

Myrna patted Mercier's hand, and Mercier stared back at her.

"Now," she said. "How did you rise from the dead?"

Mercier looked at her like she was the crazy one, then his eyes shifted, and both Gamache and Myrna turned to follow his gaze out the window.

Another vehicle had pulled up. A pickup truck. And out hopped a young man, his mitts falling into the snow. But he swiftly stooped and picked them up.

Armand caught Myrna's eye.

The newest arrival wore a long red-and-white-striped hat. So long that it tapered to a pom-pommed tail that trailed down his back and dragged in the snow as he stepped away from his truck.

Noticing this, the young man lifted the end of the tuque and wrapped it once around his neck like a scarf before tossing it over his shoulder in a move so rakish that Myrna found herself smiling.

Whoever this was, he was as vibrant as their dead host was desiccated.

Dr. Seuss meets Charles Dickens.

The Cat in the Hat was about to enter Bleak House.

There was a knock on the door, then he walked in. Looking around, his eyes fell on Gamache, who'd gotten to his feet.

"*Allô, bonjour,*" said the cheerful young man. "Monsieur Mercier?"

He put out his hand. Gamache took it.

"*Non.* Armand Gamache."

They shook hands. The newcomer's hand was callused, strong. His grip was firm and friendly. A confident handshake without being forced.

"Benedict Pouliot. *Salut.* Hope I'm not late. Traffic over the bridge was awful."

"This is Maître Mercier," said Armand, stepping aside to reveal the notary.

"Hello, sir," said the young man, shaking the notary's hand.

"And I'm Myrna Landers," said Myrna, shaking his hand and smiling, Armand thought, just a little too broadly.

Though it was hard not to smile at the handsome young man. Not that he was laughable. But he was affable and almost completely without affectation. His eyes were thoughtful and bright.

Benedict took off his hat and smoothed his blond hair, which was cut in a fashion Myrna had never seen before and hoped never to see again. It was buzz-cut short on the top then, at his ears, it became long. Very long.

"So," he said, rubbing his hands together in anticipation and perhaps because it was so cold. "Where do we begin?"

They all looked at Mercier, who continued to stare at Benedict.

"It's the haircut, isn't it?" said the young man. "My girlfriend did it. She's taking a stylist course, and the final exam is to create a new cut. What do you think?"

He ran his hands through it as the others remained silent.

"Looks great," said Myrna, confirming for Armand that love, or infatuation, was indeed blind.

"Did she also make your hat?" Armand asked, pointing to what was now a large red-and-white lump of wet wool at the end of the table.

"Yes. Final marks in her design class. Do you like it?"

Armand gave what he hoped might be a noncommittal grunt.

"You sent the letter, didn't you, sir?" Benedict said to Mercier. "Now, do you want to show me around first, or should we look at plans? Is this your house?" he asked Armand and Myrna. "To be honest, I'm not sure it can be saved. It's in pretty rough shape."

Gamache and Myrna looked at each other and realized what he was saying.

"We're not together," said Myrna, laughing. "Like you, we were invited here by Maître Mercier."

She brought out her letter, as did Armand, and they placed them on the table.

Benedict bent over, then straightened up. "I'm confused. I thought I was here to bid on a job."

He put his own letter on the table. It was, except for his name and address, identical to the other two.

"What do you do?" Myrna asked, and Benedict handed her one of his cards.

It was bloodred and diamond shaped, with something unreadable embossed.

"Your girlfriend?" asked Myrna.

"Yes. Her business class."

"Final marks?"

"*Oui.*"

Myrna handed it to Gamache, who had to put on his reading glasses and tip the card toward the window to have any hope of reading the bumps.

"'Benedict Pouliot. Builder,'" he read out loud, then turned it over. "There's no phone number or email."

"No. Marks were deducted. So am I here to bid on a job?"

"No," said Mercier. "Sit."

Benedict sat.

More like a puppy than a cat, really, thought Gamache as he took the seat next to Benedict.

"Then why am I here?" Benedict asked.

"We want to know too," said Myrna, ripping her eyes off Benedict and directing them back to the notary.

15

CHAPTER 3

—⁓—

"State your name, please."

"You know my name, Marie," said Jean-Guy. "We've worked together for years."

"Please, sir," she said, her voice pleasant but firm.

Jean-Guy stared at her, then at the two other officers assembled in the boardroom.

"Jean-Guy Beauvoir."

"Rank?"

He gave her a filthy look now, but she just held his stare.

"Acting head of homicide for the Sûreté du Québec."

"*Merci.*"

The inspector gazed at the laptop in front of her, then back at him.

"This isn't about you, you'll be happy to hear." She smiled, but he did not. "Your suspension was lifted several months ago. But we still have serious questions about the decisions and actions of Monsieur Gamache."

"Chief Superintendent Gamache," said Beauvoir. "And how can you still have questions? You've asked, and he's answered, every possible question. You must've cleared him by now? It's been almost six months. Come on. Enough."

Again he looked at who he thought were his colleagues. Then back at her. His gaze becoming less hostile and more baffled.

"What is this?"

Jean-Guy had been in many such interviews and had felt confident he could control the situation, knowing they were all on the same side.

But as they stared at him from the other side of the table, he realized his mistake.

He'd entered the room expecting this would just be a formality. A last interview before, like him, the Chief was exonerated and returned to work.

The atmosphere had indeed been convivial, almost jovial. At first.

Beauvoir was sure they'd tell him that a sternly worded statement was being drafted, explaining that a rigorous investigation had been held. It would lament the fact that the covert Sûreté operation in the summer had ended with such bloodshed.

But it would, ultimately, voice support for the unconventional and bold decisions taken by Chief Superintendent Gamache. And unwavering support for the Sûreté team involved in what turned out to be a wildly successful action. A commendation would be given to Isabelle Lacoste, the head of homicide, whose actions had saved so many lives but who'd paid so high a price.

It would end there.

Chief Superintendent Gamache would go back to work, and all would return to normal.

Though the fact an investigation that had begun in the summer was still going on in the depth of the Québec winter was disconcerting.

"You were second-in-command to your father-in-law when decisions were taken leading to the action we're investigating?" the inspector asked.

"I was with Chief Superintendent Gamache, yes. You know that."

"*Oui*. Your father-in-law."

"My boss."

"Yes. The person responsible for what happened. We all know that, Chief Inspector, but thank you for clarifying."

The others nodded. Sympathetically. Understanding the delicate position Beauvoir found himself in.

They were, Beauvoir realized with some surprise, inviting him to distance himself from Gamache.

It would be easier to distance himself from his hands and feet. His position was not at all delicate. It was, in fact, firm. He stood with Gamache.

But he was beginning to get a sick feeling deep in his gut.

"Neither of us is guilty, *mon vieux*," Gamache had said months earlier, when the inevitable investigation had begun. "You know that. These are just questions that need to be asked after what happened. There's nothing to worry about."

Not guilty, his father-in-law had said. What he didn't say was that they were innocent. Which, of course, they were not.

Jean-Guy Beauvoir had been cleared and had accepted the post as acting head of homicide.

But Chief Superintendent Gamache remained on suspension. Though Beauvoir had been confident that was about to end.

"One last meeting," he'd said to his wife that morning as they fed their son, "and your father will be cleared."

"Uh-huh," said Annie.

"What?"

He knew his wife well. Despite the fact she was a lawyer, a less cynical person would be hard to find. And yet he could tell there was doubt there.

"It's taken so long. I'm just worried it's become political. They need a scapegoat. Dad let a ton of opioids through his hands. Drugs he could've stopped. Someone has to be blamed."

"But he's got most of it back. And he had no choice. Really." He stood up and kissed her. "And it wasn't quite a ton."

A clump of oatmeal Honoré had flung hit Jean-Guy's cheek, then dropped onto the top of Annie's head.

Picking the glop out of her hair, Jean-Guy looked at it, then put it into his mouth.

"You'd have made a great gorilla," said Annie.

Jean-Guy started searching her scalp, aping a gorilla grooming its mate, while Annie laughed and Honoré flung more oatmeal.

Jean-Guy supposed he knew that Annie would never be the most beautiful woman in any room. A stranger wouldn't look at her twice.

But if one did, he might discover something it had taken Jean-Guy many years and one failed marriage to see. How very beautiful happiness was. And Annie Gamache radiated happiness.

She would always be, he knew with certainty, not just the most intelligent person in any room but also the most beautiful. And if anyone didn't see it, it was their loss.

He unbuckled Honoré and walked to the door with him in his arms.

"Have fun today," he said, kissing both of them.

"Just a moment," said Annie.

She took off Jean-Guy's bib, wiped his face, and said, "Be careful. I think this might be a two-holer."

"Deep *merde*?" Jean-Guy shook his head. "*Non*. This's the last of it. I think they just have to make it clear that there was a thorough investigation. And there was. But believe me, after looking at the facts, they'll be thanking your father for what he did. They'll understand that he faced a shitty choice and did what had to be done."

"Please, no swearing in front of the kid. You'd hate his first word to be 'shit,'" she said. "I agree with you. Dad had no choice. But they might not see it that way."

"Then they're blind."

"Then they're human," said Annie, taking Honoré. "And humans need a place to hide. I think they're hiding behind him. And preparing to shove Dad to the predators."

Beauvoir walked briskly to the subway and what he knew would be the final internal-affairs interview before all returned to normal.

His head was down, and he concentrated on the sidewalk and the soft, light snow hiding the ice below.

One misstep and bad things happened. A turned ankle. A wrist broken trying to break the fall. Or a fractured skull.

It was always what you couldn't see that hurt you.

And now, sitting in the interview room, Jean-Guy Beauvoir was wondering if Annie had been right and he had, in fact, missed something.

CHAPTER 4

———

"Who are you?" Gamache asked, leaning forward and staring at the man at the head of the table.

"We already know, sir," said Benedict.

He spoke slowly. Patiently. Myrna had to drop her head to hide her amusement and delight.

"He's. A. Notary." The young man all but patted Armand's hand.

"Oui, merci," said Armand. "I did just get that. But Laurence Mercier died six months ago. So who are you?"

"It says it right there," said Mercier. He pointed to the illegible signature. "Lucien Mercier. Laurence was my father."

"And are you a notary?"

"I am. I've taken over my father's practice."

In Québec, Gamache knew, notaries were more like solicitors than clerks. Doing everything from land transactions to marriage contracts.

"Why're you using his stationery?" asked Myrna. "It's misleading."

"It's economical and environmental. I hate waste. I use my father's letterhead when I'm doing business that was his. Less confusing for the clients."

"Can't say that's true," muttered Myrna.

Lucien brought four file folders from his briefcase and handed them around. "You're here because you're named in the last will of Bertha Baumgartner."

There was silence as they absorbed that, then Benedict said, "Really?" at the same time both Armand and Myrna said, "Who?"

"Bertha Baumgartner," the notary repeated. And then said the name a third time when the two older *invités* continued to stare at him.

"But I've never heard of her," said Myrna. "Have you?"

Armand thought for a moment. He met a lot of people and felt fairly certain he'd remember that name. But he was drawing a blank. It meant absolutely nothing.

Armand and Myrna turned to Benedict, whose handsome face was curious, but not more.

"You?" Myrna prompted, and he shook his head.

"Did she leave us money?" Benedict asked.

It wasn't said with greed, Gamache thought. More amazement. And yes, perhaps some hope.

"No," Mercier was happy to report, and then unhappy to see that the young man didn't seem at all disappointed.

"So why're we here?" asked Myrna.

"You're the liquidators of her estate."

"What?" said Myrna. "You're kidding."

"Liquidator? What's that?" asked Benedict.

"It's called 'executor' in most places," Mercier explained.

When Benedict continued to look confused, Armand explained. "It means Bertha Baumgartner wants us to oversee her will. Make sure her wishes are carried out."

"So she's dead?" asked Benedict.

Armand was about to say yes. That much seemed obvious. But "dead" had already proved less than obvious that day, so perhaps Madame Baumgartner . . .

He turned to the notary for confirmation.

"*Oui*. She died just over a month ago."

"And she was living here until then?" asked Myrna, looking up at the sagging ceiling and calculating how long it would take to get out the door if the sag became a collapse. Or maybe she could just fling herself through the window.

Between the new snow and the fact she was made almost entirely of gummy bears, it would probably be a soft landing.

"No, she was in a seniors' home," said Mercier.

"So is it like jury duty?" asked Benedict.

"*Pardon?*" asked the notary.

"You know, people whose names just come up. Our civic duty, that sort of thing. To be . . . what did you call it?"

"A liquidator," said Mercier. "No. It's not at all like jury duty. She chose you specifically."

"But why us?" asked Armand. "We didn't even know her."

"I have no idea, and, sadly, we can't ask her," said Mercier, who did not look at all sad.

"Your father didn't say anything?" asked Myrna.

"He never spoke about his clients."

Gamache looked down at the brick of papers in front of him and noticed the red stamp in the upper left corner. He was familiar with wills. You didn't generally get into your late fifties without having read a few. And Gamache had read a few, including his own.

This was indeed a legitimate, registered will.

Scanning the top page quickly, he noted that it had been written two years earlier.

"Turn to page two, please," said the notary. "You'll see your names in section four."

"But wait a minute," said Myrna. "Who was Bertha Baumgartner? You have to know something."

"All I know is that she's dead and my father looked after the estate. And now I have it. And now it's yours. Page two, please."

And sure enough, there they were. Myrna Landers of Three Pines, Québec. Armand Gamache of Three Pines, Québec. Benedict Pouliot of 267 rue Taillon, Montréal, Québec.

"This is you?" Mercier watched as each of them nodded. He cleared his throat and prepared to read.

"Wait a minute," said Myrna. "This's crazy. Some stranger picks us at random and makes us liquidators? Can she do that?"

"Oh yes," said the notary. "You can name the pope if you want."

"Really? That's pretty cool," said Benedict, his mind whirring at the possibilities.

Gamache didn't completely agree with Myrna. He doubted it was random. He looked down at the names in Bertha Baumgartner's will.

Their names. Very clear. There for a reason, he suspected. Though that reason was anything but clear.

A cop, a bookstore owner, a builder. Two men, one woman. Different ages. Two lived in the country, one in the city.

There was no pattern. They had nothing in common except their names on this document. And the fact none of them knew Bertha Baumgartner.

"And whoever is named has to do it?" asked Myrna. "We have to do it?"

"Of course not," said Mercier. "Can you imagine the Holy Father liquidating this estate?"

They tried. Only Benedict seemed, by the smile on his face, to be succeeding.

"So we can refuse?" asked Myrna.

"*Oui.* Would you like to refuse?"

"Well, I don't know. I mean, I haven't had a chance to think about it. I had no idea why you wanted me here."

"What did you think?" asked Mercier.

Myrna sat back in her chair, trying to remember.

She'd been in her bookstore the morning before when the mail arrived.

She'd poured a mug of strong tea and sat in the comfortable armchair with the indentation that fit her body like a mold.

The woodstove was on, and beyond her window was a brilliant winter day. The sky was a deep perfect blue, and the sun bounced off the snow-covered lawns, the road, the ice rink, and the snowmen on the village green. The whole village gleamed.

It was the sort of day that drew you outside. Even though you knew better. And once you were outside, the cold gripped you, burning your lungs, soldering your nostrils together with every breath. It brought tears to your eyes. Freezing the lashes so that you had to pry your lids apart.

And yet, gasping for breath, you still stood there. Just a little longer. To be part of such a day. Before retreating back inside to the hearth and hot chocolate, or tea, or strong, rich café au lait.

And the mail.

She'd read and reread the letter, then called the number to ask why this notary wanted to meet her.

Getting no answer, she took the letter with her to meet her friends and neighbors, Clara Morrow and Gabri Dubeau, for lunch in the bistro.

As Clara and Gabri discussed the snow-sculpture themes, the ball-hockey tournament, the tuque judging, and the refreshments for the upcoming winter carnival, Myrna found her attention wandering.

"Hello," said Gabri. "Anybody home?"

"Huh?"

"We need your help," said Clara. "The snowshoe race around the village green. Should it be one circuit or two?"

"One for the under-eights," said Myrna. "One and a half for the under-twelves, and two for everyone else."

"Well, that was decisive," said Gabri. "Now, teams for the snowball fight . . ."

Myrna's mind drifted again. She vaguely noted Gabri getting up and tossing more logs onto the fires in the open hearths at either end of the bistro. He paused to chat with customers as more villagers came in from the cold, stamping their feet and rubbing their freezing hands.

They were met with warmth and the scent of maplewood smoke, tourtières just out of the oven, and the permanent aroma of coffee embedded into the beams and wide-plank floors.

"I have something I need to show you," Myrna whispered to Clara while Gabri was occupied.

"Why're you whispering?" Clara also lowered her voice. "Is it dirty?"

"Of course not."

"Of course?" said Clara, raising her brows. "I know you too well for the 'of course.'"

Myrna laughed. Clara did know her. But then she also knew Clara.

Her friend's brown hair stuck out from her head, as though she'd had a mild shock. She looked a little like a middle-aged Sputnik. Which would also explain her art.

Clara Morrow's paintings were otherworldly. And yet they were also achingly, profoundly human.

She painted what appeared to be portraits, but that was only on the surface. The beautifully rendered flesh stretched, and sometimes sagged, over wounds, over celebrations. Over chasms of loss and rushes of joy. She painted peace and despair. All in one portrait.

With brush and canvas and oils, Clara both captured and freed her subject.

She also managed to get paint all over herself. On her cheeks, in her hair, under her nails. She was herself a work in progress.

"I'll show you later," said Myrna as Gabri arrived back at their table.

"Better be dirty, after that buildup," said Clara.

"Dirty?" said Gabri. "Spill."

"Myrna thinks the adults should do their snowshoe race naked."

"Naked?" asked Gabri, looking at Myrna. "Not that I'm a prude, but the children . . ."

"Oh for God's sake," said Myrna. "I didn't say that at all. Clara's making it up."

"Of course, if we held it at night, after the kids were asleep," said Gabri. "Put torches around the village green, it could work. We'd certainly set some speed records."

Myrna glared at Clara. Gabri, the president of the Carnaval d'hiver, was taking it seriously.

"Or maybe, instead of naked, because—" Gabri looked around at the bistro crowd, imagining them without clothing. "Maybe they have to wear bathing suits."

Clara frowned, not in disapproval but in surprise. It actually wasn't a bad idea. Especially given that most of the conversation in the bistro through the long, long, dark, dark Québec winter was about escaping to the sun. Lying on some beach, roasting.

"We can call it Running Away to the Caribbean," she said.

Myrna let out a sigh.

Across the bistro an elderly woman saw this and thought the dismissive look had been directed at her.

Ruth Zardo glared back.

Myrna caught this and thought of the unfairness of nature, that the old poet should be wizened without being wise.

Though there was wisdom there, if you could get beyond the haze of scotch.

Ruth returned to her lunch of booze and potato chips. Her notebook, on the table, contained neither rhymes nor reason but held, between the worn pages, the lump in the throat.

She looked out the window, then wrote:

> *Sharp as thin ice*
> *the clear cries of children pierce the sky . . .*

Rosa, on the sofa beside Ruth, muttered, "Fuck, fuck, fuck." Or it might have been, "Duck, duck, duck." Though it seemed silly that a duck would actually say "duck." And those who knew Rosa felt that "fuck" was much more likely.

Rosa leaned her long neck over and delicately took a potato chip out of the bowl while Ruth watched the children tobogganing down from the chapel to the village green. She scribbled:

> *Or in the snow-lapped country church,*
> *kneeling at last to pray*
> *for what we could not have.*

Lunch arrived. Clara and Myrna had both ordered the halibut, with mustard seeds, curry leaves, and grilled tomato. And for Gabri, his partner, Olivier, had made grouse with roasted figs and cauliflower puree.

"I'm going to invite the Prime Minister," said Gabri. "He could open the *carnaval*."

He invited Justin Trudeau every year. And never heard back.

"And maybe he could take part in the race?" asked Clara.

Gabri's eyes widened.

Justin Trudeau. Racing around the village green. In a Speedo.

From there the conversation went south.

Myrna's heart wasn't in it, and neither was her mind, though she had paused for a moment on the Trudeau image before her thoughts went back to the letter folded in her pocket.

What would happen if she didn't show up?

The sun was turning the snow outside pink and blue. Shrieks of children could be heard, giddy with that intoxicating mix of fun and fear as their toboggans plunged down the hill.

It looked so idyllic.

But.

But if, by chance or fate, you got caught too far from home as clouds rolled in, as a flurry blew into a blizzard, then all bets were off.

A Québec winter, so cheerful and peaceful, could turn on you. Could kill. And each winter did. Men, women, children alive in the autumn did not see the blizzard coming and never saw the spring.

In the countryside, winter was a gorgeous, glorious, luminous killer.

Québécois with gray in their hair and lines in their faces got there by being wise enough and sensible enough and prudent enough to get back home. And watch the blizzard from beside a cheery hearth, with a hot chocolate, or a glass of wine, and a good book.

While there were few things more terrifying than being outside in a blizzard, there were few things more comforting than being inside.

As with so much in life, it was, Myrna knew, a matter of inches between safe and sorry.

While Gabri and Clara debated the merits of all-inclusives versus other resorts versus cruises, Myrna thought about the letter and decided to leave it up to fate.

If it was snowing, she'd stay home. If it was clear, she'd go.

And now, as she sat in the off-kilter kitchen, with the off-kilter table, and the off-kilter notary, and the wacky young builder, Myrna looked out at the worsening snow and thought—

Fucking fate. Tricked again.

"Myrna's right," said Armand, laying a large hand on the will. "We need to decide if we even want to do it." He turned to the other two. "What do you think?"

"Can we read the thing first?" said Benedict, patting the will. "Then decide?"

"No," said the notary.

Myrna got up. "I think we should talk about it. In private."

Armand walked around the table and bent down beside Benedict, who was still sitting there, and whispered, "You're welcome to join us."

"Oh great, yes. Good idea."

CHAPTER 5

As Gamache passed from the kitchen into the dining room, he paused to look at the doorframe and the marks.

Bending closer, he noted faint names beside the lines.

Anthony, aged three, four, five, and so on up the doorjamb.

Caroline, at three, four, five . . .

And then there was Hugo, three, four, five, and so on. But his lines were denser. Like the rings of some old oak that wasn't growing very fast. Or very tall.

Hugo lagged far behind where his brother and sister were at the same age. But, uniquely, beside his name, at each faint line, there was a sticker. A horse. A dog. A teddy bear. So that while little Hugo might not stand tall, he did stand out.

Armand looked back into the kitchen, stripped bare. Then into the empty dining room, its wallpaper stained with moisture.

What happened here? he wondered.

What happened in Madame Baumgartner's life that she had to choose strangers to enact her will? Where were Anthony and Caroline and Hugo?

"Roof leaking," said Benedict, splaying his large hand on a stain on the dining-room wall. "It's getting between the walls. Rotting. A shame. Look at these floors."

They did. Old pine. Warping.

Benedict walked around, inspecting the room, staring up at the ceiling.

He'd unzipped his winter coat to reveal a sweater that was alternately fuzzy and tight-knit, and one section looked like it was made of steel wool.

Myrna could not believe it was comfortable, but she could believe it was made by his girlfriend.

He must love her, she thought. A lot. And she him. Everything she created was for him. The fact it was awful didn't take away from the thought. Unless, of course, she did it on purpose. To not only make him look foolish but to cause him actual pain, as the steel-wool sweater scratched and rubbed the young flesh beneath.

She either loved Benedict a lot or despised him. A lot.

And he either didn't see it or was drawn to pain, to abuse, as some people were.

"So," said Myrna. "Do you want to be a liquidator?"

"What's involved?" asked Benedict. "What do we have to do?"

"If the will's simple, not much," said Armand. "Just make sure the taxes and bills are paid and any bequests get to the right people. Then wrap up the estate. The notary helps with that. Liquidators are generally family members and friends. People who're trusted."

They looked at each other. They were none of those things to Bertha Baumgartner. And yet here they were.

Armand glanced around for a photograph left behind on the damp walls or fallen to the floor. Something that might tell them who this Bertha Baumgartner was. But there was nothing. Just the smudged lines on the door. And the horsey, doggy, teddy bear.

"That doesn't sound so bad," said Benedict.

"That's if it's simple," said Armand. "If it isn't, it could take a lot of time. A long time."

"Like days?" asked Benedict. When there was no answer, he added, "Weeks? Months?"

"Years," said Armand. "Some wills take years, especially if there're any arguments between the heirs."

"And there often are," said Myrna. She turned full circle. "Greed does that. But it looks like they've already stripped the place. And I can't imagine there's much left to divide."

Beside her, Armand made a noise like a rumble.

She looked at him and nodded. "I know. It might not seem like much to us, but to people who have little, a little more can seem a fortune."

He remained silent.

That wasn't exactly what he was thinking. A will, an estate, could become about more than money, property, possessions. Who was left the most could be interpreted as who was loved the most. There were different sorts of greed. Of need.

And wills were sometimes used as a final affront, the last insult delivered by a ghost.

"Do we get paid?" asked Benedict.

"Maybe a little. It's normally done as a favor," said Armand.

Benedict nodded. "So how do we know if this's simple?"

"We can't know until we read the will," said Myrna.

"But we can't read the will until we decide," Benedict pointed out.

"Catch-22," said Gamache, to the young man's blank face. "I think we have to assume the worst and decide if we still want to do it."

"And if we don't?" asked Myrna. "What happens?"

"The courts will appoint other liquidators."

"But she wanted us," said Benedict. "I wonder why. She must've had a reason." He stopped, deep in thought. They could almost hear the wheels grinding. Finally he shook his head. "Nope. Can't think what it would be. You two know each other, don't you?"

"We're neighbors," said Myrna. "Live in the same village about twenty minutes away."

"I live in Montréal with my girlfriend. I've never even been out this way. Maybe she meant another Benedict Pouliot."

"You live on rue Taillon in Montréal?" asked Armand, and when the young man nodded, he went on. "She meant you."

Benedict focused on Armand, as though really seeing him for the first time. He brought his hand up to his own temple, placing a finger there. "That looks nasty. What happened? An accident?"

Armand raised his hand and brushed it along the furrow of the scar. "*Non*. I was hurt once."

More than once, Myrna thought, but didn't say it.

"It was a while ago," Armand assured the young man. "I'm fine now."

"Must've really hurt."

"It did. But I think it hurt others more."

He obviously has no idea who Armand is, thought Myrna. And saw that Armand had no intention of telling him.

"Either way, we should decide," she said, walking over to the window. "Snow's getting heavier."

"You're right," said Armand. "We need to get going soon. So are we in or out?"

"You?" Myrna asked him.

He already had his answer. Had it from the moment the notary explained why they were there.

"I have no idea why Madame Baumgartner chose us, but she did. I don't see any reason to refuse. I'm in. Besides"—he smiled at Myrna—"I'm curious."

"You are that," she said, then looked at Benedict. "You?"

"Years, you say?" he asked.

"Worst case," said Gamache. "*Oui*."

"So it could take years and we don't get paid," Benedict recapped. "Oh, what the hell. I'm in. How bad can it be?"

Myrna regarded the handsome young man with the grievous haircut and the steel-wool sweater. If he could put up with that, she thought, he could put up with irritating strangers fighting over a pittance.

"You?" Armand asked Myrna.

"Oh, I was always in," she said, smiling. And then there was a shudder and the rattle of windows as wind rocked the house. It gave a creak, then a sharp crack.

Myrna felt panic rise up. And spike. They weren't safe in the house. But neither were they safe outside.

And they still had the drive home to Three Pines.

"We need to leave."

Walking rapidly back into the kitchen, she looked out the window. She could barely see her car, now buried under blowing and drifting and eddying snow.

"We're in," she said to Lucien. "And we're leaving."

"What?" said Lucien, getting up.

"We're leaving," said Armand. "And you should too. Where's your office?"

"Sherbrooke."

It was an hour's drive away, at least.

They hadn't taken off their coats or boots, and now they grabbed their mitts and hats and made for the back door.

34

"Wait," said Lucien, sitting down again. "We have to read the will. Madame Baumgartner stipulated that it be done here."

"Madame Baumgartner's dead," said Myrna. "And I plan on living through the day."

She rammed a tuque onto her head and followed Benedict out of the house.

"Now, *monsieur*," said Armand. "We're leaving. And that means you."

Benedict and Myrna were wading through the snow, already knee-deep in places, toward her car. The young man had yanked a shovel from the snowbank and was starting to dig her car out.

Lucien leaned back in his chair and crossed his arms.

"Up," said Armand, and when the notary didn't move, he grabbed Lucien by the arm and pulled him to his feet.

"Put your things on," he ordered, and after a moment's shocked pause, Lucien did.

Armand checked his iPhone. There was no signal. The storm had knocked everything out.

He looked out at the blizzard, then around at the creaking, cracking, crooked home.

They had to leave.

He thrust the paperwork back into the briefcase, which he handed to the notary. "Come on."

When Gamache opened the door, the snow whacked him in the face, taking his breath away. He closed his eyes and winced against the pellets that all but blinded him.

The sound was deafening.

Howling, hitting, furious movement. It burst in on them and over them. The world unraveling. And them in the middle of it.

As the snow plastered itself against Gamache's face, he turned his head away and saw Benedict furiously shoveling, working to free Myrna's car from the snowdrifts that had formed around it. No sooner had the young man dug out one section than the wind picked up the snow and filled it back in.

The only thing not white in the landscape was Benedict's tuque, its long red-striped tail looking like lashes of blood on the snow.

Myrna was using her hands to scoop snow off the windshield.

Benedict's own truck, parked in the open, was already covered, and the notary's car had disappeared completely.

By the time he reached the others, Armand could feel snow down his boots, and down his collar, and up his sleeves, and under his tuque.

Myrna was trying to yank her car door open, but the snow, blown against it, was trapping it shut.

"It's too deep," Armand called into Myrna's ear. "Leave it." Then he trudged to the back of the car and grabbed Benedict's arm, stopping the shovel. "Even if we could dig everyone out, the roads are too bad. We need to stay together. Your truck's probably the best bet."

Benedict looked over at it, then back at Armand.

"What is it?" shouted Armand, sensing there was an "it."

"I don't have snow tires."

"You don't—" But he stopped himself. When the house was burning, it was not the best time to lay blame. "Okay." He turned to Myrna and Lucien. "My car is slightly protected by Myrna's. Hers is acting as a windbreak. We can probably get mine out."

"But I need to get back to Sherbrooke," said Lucien, waving behind him to his vehicle, which was now just another white lump in the yard.

"And you will," Myrna shouted. "Just not today."

"But—"

"Dig," said Myrna, waving toward Armand's Volvo.

"With what?"

Armand pointed to Lucien's briefcase.

"No," said the notary, hugging it to him like a teddy bear.

"Fine," said Myrna.

Yanking it away from him, she went to work, using the briefcase to push the snow from around the doors while Benedict shoveled and Armand ripped wooden planks from the front steps of the house and pushed them under the rear wheels, using his boots to kick them firmly into place.

And Lucien stood there.

Finally they managed to get the doors open.

Myrna all but rammed the notary into the backseat, then got in beside him.

"You drive," shouted Benedict to Armand, motioning to the driver's side. "I'll push."

"*Non*. When we get moving, we can't stop. We'll sink in again. Whoever pushes will be left behind."

Benedict paused.

My God, thought Armand. *He's actually considering it.*

"In," he commanded.

The young man stared at the older man, still undecided.

"This will work," said Gamache, softly this time, while the snow piled up around them again and the precious moments ticked by. "Get in."

Benedict reached for the driver's-side door, but Armand stopped him.

"In," he said, with a smile, and pointed to the passenger door.

Myrna double-checked her seat belt, then closed her eyes and breathed. Deeply. And prayed.

The car started to back up, and Gamache slowly, slowly, gently, gently pressed the gas.

There was a hesitation as the tires worked to mount the planks.

They caught and climbed the inch or so out of the snow and ice and onto the wood.

With traction now, the car moved. An inch. Six inches. A foot.

Benedict exhaled. Myrna exhaled. The notary hyperventilated.

Then Armand put it in gear and gently turned the wheel, so that they were headed back down the pine drive.

"Oh, *merde*," said Benedict.

Myrna leaned forward between the seats and saw what he saw.

A wall of snow blocked their way out. So high they couldn't see the road beyond.

"It's okay," said Gamache. "It means the plow's been by. This is good."

"Good?" asked Benedict.

"Look what it did," said the notary, finding his voice. Or someone's. It was unnaturally high and breathy. "We can't get through that."

The plow had pushed snow across the entrance to the driveway, creating a barrier. There was no way to tell how thick, how packed it would be. Or what was on the other side.

But they had no choice. There was only one way to do this.

"Hold on," said Armand, and pressed his foot on the gas.

"Are you sure?" said Benedict as they headed straight for the wall of snow.

"Oh shit," said Myrna, bracing herself.

And then they hit.

The snow exploded, plastering itself against the windshield and blinding them as the car skewed violently one way, then the other.

And then, to Benedict's horror, Armand leaned back in his seat.

"Hit the brake," Benedict screamed.

Benedict reached for the wheel, but Armand grabbed his wrist in a grip so tight the young man flinched.

A chunk of snow flew off the windshield, and they could see the forest—trees, trunks—heading toward them.

Benedict gasped and put his hands against the dashboard while Armand stared ahead, waiting. Waiting. And then, just when it appeared too late, he gently, gently, pumped the brakes.

The car slowed. Then stopped. Its nose just touching the other bank.

There was complete silence, then long exhales.

They were right across the road, blocking it. Armand quickly looked left and right, to see if there were any oncoming cars. But the road was empty.

Only fools would be out in a blizzard.

There was quiet, giddy laughter.

"Oh shit," sighed Myrna.

Armand backed the car up and pointed it toward home. Putting on the warning flashers, he got out to inspect for damage.

"What the fuck was that?" demanded Benedict, marching around the car to confront Armand. "You gave up. You almost killed us."

Armand gestured with both hands toward the car.

"Yeah," shouted Benedict. "Dumb luck."

"There was that." Had there been another vehicle coming or the plow returning—

"You froze," shouted Benedict as Armand began digging snow out of the grille of the car. "I saw you."

"What I did and what you saw seem to be two different things. Sometimes the best thing we can do is nothing."

"What sort of Zen bullshit is that?"

Snow whipped around Benedict, his fists clenched as he stared at Gamache.

"You want to know why I did what I did?"

"You panicked."

"Did no one teach you how to drive in snow?" Gamache shouted into the blizzard.

"I can do it better than you."

"Then you can give me a lesson. But perhaps not today."

They got back into the car, and Gamache put it in gear.

"And," he said, concentrating on the road, "just so you know. I never give up."

"Where're we going?" asked Lucien from the backseat.

"Home," said Myrna.

CHAPTER 6

"Are we there?" asked the notary. Again.

"*Oui.*"

"Really?"

The answer was so unexpected it silenced him. Lucien used his sleeve to wipe the condensation from the car window and peered out. And saw . . . nothing.

And then the blowing snow momentarily shifted, and for a split second, through a tear in the blizzard, he could see a house. A home.

It was made of fieldstone, and there was soft light coming through the mullioned windows.

And then it was gone, swallowed by the storm. The sighting was so brief, Lucien wondered if desperation and imagination had conjured a fairy-tale cottage.

"Are you sure?" he asked.

"Pretty sure."

Less than an hour later, Armand and his guests were showered and changed into clean, dry clothing. Except Lucien, who'd refused all offers.

They were seated at the long pine table in the kitchen while the woodstove pumped out heat at the far end of the room. Snow had piled up on the frames of the windows on either side of the fireplace, making it difficult to see out.

Benedict wore a borrowed T-shirt, sweater, and slacks and had calmed down since the drive. The hot shower and the promise of food had lulled him.

He looked around.

This place didn't shudder, the windows didn't rattle, despite the fury outside. It had been built to last, and lasted it had. He figured it was more than one hundred, perhaps even two hundred years old.

Even if he tried, if he really, really tried, he doubted he could build a home this solid.

He looked across the room, at Madame Gamache serving up soup and Armand cutting bread. Occasionally consulting. Their bodies just touching in an act both casual and intimate.

Benedict wondered if he tried, really, really tried, if he could build a relationship that solid.

He scratched his chest and winced.

A few minutes earlier, while standing under the hot stream of the shower, Armand had asked Reine-Marie, "Does the name Bertha Baumgartner mean anything to you?"

"Wasn't she a cartoon character?" said Reine-Marie. "No, that was Dagwood. Was she a villain in *Doonesbury*?"

He turned off the shower and stepped out, taking the towel she handed him.

"*Merci.*" As he rubbed his hair dry, he looked at her, amused, but then saw she was serious. "No, she was a neighbor, sort of."

He put on cords, a clean shirt, and a sweater and told her why he'd been summoned to the remote farmhouse.

"A liquidator? But you must've known her, Armand. Why else would she choose you?"

"I have no idea."

"And Myrna doesn't know her?"

"Neither does the young fellow. Benedict."

"How do you explain that?" she asked.

"I can't."

"Huh," said Reine-Marie.

When they had their soups and sandwiches and beer, Reine-Marie left them at the kitchen table, taking her own lunch into the living room.

Sitting by the fireplace with Gracie, their little foundling, beside her, Reine-Marie stared into the flames and repeated:

Bertha Baumgartner. Bertha Baumgartner.

Still the name meant nothing.

"Now," said Lucien, adjusting his glasses. "You've all agreed to be liquidators of the estate of Bertha Baumgartner. Is that correct?"

What sounded like "Yes" came from Benedict, but his mouth was so full of roast-beef sandwich it came out as a muffled "Woof."

Henri, lying at Armand's feet, perked up his ears, his tail swishing slightly.

"That is correct," said Myrna, using the same tone as the notary, though he didn't seem to notice.

The chair creaked as she sat back, a warm mug of pea soup in her hands. She longed to reach for the beer, but the mug was so comforting she didn't want to let it go.

Armand had dropped her at the door into the bistro, her bookstore being snowed in, so she could have a hot shower and change before heading to their place.

"Oh for Christ's sake," said Clara as she hugged her friend. "We were so worried."

"I wasn't," said Gabri, though he also hugged her tight. "You okay?" he said. "You look like shit."

"Could be worse."

"Where were you?" asked Olivier.

Myrna saw no reason not to tell them.

"Bertha Baumgartner?" said Gabri. "Bertha Baumgartner? Really? There was someone around here named Bertha Baumgartner and I didn't know her? Who was she?"

"You don't know?" asked Myrna. Gabri and Olivier knew everyone.

"Don't you?" asked Clara, following her to the door connecting the bistro to the bookstore.

"No. Not a clue." She stopped and looked at their astonished faces.

"You say that Armand is also a liquidator?" asked Olivier. "He must know her."

"No. None of us do. Not even the notary."

"And she lived just down the road?" asked Clara.

"Well, about twenty minutes from here. You sure the name doesn't sound familiar?"

"Bertha Baumgartner," said Gabri again, clearly enjoying the sound of it.

"Don't you dare," said Olivier. He turned to Clara and Myrna. "He's been looking for another name to sign to the letter inviting Prime Minister Trudeau to the carnival. We suspect Gabri Dubeau is on the straight-to-garbage list."

"I have sent him a few letters," admitted Gabri. "And a couple photographs."

"And?" said Olivier.

"A lock of hair. In my defense," said Gabri, "it was Olivier's."

"What? You bastard." Olivier touched his head. Already thinning, each blond strand was precious.

When Myrna came back down from her loft twenty minutes later in warm dry clothes, she discovered that Gabri and Olivier were out clearing paths.

"They're not digging out Ruth?" Myrna said to Clara.

It was like releasing a chimera. Not something done lightly. And very hard to put back, once out.

"Afraid so. And feeding her too. They took over soup in a scotch bottle, hoping she won't notice the difference."

"Ruth might not, but Rosa will."

The duck was discerning.

"Where're you going?" asked Clara, following her to the door.

"To Armand's. We're going to read the will."

"Can I come?"

"Do you want to?"

"Yes, I'd far prefer to walk into a blizzard than sit by the fire with my book and a scotch."

"Thought so," said Myrna as she yanked open the door. Bending into the wind, she trudged through the thick snow.

She did not know Bertha but was growing to dislike her. Intensely.

Armand stood in the study, the phone to his ear.

He could just see, through gaps in the blowing snow, Myrna making her way around the village green to their home.

Reine-Marie had told him the phone was dead, but he thought he'd just check to see if the line had been restored.

It had not.

He looked at his watch. It was one thirty in the afternoon but felt like midnight.

Three and a half hours since he'd received the call while sitting in his car outside Bertha Baumgartner's home. Three and a half hours since the angry exchange of words.

Thinking of it conjured the smell of wet wool, the sound of snow tapping his car.

He'd said he'd get back to them. Made them promise not to do anything until they heard from him. And now this.

Reine-Marie greeted Myrna, and, after replacing the dead phone, Armand joined them in the warm kitchen, for soup, sandwiches, beer, and the reading of the will.

"Heard on the radio that the blizzard's all over southern Québec," said Myrna, trying to repair her hat head. "But should blow itself out sometime in the night."

"That widespread?" asked Armand.

Reine-Marie examined his face. Instead of concerned, he seemed relieved.

The lights of Annie and Jean-Guy's apartment in the Plateau *quartier* of Montréal flickered.

They stopped what they were doing to stare at the overhead light.

It wavered. Wavered.

Then held.

Annie and Jean-Guy exchanged glances and raised their brows, then went back to their conversation. Jean-Guy was telling her about his meeting that morning with the investigators.

"Did they ask you to sign anything?" asked Annie.

"How did you know about that?"

"So they did?"

He nodded.

"Did you?"

"No."

"Good."

Once again he saw the sheets of paper pushed across the table at him, and their expectant faces.

"You were right. They have an agenda. I think your father might be facing more than suspension or even being fired."

"Like what?"

"I don't really know. They didn't make any accusations, but they kept going back to the drugs. The ones he let through."

"They already knew about that," said Annie. "He told them right away. Alerted cops across the country and into the States. The DEA got back the junk that crossed the border, right?"

"With your father's help, yes."

"And yours."

"*Oui*. But there's a whole lot still missing. Kilos of it. Here. In Montréal. Somewhere. We've spent months looking. Using all our informants. And nothing. When that shit hits the streets . . ."

He left it hanging there, not sure how to finish the sentence.

"It's terrible stuff, Annie."

"I know."

He shook his head. "You think you do, but you don't. Think of the worst. The very worst."

She did.

"That would be the very best that could happen," he said.

Annie smiled, thinking he was kidding. Certainly exaggerating. And then her smile faded.

That bad.

"I think they know there's going to be a shitstorm once the stuff hits the streets. They need someone to blame."

"They?"

"Them." He lifted his hands. "I don't know. I'm not good at this political crap. That was your dad's job."

"But it is political?"

"I think so. No one seems particularly worried about the poor sons

46

of bitches who're going to take the stuff. They're all covering their own asses."

"Does Dad know?"

"I think he suspects. But he's still trying to get the stuff back. He isn't looking in that direction. I honestly thought when I walked in there this morning that they were going to tell me they were ending the investigation and reinstating your father."

"Now what?" asked Annie.

"I don't know," he said, leaning back heavily. "I'm tired of all this, Annie. I've had it."

"I know. It sucks. Thank you for sticking by Dad."

Jean-Guy nodded but didn't say anything.

He again heard Marie's reassuring voice. *All this will go away, Chief Inspector. Once you sign. Then you can get on with your life.*

CHAPTER 7

⁓

Benedict, Myrna, and Armand stared down at the page in front of them.

Then they looked up, and at each other.

Then, as one, they turned to Lucien.

"This's a joke, right?" asked Myrna while, beside her, Armand took off his reading glasses and watched the notary.

"I don't understand," said Benedict.

"It's all very clear," said Lucien.

"But it's nonsense," said Myrna. "It makes no sense."

Armand looked back down at the document in front of him. They'd finally reached the eighth section of the will, with the notary having read every preceding section, every clause, every word, in a sonorous voice. Given their exhaustion after the stresses of the morning, the meal they'd just had, the warmth from the woodstove, and now Lucien's voice droning on, it was all they could do to remain conscious.

Armand had noticed Benedict's eyelids fluttering and his head drooping more than once, and then the young man had fought his way back to them. Opening his eyes wide, before the heavy lids slowly lowered again.

But he was wide awake now. They all were.

"It says here," Myrna looked back down and put her finger under the line as she read, "'I bequeath to my three children the sum of five million dollars each.'"

She looked up again, hard, at Lucien.

"Five. Million. Dollars," she repeated. "And that makes sense to you?"

"Each," Benedict pointed out. "That's . . . fifteen million."

"Five million, fifteen million, a hundred million," said Myrna. "It's all the same. Nonsense."

"Maybe she meant Canadian Tire money," said Benedict, trying to be helpful.

It was not.

"What're we supposed to do with this?" Myrna asked.

She gestured toward the will, then appealed to Armand, who looked at the notary and raised his brows.

"Does she have it?" he asked.

"Bertha Baumgartner?" asked Myrna. "Were we in the same house this morning? That woman, while apparently rich in imagination, was obviously not a multimillionaire."

"She might've been a . . . what's the word?" said Benedict.

"Miser?" asked Armand.

"Lunatic," said Benedict.

"We haven't finished yet," said Lucien.

His voice droned on, but now they were alert, following closely, as bequest followed bequest.

Her home in Switzerland was to be sold, as was the building in Vienna. The proceeds to be divided among her children and grand-children. With a million dollars going to the local animal shelter.

"That's nice," said Benedict.

Section 8, thought Armand, scanning the figures on the page. In the U.S. military that was the section for the mentally unfit. Benedict might have found exactly the right word.

"'The title will, of course,'" the notary read, "'be passed to my eldest son, Anthony.'"

"Huh?" said Myrna.

By now words had failed her, and she could just make sounds.

"Title?" asked Benedict. "What's that?"

"Must be the title to the property," said Armand.

All the lights in the kitchen flickered.

All the people in the kitchen fell silent, staring up at the chandelier over the pine table. Willing it to stay on.

But willing something to happen, as they were discovering with

50

Madame Baumgartner, and having it happen were often two different things.

The lights wavered again, then came back to full brightness.

They looked at one another and breathed a sigh of relief.

Then the lights, all at once, went out.

No flicker this time. Just gone. And with it went all sound. No hum of the fridge, no rumble of the furnace. No tick of a clock. They sat at the kitchen table in silence.

Sunlight still struggled through the windows of the kitchen. But it was weak. As though it had fought long and hard to get that far.

Before it too died.

Armand struck a match and lit the storm lamps at either end of the table while Myrna lit the candles on the kitchen island. Put there in case.

"You okay?" Armand asked, going to the door between the kitchen and the living room.

There he saw the fire in the hearth and one lantern already lit.

"No worries," said Reine-Marie. "And no surprise."

"We're almost finished. Be with you in a few minutes."

He took two small logs off the neat pile in the kitchen and shoved them into the woodstove. It was now their main source of heat. There was no emergency, yet. But if this blackout lasted a long time, days even, and the temperature dropped still further, and the fire went out . . .

"Well, this's nice," said Benedict, looking around at the pools of light.

"Let's call it a day," said Armand, and when Lucien protested, Myrna hauled herself out of the chair and just left. Taking her beer into the living room to join Reine-Marie.

Benedict followed.

Armand held his arm out, inviting Lucien to join them. After a moment's hesitation, he grudgingly got up.

Once seated, Myrna asked, "How're we supposed to liquidate a will that makes no sense? We can't give away money that isn't there."

"Madame Baumgartner overestimated her estate?" asked Reine-Marie.

"By about twenty million," said Myrna.

Reine-Marie grimaced. "That is overshooting."

51

"We're all assuming she didn't have the money," said Lucien. "Maybe she did."

"You think so?" asked Armand.

"Conrad Cantzen."

"I beg your pardon?" said Armand.

"Conrad Cantzen," the notary repeated. "My father told me about him. Monsieur Cantzen was a bit actor on Broadway back in the 1920s. He'd beg for money and go through the garbage for food, and when he died, he left a quarter of a million dollars. It's a lot of money today. Back when he died, that was a fortune."

They were silent, absorbing this.

"You just never know," said Lucien.

CHAPTER 8

———

"Armand, are you awake?"

"Hmmmm."

He turned over so that he was on his side, facing Reine-Marie. The air was chilly, but the duvet was warm. He reached under the covers for her hand.

They'd moved their mattress down to the kitchen and were camped by the woodstove. So that they could get up in the night and feed more logs into it.

"This afternoon, when you heard that the blizzard covered most of Québec, you seemed pleased."

"Relieved," he admitted.

"Why?"

That, he thought, was harder to explain.

Henri and Gracie, curled on the floor beside them, stirred, and then, with reassuring pats from Armand and Reine-Marie, they went back to sleep.

"I needed to go to the Sûreté Academy yesterday afternoon, to a meeting," Armand whispered. "I told them not to do anything until I arrived. Then the storm hit and the phones went out, and I was worried that they'd proceed without me. But with the blizzard being so big, I knew nothing could happen. They were snowed in too."

And he could relax. Knowing for the next number of hours, as the blizzard howled, the world was on hold. Frozen in place.

In the hectic, often frantic pace of life, there was something deeply peaceful about not being able to do anything. No Internet, no phone, no TV. No lights.

Life became simple, primal: Heat. Water. Food. Companionship.

Armand crawled out of bed, feeling the chill immediately as the warmth of the duvet slid off and the cold took hold.

Stepping over the other mattress on the kitchen floor, he fed more split logs into the fire.

Before returning to the warm bed, Armand stared out the mullioned windows into the darkness. Then bent and tucked the duvet around Reine-Marie.

As he did that, a voice, sharp and unexpected, came to him out of the darkness.

The evening before, those who weren't snowed in dug out those who were, clearing paths from homes to the road.

Gabri and Olivier had been invited over to the Gamaches' after they'd finished but had declined.

"Want to keep the bistro open," Olivier explained.

"And we have unexpected guests at the B&B," Gabri shouted into the battering wind. "Can't get their cars out to drive home."

"Can't find their cars." Olivier used his shovel to point to the burial mounds around the village green.

"Do you think we can get kids to do it? Convince them that it's a game?" Gabri yelled into Olivier's tuque. "Whoever digs a car out first wins a prize?"

"The prize would have to be a brain," said Olivier.

A path had been shoveled to Ruth's home, and Reine-Marie had knocked, but the old woman had refused to open the door.

"Come to our place for dinner," Reine-Marie shouted through it. "Bring Rosa. We have plenty of food."

"And drink?"

"Yes."

"No, I don't want to leave."

"Ruth, please. You shouldn't be alone. Come over. We have scotch."

"I don't know. The last bottle I had tasted strange."

Reine-Marie could hear the fear in her voice. An old woman leaving her home to venture into a blizzard. Every survival instinct screamed no. While Ruth Zardo was not well endowed with survival instincts, she still had managed to claw her way into her eighties.

And not by walking into snowstorms.

One by one over the course of the early evening, they'd gone over to Ruth's, clearing the fresh snow ahead of them. And one by one they'd been rebuffed.

"Okay, enough of this," said Armand, getting up.

He grabbed a Hudson Bay blanket before heading to the door.

"What're you going to do?" asked Reine-Marie.

"I'm going to get Ruth here, if I have to break down her door."

"You're going to kidnap her?" asked Myrna.

"Isn't that against the law?" asked Reine-Marie.

"It is," said Lucien, who had no ear for sarcasm. "Who's this Ruth? Why's she so important?"

"She's a person," said Armand, his parka and boots now on.

"But is she really?" Myrna mouthed to Reine-Marie.

"You do know if you kidnap her, no one will pay the ransom," said Reine-Marie. "And we'll be stuck with her."

"Ruth's not so bad," said Myrna. "It's the duck that worries me."

"Duck?" asked Lucien.

"I'll go with you, sir," said Benedict.

"You don't think I can take her on my own?" asked Armand with some amusement.

"Her, yes," said Benedict. "But the duck?"

Armand looked at him for a moment, then laughed. Unlike Lucien, Benedict had slipped easily into the stream of conversation. Understanding what was banter and what was important.

Benedict got his boots, parka, tuque, and mitts on, and Gamache opened the door. Only to step back in surprise.

Ruth was standing there, covered in snow. Her heavy winter coat bulging and squirming.

"I hear there's scotch," she said, walking past them as though they were the guests and she the owner of the place.

As she walked, she dropped tuque, mitts, coat on the floor. And left puddles from her huge boots.

"Who're they?" Ruth used Rosa to indicate Lucien and Benedict.

Reine-Marie introduced them. "They're not drinking scotch," she said, rightly assuming that was all Ruth really wanted to know.

A buffet of bread, cheese, cold chicken, roast beef, and pastries had been set out on the dining table at the far end of the living room, with storm lanterns and candles placed on it.

"Does the name Bertha Baumgartner mean anything to you?" Armand asked Ruth as he handed her a plate he'd made for her and joined her on the sofa.

"No," said Ruth.

Myrna stepped from the buffet table long enough to whisper into Armand's ear. "Unless it's Johnnie Walker or Glenfiddich, she's not interested. Watch and learn."

Going back to the table, Myrna placed a chicken leg, some camembert, and a slice of baguette on her plate and said, "Bertha Baumgartner? Olivier just got a case in. Twenty-five years old. Slow-aged in oak. Very smooth."

"Bertha Baumgartner's booze?" asked Ruth, rejoining the conversation.

"No, she isn't, you old drunk," said Myrna. "But we wanted your attention, as wavering as it is."

"You're a cruel woman," said Ruth.

"We're liquidators of her estate," said Armand. "But we've never met her. She lived locally."

"An old farmhouse down Mansonville way," said Myrna.

"Bertha Baumgartner? Means nothing to me," said Ruth. "You the notary?"

"Me?" asked Benedict, his mouth full of bread. Again.

"No, not you." Ruth eyed him. And his hair. "I see Gabri has competition for village idiot. I meant him."

"Me?" asked Lucien.

"Yes, you. I knew a Laurence Mercier. He came to discuss my will. Your father?"

"Yes."

"I see the resemblance," she said. It did not sound like a compliment.

"You've made a will?" asked Reine-Marie, carrying her plate back to her seat by the fireplace.

"No," said Ruth. "Decided not to. Nothing to leave. But I have written instructions for my funeral. Flowers. Music. The parade. Tributes from dignitaries. The design of the postage stamp. The usual."

"Date?" asked Myrna.

"Just for that, I might not die," said Ruth.

"Unless we can find a wooden stake or a silver bullet."

"Those are just rumors." Ruth turned to Armand. "So this Bertha person made you her liquidators and you never even knew her. She sounds batty. Wish I'd met her."

"Though she wouldn't be the first person to leave something strange in a will," said Reine-Marie. "Wasn't there something in Shakespeare's?"

"*Oui*," said Lucien, finally on familiar ground. "It was fairly standard until the end, where he wrote, 'I give unto my wife my second best bed.'"

This brought laughter, then silence, as they tried to figure out, as scholars had for centuries, what that meant.

"How about Howard Hughes?" said Myrna. "Didn't he die without a will?"

"Yeah, well, he really was crazy," said Ruth.

"My favorite Hughes quote was when he said, 'I'm not a paranoid deranged millionaire. Goddamn it, I'm a billionaire,'" said Reine-Marie.

"Now, that sounds familiar," said Ruth.

"His will was finally settled," said Lucien.

"Yeah," said Ruth. "After about thirty years."

"Holy shit," said Benedict, turning to Armand. "Hope it doesn't take us that long."

"Well, it probably won't take me that long," said Armand, doing the math.

As the room grew colder, they leaned closer to the fire and listened as Lucien Mercier told them about the man who'd left a penny to every child who attended his funeral and about the husbands who punished wives and children from beyond the grave.

"'They fuck you up, your mum and dad. / They may not mean to, but they do,'" Ruth quoted.

"I know that poem," said Benedict, and all eyes swung to him. "But that's not the way it goes."

"Oh really?" said Ruth. "And you're a poetry expert?"

"No, not really. But I know that one," he said. If not oblivious to sarcasm, at least impervious to it. A useful trait, thought Armand.

"How do you think it goes?" asked Reine-Marie.

"'They tuck you up, your mum and dad,'" said the young man, reeling it off easily. "'They read you Peter Rabbit, too.'"

All around the hearth, eyebrows rose.

"'They fill you with the faults they had,'" said Ruth, squaring herself to Benedict, like a duelist. "'And add some extra, just for you.'"

"'They give you all the treats they had,'" he replied. "'And add some extra, just for you.'"

Ruth glared at him. While the others stared in open amazement.

"Go on," said Reine-Marie.

And Ruth did.

> "Man hands on misery to man.
> It deepens like a coastal shelf.
> Get out as early as you can,
> And don't have any kids yourself."

Their eyes swung back to Benedict.

> "Man hands on happiness to man.
> It deepens like a coastal shelf.
> So love your parents all you can,
> And have some cheerful kids yourself."

"Is he for real?" Ruth demanded, going back to her scotch.

The fire muttered in the hearth, and the wind howled outside, and the blizzard settled in, trapping everyone in their homes.

And Armand thought that was a pretty good question.

Was Benedict for real?

It had been decided that Lucien, Myrna, and Benedict would stay the night, as would Ruth. She and Rosa were put on the mattress closest to the woodstove in the kitchen.

In the early-morning hours, after stoking the fire, Armand bent down and tucked the duvet closer around Reine-Marie.

Man hands on happiness to man.
It deepens like a coastal shelf.

Oddly enough, Benedict's version of the famous poem now pushed the original to the back of his mind.

Then he heard a stirring in the other bed. And a voice came to him out of the darkness.

"I think I know who Bertha Baumgartner was," said Ruth.

CHAPTER 9

Reine-Marie, eyes half open, half asleep and half awake, slid her hand along the bedding toward Armand, feeling the curved ridges of the blow-up mattress.

But that side of the bed was cold. Not simply cooling. Cold.

She opened her eyes and saw soft early-morning light through the windows.

Flames were roiling in the woodstove. It had been stoked recently.

She got up onto one elbow. The kitchen was empty. Not even Ruth and Rosa. Or Henri and Gracie.

Putting on her dressing gown and slippers, she tried the light switch. The power was still out. Then she noticed a note on the pine kitchen table.

> *Ma Chère,*
> *Ruth, Rosa, Henri and Gracie and I have gone to the bistro to talk to Olivier and Gabri. Join us if you can.*
>
> > *Love, Armand*
> > *(6:50 a.m.)*

Reine-Marie looked at her watch. It was now 7:12.

She went over to the window. Snow had climbed halfway up, blocking most of the light and almost all the view. But Reine-Marie could see that the blizzard had blown itself out and left in its wake, as the worst storms often did, a luminous day.

Though it was, as any good Quebecker knew, an illusion. The sun was gleaming off its fangs.

"My God," Reine-Marie gasped as the warmth of the bistro enveloped her. "Why do we live here?"

Her cheeks were bright red and her eyes, tearing up, took time to adjust to the dim light. The short walk over to the bistro through the brilliant sunshine had rendered her almost snow-blind. It wasn't enough that the bitter winter wanted to kill them, first it had to blind.

"Minus thirty-five," said Olivier proudly, as though he were responsible.

"But it's a dry cold," said Gabri. "And no wind."

It was their refrain when trying to comfort themselves as they looked out on a day so inviting and so brutal.

"I smell something," said Reine-Marie after taking off her coat and hat and mitts.

"It's not me," said Ruth. But Rosa was looking a little sheepish. Though ducks often did.

"I was wondering why you two braved the cold to come here," said Reine-Marie, following her nose, and the aroma, to the table and the empty plates smeared with maple syrup.

Armand shrugged in an exaggerated Gallic manner. "Some things are worth risking life and limb."

Olivier came out of the kitchen with a plate of warm blueberry crêpes, sausages, and maple syrup, and a café au lait.

"We left some for you," said Gabri.

"Armand made us," said Ruth.

"Oh heaven," she said, sitting down and putting her hands around the mug. "*Merci.*" Then a thought struck her. "Do you have power?"

"*Non.* A generator."

"Hooked up to the espresso machine?"

"And the oven and fridge," said Gabri.

"But not the lights?"

"Priorities," said Olivier. "Are you complaining?"

"*Mon Dieu*, no," she said.

Her eyes settled on Armand. For all the kidding, she knew her

62

husband would not bring an elderly woman into the bitter cold without a good reason.

"You came here with Ruth for more than crêpes."

"*Oui*," he said. "Ruth knows who Bertha Baumgartner was."

"Why didn't you tell us last night?"

"Because it only came to me this morning. But I wasn't really sure."

Reine-Marie raised her brows. It was unlike Ruth to be anything other than absolutely sure of herself. It was others she doubted.

"I needed to speak to Gabri and Olivier, to see what they thought," said Ruth.

"And?"

"Did you ever hear of the Baroness?" asked Gabri, taking a seat beside Reine-Marie.

It did sound vaguely familiar. Like a memory of a memory. But it was so removed that Reine-Marie knew she would never get it.

She shook her head.

"We were introduced to her when we first moved here," said Olivier. "Years ago. By Timmer Hadley."

"The woman who used to own the old Hadley house," said Reine-Marie.

She gestured in the direction of the fine house on the hill, overlooking the little village. The house where the "rich" family had once lived and had, a century ago, lorded it over the great unwashed below.

"I met the Baroness at Timmer's home," said Ruth.

"And she came to us too," said Gabri. "When we opened the B&B."

"A regular? A friend?" asked Reine-Marie.

"A cleaning woman."

"Hurry up," called Myrna, tugging at Benedict's arm.

Lucien was a few paces ahead, but Benedict had stopped and Myrna had had to backtrack to get to him.

It felt akin to running back into a flaming building.

The skin on her face was so cold it burned. It had even penetrated her thick mittens and was biting at her fingers. She squinted through the searing sunlight.

But Benedict, instead of hurrying to the bistro like any sensible

Québécois, had stopped. His back to the shops, his immense red-and-white tuque dragging on the ground, he was staring at the three huge pine trees, laden with snow, and the cottages that ringed the village green.

"It's beautiful."

His words came out in a puff, like a dialogue cloud in a cartoon.

"Yes, yes, beautiful, beautiful," said Myrna, pulling at his arm. "Now, hurry up before I kick you where it hurts."

They'd arrived in the blizzard, so this was Benedict's first look at Three Pines. The ring of homes. The smoke drifting out of the chimneys. The hills and forests.

He stood and looked at a view that hadn't changed in centuries.

And then he was tugged away.

A few minutes later, another table had been dragged over to the open fire, and they too were enjoying breakfast and coffee in the bistro.

Clara, having seen everyone running over, had joined them.

"If it's this cold for *carnaval*, I'm not taking my clothes off," she said, rubbing her arms.

"Excuse me?" said Armand.

"Nothing," said Gabri. "Never mind."

"What were you talking about when I came in?" asked Clara, accepting the mug of hot coffee. "You were all looking pretty shocked."

"Ruth figured out who Bertha Baumgartner was," said Armand.

"Who?"

"Do you remember the Baroness?" asked Gabri.

"Oh, yeah. Who could forget her?"

Clara lowered her fork and locked eyes with Ruth.

Then her gaze traveled across the bistro, to the windows. But she didn't see the sun hitting the frost-etched panes. She didn't see the village under the deep snow and the impossibly clear blue sky.

She saw a plump older woman, with small eyes, a big smile, and a mop she held like a North Pole explorer about to plant a flag.

"Her name was Bertha Baumgartner?" asked Clara.

"Well, you didn't think it was the 'Baroness,' did you?" asked Ruth.

Clara frowned. She'd actually given it no thought.

"Do you know why she was called the Baroness?" asked Armand.

They looked at Ruth.

"How the hell should I know? She never worked for me." She looked at Myrna. "You're the only cleaning woman I've ever had."

"I'm not—" Myrna began, then said, "Why bother?"

"Then why do you think this Bertha and the Baroness are the same person?" asked Armand.

"You said her home was down Mansonville way?" said Ruth, and he nodded. "An old farmhouse by the Glen?"

"*Oui.*"

"I dropped the Baroness off once, when her car broke down, years ago," said Ruth. "It sounds like the same place."

"What was it like? Can you remember?"

But, of course, Ruth remembered everything.

Every meal, every drink, every sight, every slight, real and imagined and manufactured. Every compliment. Every word spoken and unspoken.

She retained it all and rendered those memories into feelings and the feelings into poetry.

> *I prayed to be good and strong and wise,*
> *for my daily bread and deliverance*
> *from the sins I was told were mine from birth,*
> *and the Guilt of an old inheritance.*

Armand didn't have to think hard to know why that particular poem of Ruth's, a fairly obscure one, came to mind.

"Her house was small, sort of rambling. But inviting," said Ruth. "Window boxes planted with pansies and barrels of flowers on either side of the steps up to the porch. I could see a cat lying in the sun. There were all sorts of trucks and farm equipment in the yard, but there always are in these old farmhouses."

Once Armand stripped away the snow and straightened the crooked house, he could just about see it. As the home had been, once. On a warm summer day. With a younger Ruth and the Baroness.

"You haven't seen her lately?" he asked.

"Not for years," said Gabri. "She stopped working, and we lost contact. I didn't know she'd died. Did you?"

Clara shook her head and dropped her eyes.

"My mother was a cleaning lady," said Reine-Marie, rightly interpreting how Clara was feeling. "She grew close to the families she worked for, while she worked for them. But then she lost track of them. I'm sure many died and she had no idea."

Clara nodded, grateful to her for pointing out that it went both ways.

"Do you think if the Baroness Baumgartner wrote to Justin—" Gabri began.

"*Non.*"

"What was she like?" Armand asked.

"A strong personality," said Olivier. "Liked her own voice. Used to talk about her kids."

"Two boys and a girl," said Gabri. "The most wonderful children on earth. Handsome, beautiful. Smart and kind. Like their mother, she used to say, then laugh."

"And we were always expected to say, 'Don't laugh, it's true,'" said Olivier.

"And did you?" asked Reine-Marie.

"If we wanted our house cleaned, we did," said Gabri.

As they described the Baroness's personality, Clara could see her. Almost always with a smile. Sometimes warm and kind. Often with a touch of cunning. But never malicious.

A woman who was less like a baroness would be hard to find.

And yet Clara also remembered the Baroness really leaning into the mop or brush. Working hard.

There was a nobility in that.

Clara wondered why it had never occurred to her to paint the Baroness. Her small, bright eyes, at once kind and needy. Cunning, but also thoughtful. Her worn hands and face.

It was a remarkable face, filled with generosity and bile. Kindness and judgment.

"Why're you asking?" asked Gabri. "Does it matter?"

"Not really," said Armand. "It's just that the provisions of her will are a little odd."

"Oooh, odd," said Gabri. "I like that."

"You like queer," said Ruth. "You hate odd."

"That is true," he admitted. "So what was odd about the will?"

"The money," said Benedict.

"Money?" asked Olivier, leaning forward.

Lucien told them about the bequests.

Olivier's expressive face went from dumbfounded to amused and back to dumbfounded.

"Fifteen million? Dollars?" He looked at Gabri, who was also gaping. "We should've kept in touch."

"*Oui*," said Lucien, pleased with the reaction. "And a home in Switzerland."

"And one in Vienna," said Myrna.

"She was always a little loopy," said Gabri, "but she must've gone right around the bend."

"No. My father would never have allowed her to sign the will if he thought she wasn't clearheaded."

"Oh come on," said Ruth. "Even I can see it's madness. And not just the money, but choosing three people she didn't even know to be her liquidators? Why not one of us?"

Armand looked at Gabri, Olivier, Ruth, and Clara.

They'd known her. And hadn't known her.

They knew the Baroness. Not Bertha Baumgartner.

Is that why?

He and Myrna had no preconceptions. They saw her as a woman, not a cleaning woman, and certainly not a baroness.

But why would that matter?

Maybe it was their skill set. He was a cop, an investigator. Myrna was a psychologist. She could read people. They both could. But again, why would that matter to Madame Baumgartner in the execution of her will?

And how did she even know about them, when they didn't know her?

And what about . . . ? Armand turned to Benedict. How do you begin to explain him as liquidator?

"Who were the witnesses?" he asked, sitting forward again.

"Neighbors," said Lucien. "Though they wouldn't have seen the contents of the will."

Armand looked at his watch. It was coming on for eight thirty in the morning. The power hadn't yet been restored, but the tiny village of Three Pines was often among the last to be remembered by Hydro-Québec.

"You need to go?" asked Reine-Marie, remembering their conversation of the evening before.

"I'm afraid so."

"What about us?" asked Lucien.

"I'll drive you back to the farmhouse. We can dig your cars out together."

"The heirs need to be contacted," said Lucien. "I'll try to set something up for this afternoon. No use waiting."

"Sounds good to me," said Benedict.

Armand nodded. "Just let me know when and where."

"The Guilt of an old inheritance," he thought as he walked toward his car, his boots squealing on the hard-packed snow.

Is that what was in the crumbling farmhouse? Guilt, and sins that were there from birth?

CHAPTER 10

―――

"Come in, come in," said the neighbor, gesturing. "Get out of the cold."

She was young, in her mid-thirties, Gamache guessed. Only slightly older than his own daughter, Annie. And she probably shouldn't be letting complete strangers into her home.

But by the way she'd looked at him when she'd answered his knock, Gamache suspected he wasn't a complete stranger. And that was confirmed a moment later when he took off his gloves and offered his hand as they crowded into her vestibule.

"*Désolé,*" he said. "Sorry to disturb you, especially on a day like this. My name is Armand Gamache. I live down the road, in Three Pines."

"Yes, I know who you are. I'm Patricia Houle."

She took his hand, then turned to Myrna. "I know you too. You run the bookstore."

"I do. You've been in quite a few times. Nonfiction. Gardening books. But also biography."

"That's me."

Lucien introduced himself, and then she turned to Benedict.

"Benedict Pouliot," he said. "Builder."

"Come in, get warm."

They followed her into the heart of the home, the kitchen, where a large woodstove was throbbing out heat.

As with her home, there was nothing pretentious about Madame Houle. She seemed to be someone without need to impress, who, because of that, was impressive. Like her strong, simple home.

"I have a pot of tea on. Would you like a cup?"

"Not for me, thank you," said Myrna. The others also declined.

"We won't take much of your time," said Armand. "We just have a couple of questions."

"*Oui?*" asked Patricia.

"Did you know the woman who lived next door?" Myrna asked.

"The Baroness? Oh yes, though not well. Why?"

She'd noticed her visitors exchanging glances but could not have known the significance of what she'd just said. Patricia Houle had just confirmed that Ruth was right. Bertha Baumgartner was the Baroness.

"Nothing," said Myrna. "Go on."

"Was it that I called her the Baroness?" asked Patricia, looking from one to the other. "It wasn't our nickname for her. Believe me, we wouldn't have chosen that one. She called herself that."

"How long have you known her?" Lucien asked.

"A few years. Is everything all right?" She looked at Armand. "You're not here officially, are you?"

"Not in the way you think," he said. "We're liquidators of her estate."

"She died?"

"Yes, just before Christmas," said Lucien.

"I hadn't heard," said Patricia. "I know she moved into a nursing home a couple of years ago, but I didn't know she'd passed away. I'm sorry. I'd have gone to the funeral."

"You witnessed her will?" asked Armand. When she nodded, he went on. "Did she strike you as competent?"

"Oh yes," said Patricia. "She was all there. She was a little odd, granted. She did insist on being called Baroness, but we all have our eccentricities."

"I bet I can guess yours," said Myrna.

"I bet you can," said Patricia.

"You like poisonous plants. Probably have a bed dedicated to them."

"I do," Patricia admitted with a laugh.

"How did you know that?" Benedict asked.

"The books she bought," said Myrna. "*The Poison Garden* was one, as I remember. Another was . . ." Myrna strained her memory.

"Deadliest Garden Plants," said Patricia. She looked at Armand and cocked her head. "Bit of a clue, that."

Armand smiled.

"That's how I first got to know the Baroness and how I learned about poison gardens. She had one. Walked me through it and pointed out that foxglove is digitalis. Deadly. She also had monkshood, and lily-of-the-valley, and hydrangea. All toxic. Among other perennials, of course. But, strangely enough, the poisonous ones are the most beautiful."

Myrna nodded. She was also a keen gardener, though it had never occurred to her to dedicate a bed to plants that kill. But enough people did so that there were a number of books written about it. And Patricia Houle was right. The deadly flowers were among the most beautiful. And, perversely, the longest-lived.

"There're flowers that'll really kill someone?" asked Benedict.

"Supposedly," said Patricia, "though I wouldn't know how to get the poison out. You probably need a chemistry degree."

"And a desire," said Gamache.

His voice was pleasant, but his eyes took in Patricia Houle, and he amended his earlier impression. She gave off an aura not just of confidence but of competence.

He'd noticed her car parked outside, completely cleaned off. The snow around it shoveled with crisp, straight lines.

When she did a job, she did it well and she did it thoroughly.

He suspected if she needed to, she could figure out how to squeeze poison from a daffodil.

Thanking her for her help and hospitality, they left Madame Houle and headed next door.

Bertha Baumgartner's home seemed to be tilting even further under the weight of the new snow. It would be folly to go anywhere near it, and Gamache made a note to call the local town hall and get warning tape put up. And, as soon as possible, a bulldozer should be brought in.

They dug out Myrna's and Lucien's cars, but when they'd cleared off Benedict's pickup truck, Armand stopped the young man from getting in.

"You can't drive without winter tires."

"But I have to. I'll be fine."

Those were, Gamache knew, the last words of too many young people.

"Yes, you will be fine," he said. "Because you're not going anywhere in that."

"And if I do drive?" asked Benedict. "What're you going to do? Call the cops?"

"He wouldn't need to call," said Lucien, and saw that Benedict still didn't get it. "You really don't know who he is?"

Benedict shook his head.

"I'm the head of the Sûreté du Québec," said Armand.

"Chief Superintendent Gamache," said Lucien.

Benedict said either "Oh shit" or "No shit." Either way, *merde* was involved.

"Really?"

Gamache nodded. *"C'est la vérité."*

Benedict looked behind him, to his pickup, and mumbled something that sounded like "What fucking luck."

Gamache grinned. He'd had luck like this too, when he was Benedict's age. Took a long time before he realized it was, in fact, good luck.

"I guess I have no choice," said Benedict.

"Bon. Call the CAA when the phones come back. Have it towed to a garage and decent winter tires put on. Not the cheap ones. *D'accord?"*

"Got it," Benedict mumbled to the snow on his boots.

"It's all right," said Gamache quietly. "We'll pay for the tires."

"I'll pay you back."

"Just give me that lesson in driving on snow you promised. We'll call it even."

"Merci."

"Good." Gamache turned to Lucien. "Let me know about the meeting with Madame Baumgartner's children."

"I will," said Lucien.

As she drove Benedict back to Three Pines, Myrna looked at the thick snow in the yard. And thought of the poisonous plants buried there. Frozen, but not dead. Just waiting.

Though the real threat, Myrna knew, didn't come from the poison flowers. Those you could see. Those you knew about. And besides, they at least were pretty.

No. The real danger in a garden came from the bindweed. That moved underground, then surfaced and took hold. Strangling plant after healthy plant. Killing them all, slowly. And for no apparent reason, except that it was its nature.

And then it disappeared underground again.

Yes, the real danger always came from the thing you couldn't see.

CHAPTER 11

⁓

"So what's the problem?"

"What makes you think there's a problem?" Armand asked.

"You aren't eating your . . . éclair."

Each of her words was carefully enunciated, though they were still muffled, as though wrapped in too much care and cotton batting.

And her movements, as her hand brought her own pastry to her mouth, were also considered. Deliberate. Precise. Slow.

Gamache visited Isabelle Lacoste at least once a week at her home in Montréal. When the weather was good, they'd go for a short walk, but mostly, like today, they sat in her kitchen and talked. He'd gotten into the habit of discussing events with her. Getting her take on things. Her opinions and advice.

She was one of his senior officers.

He looked now, as he always did, for any sign of improvement. Real was best, but he'd even settle for imagined. He thought perhaps her hands were steadier. Her words clearer. Her vocabulary richer.

Yes. Without a doubt. Maybe.

"Is it the internal investigation?" she asked, and took a bite of the mille-feuille that Armand had brought her from Sarah's Boulangerie, knowing it was her favorite.

"No. That's just about over."

"Still, they're taking their sweet time. What's the problem?"

"We both know the problem," he said.

"Yes. The drugs. Nothing more there?"

She studied him. Looking for signs of improvement. Of reason to hope this really would all go away soon.

The Chief looked relaxed. Confident. But then he almost always did. It was what he hid that worried her.

Isabelle's brow furrowed in concentration.

"I'm tiring you out," he said, and made to get up. "I'm sorry."

"No, no, please." She waved him back down. "I need . . . stimulation. The kids are off school because of the storm and have decided I need to learn to count to a . . . hundred. We did that all morning before I kicked them outside. I tried to explain that I can count. Have been able to for . . . months, but still, they insisted." She looked into Armand's eyes. "Help me."

It was said with a comically pathetic inflection, intentionally exaggerated. But still, it broke his heart.

"I'm kidding, *patron*," she said, sensing more than seeing his sorrow. "More coffee?"

"Please."

He followed her to the counter. Her gait was slow. Halting. Deliberate. And so much better than anyone, including her doctors, had dared hope.

Isabelle's son and daughter were outside, building snow forts with the neighborhood children. Through the windows Armand and Isabelle could hear shrieks as one "army" attacked those who held the fort.

Playing the same games Armand had played as a child. The same ones Isabelle, twenty-five years later, had played. Games of domination and war.

"Let's hope they never know . . . what . . . it's really like," said Isabelle, standing by the window, next to her boss and mentor.

He nodded.

The explosions. The chaos. The acrid stink of gun smoke. The blinding grit as stone and cement and brick were pulverized. Choking the air.

The screams. Choking the air.

The pain.

His grip tightened on the counter as it washed over him. Sweeping him up. Tossing and spinning. Drowning him.

"Does your hand still tremble?" she asked quietly.

He gathered himself and nodded.

"Sometimes. When I'm tired or particularly stressed. But not like it used to."

"And the limp?"

"Again, mostly when I'm tired. I barely notice it anymore. It was years ago." Unlike Isabelle's wounds, which were mere months old. He marveled at that. It seemed both ages ago and yesterday.

"Do you think about it?" she asked.

"What happened when you were hurt?"

He turned to look at her. That face, so familiar from across so many bodies. So many desks, conference tables. So many hastily set-up incident rooms in basements and barns and cabins across Québec. As they'd investigated murders. Isabelle. Jean-Guy. Himself.

Isabelle Lacoste had come to him as a young agent, barely twenty-five. Rejected by her own department for not being brutal enough, cynical enough, malleable enough to know what was right and to do wrong.

He'd been the head of homicide then and given her a job in his department, the most prestigious within the Sûreté du Québec. To the astonishment of her former colleagues.

And Isabelle Lacoste had risen through the ranks, eventually taking over from Gamache himself when he'd become head of the academy and then head of the whole Sûreté. As he was now.

Sort of.

She'd aged, of course. Faster than she should have, would have, had he not brought her on board. Had he not made her Chief Inspector. And had that last action against the cartels not taken place. Mere months ago.

"Yes," he said. "I think about it."

Isabelle hitting the floor. Shot in the head. What had seemed her last act had given them a chance. Had, in fact, saved them all. But still, it had been a bloody nightmare.

He remembered that, the most recent action. But he also remembered, equally vividly, all the raids, the assaults, the arrests. The investigations over the years. The victims.

All the sightless, staring eyes. Of men, women, children whose murder he'd investigated. Over the years. Whose murderer he'd hunted down.

All the agents he'd sent, often led, into the gun smoke.

And he remembered his hand raised, ready to knock on the closed door. The rapping of the Grim Reaper. To do murder himself. Not physically, but Armand Gamache was realistic enough to know this was a killing nevertheless. He carried with him always the faces of fathers, mothers, wives, and husbands. Inquisitive. Curious. Politely they opened the door and looked at this stranger.

And then, as he spoke the fateful words, their faces changed. And he watched their world collapse. Pinning them under the rubble. Crushed under a grief so profound most never emerged. And those who did came out dazed into a world forever changed.

The person they were before his arrival was dead. Gone.

When a murder was committed, more than one person died.

Yes. He remembered.

"But I try not to dwell on it," he said to Isabelle.

Or, worse, dwell in it. Take up residence in the tragedies, the pain. The hurt. To make a home in hell.

But leaving was hard. Especially his agents, men and women whose lives were lost because they'd followed his orders. Followed him. He'd felt, for a long time, that he owed it to them to not leave that place of sorrow. To keep them company there.

His friends and therapists had helped him to see that that was doing them a disservice. Their lives could not be defined by their deaths. They belonged not in perpetual pain but in the beauty of their short lives.

His inability to move on would trap them forever in those final horrific moments.

Armand watched as Isabelle carefully lowered her mug to the kitchen table. When it was just an inch away from the surface, her grip slipped and the coffee spilled. Not much, but he could see her anger. Frustration. Embarrassment.

He offered her his handkerchief to sop it up.

"*Merci.*" She grabbed it from him and wiped. He put out his hand to take it back, but she kept it. "I'll w-w-w . . . wash it and get it back to you," she snapped.

"Isabelle," he said, his voice calm but firm. "Look at me."

She lifted her eyes from the soiled handkerchief to his face.

"I hated it too."

"What?"

"My body. I hated it for letting me down. For letting this happen." He ran his finger along the scar at his temple. "For not moving fast enough. For not seeing it coming. For being on the ground, not being able to get up to protect my agents. I hated it for not healing fast enough. I hated when I stumbled. When Reine-Marie had to hold my hand to keep me steady. I could see people staring at me with pity as I limped or searched for a word."

Isabelle nodded.

"I wanted my old body back," said Armand. "The strong and healthy one."

"Before," she said.

"Before," he nodded.

They sat in silence, except for the far-off laughter of the children.

"That's how I feel," she said. "I hate my . . . body. I hate that I can't pick up my kids or play with them, or if I do get onto the floor with them, they have to help me up. I hate it. I hate that I can't . . . read them to sleep, and that I get tired so easily, and lose my train of thought. I hate that some days I can't add and some days I can't . . . subtract. And some days—"

Isabelle paused, gathering herself. She looked into his eyes.

"I forget their names, *patron*," she whispered. "My own children."

It was no use telling her he understood. Or that it was all right. She'd earned the right to no easy answer.

"And what do you love, Isabelle?"

"Pardon?"

Gamache closed his eyes and raised his face to the ceiling. "'White plates and cups, clean-gleaming, / Ringed with blue lines; and feathery, faery dust; / Wet roofs, beneath the lamp-light; the strong crust / Of friendly bread.'"

He opened his eyes, looked at Isabelle, and smiled, deep lines forming at his eyes and down his worn face.

"There's more, but I won't go on. It's a poem by Rupert Brooke. He was a soldier in the First World War. It helped him to th things he loved. It helped me too. I made mental lists and followed the things I love, the people I love, back to sanity. I still do."

He could see her thinking.

What he was suggesting wasn't a magic cure for a bullet to the brain. A huge amount of work, of pain, physical and emotional, lay ahead. But it might as well be done in the sunlight.

"I'm stronger, healthier now than I was before any of that happened," said Gamache. "Physically. Emotionally. Because I've had to be. And you will be too."

"Things are strongest where they're broken," said Lacoste. "Agent Morin said that."

Things are strongest where they're broken.

Armand heard again the impossibly and eternally youthful voice of Paul Morin. As though he were standing right there, in Isabelle's sunny kitchen with them.

And Agent Morin had been right. But oh the pain of mending.

"I'm lucky in a way," Isabelle said after a few moments. "I can't remember anything about that day. Nothing. I think that helps."

"I think it does."

"My kids keep wanting to read me . . . Pinocchio. Something to do with what happened, but damned if it makes sense to me. Pinocchio, *patron*?"

"Sometimes being shot in the head is a blessing."

She laughed. "How do you do it?"

"Remember?"

"Forget."

He took a breath, looked down at his feet, then back up, into her eyes.

"I had a mentor once—" he said.

"Oh Jesus, not the one who taught you poetry," she said in mock panic. He had that "poetry" look about him.

"No, but just for that." He cleared his throat. "'The Wreck of the Hesperus,'" he announced, and opened his mouth as though to launch into the epic verse. But instead he smiled and saw Isabelle beaming with amusement.

"What I was going to say is that my mentor had this theory that our lives are like an aboriginal longhouse. Just one huge room." He swept one arm out to illustrate scope. "He said that if we thought we could compartmentalize things, we were deluding ourselves. Everyone we meet, every word we speak, every action taken or not taken lives in our longhouse. With us. Always. Never to be expelled or locked away."

"That's a pretty scary thought," said Isabelle.

"*Absolument*. My mentor, my first chief inspector, said to me, 'Armand, if you don't want your longhouse to smell like *merde*, you have to do two things—'"

"Not let Ruth Zardo in?" asked Isabelle.

Armand laughed. "Too late for that. For both of us."

In a flash he was back there. Running toward the ambulance. Isabelle on the gurney, unconscious. The old poet's bony hands holding Isabelle's. Her voice unwavering as she whispered to Isabelle over and over again the only thing that mattered.

That she was loved.

Isabelle would never remember that, and Armand would never forget it.

"*Non*. He said, 'Be very, very careful who you let into your life. And learn to make peace with whatever happens. You can't erase the past. It's trapped in there with you. But you can make peace with it. If you don't,' he said, 'you'll be at perpetual war.'"

Armand smiled at the memory.

"I think he knew what an idiot he was dealing with. He could see I was getting ready to tell him my own theory of life. At twenty-three. He showed me the door. But just as I was leaving, he said, 'And the enemy you'll be fighting is yourself.'"

Gamache hadn't thought of that encounter for years. But he had thought of his life, from that moment forward, as a longhouse.

And in his longhouse, as he glanced back down it now, he saw all the young agents, all the men and women, boys and girls, whose lives he'd affected.

He could also see, standing there, the people who'd hurt him. Badly. Almost killed him.

They all lived there.

And while he would never be friends with many of those memories, those ghosts, he had worked very hard to make peace with them. With what he'd done and what had been done to him.

"And are the opioids there, *patron*? In your longhouse?"

Her question brought him back with a jolt, to her comfortable home.

"Have you found them?"

"Not all, *non*. The last of it, here in Montréal, has disappeared," he admitted.

"How much?"

"Enough to produce hundreds of thousands of hits."

She was silent. Not saying what he knew better than anyone.

Each one of those hits could kill.

"*Merde*," she whispered, then immediately apologized to him. "*Désolée*."

She rarely swore and almost never in front of the Chief. But this one escaped, riding the wave of revulsion.

"There's more," she said, studying the man she'd gotten to know so well. Better than her own father. "Something else is bothering you."

Weighing on him, was more like it, but she could not quite come up with that word.

"*Oui*. It's about the academy."

"The Sûreté Academy?"

"Yes. There's a problem. They want to expel one of the cadets."

"It happens," said Isabelle. "I'm sorry, *patron*, but why is it your concern?"

"The one the Commander called me about, and wants to expel, is Amelia Choquet."

Isabelle Lacoste settled back in her chair and considered him closely. "And? Why would he call you about this? You're no longer head of the academy."

"True."

And she saw that this wasn't just a weight on Gamache. It was close to crushing.

"What is it, *patron*?"

"They found opioids in her possession."

"Christ." And this time she didn't apologize. "How much?"

"It seems to be too much for personal consumption."

"She's trafficking? At the academy?"

"It would appear so."

Now Isabelle was quiet. Absorbing. Thinking.

Armand gave her time.

"Is it from your shipment?" she asked. She hadn't meant to give him ownership, but that was the way it came out. And they both knew he did have ownership, if not of the actual drugs then of the situation.

"They haven't been sent to the lab yet, but it's possible, yes." He looked down at his hands, one clasping the other. "I have a decision to make."

"About Cadet Choquet."

"*Oui.* And frankly, I don't know what to do."

She wished with all her heart she could help him.

"I'm sorry, Chief, but surely this is up to the Commander. Not you."

Watching Chief Superintendent Gamache, Lacoste couldn't fathom what he was thinking. He seemed to be asking for her help and yet keeping some information from her.

"There's something you're not telling me."

"Let me ask you this, Isabelle," he said, ignoring her statement. "What would you do if you were me?"

"And a cadet was found with drugs in her possession? I'd leave that up to the Commander of the academy. It's not your business, *patron.*"

"Oh, but it is, Isabelle. If it's my opioids, as you put it, in her possession."

"Where did she get the drugs from?" Isabelle asked. "Has she told you?"

"The Commander hasn't interviewed her yet. As far as he knows, Cadet Choquet doesn't even realize they've been found. I'm going there now. If he expels her, she'll die. I know that much."

Lacoste nodded. She knew it too. What most didn't know was why Gamache had let Amelia Choquet into the academy in the first place. Why that messed-up young woman, with the history of drug abuse and prostitution, had been given a coveted place at the Sûreté school.

But Isabelle knew. Or thought she knew.

The same reason he'd reached down into the bowels of her own career and given her a job.

Had reached down and dragged Jean-Guy up, a moment from being fired himself.

It was the same reason Chief Superintendent Gamache was now considering convincing the current Commander to keep Cadet Choquet.

This was a man who profoundly believed in second chances.

Except this wouldn't be Amelia Choquet's second chance. It would be her third.

And that was, in Lacoste's view, one too many.

There was grace in second chances and foolishness in third. And perhaps worse than foolishness.

There was, or could be, outright danger. Believing a person capable of redemption when they'd proven they were not.

Amelia Choquet hadn't been caught cheating on an exam or stealing some trinket from a fellow cadet. She'd been caught with a drug so potent, so dangerous, it eventually killed almost everyone who took it. Amelia Choquet knew that. Knew she was trafficking in death.

Chief Inspector Lacoste regarded the steady man in front of her, who believed everyone could be saved. Believed he could save them.

It was both his saving grace and his blind spot. And few knew better than Isabelle Lacoste what that meant. Some things hurtled. Some slithered. But nothing good ever came out of a blind spot.

Isabelle noticed that Gamache's right hand wasn't trembling. But it was clenched into a fist.

CHAPTER 12

"Sit."

The Commander of the Sûreté Academy did not stand when Cadet Choquet entered the office, and neither did Chief Superintendent Gamache.

Amelia waited at the door, defiant as ever, then walked across the room and dropped into the chair indicated, crossing her arms tight over her chest. Glaring straight ahead.

She looked exactly as Gamache remembered her.

Hair jet-black and spiky. Though perhaps not quite as belligerent in its cut. She was not, he suspected, softening so much as maturing. Or perhaps he was just getting used to it.

Cadet Choquet was in the final year of her training. Within months of graduation.

She was small but powerful. Not in her build but in her presence. She radiated aggression.

Fuck off.

The words fairly pulsed off her, a spiky aura.

Was a time, when Gamache first met her, that she'd actually say it. To his face. To anyone's and everyone's face. But now she simply thought it. Such was the force of the petite woman, though, that she might as well be screaming it.

Still, thought Gamache, it was progress. Of sorts.

She gave him one curt nod.

Fuck off.

He didn't respond. Simply watched her.

The piercings were still in place. Through her eyebrow, her nose and cheek. Along the gristle of her ears.

And . . . ? Yes. There it was.

The click, click, click as she moved the post in her tongue up and down, knocking it against her teeth.

In poker it would be considered a "tell."

Click, click, click. Amelia's unconscious Morse code.

One day he might tell her about her tell. But not just yet. Right now it served a purpose. His purpose.

Click. Click. Click.

SOS.

Clean sheets, thought Gamache. *The scent of wood smoke. Feeling Henri's head on my slippers.* He went through his own private code. A sort of rosary.

Flaky croissants.

"Do you know why you're here?" the Commander asked the cadet.

When Gamache had left the academy to take up the job of chief superintendent of the Sûreté, he'd had long discussions with his successor about the cadets. Including the suggestion that the students be allowed to be individuals. Amelia Choquet was certainly that. And more.

"No, I do not know why you wanted to see me." Pause. "Sir."

The Commander picked up an envelope from his desk, and from it he took a baggie.

"Recognize this?"

"No."

The answer came too quickly for her to be surprised. She knew exactly why she was there. And she knew exactly what was in that little plastic bag.

Gamache knew Amelia well enough to know she'd prepared for this encounter. Perhaps a little too much. She wasn't showing the natural curiosity, even astonishment, of the innocent.

Instead she displayed the rehearsed answers of the guilty.

He glanced at the Commander to see if he'd picked up on the same thing and saw that he of course had.

Gamache felt his heart speed up as he saw the point of no return approaching. He'd made up his mind what had to be done, though it seemed his heart remained unconvinced. But he knew he had to see this through.

Amelia Choquet's breathing had changed. Shorter, more rapid.

She too could see the point of no return. Just there. On the horizon. Getting closer. Fast.

The clicking had stopped. She was alert. An animal who, after living with smaller creatures, suddenly discovered a world of giants. Suddenly discovered it was tinier than it realized. More vulnerable than it thought. More threatened than it believed possible. A creature looking for escape and finding only a cliff.

"It was in your room, under your mattress," said the Commander.

"You searched my room?" She sounded indignant, and Gamache almost admired her rally.

Almost.

"That's not exactly the lede, is it, Cadet Choquet?" The Commander lowered the baggie to his desk. "This is a narcotic. Enough to traffic."

"It's not mine. I have no idea where it came from. If I was going to do something as stupid as having shit in the academy, I'd find a better hiding place. Like maybe someone else's room."

"Are you suggesting someone planted it?" asked Gamache.

She shrugged.

"Intentionally?" he persisted. "Trying to set you up? Or just wanting to get it out of their own room?"

"Take your pick. All I know is, it isn't mine."

"The bag has been fingerprinted—"

"Clever."

The Commander stared at her. Amelia, Gamache knew, had a rare ability to get up people's noses. Though why she'd want to be there was anyone's guess.

"—and we'll have the results soon. Where did you get it from?"

"It's. Not. Mine."

The clicking had begun again. A rat-a-tat-tat now, designed to annoy.

Gamache could see the Commander struggling not to claw his way across his desk and reach for her throat.

And Cadet Choquet was doing nothing to save herself. In fact, just the opposite. She was taunting them. Arrogant, smug, almost certainly deceitful, she was demanding to be doubted. And worse.

An innocent cadet, when a Schedule 1 drug was discovered in her room, would protest innocence and try to work with them to find out whose it was.

A guilty cadet would almost certainly at least pretend to do the same.

But she was doing neither.

She'd gone from a vulnerable creature, trapped and frightened, to an aggressor, throwing out ridiculous and obvious lies.

Amelia Choquet was a senior cadet. She'd matured into a natural leader, not the bully Gamache feared she'd become.

She was quick-witted, alert. Someone others instinctively wanted to follow.

Which made Cadet Choquet as trafficker in narcotics all the more dangerous. But not, with her background, completely unbelievable.

Leaning closer to her, he saw the tattoos on her wrists and forearms, where the sleeves of her uniform had ridden up. Then his sharp gaze traveled to her face, and he saw something else. Something that might explain her lack of judgment, her self-destructive, erratic behavior in this meeting.

Her reactions had been wild. Unpredictable. The reactions of a junkie.

She hadn't . . . ?

His own eyes widened a little.

"You foolish, foolish woman." His voice was practically a snarl. Then he turned to the Commander. "We need a blood test. She's high."

"Fuck you."

He glared at her. "When did you last use?"

"I've taken nothing."

"Look at her," Gamache said to the Commander before turning back to Amelia. "Your pupils are dilated. You think I don't know what that means? Search her room again," he said, and the Commander placed a call.

"I have a mind to end it right now," Gamache said, turning back to Amelia.

"Don't you dare. I've come too far. We're so close. I can do this."

"You can't. You've messed up. You're messed up. You've gone too far."

"No, no. These are eyedrops. Only eyedrops." She was almost begging. "It looks like I'm stoned, but I'm not."

"Tell the agents searching her room to look for eyedrops," said Gamache, who wanted, was almost desperate, to believe her. To believe she hadn't taken any of the drug herself.

"They won't find any," said Amelia. "I threw them away."

There was silence as Gamache stared deep into the dilated eyes of the cadet.

Seeing the look on Gamache's face, she turned away from him and spoke to the Commander. "If you think I'd deal in that shit, you're a worse judge of character than I thought."

"Drugs change people," said the Commander. "Addiction changes people. As I think you know."

"I've been clean for years," she said. "I'm not stoned. Why the fuck would I enroll in the Sûreté, for God's sake, if I was still a junkie?"

Gamache started to laugh. "You're kidding, right? You get a gun and access to any amount of drugs. Most dirty agents at least have the sense to wait until they've graduated and are on the street before they turn. But then most don't arrive as addicts."

"I was never an addict, and you know it." She was all but screaming at him now. "I used, yes. But I was never addicted. I quit. In time."

Her own words seemed to give her pause as she remembered how and why she quit. In time.

It was because of this man. Who'd given her a home here. A purpose and a direction. A chance.

"I'm not trafficking," she said. Her voice quieter. "I'm not using."

Gamache examined her. Studied her. So much was riding on this.

He'd known, when he'd let her into the academy, that if she succeeded, she had the makings of a remarkable Sûreté officer. A street kid, a junkie turned cop.

It had given her a huge advantage. She knew things other agents never could. She knew them not just in her intellect but deep in her gut. She had contacts, credibility, the language of the streets etched into her very skin. She could get to places and people no one else could reach.

And she knew the despair of the streets. The cold, lonely deaths of opioid addicts.

Gamache had hoped Amelia Choquet shared his profound desire to stop that plague. But now he wondered just how big a misjudgment he'd made. And how big a mistake he was about to make.

While in the gutter, Amelia Choquet had read the poets, the philosophers. She was an autodidact, who'd taught herself Latin and Greek. Literature. Poetry.

Yes, if she succeeded, she'd go far. In the Sûreté. In life.

But he'd also known if she failed, it would be equally spectacular.

And it seemed, so close to the finish line, Amelia Choquet had failed. Spectacularly.

She knew, of course, when she walked in that they'd found the drugs. Having them there was an act of self-destruction.

Gamache closed his eyes. A decision had to be made. No, he realized, that was wrong. The decision he'd already made had to be carried out. No matter how distasteful.

Sitting in the Commander's office, he could smell wet wool and hear the tapping of snow as it fell.

Opening his eyes, he turned to the Commander. "We need a blood test, to confirm and to build the case against Cadet Choquet."

"Look, give me another chance," she said. "It was a mistake."

"A mistake?" said Gamache. "Is that what you call it? A parking ticket is a mistake. This is . . . ." He searched for the word. "Ruinous. You've ruined your life, and this time there'll be no more chances. You'll be arrested and you'll be charged. Like anyone else."

"Please," she said.

Gamache looked at the Commander, who made a subtle gesture. It was the Chief Superintendent's call.

"Where did you get the stuff?" Gamache asked.

"I can't tell you that."

"Oh, I think you can, and you will. Tell us that and we might go easier on you."

There was a pause, as everything hung in the balance.

And then Amelia Choquet tipped that balance.

"I got it from you."

Gamache's eyes widened just a little as he glared at her. Warning her. Go no further.

The scent of fresh croissants. Holding Reine-Marie in my arms, in bed, on a rainy morning. Driving across the Champlain Bridge and seeing the Mon-tréal skyline.

"What do—" began the Commander.

"You don't even know, do you?" she said to Gamache, cutting off the Commander. "You don't know if this's the shit you let in. You've lost track of it, haven't you?" Now she leaned toward Gamache, her pupils dilated. "What the fuck did you think would happen when you made that choice? Is that why you're so angry? Is that why you want to punish me? For your own mistake?"

"This isn't a punishment, Cadet, it's a consequence. Do I want to find the drugs? Absolutely. But I never thought it would start with you."

"Save it. You knew who I was when you let me in."

"We should consider ourselves lucky, I suppose, that you didn't burn the place down."

"How do you know I haven't?"

Her words froze him for a moment.

"Where did you get it from? Who sold it to you?" he asked, menace in his voice now.

"What a fucking shitshow you've made of being Chief Superinten-dent."

"Cadet," warned the Commander.

"Why're you even consulting him?" she asked the Commander, ac-knowledging him again, jabbing her finger at Gamache. "He's on suspension. You're nobody now, *patron*."

The last word was spit out. And in the silence the clicking began again. This time metronome-slow. Counting the passing moments. While Gamache sat perfectly still.

"If I'm going down, I'm just following you," Amelia said, leaning even further forward. "You're a ruin, old man."

She must be out of her mind, thought the Commander. Stoned. Sui-cidal. Insane.

"Feel better?" asked Gamache, his voice steady. "Getting the bile out? Spewing over someone else?"

"At least I chose someone my own size," said Amelia.

"Good. And now we can talk reasonably."

While Chief Superintendent Gamache's voice was calm, the Com-mander felt the force of his personality. So much stronger than the young cadet's. If he wanted to, the Commander knew, Gamache could crush her.

But what he felt vibrating off the Chief Superintendent wasn't what he expected. He expected anger, rage.

There was, certainly, some of that, but there was something else. Something even more powerful.

Concern. Far greater than Gamache's anger was his caring.

Good God, thought the Commander. *He's going to try to talk sense into a junkie.*

But the Commander was wrong.

"We will take a blood test," said Gamache.

"You don't have my permission," said Amelia. "And unless you're willing to tie me down, you won't get anything out of me. And I'll sue your ass."

Gamache nodded. "I see." He turned to the Commander. "I suggest Cadet Choquet wait outside, supervised, while we talk."

Myrna set down her ham sandwich on croissant as the phone rang.

From deep in the armchair in her bookstore, she looked over at it. Hauling herself up with a grunt, she went to the counter.

"Oui, allô."

"I spoke to the oldest son. Anthony Baumgartner. He's arranged for his brother and sister to be at his place today at three o'clock."

"Who is this?" asked Myrna pleasantly, though she knew perfectly well who it was.

"It's Lucien Mercier. The notary."

Out the bay window of her shop, Myrna Landers saw puffs of snow being lifted, then falling onto the massive banks that now circled the village green. They were so high, Myrna could no longer see who was doing the shoveling. Just the bright red shovel and the cloud of snow.

It felt as though she was ringed in by a newly formed mountain range.

"Three o'clock," repeated Myrna, writing it down. She glanced at the clock. It was now one thirty. "Give me the address." She wrote it too. "I'll let Armand know to meet us there."

Myrna replaced the phone and turned to look out the window again, watching the small eruptions all around the village green.

Then she put in a quick call to Armand, giving him the time and place of the meeting with the Baroness's family. After wolfing down the last of her sandwich, she headed back outside.

"My turn," said Myrna, taking the shovel from Benedict, who was both sweating and freezing.

"My God," said Clara, leaning on her shovel and surveying the amount still left to be cleared. "Why do we live here?"

The day sparkled and their noses dripped and their feet froze, and their inner layer of clothing clung to their bodies in perspiration while their outer layer froze brittle. As they dug the village out.

Beside her, Myrna heard Clara muttering. Each word contained in a puff, accompanied by a shovelful of snow.

"Barbados."

"St. Lucia," said Myrna.

"Jamaica," came the response.

"Antigua," both women said, leaning into their job.

When they'd run out of Caribbean islands, they went on to food. Mille-feuilles.

Lobster. Lemon posset.

These things they loved.

Armand hung up just as the Commander returned to his office.

"She's sitting on the bench in the anteroom. My assistant is watching her."

"Does your assistant have a Taser?"

The Commander gave one brief laugh and pulled a chair up to face Gamache.

"So what're we going to do with her?"

"What would you suggest?" asked Gamache. "This is your academy. She's one of your cadets."

The Commander paused for a moment, watching the Chief Superintendent.

"Is she, Armand? She seems yours."

Gamache smiled. "Do you think it was a mistake, letting her in?"

"A stoned former prostitute junkie who's dealing opioids in the academy? Are you kidding? She's a delight."

Armand gave one, not altogether amused, chuckle.

"And yet not everyone sees it that way," he said before his face grew serious again.

"You know, the truth is," said the Commander, "until this happened, Cadet Choquet was a standout. Unconventional. Annoying as hell. But brilliant. And not given to deceit. I thought."

The Commander looked at the door and imagined the once-promising young woman sitting on the other side.

Once again the fate of reckless youth was being decided by old men behind closed doors. Though neither man was old, they were probably, he thought, older than she would ever be.

Cadet Choquet hadn't been just reckless. Chief Superintendent Gamache was right. Her actions had been ruinous. But ruins could, with great effort, be restored. Or they could collapse entirely, hurting everyone trying to help.

"What're you thinking?" the Commander asked.

For Gamache was thinking something. Considering something.

"What would happen," Gamache asked, "if we cut her loose?"

"Expel her, you mean."

It was certainly one of the few options open to them.

He went through the possibilities. They could give Cadet Choquet a warning and forget this ever happened. Sweep it under an already fairly lumpy academy carpet.

Kids made mistakes and should not be handicapped the rest of their lives for them. Though this seemed considerably more than a "mistake."

Or they could kick her out of the academy.

Or they could have her arrested and tried for possession and trafficking.

Chief Superintendent Gamache was considering the middle option. What would be, with any other cadet, a reasonable, even kind response.

It would be punishment, a consequence, but it would not blight the rest of their life.

Except they were talking about Amelia Choquet. A young woman with a history of prostitution. Of drug abuse. Who had fallen back into old habits.

The Commander reflected. "I've begun researching rehabs. Whichever route we choose, that'll be necessary."

When there was no response, he looked over at the Chief Superintendent, who was staring at him.

The Commander's eyes widened.

"*Non?* But if we don't—"

His mind retreated, back to the fork in the road. And then he took the other route.

His face flattened, all expression sliding from it, as he stared into Cadet Choquet's future. If they took that road.

"You'd do that?" he asked, quietly. "Not even try to get her help?"

"I helped once, and look where it got us. If she wants help, she has to come to it herself. It's more effective. We both know that."

"No we don't. What we know is that she's a junkie who's slipped. She's our responsibility, Armand. We have to help her up."

"She isn't ready. You can see that. It would be wasting a precious rehab place. A place another kid could use. A kid who is ready."

"Are you kidding me?" It was all the Commander could do to get the words out. "Are you trying to convince me, or yourself, that this is some big favor you're doing?"

"Carrying her is no favor."

"Seems to me when you were hurt, you were carried to safety. No one expected you to crawl to the emergency ward."

Gamache sat there, his entire body tingling. With the truth of it. But he needed to remain firm. Resolute.

"She's wounded, Armand. Deep down. As surely as if she'd been shot. She needs our help."

"She needs to know she can do this herself. If she can, there'll be no more slips. That's the help we give her now."

"For God's sake, Armand, if you cut her loose, you kill her. You know that."

"No. If I cut her loose, I allow her to own her own life. She can do it. I know she can."

"You came to that conclusion sipping scotch beside your fireplace, did you?"

The two men stared at each other. What the Commander said wasn't far from the truth. Armand had sat in his living room, Henri's head on his feet, Reine-Marie reading archive files across from him. While outside, snow gently fell. And Chief Superintendent Gamache considered the fate of reckless youth.

Amelia. And thousands of others. Maybe hundreds of thousands of others.

He'd weighed the options. In front of the hearth.

Safe and sound. Warm and loved. He'd considered his options and the atrocity he was about to commit.

Twenty minutes later they stood in the long hallway by the entrance, and exit, to the Sûreté Academy.

Amelia Choquet, no longer in her uniform, walked toward them, a member of staff on either side of her. A large knapsack was slung over her shoulder, bulging not with clothes, Gamache suspected by the sharp angles of the canvas bag, but with the only things Amelia considered worth keeping.

Books.

He watched her progress, and as she passed him, neither said a word.

She'd return to the streets, of course. To the gutter. To the drugs and prostitution necessary to pay for the next hit. And the next.

A few paces from them, Amelia stopped. She reached into her bag, then in one fluid motion she turned and threw something at them. It spun through the air with such speed the Commander, standing next to Gamache, barely had time to duck away.

But Gamache's instincts were different.

He didn't flinch. Instead his right hand shot up, and just before the object struck him in the face, he caught it.

The last he saw of Amelia Choquet was a sneer as she turned her back on him and, lifting her middle finger, she walked into her new life. Her old life.

Gamache stood there contemplating the empty rectangle of light, until the door closed and the place fell dark. Only then did he look down at the book in his hand. It was the small book he had offered her that first day at the academy. A lifetime ago.

His own copy. Marcus Aurelius. *Meditations.*

She'd turned it down, sneering at the offer. But now he looked at the slim volume. Amelia had gone out and bought her own. And hurled it in his face.

"*Excusez-moi,*" he said to the Commander, who was staring at him with something close to loathing. "May I use your office? Privately?"

"Of course."

Gamache placed a call, though the door wasn't quite closed and the Commander heard. Because he was listening.

"She's left. Follow her."

The Commander understood then what Gamache had done. What he was doing. What had almost certainly been the plan all along.

Chief Superintendent Gamache was releasing the young woman into the wild. And where would she go? Back to the gutter, certainly. And there, amid the filth, she would search out more dope.

She would lead them to the trafficker. And perhaps the rest of the opioids that the head of the Sûreté du Québec had allowed into the country.

Chief Superintendent Gamache would recover the drugs and save any number of lives. But he would have to step over the body of Amelia Choquet to do it.

As he watched Gamache leave the academy, the Commander didn't know if he admired the head of the Sûreté more. Or less.

He also harbored an unworthy thought. And as much as he tried to dismiss it, the idea refused to leave.

The Commander wondered if the Chief Superintendent had planted the drugs himself. Knowing this would happen.

In his car, before heading to the rendezvous with Myrna and the others, Armand took off his gloves, put on his reading glasses, and held the book between his large hands.

Then he opened it, revisiting the familiar passages. An old friend.

As he flipped through the dog-eared pages, he found lines she'd underlined.

"It is not death that a man should fear, but he should fear never beginning to live."

And he thought of the click, click, clicking he'd heard as Amelia had passed him in the hallway. Her tell.

Save Our Souls.

CHAPTER 13

⁓

"Armand, you need to hear this."

Gamache had barely arrived at the home of Bertha Baumgartner's eldest son when Myrna dragged him into the living room, where they'd all assembled.

He'd taken off his coat, tuque, mitts, and boots and now stood in stocking feet quickly taking in the room. Bookshelves were built along the far wall, with books and framed photos and the mementos people accumulate. There was art on the other walls. None of it avant-garde, but some decent watercolors, a few oil paintings, some numbered prints. Windows looked onto the backyard, with mature trees and lawn covered in deep, bright snow. A fire was in the grate.

The room was done in muted, slightly masculine shades of beiges and blues. It was a room, a home, that whispered comfort and success.

"Armand Gamache," he said, extending his hand to the three Baumgartner siblings. "I'm so sorry for your loss."

There was a slight hesitation as they stared at him. That now-familiar look of surprise as someone they saw in their living rooms on TV appeared unexpectedly in their living room in person. In three dimensions.

Walking and talking.

They shook hands.

Anthony, Caroline, and Hugo.

Tall, fine boned. The healthy complexions of people who ate well and looked after themselves.

Except Hugo.

He seemed to take after his mother. He was short, round, ruddy. A duckling among swans. Though, really, he more resembled a toad.

At fifty-two, Anthony Baumgartner was the oldest, followed by Caroline, and finally Hugo. Although Hugo seemed much older than the others, with features that looked like they'd been worn down by the elements. A sandstone statue left out too long. His hair was iron-gray. Not the distinguished gray-at-the-temples of Anthony or the soft dyed-blond of Caroline.

Anthony held himself with ease and even a certain grace. But it was Caroline who'd moved forward first, her hand extended.

"Welcome, Chief Superintendent," she said, using his rank though he himself had not. Her voice was warm, almost musical. "We didn't realize my mother knew you. She never mentioned it."

"Which was strange, for her," said Hugo. His voice was unexpectedly deep, rich. If a trench in the earth could speak, it might sound like this man.

"We never actually met," said Armand. "None of us knew your mother."

"Really?" said Anthony, looking from one to the other. "Then why are you liquidators?"

"We were hoping you could tell us," said Myrna.

The siblings consulted one another, perplexed.

"To be honest," said Anthony, "we thought we were the liquidators. Came as a surprise when Maître Mercier here called."

"Well, the Baroness must've had her reasons," said Caroline. "She always did. There must be a connection."

"Madame Landers and I live in a village called Three Pines," said Gamache. "I believe your mother worked there."

"That's right," said Hugo. "She said it was a funny little village in a sort of divot in the ground."

He cupped his hand as he spoke.

While the word "divot" didn't make it sound attractive, the actual gesture did. His strong hand cupped was suggestive not of emptiness but of holding something precious. Water in a drought. Wine at a celebration. Or some creature, near extinction, that needed protection.

And it struck Armand how very expressive this rough man was. With a small, common gesture, he'd conjured a world of meaning.

Like Armand, Myrna was watching these people closely. Not with any suspicion, more a professional interest in dynamics. Of groups. Of families. And what happened when strangers came into their midst.

These three seemed comfortable with one another. Though there was a hierarchy, with Anthony clearly at the top.

"Would you like something to drink?" Caroline asked their guests. "Coffee, tea? Something stronger perhaps."

"I think we should get started," said Lucien.

"I'll take a beer," said Hugo, and went into the kitchen.

"A tea would be nice," said Myrna, and Armand agreed.

"I'll take a beer too, if you're offering," said Benedict.

Caroline and Anthony followed Hugo into the kitchen while Armand joined Myrna at the bookcase.

"You said there was something I need to hear. What is it?"

"It's about the Baroness. Why she's called that."

"Yes?"

Myrna gave him such a pained expression he wondered if she wasn't in some sudden acute agony. Which, it turned out, she was, though not the physical kind.

"I can't tell you."

"Why not? You just said I had to hear it."

"You do, but you have to hear it from them." She tilted her head toward the kitchen. "It's kinda amazing. I wonder if it's true."

"Oh come on," said Armand. "Now you're just being annoying."

"Sorry, but actually, they didn't get to the full story before you arrived." She looked toward the kitchen again. "What do you make of them?"

"The Baumgartners?" He glanced over there too. "I have no real opinion yet. They seem nice enough. You?"

"I'm always looking for psychoses," Myrna admitted. "Too many years digging around people's brains. If you search long enough and deep enough, you're sure to find something. Even in the most well balanced of people."

She gave him a meaningful look and he grinned.

"I'm glad it's their turn now. And? Have you unearthed any psychoses in these nice people?"

"None. Which I find quite unsettling."

He laughed. "Not to worry. If anything can expose craziness, it's a will."

"We already have plenty of that," she agreed. "Do you think they're upset that we're the liquidators?"

"I'm not sure. They were certainly surprised. I wonder why their mother didn't tell them they'd been replaced."

"I wonder why she did it," said Myrna, glancing through the open door into the kitchen. "Do you think one of them's a little off?" She lifted her hand to her temple and rotated it. "But she felt she couldn't just drop him, so she replaced them all?"

"Him? Do you have someone in mind? Hugo, maybe?"

"Because he looks the part? Poor fellow, imagine being raised with two gorgeous siblings. It could warp a person. But my money's on Anthony."

Armand watched the three Baumgartners prepare the refreshments. Caroline and Anthony together making the tea and putting out cookies. Hugo alone, farther down the counter, pouring two beers.

On the surface, friendly. And yet they barely said a word to one another.

"Why Anthony?" he asked.

"Because he doesn't look the part. I'm always suspicious of people who seem too well balanced."

"Sometimes a cigar . . ." said Armand, to Myrna's laugh.

He noticed something behind her, on the bookcase, and reached to pick it up.

It was a small photo. The silver frame was tarnished, and the black-and-white snapshot had faded, but he knew who they were and where it was taken.

The three Baumgartner children, two skinny, one plump, arms lazily slung over one another's shoulders, stood in front of the farmhouse. It was summer, and they wore sagging bathing suits and huge, toothy grins.

Behind them, in the garden, he saw tall spires of foxglove and the easily identified monkshood.

"What's that?" He pointed to another clump.

"Huh," said Myrna. "The Baroness must've been quite a gardener. I didn't think that would grow here, but I guess the house protects it.

Or maybe she planted it as an annual. That's deadly nightshade. Also known as belladonna."

Armand replaced the photo of the three kids, growing like weeds amid the poisonous plants.

"Here you go," said Caroline as Anthony carried in a tray with tea things and Hugo followed with the beers.

It did seem his natural place, Gamache was beginning to see. A few steps behind his brother and sister. Separated from them. Just a little. Close enough to see their closeness but far enough away not to be included.

"Can we continue?" asked Lucien, who'd refused all offer of refreshments.

"I think we need to back up a bit, now that Armand is here," said Myrna. "He didn't hear what Caroline said just before he arrived."

"It's not pertinent," said Lucien. "We're here to read the will and that's all."

"You were telling us why your mother liked to be called Baroness," Myrna prompted Caroline.

"Liked?" Anthony threw another log on the fire. "She didn't 'like' to be called Baroness, she insisted."

He settled back into his chair.

Caroline turned to face their guests, tucking her skirt in. Her knees together, her ankles crossed. The doyenne entertaining.

"Our mother called herself Baroness because she was one."

Armand stared at her, then at the others. His mouth didn't exactly drop open, but his eyes certainly widened.

Myrna turned to him. She was beaming. If she could have combusted with pleasure, she would have. What had started as a chore, accepting to be the liquidator of a stranger's will, was quickly becoming not just entertaining but kind of wonderful.

A baroness, her glowing eyes said. A noble cleaning woman. Does it get better than this?

Across from them the Baumgartner siblings had their own reactions. Anthony seemed to share the joke and had raised his brows in a *Parents. What can you do?* expression.

Caroline was composed, but her complexion betrayed her. Little pink patches had appeared on her cheeks.

And Hugo—

"She might be," he said. "We don't know."

"I think we do," said Anthony. "Some things just have to be faced, Hug. No matter how unpleasant."

He pronounced it as "Oog" and was staring at his brother.

"I've never met a real baroness," said Benedict. "This's kinda cool."

"And you still haven't," Myrna pointed out.

"Why would she think she's a baroness?" asked Armand.

"Well, among other things, there's the family name," said Anthony.

"Baumgartner?" asked Benedict.

"No," said Caroline. "That was our father's name. Her maiden name was Bauer. But her grandfather, our great-grandfather, was a Kinderoth."

She looked at them intently, apparently expecting something.

"Kinderoth," Hugo repeated.

"We heard," Myrna said. "Is there something you're trying to say?"

Benedict's eyes were narrowed, and his lips moved as he lifted his fingers. Obviously trying to work out the relationship.

"Kinderoth," he finally said. "Child roth."

"Child roth," Armand repeated, then paused. "Roth child? Roth-schild?"

Hugo nodded.

"That's ludicrous," said Lucien with a snort. Then he looked at the Baumgartner siblings. "You're not saying that Bertha Baumgartner was a Rothschild?"

Anthony leaned back in his chair, apparently distancing himself from the claim.

Caroline looked politely defiant, as though daring them to challenge it. And Hugo looked triumphant.

"Yes."

"The Rothschilds?" asked Myrna. "The banking family? Worth billions?"

"Well, a branch of the family," said Caroline. "The one that came to Canada in the 1920s and decided to invest everything in the stock market."

"They were the lucky ones," said Anthony. "They at least got out."

"And there was no 'everything,'" said Hugo. "They came here because it'd all been stolen from them. Us."

"Enough," said Anthony, lifting his hand. "We've been through this all our lives. It hounded our parents, our grandparents. It drove them near mad with resentment. Let's just stop."

"Anthony's right," said Caroline. "Even if it's true, there's nothing we can do about it."

"Maman said—" Hugo began.

"Maman was an embittered old woman who made things up to make her feel better about cleaning other people's toilets," she said. "She raised us with love and bile and made us promise to continue the fight. But we were children when we made that promise."

"*Kinder,*" said Benedict.

Caroline looked at him with some annoyance.

"How do you know that word?" asked Myrna.

"*Kinder?*" said Benedict. "My girlfriend's family is German. Besides, I went to kindergarten. Didn't everyone?"

Kindergarten, thought Gamache, and glanced over at the bookshelf where the tarnished frame sat. The photo of children in a deadly garden.

"We're not German," said Hugo. "Austrian."

"Ahh," said Benedict, then he lowered his voice. "Were they convicts?"

"Of course not," said Caroline.

They stared at him for a moment before Myrna got it.

"Not Australian. Austrian. Like the von Trapp family." When he looked blank, she went on. "*The Sound of Music? 'The hills are alive'*? Help me, Armand."

"Oh, I think you're doing just fine."

From off to his left, he heard the thin strains of a voice singing, "'*Edelweiss, Edelweiss . . .*'" before it petered out.

They looked over, and Hugo dropped his head, apparently studying his hands.

"Maman used to sing it to us," Anthony explained. "We must have watched that movie a hundred times."

Armand had seen the movie too. More times than he could count, with his children. And now his grandchildren. And he'd sung that haunting song to them as they fell asleep.

Edelweiss. Their heavy lids would close. *Edelweiss.*

"Can we continue?" asked Lucien. He handed around copies of Bertha Baumgartner's will to her children, while the liquidators brought out their own copies.

"Please turn to page fifteen," said Lucien. "I'll go over the highlights. She leaves each of her three children five million dollars, as well as buildings in Geneva and Vienna."

"And the title goes to the eldest son," said Lucien, speaking earnestly, as though the title actually existed. He looked at Anthony. "To you."

"Merci," he said.

It could have come out as sarcastic, but instead he just sounded sad. And he wasn't alone. Armand looked at the others. Their sorrow was palpable.

The Baroness might've been delusional. Might've even been bitter. But she loved these three, and they loved her.

Lucien read the rest of the document, and when he'd finished, he looked at them.

"Any questions?"

Benedict raised his hand.

"From the family," said Lucien.

"How does this work?" Caroline asked. "Given that none of this exists?"

"And what about what does exist?" asked Anthony. "She had some small investments, a little in the bank. The home? We didn't sell it while she was alive. Out of respect. She always hoped maybe she'd return."

"I'm glad you mentioned the farmhouse," said Gamache. "We were there yesterday. It's in pretty bad shape and should probably be torn down."

"No," said Hugo. "I'm sure it can be saved."

Armand shook his head. "It's too dangerous. Especially with the weight of this snow. I'm afraid I'm going to have to make a call to have it inspected and possibly condemned."

"That's fine with me," said Caroline. "We can just sell the land.

Maman hadn't lived there for a couple of years. I have no sentimental attachment."

"You grew up there?" asked Myrna.

It was rare that kids, no matter how old they were, held absolutely no attachment to their childhood home. Unless it had been an unhappy place.

"Your father—" she began.

"What about him?" asked Anthony.

"Your mother was widowed, it says in the will."

"Yes, he died thirty years ago."

"Thirty-six," said Hugo.

"Accident on the farm," said Caroline. "He was run over by the combine while haying."

Myrna winced, and while Armand's professional face held, his mind conjured the image.

"Tony found him," said Hugo. "Went out looking when he didn't come in for lunch. He died right away. Probably didn't feel a thing."

"Probably not," said Armand, and hoped his tone didn't betray what he really thought.

"That's when the Baroness went out to work," said Caroline. "Had to support us."

"I got a job bagging groceries at the IGA," said Anthony. "And, Caroline, you went out babysitting."

"Remember when that couple hired you to look after their goats?" asked Hugo with a laugh.

"Oh Jesus, yeah," said Anthony, also laughing, as was Caroline. "You'd put up a notice in the church hall saying you loved kids and would like to look after them."

"Hey, those kids were way better behaved than the human ones," said Caroline. Relaxing back in her seat, her smile wide, her eyes gleaming.

"Except when they kicked," said Hugo. "I remember going with you a few times to help."

He rubbed his shins.

"They just didn't like you."

Armand listened as the brothers and their sister went over clearly familiar ground. Part of the family liturgy. The same stories, told over and over. They looked, for a moment, like the children in the photo.

For his part, Armand kept his eyes on Anthony Baumgartner.

He must have been all of sixteen when he found his father in the field.

That was a sight that could never be unseen. A memory that would take up more than its fair share of Anthony's longhouse. Squeezing other, happy childhood memories into corners.

Armand's own parents had died, in a car accident, when he was a child. And to this day he could remember every moment of when the police arrived at the door.

That day, that moment, had affected every moment of the rest of his life.

And he hadn't found his parents. Had not seen their bodies. He remembered the scent of the peanut-butter cookies that had been baking, and to this day it made him nauseous.

This man remembered the mangled, bloody body of his father.

"I think we should try to save the place," Hugo was saying.

"Why don't you stay behind after everyone leaves," said Anthony. "We can discuss it then."

"As for the rest of her assets," said Lucien, "we'll do an inventory, and you can sign off."

"Do you have any photographs of your mother?" Armand asked.

He followed Anthony to the fireplace, where there was a framed picture on the mantel.

"May I?" When Anthony nodded, he picked it up.

"That was taken last Christmas," said Caroline, who'd joined them.

Armand recognized the hearth he was standing in front of. In the picture it was decorated with garlands of pine and bright red bows, and in the background stood a Christmas tree heavy with baubles and strings of popcorn and candy canes. Brightly wrapped gifts tumbled out from beneath the tree. But the focal point of the photo, the point of the photo, was the elderly woman in the large chair. Children were festooned over it and around her, and her own three stood behind the chair. Everyone was smiling. Some were laughing.

The Baroness wore a paper crown from a Christmas cracker and a beaming smile and looked not unlike Margaret Rutherford.

White hair. Jowls. Bright blue eyes sagging like a bloodhound's. Huge bosom and trunk, made for wiping off flour-caked hands and hugging grandchildren.

Looking at it, Armand could almost smell the vanilla extract.

He found himself smiling, then handed it to Myrna.

"Grand Duchess Gloriana," he suggested, and her smile grew all the broader as she nodded.

"*The Mouse on the Moon*." Then Myrna's expression became wistful as she studied the photo that had pride of place in her son's living room. "Or *Harvey*."

"You'll take them, right," said Lucien a few minutes later, when they were about to leave.

It was a statement, not a question. "Them" being Myrna and Benedict. Like bags of salt. Only less useful.

"I have a few more things to go over with Anthony Baumgartner," said the notary.

"*Oui*," said Armand.

Caroline was leaving with them, but Hugo had stayed behind with Anthony, to talk about the future of the farmhouse.

A little while later, Myrna, Benedict, and Armand sat with Reine-Marie by the fire in the bistro. Clara, Ruth, and Gabri joined them, and drinks were ordered.

The power was back on, and the phones repaired.

"They can't come until tomorrow afternoon," Benedict reported, returning from the phone on the bistro bar.

"Who?" asked Clara.

"The garage," said Benedict. "My pickup's still at Madame Baumgartner's farmhouse. It needs towing. And new tires."

He shot a look at Armand, who nodded approval.

"I've called the township and strongly suggested they send inspectors to her home," said Armand. "I think it needs to be condemned."

"It might be savable," said Benedict. "If the Baumgartners would like me to try."

"Don't even think about it," said Armand. "Caroline was right. They should just tear it down and sell the land."

The sun was setting, the sky a soft blue before fading to black.

"You'll stay with us another night," Reine-Marie said to Benedict.

"But I don't have any clothes."

"We'll give you some," said Gabri, assessing the young man. "I think you're about Ruth's size. Though she is a bit more masculine."

Over drinks they told the others about the meeting with the Baroness's family and the fact she seemed to think she was an actual baroness. Descended from the Rothschilds.

"Quite a descent," said Ruth.

"But even if it is true," said Reine-Marie, "that wouldn't necessarily mean there was a title and money."

"Or maybe it does," said Clara. "How do you find out?"

"Lucien's checking into it," said Myrna.

"Sounds strange to hear her called 'Madame Baumgartner,'" said Clara. "I know the Baroness, but this Bertha Baumgartner's a stranger."

"I liked what you said." Myrna turned to Armand. "She did look like Margaret Rutherford."

Ruth snorted scotch back into her glass and laughed. "Yes, that's it. That's who she reminded me of."

"But still," Armand said to Myrna, "I think you were closer to the heart of the matter. Not her looks but her personality."

"How so?" asked Gabri.

"*Harvey,*" said Myrna. "The whole meeting with the family reminded me of that movie."

Clara smiled. "Elwood P. Dowd."

"That's just stupid," said Ruth. "The Baroness looked nothing like Jimmy Stewart."

On seeing Benedict's blank expression, Reine-Marie explained. "*Harvey* is an old movie. It's about a man—"

"Elwood P. Dowd," said Myrna.

"—whose best friend is a six-foot rabbit," continued Reine-Marie.

"Harvey," said Myrna.

"They go everywhere together," continued Reine-Marie. "But no one else can see him."

"Obviously," said Ruth. "He's a six-foot white rabbit."

"They try to convince Elwood that Harvey doesn't exist," said Clara.

"They think he's crazy," said Ruth, stroking Rosa. "Try to have him committed."

"It's a reminder that if someone's happy, maybe that's the only reality that matters," said Reine-Marie. "What harm is there in believing in a giant white rabbit?"

"Or a title," said Clara, raising her glass. "The Baroness."

"The Baroness," they said.

"But it's not just the title, is it," said Benedict. "It's the money too. Millions. I wonder if there's harm in believing in a fortune that doesn't exist."

"'You have a lot to learn,' young man," said Ruth, quoting the movie. "'And I hope you never learn it.'"

CHAPTER 14

"So what're you going to do?" asked Annie as their car crept carefully down the hill into Three Pines. "Are you going to tell him?"

"Which part?" asked Jean-Guy. "The investigation or—"

He could feel the rear of the vehicle begin to slide sideways on the snow and ice, and he stopped talking to concentrate. His eyes sharp on the road, his focus complete. His hands gentle on the steering wheel.

He glanced swiftly into the rearview mirror and saw Honoré buckled into his car seat, looking out the window.

"I think it's up to us to decide first, don't you?" he finally said as the car made it safely down the hill, and they drove around the village green.

Walls of snow mounted on either side so that nothing beyond was visible except the glow of hidden homes.

Jean-Guy had never seen anything like it. It was both beautiful and alarming. Comforting and ominous. As though nature were trying to decide whether to protect or consume the little village.

He pulled the car up to the opening chiseled into the banks, a snow tunnel leading to the Gamache home. But instead of getting out, Annie sat there, her face lit by the headlights bouncing back from the snow.

"It'll be all right," she said, and, leaning over, she kissed him on the cheek.

It was an act of such simplicity it would have been easy for Jean-Guy to overlook the glory of it.

To be kissed. For no reason.

For a man of reason, it was staggering.

"How did the meeting go yesterday?" asked Gamache as he and Jean-Guy settled into the study.

They'd had their dinner. Shepherd's pie and chocolate cake. Honoré was asleep in his room.

The Gamaches' unexpected guest, the young man with the weird hair, Benedict, had gone off to the bistro for a few drinks. He'd spent much of the time, after being introduced to Annie and Jean-Guy, playing with Honoré. Once Honoré was put to bed for the night and they'd had dinner, Benedict asked if they'd mind if he went out for a beer.

"Nice kid," said Jean-Guy.

"Yes," said Armand.

"What do you know about him?" Jean-Guy's voice was casual, but Armand knew him too well to be fooled.

"You mean, is he likely to kill us in our sleep?"

"Just wondering," said Jean-Guy.

It wasn't as though this Benedict had been found hitchhiking, wearing a ski mask and carrying a machete. But really, what did Armand know about him?

"I did a quick check," said his father-in-law. "He is who he says he is. A builder. Lives in Montréal, apparently with a girlfriend."

"Apparently?"

"Well, that is a little odd," admitted Armand as they took their seats. "When the power and phones were out, Benedict didn't seem at all stressed about not being able to contact his girlfriend to tell her where he was and that he was safe. Or in making sure she was okay. If it was me, cut off from Reine-Marie in a storm, I'd move heaven and earth to make sure she was safe."

Jean-Guy nodded. The same for him and Annie. It wasn't even a choice, it was instinctive.

"Maybe they're not in love," he said. "You think it's something else?"

"I think she might be a convenient fabrication," said Armand with a smile. "I think he's a handsome kid who needs a way to get out of uncomfortable situations."

"So he created a fictional girlfriend?" He looked at his father-in-law closely. "Don't tell me you once had one?"

Armand laughed. "When I was young, I had quite a few. Getting a real one was the problem."

"I can see why you'd have trouble, but why would this kid make up a girlfriend? I doubt he has any problem getting girls."

"And that might be why. This way he can fend off unwanted advances."

"The fictional lover. Clever."

He wished he'd thought of that, back in the day. Invitations to social events he didn't want to attend, declined. Blamed on the girlfriend.

Damn. If it was true, that Benedict was smarter than he looked. Though that would not be difficult.

"Well, if she doesn't exist, how do you explain that haircut?" Jean-Guy asked. "She did it, didn't she?"

"It is hard to explain. You didn't see the sweater he was wearing yesterday. She'd made it out of steel wool."

"Then she must exist. What a young man will do for sex. I remember—" Just in time he realized who he was speaking to. And stopped.

"Do you want me to check him out, *patron*?"

"No, don't bother. It's none of our business."

"Of course, the other question is why he was chosen to be a liquidator of the woman's will," said Jean-Guy. "Why any of you were. Do you think she really was a baroness?"

"No," said Armand. "I don't. I think her daughter was right. She made it up to comfort herself. We all have fantasies, especially when we're children. But most grow out of it. I think Madame Baumgartner never did."

"And she passed it along to her own children."

"I'm not so sure about that. I think the daughter might've let it go, and the eldest son, Anthony, seemed amused by it, but the youngest son? Hugo? I don't know."

"Maybe that's why she chose you and Myrna. In a moment of sanity, she got that she'd really messed them up with her fantasies. Can you imagine the fighting if her kids were in charge of the will?"

"But that doesn't explain why us specifically," said Armand. "And it sure doesn't explain Benedict."

"No." Jean-Guy thought for a moment. "Honoré likes him."

It seemed a non sequitur, but Armand knew it wasn't. He'd noticed that too. It would be folly to trust the instincts of a baby. But it would also be a mistake to completely dismiss them.

Armand shifted in his chair and then asked the question. "How did the meeting go yesterday?"

"The one with the investigators?"

There was a pause, and Jean-Guy immediately understood his mistake. In asking that question, he'd let drop that there'd been another meeting.

Beauvoir waited for his father-in-law to ask.

Had there been another meeting?

But Gamache did not ask. Instead he crossed his legs and waited.

"It went okay."

"Now, don't forget who you're speaking to."

It was said calmly, conversationally. But the warning was clear.

Do not lie.

Through the closed door, they could hear voices in the next room. Annie and Reine-Marie.

There were few things more soothing, Jean-Guy thought, than hearing people you love talking softly in another room.

Instead of a white-noise machine, or recordings of rain or the ocean, if he ever needed help falling asleep, he wanted the sound of these two women. He'd drift off, the unintelligible murmurs on a loop. Reminding him he was no longer alone.

And the truth was, he hadn't slept well the night before. He had a decision to make and was worried.

Beauvoir cast his mind back to his meeting with the Sûreté investigators the day before. Wanting to be accurate. "They were friendly," he said, his voice slow, careful. "But they seemed to be offering me an out. A lifeboat."

"And you didn't realize the ship was sinking?"

Beauvoir nodded. "I thought it was over. I really did. I expected to walk into the meeting and be told it was all cleared up. You'd be reinstated."

"Do you really expect that?"

"Don't you?"

Gamache considered. Maybe, at first, he'd thought that was a possibility.

Then, as more and more questions were asked, as he'd explained what happened and why, over and over again, he could see their minds working. And he could hear it, from their point of view.

This whole thing had given him an interesting perspective on being a suspect. Trying to explain something that, in the cold light of day, seemed inexplicable.

Though his thinking had been clear at the time.

"I think, at this stage, anything is possible," he said to Jean-Guy.

Through the door the voices continued. They could hear soft laughter as one or the other said something amusing.

There was silence in the small room. A silence like Jean-Guy had rarely experienced, though it reminded him a little of their time in the remote monastery. Saint-Gilbert-Entre-les-Loups. Where the quiet had been so profound he'd found it disquieting.

He wanted to break this silence but knew instinctively that it was not his to break.

And so he waited.

Gamache sat in the familiar chair, and yet everything, for a moment, felt unfamiliar. And he realized he had, in fact, harbored a hope that he'd be exonerated.

That Jean-Guy would call yesterday after his meeting with the investigators to tell him it was over. And then he'd get a call from the Premier Ministre, telling him he'd been cleared and would be reinstated.

The call hadn't come. But then the phones had been down, allowing this phantom hope to remain alive.

Gamache smiled to himself and understood Madame Baumgartner a little better. We all had our delusions.

He could see now how wrong he'd been.

Someone had to be blamed. If the drugs hit the streets, as they surely would any day now, they'd throw the book at him. And why not? The blame was, after all, his. Alone.

That much was a comfort. When the ship did sink, he'd take no one else down with him. It would be a result of his own decisions. And friendly fire.

He saw his mother kneeling beside him, adjusting his mitts and cap. Tying his huge scarf at his neck and patting it as he headed out into the bitter-cold Montréal morning, to school. She looked at him and said, "Remember, Armand. If you're ever in trouble, you find a police officer."

She'd held his eyes, as serious as he'd ever seen her, and didn't smile again until he'd solemnly agreed.

Cross my heart and hope to die.

And now, fifty years later, he sat in his own home and smelled a slight scent of peanut-butter cookies.

Then he heard, through the door, the soft laughter of his wife and daughter. He thought of his grandson, asleep. He thought of his son, Daniel, and daughter-in-law and two granddaughters in Paris.

He looked into the eyes of his son-in-law. His second-in-command. His friend.

Safe. And he had no regrets.

Then Armand glanced at his desk and the book sitting there. The one that had, literally, been thrown at him earlier in the day.

It is not death that a man should fear, but he should fear never beginning to live.

"Your old room," said the landlady.

Her pudgy hand with its nicotine-yellowed fingers was splayed on the door as it swung open, releasing a stale odor.

Despite the bitter-cold night, the place was stifling, the old iron radiators unregulated. Pumping out heat that only hurried the decay. It smelled like something decomposing.

In the time since Amelia had lived in the rooming house in East End Montréal, very little had changed.

There was still the reek of urine. Still the moans, groans, of men. As their lives slipped away. Through their fingers and down the drain.

The landlady had grown fatter, softer. A single tooth hung by a thread of gum, waving as she chortled. Her breath like a slaughterhouse.

The door closed, and Amelia could hear her shuffling back down the hallway.

Amelia breathed through her mouth, and clicked the stud against her teeth, and tossed the book-laden knapsack onto the single bed.

Regretting throwing that book at Gamache. Not the act of violence. That had felt good. But she regretted not having Marcus Aurelius to keep her company.

When she opened the door to leave, Amelia almost tripped over the mop and pail. The landlady must've left it there. Her job, in exchange for a room, was to clean. A place that had not, it appeared, been cleaned since she'd last lived there.

"Fuck it," she said, kicking the bucket over and watching the suds rush down the hallway.

That would wait. She had far more pressing things to do than hang around this shithole.

"Walk with me," said Gamache, and to Jean-Guy's surprise, and disappointment, he saw that Armand did not mean walk into the kitchen for more chocolate cake.

Instead Armand went to the front door and took his parka off the hook.

"Going somewhere?" asked Reine-Marie, turning in her seat to watch them.

"Just a stroll."

"To the bistro?" asked Annie, getting up to join them.

"No. Around the village green."

She plunked back down onto the sofa. "Bye."

Henri and Gracie raced to the front door, expecting yet another walk, but Armand explained it was too cold for them.

"But not for us?" asked Jean-Guy. Yet followed him anyway.

Once outside, they walked down the snow tunnel to the road. There was no need of a flashlight. It was a clear night, and quiet. Just the squeal and crunch and munch of their heavy winter boots on the snow.

The Chief often said that everything could be solved by walking. For himself, Beauvoir was pretty sure everything could be solved in the kitchen with a piece of cake.

"Ready yet?"

"Huh?"

"You do know we're going to go round and around until you tell me the other thing on your mind."

"You—"

"Ahhh," warned Armand.

"Ahhh nothing," said Beauvoir. "I can't feel my feet, my fingers are numb. My nose is frozen shut, and my eyes are watering from the pain in my sinuses."

"Then you're probably ready to talk."

"This is torture," said Jean-Guy.

"I'm not very good at it, then," said Armand, his voice friendly. "Since I'm out here too."

Squeak. Squeak. Squeak.

Gamache's pace was measured. His mittened hands clasped each other behind his back as he walked. As though it weren't minus a thousand. As though the cold weren't scraping his face as it was Jean-Guy's.

"There's something else, isn't there? There was another meeting."

"Just with our bank. We're thinking of buying a home."

Squeak. Squeak. Squeak.

"Well, that's exciting."

Squeak.

"I didn't want to tell you until all the finances were in place," said Jean-Guy. Willing himself to stop talking. To stop lying.

"I see."

Armand had stopped and tilted his head back. "Look at that, Jean-Guy."

And he did.

What he saw were northern lights. The aurora borealis. Otherworldly green light, flowing across the night sky.

Then Jean-Guy lowered his gaze and saw that Armand was looking at him. The older man's face clear in the remarkable dancing light.

In those gentle eyes, he saw himself reflected.

And he knew that what his father-in-law saw, when he looked at him, was a man in a lifeboat. Getting further and further away.

CHAPTER 15

—

"Can someone go and wake up Benedict?" asked Jean-Guy as he pushed the bacon around the cast-iron skillet with a fork.

The kitchen smelled of maple-smoked bacon and fresh-perked coffee. The eggs were ready to go on.

It was eight fifteen in the morning, and the sun was up. But Benedict was not.

"I'll go," said Armand.

He'd just emerged from his study, having made a private call. He looked slightly distracted, his attention elsewhere, as he walked up the stairs.

They heard a knocking on the bedroom door and Armand calling, "Benedict. Breakfast's ready."

Then more knocking. "Up and at 'em."

Reine-Marie smiled. How often had she heard Armand saying the same thing? *Up and at 'em.* Outside their son Daniel's door?

Though the final few months Daniel had been at home had been less than amusing, given the reason he was passed out at ten in the morning. And she remembered the rage their son had felt when his father entered his room to wake him up.

It had verged on violence.

But still Reine-Marie smiled. It had started out as normal, and natural, for a young fellow to sleep in. And had been that way for a long while. Before it all changed.

"Can you come here, please?" Armand called down.

They looked at one another, then Annie gathered Honoré in her arms and they all walked upstairs.

"He's not here," said Armand, stepping aside so they could look through the open door.

They peered in. Not only was he not there but the bed hadn't been slept in. Armand stepped into the room and looked around.

"His things?" asked Jean-Guy.

"Still here."

Sure enough, the room was exactly as Benedict had left it the night before.

"I'll make some calls," said Reine-Marie, heading down the stairs and into the living room, picking up the phone while Armand and Jean-Guy put on their coats, tuques, mitts, and boots.

Armand had already been outside once that morning, walking around the village green with Henri and Gracie. But the sun had been barely up, and it was possible Armand had missed something. Someone. In a snowbank.

The bitter-cold snap had broken, and now it was merely cold. Once outside, Gamache glanced at the thermometer on the verandah. Minus six Celsius.

Cold enough.

The men broke into a trot, Armand pointing clockwise while he went counterclockwise around the village green.

He forced himself to slow to a rapid walk. He didn't want to miss anything.

His eyes were sharp, scanning. His mind on the search. Trying to divorce action from emotion. Trying not to imagine Benedict curled up by the side of the road.

If that was the case, then there was no hurry, and yet they hurried. In case.

Jean-Guy came around the bend. "Nothing, *patron*."

They went around again, slower this time. The snowbanks were steep, but Jean-Guy managed to scramble, with Armand's help, to the top and walk, like a man on a tightrope, across the jagged ridge. Peering on either side.

Clara came out of her cottage, soon joined by Myrna from her bookshop. Even Ruth appeared.

"Reine-Marie called," said the old poet. "Anything?"

"Nothing."

Reine-Marie joined them. "I just spoke to Olivier. Benedict was in the bistro last night. He had a few beers but wasn't drunk."

She knew as well as Armand that sometimes people got disoriented in the cold and dark. Often helped along by drink and drugs.

"Nothing here," said Jean-Guy, sliding off the snowbank.

"We need to split up," said Armand. "Check the roads in and out of town."

"I'll take the Old Stage Road," said Clara, not waiting for a response but heading in that direction.

They divvied up the paths while Ruth went into the bistro to talk to Olivier.

A few minutes later, they heard a sharp whistle. Ruth was calling them back to the bistro.

Their skin tingled and ached as they stepped into the warmth.

"He was here last night," Olivier confirmed. "I didn't see him leave—"

"But I did," said Gabri, wiping his hands on his apron. "He left with Billy Williams. They'd been talking, and the two went out together."

"Where did they go?"

"I have no idea, but I did see Billy's truck drive away. I don't know if the kid was with him."

Gabri picked up the phone on the bistro bar and called. They saw him nod, listen, then hang up.

"Billy says he gave Benedict a lift to Madame Baumgartner's farmhouse."

Myrna stopped rubbing her hands by the fire and turned to him. "Why would he do that?"

"Benedict asked to go," said Gabri. "Something about the kid's truck. It's on Billy's way home, so he drove him over."

"And just left him there?" asked Clara.

"I guess so," said Gabri. Though it didn't sound like Billy Williams. He maintained the roads and did odd jobs around the area, and he was well aware that the cold kills. "That's all Billy knows."

"Benedict must've driven back to Montréal," said Olivier.

"Maybe," said Armand.

"What is it?" asked Clara as Myrna went into her shop to get the papers from the notary, with Benedict's phone number.

"He promised he wouldn't drive his truck," said Armand. "That's why we left it behind. It doesn't have winter tires."

"Don't tell me someone lied to you?" Ruth thrust out her lower lip and made a sad face.

"Did he cross his heart?"

And hope to die?

But she stopped short of saying that, to Armand's surprise. Seemed Ruth had a filter after all.

"Wouldn't he have told us if he'd returned to Montréal?" asked Reine-Marie.

"He's probably still asleep in his apartment," said Clara. "You'll get a call when he wakes up."

"Well, I'm not waiting," said Myrna, waving the papers she'd retrieved and going to the phone. "I'm calling his cell."

She placed the call. They watched. And waited. And waited.

She spoke into the receiver, then hung up.

"It clicked over to voice mail. I told him to call here."

"There's just the one number for him?" asked Jean-Guy, looking over Myrna's shoulder at the papers. "No home phone?"

"Kids today don't have home phones, numbnuts," Ruth explained to Jean-Guy. "You're old, so you wouldn't know that."

"We have to go to the farmhouse," said Armand, heading to the door. "And make sure."

"I'll come with you," said Myrna. "We're a team. Liquidators stick together." She returned Armand's stare. "What? It's a thing."

"It's a nothing," said Ruth.

"I know," said Myrna, responding more to Armand's eyes than Ruth's words.

He nodded. They both knew what they might find. And of the group, he and Myrna were closest to Benedict. The young man invited a kind of intimacy, a near-immediate affection. And Myrna was right. They did feel like an odd little team.

"I'm coming too," said Beauvoir, walking to the car with them.

"So am I," said Reine-Marie.

"Can you stay at home?" Armand asked her. "In case he calls there?"

"Let me know," she said as they got into the car.

"Oh Christ," said Myrna, straining forward in her seat belt as they turned the corner and saw the farmhouse.

"I'll call 911," said Jean-Guy.

Armand grabbed the shovel from the trunk of his car.

Benedict's truck was parked where they'd left it. Armand walked quickly over and looked into the cab.

Empty. The keys were in the ignition, and it had been turned on but must've run out of gas. He pulled the keys out and pocketed them.

"Rescue team's on its way," said Beauvoir, catching up.

"No one here," called Myrna. She was standing next to the other vehicle in the yard. Not one Armand recognized. "This wasn't here when we left yesterday, was it?"

"*Non*," said Armand.

Beauvoir had pulled a shovel out of the snowbank by the front steps and now held it like a weapon.

Myrna joined them, and all three stared.

Madame Baumgartner's home had collapsed.

The roof and second floor had caved in, part of it crushing the main floor, part of it hanging loose, barely holding together.

"Call back. Tell them to bring the dogs," said Gamache as he advanced, slowly.

Beauvoir made the call.

"Is he inside?" Myrna whispered.

"I think so." Gamache glanced behind him, at the other car. "And he's not alone."

He took off his tuque and cocked his head toward the farmhouse.

"Did you hear that?"

Jean-Guy and Myrna took off their hats and listened.

Nothing.

Gamache strode over to his car and hit the horn. Two quick blasts, then stopped. And listened.

125

But there was only grim silence.

Nothing. Nothing.

Something.

A knock. A crack?

They looked at one another.

"It could be a beam breaking, *patron*."

"Or it could be Benedict," said Myrna. "Or someone else, trying to signal. What do we do? We can't just stand here."

Help was on the way, but it could be twenty or thirty minutes before it arrived. The difference, in this cold, between life and death. If someone had survived this long through the bitter night, they must be close to the end.

"We have to make sure that someone's alive in there before we decide what to do," said Armand. He cupped his hands around his mouth and shouted, "Benedict!"

"*Allô!*" called Beauvoir.

They fell silent. Listening.

There was a knock. Definite this time. Then another. A rat-a-tat. No mistaking it. Someone was alive. And afraid.

It reminded Gamache, just for a moment, of someone else. Amelia and her tongue stud. Rat-a-tat. Her tell.

Save Our Souls.

"He has to stop," said Myrna, her eyes wide, her breathing rapid. "He'll bring the whole place down." She shouted, "Stop it."

"We hear you," Gamache called. "We're coming. Stop knocking."

He turned to them and saw the fear in their faces.

"We have to go in, don't we?" said Beauvoir.

Armand nodded. Their fear, and one he shared, was that the place they were about to enter would collapse completely. But while he and Myrna were afraid, Jean-Guy was terrified.

He had claustrophobia. This was, quite literally, his nightmare.

Beauvoir gave a curt nod, gripped the shovel even tighter, and took a step toward the ruin.

"I think you should—" Gamache began, but stopped when he heard a sound.

They turned to look back down the drive. A pickup truck had arrived. Jean-Guy lowered his shovel and almost wept.

126

Help. Rescuers. Who actually knew what they were doing. Who could go in instead of them.

The truck stopped, and a single man got out. And Beauvoir could have wept again.

It wasn't help. It was Billy Williams.

"Heard the boy was missing. Came to see if I could help." He stood beside his vehicle and stared at the house. Then said something else that sounded to Gamache like "Whale oil beef hooked."

Gamache turned to Myrna. "What did he say?"

For reasons that baffled Gamache, he seemed the only person on earth who could not understand a word Billy Williams said. Not a word. Not even close.

"Not important," she said.

"Boy alive in there?"

"We think so," said Myrna. "Someone is. Either Benedict or someone else. Was that here when you dropped him off last night?" She pointed to the car, parked off to the side.

"Not so's I noticed." He turned to the house again. "But it were dark. Right. I should go in and get him. My fault he's here."

Gamache, trying to follow this exchange, looked at Myrna. "Ask if he has any training. In rescuing people out of buildings. Does he know what he's doing?"

Now Billy turned to Gamache. "You think I don't understand you? I understand perfectly."

Billy's face was so weathered and worn that it was impossible to say if he was thirty-five or seventy-five. His body was cord-thin, and even through the heavy winter clothing there was a sense of taut muscle and sinew.

But his eyes were soft as he looked at Armand, with an expression of tenderness. Billy smiled.

"One day, old son, you'll understand me."

But Gamache did understand.

What he understood, and had from the first moment he'd met the man, was that Billy Williams had more than the average measure of the divine.

Billy's face grew grim as he studied the heap of house, and then he turned back to Armand.

"When this is over," he said, picking up a huge tire iron from his truck, "you owe me a lemon meringue pie."

Myrna didn't bother to translate that.

Billy took a step forward, and Gamache reached out to stop him, but Billy shook him off.

"I dropped the kid here last night. Boosted his truck to get it going. Then I left. I should never have left him. So I've come back. To get him. To bring him home."

Gamache didn't need Myrna this time to translate. It didn't matter what Billy said—all that mattered now were actions.

"You can't go in alone. You need help. I'll come with you." Armand turned to Jean-Guy and Myrna. "Wait for the emergency team. They should be here soon. Let them know what's happening."

"If you're going, so am I," said Myrna.

"No you're not."

"There're two people trapped in there," she said. "You need more help." When Armand still hesitated, she said, "This isn't your decision, Armand. It's mine. Besides, I'm stronger than I look."

His brows rose. She looked pretty strong.

Gamache nodded. She was right. They would need her. And it wasn't his decision.

"*Patron?*" said Jean-Guy. He looked in torment.

"You get the heights, *mon vieux*," said Armand quietly. "And I get the holes. Remember? That's the deal."

"Are you coming?" called Billy, already at the front steps. "Hurry up."

Beauvoir stepped back.

"He says be careful," said Jean-Guy, but Armand had already squeezed into the semicollapsed doorway behind Billy and Myrna.

It was darker in there, though shafts of sunlight from openings above them were hitting the floor. Snow trickled down in drifts as it slid off the roof and through the jagged holes.

It was quiet too. Except for their breathing and the sound of their footfalls as they made their way forward, squeezing along narrow, debris-clogged passages.

They moved as quickly and quietly as possible.

And then came to a halt.

A bathroom above had fallen into what had been the kitchen. The debris, including a claw-foot tub, blocked their way forward.

Gamache tapped his shovel, softly, on the tub and waited.

There was silence, and just as Armand's heart was sinking, there was a knock. Then another.

Billy pointed in the direction of the sound.

Exactly where the debris blocked their path.

Billy muttered something that Gamache completely understood. Some oaths needed no translation.

Then Gamache watched in surprise as Billy dropped to his knees. Catching Myrna's eyes, Armand saw she was thinking the same thing.

Was the man praying? Armand was all for that, but now might not be the time. Besides, he suspected that God knew exactly how they felt and how they wanted this to go.

But he also knew praying was more to steady the person than inform the deity.

Then he noticed that Billy had shoved his tire iron under the tub and was trying to get leverage. He put down his shovel and went to help. The two men leaned. Armand straining, pushing down with all his might.

The cast-iron tub moved, but only slightly.

"Wait, hold it," said Armand, stepping back and catching his breath. Then he nodded to Billy, and the two of them went at it again.

But the tub, crushed under tons of debris, barely budged.

"Can you help over here?" asked Myrna.

"Just. A. Moment," said Armand, through gritted teeth. Pushing. Pushing. Before staggering back. Defeated. Staring at the solid barrier between them and whoever was alive behind it.

There was a creaking, groaning sound. The wall of rubble was moving. Shifting.

Gamache took a half step back, sweeping Billy back with him.

He turned to warn Myrna. But stopped. His face opening in astonishment. It looked as though Myrna was single-handedly lifting the debris. Then he looked more closely.

Where he'd grabbed a shovel and Billy a tire iron, Myrna had quietly picked up the jack from Armand's car and now had it wedged under a beam. And was leaning on the arm.

The beam was lifting, inch by precarious inch.

"I need help," she called.

The two men joined her and leaned into the arm of the jack. One. Two pumps. More snow drifted down, and they paused. Three.

There was a cracking as rafters and crossbeams shifted.

Gamache, his breathing shallow, his eyes sharp, his hearing keen, waited. For it to either collapse or stabilize.

Then he heard, through the shifting debris, more tapping. Increasingly frantic.

"Stop," he called. One sharp word. And the tapping stopped.

Myrna, with their help, had jacked up the beam as high as they dared. The opening was about eighteen inches.

Gamache stared at it, then at Myrna.

"You're not leaving me behind," she said, reading his thoughts.

"You won't make it through."

"And you will?"

Armand was taking off his heavy parka. "I will."

"Then so will I. We go together." She took off her coat and hugged it to her.

"Ego?" asked Armand.

"Practicality," she said. "You need me."

"If I have a choice, I'd take her over you any day," said Billy, smiling at Myrna. "Mighty fine woman."

"What did he say?" asked Armand.

She told him.

"You must've misheard," said Armand. But he was smiling.

"Oh for fook's sake," said Billy. "Let's try again. Another coupla inches should do it."

He grabbed the lever and pushed. Armand and Myrna joined him.

More groaning. Some from the house. Most from them.

But it shifted. Just enough. They figured. They hoped.

"I'll go first," said Armand.

He glanced behind him, down the narrow, rubble-strewn passage they'd just come through. They were, he knew, in what had been the kitchen. Heading, it seemed, toward the dining room. Via the second-floor bathroom.

He turned again toward the opening. It looked like a mouth, ready to clamp shut. Every survival instinct cried out for him not to do it.

Getting onto his back, faceup, he pushed himself into the opening. His eyes within centimeters of shards of wood and rusted nails, like teeth. Turning his head, closing his eyes, exhaling to make himself as flat as possible. He inched forward.

The scent of fresh-cut grass. Walking along the Seine, holding the little hands of Flora and Zora. Reine-Marie in his arms on a lazy Sunday morning.

His face was through. Then his neck. He twisted his shoulders. His chest made it through.

And then his progress stopped. His shirt was snagged on the nails.

He was too far in for Myrna or Billy to be able to help.

The place shifted again, and he felt it drop. The nails now touched his chest every time he took a shallow breath.

"Armand?" called Myrna.

"Just a moment," he said.

Closing his eyes again, he steadied his breathing. Steadied his mind.

Laundry on the line. The scent of Honoré. Sitting in the garden with an iced tea. Reine-Marie. Reine-Marie. Reine-Marie.

He pushed again and felt the nails ripping his shirt.

Tiny pieces of rubble fell onto his face, peppering his lids and lips. As he breathed, they went into his nose, and he could feel himself on the verge of a cough. Smothering it, fighting it, he pushed harder, more frantically.

The ripping stopped, and he broke free.

Scrambling to his knees, Armand bent double, hacking and coughing.

"Armand?" called Myrna, more insistent.

"I'm okay," he said, his voice raspy. "Don't come yet."

He looked around, and, finding a piece of concrete, he reached into the opening and used it to flatten the nails.

"It should be okay now."

With some effort, Myrna also made it through, then Billy, who pushed their parkas in ahead of himself.

"What's that?" asked Myrna. Her head was lifted, nose in the air.

Armand had just caught it too. A whiff of something acrid. It was familiar. Comforting, even. Except—

Wood, charred. Charring.

He and Myrna locked eyes, then over to Billy, who looked genuinely alarmed for the first time.

Gamache felt the hairs go up on his neck.

The place was on fire.

"We need to move."

"Come on, come on," said Jean-Guy, staring at the farmhouse.

His focus was so complete he barely breathed. Didn't blink. Didn't hear the vehicles arrive.

Nothing existed except the house.

The time for caution was past.

"Hello," Myrna shouted. "Where are you?"

"Here, I'm here" came the reply. The voice hoarse. Unfamiliar.

They looked in the direction of the shout. There was another barrier of debris between them and the voice.

Scrabbling with their hands, they cleared chunks of concrete and wood until they'd made a hole. Armand lay on his stomach and peered through.

And saw the long, thin tail of a tuque.

And then a familiar face.

"It's Benedict," he called to the others.

"Oh thank God," said Myrna, and hugged Billy.

Benedict had his back against a doorway. His eyes were wide, barely daring to believe that what he'd prayed for, cried out for, had actually happened.

The young man brought his hand up to his face, not able to hold back tears.

"You came. You came."

Billy enlarged the opening, and when Armand crawled through, Benedict gripped him in a tight embrace, sobbing.

Armand held him for a moment, then stepped back so he could see Benedict's face. His body. He seemed unhurt.

"There's someone else here," said Gamache. "Where is he?"

"There is?" asked Benedict. "I don't think so. I can't believe you came—"

"There's another car in the drive," said Myrna, who'd joined them, as had Billy.

"Yes, I saw that, but when I came in, I called and no one answered." Armand noticed a small circle of smoldering wood on the floor. Benedict had survived the bitter-cold night by burning whatever wood he could lay his hands on.

That had been the smell. The house wasn't on fire after all.

He began to point it out to Myrna, just as Billy touched Armand's arm. For quiet. Billy's face was tilted up, his head cocked to one side. Listening.

"Is it the rescuers?" Myrna asked.

"Rescuers?" asked Benedict. "Aren't you the—"

"Shh," hissed Billy, and they hushed.

Billy stared at the ceiling. Then Armand saw his eyes widen, at the same moment he heard a great rending. Like a scream. The house was shrieking.

"No," Jean-Guy shouted.

He started forward, but hands held him. He twisted and bucked, struggling to break free.

Members of the local Sûreté rescue team dragged him back, as the farmhouse disappeared into a cloud of snow.

"Holy hell," whispered one of the agents.

As the structure fell, Benedict pulled Armand toward him.

"Get into the doorway," the young man shouted.

Billy grabbed Myrna and just managed to leap in there before there was an almighty splitting sound.

They sank to their knees, eyes screwed shut. Clinging to each other.

The violence was overwhelming. The din deafening. Disorienting. Banging, booming. Scraping. Screaming. From the house. From them. As the house came crashing down on top of them.

Rubble fell against Armand, pushing him sideways, but there was nowhere to go. Debris, wreckage, was closing in on both sides of them now. Pinning them there. Crushing them there.

Benedict pulled him closer, and he heard the sobbing of the boy, whose body was folded over his. Protecting him from the inevitable.

He could barely breathe now. There was room for only one thought. One feeling.

Reine-Marie. Reine-Marie.

And then the unholy shrieking died down. There were thumps and thuds as rafters fell. And settled. But the great rending sound, the crashing, had slowed.

Armand opened his eyes, squinting against the grit stinging them. He lifted his head, coughing.

And looked right into Benedict's face.

There was blood on Benedict's forehead, making its way through the plaster and concrete dust. So that the handsome young man looked like a statue that had cracked.

But his eyes were bright. And blinking.

"Myrna?" Armand rasped, barely recognizing his own voice.

"Here." He felt her move against his back but couldn't turn around. They were pinned there.

"Billy?"

There was a word Armand didn't recognize, in a voice he did.

They'd all survived.

Benedict closed his eyes, shutting out the grit in the air. But Armand kept his eyes open. Staring. Peering beyond the boy who still hugged him. Through eyes, watering and burning, he could see the doorjamb that had saved their lives and the familiar marks made on it decades ago. Height charts.

Anthony. Caroline. Shooting up with each measurement. And Hugo, who was not.

But Armand was staring beyond the marks on the wood. At a gray hand thrust up through the rubble.

CHAPTER 16

———

Amelia woke up, clawing her way to the surface, to the sunlight. Her head throbbed, and her mind was numb. And her eyes refused to focus.

She looked around, blinking, until she could make out what she was seeing. And not seeing.

This wasn't her bedroom. Certainly not the small, neat room at the academy that she'd called home for the past two years.

But neither was it the shithole in the rooming house.

This was a whole other shithole.

And then she remembered. Sinking back into the grimy sheets, her face going slack, and she closed her eyes.

"What have I done?"

"What did you do, Sweet Pea?"

Marc sat on the edge of the bed in his underwear gray and sagging. His eyes were bright in their sunken sockets. Like a gleam from some deep well.

She and Marc had been toddlers in the same village. Playing in the same playgrounds, schoolyards. Streets.

Marc had come to Montréal first. Young, gay, fresh, and alive. Fit and handsome. Excited to be out. He'd made a life for himself. A male prostitute, to be sure. But clean and careful. With his own tiny place.

His dream was to find some rich old queen and settle down.

She'd followed Marc to Montréal. He'd guided her. To the best dealers. The ones who didn't cut their shit with worse shit. When she'd sunk low enough, he guided her to the best street corners. And protected her. He was like a big brother to her.

He was careful himself, teetering on the edge of addiction but not quite tipping over. Keeping himself presentable. For the nice restaurants, the private clubs, the international travel he knew was in the next car. On the next corner.

When Gamache kicked her out of the academy, Amelia had gone to the only person she knew could help her find what she needed.

They'd stared at each other, on either side of the threshold of his apartment. Barely recognizing each other. Marc's hair wasn't just greasy, it was falling out. His scabbed scalp visible in patches. His lips chapped, his skin mottled.

When he smiled, she could see gaps where teeth had once been.

"Am I so bad?" he asked, reading the look on her face.

"No, no. Am I?"

She could see herself in his eyes. A stranger. Repulsive in her cleanliness. Jet-black hair shiny. Complexion smooth.

They were no longer brother and sister. They were barely of the same species.

"Why're you here?" he asked, barring the door.

"I need your help. I got kicked out of the academy."

"Why?"

"Possession. Maybe trafficking."

He'd laughed then, relieved. "Maybe?"

Amelia might look like another species, but they shared some DNA after all. She'd come home. To him. To the gutter. Where she belonged.

"What?" he'd asked, dropping his arm and letting her in. "Hell dust? Percs?"

"Fen."

"The good stuff."

She nodded.

"Do you have it on you now?"

He reached filthy hands toward her. She backed up, tripping over a pile of clothes on the floor but quickly righting herself.

"Of course not. They took it all. I need to find some more. But there's even better shit. It's not out yet, but it will be. That's what I really want. You heard of it?"

"Yeah, I've heard the rumors, but it's bullshit. There's nothing." Marc stared at his unexpected guest. "What do you know, Sweet Pea?"

"I know it's not bullshit. Some cop let it through his fingers. And it's good, Marc."

"Really?"

"Really good. Way better than fen. Whoever has it will make a fortune. Will have everything they've ever wanted. Forever."

"Everything?"

She nodded.

"Forever?"

She nodded. "No more shitholes. No more turning tricks. No more wondering where the next hit's coming from. We'll have lots of everything."

"We?"

"I need your help. Look, I learned things in the academy. Useful things, like how to organize, how to fight. The cartels are gone. Everyone's scrambling, right?"

He nodded.

"I can take over."

"You?" He looked at the small girl and laughed.

"It's not the size of the dog in the fight . . ." she said. It was, she knew, his favorite saying.

"It's the size of the fight in the dog." He studied her for a moment. "You are quite a bitch."

She laughed. "You'll help?"

He looked at her with both hope and suspicion.

"You know people, Marc. I've been gone too long."

"Not just gone. You were a cop."

"Not quite," said Amelia. "And since when can't a cop also deal drugs? Not exactly a stretch. Will you help?"

He looked out the window, then back at her. "The streets aren't what you remember."

She needed no proof beyond what she saw in front of her. He wasn't what she remembered.

"You don't want to mess with what's out there, Amelia."

He opened his arms in display. What happened. When a tipping point was reached—and exceeded.

"Go home, Sweet Pea."

"I am home."

Marc looked at her. And his weary brain considered. "Everything?"

"Everything," she said. "All we have to do is find the shit."

He nodded, coming to a decision. "What the fuck. I have nothing to lose. Maybe that should be our motto."

Amelia grunted. "Maybe."

Thanks to Gamache, she too now had nothing to lose. It was, she realized, a very powerful place to be.

"Come with me," he said.

Marc hadn't lied. The streets of inner-city Montréal had changed. Never safe. Never clean. Never fun, now they were many degrees worse. Darker, filthier. Clogged with excrement, puke.

The faces that met her were gray. But the looks were canny. She was a stranger to them, even with Marc to vouch for her.

"Don't tell anyone where you've been," he whispered.

"No shit," she said.

"If anyone asks, I'm going to say you were in Vancouver, living on the streets."

They approached a loose knot of dealers, who stared at her.

She still had some meat on her bones. Pink in her cheeks. Clothes that hadn't hardened with a crust of frozen puke. And piss. And cum.

"If she was in Vancouver," a dealer asked Marc, as though Amelia weren't standing right in front of him, "why'd she come back?"

"I'm right here, fuckface," she said. "Talk to me."

She was at least six inches shorter. She had to tip her head back to glare up at him.

The dealer stepped forward, thrusting his pelvis into her. Pushing her until she was against the brick wall of the alley. Then he ground himself against her.

He was twenty-five at most but looked ancient. Like something dug up at some primitive burial site. They all did. A mass grave, under micrograms of fentanyl, on the streets of Montréal.

His breath on her face smelled of rotten eggs. Of sulfur. Of hell-fire.

"You know why I'm here," she snarled, not bothering to push him away. "You know what I want. What I can't get in Vancouver."

He thrust his body against her.

"You came for this, did you?" Grinding his pelvis into her. "I remember you, little girl. Amelia."

He said her name in a drawl, dragging it through the mud.

"You have one thing I want." She reached between his legs. "And it isn't this."

She squeezed. Though what she felt was soft. Like a mitten in his pants.

"That's it, little girl. Squeeze harder."

She brought her hand up from his crotch to his throat and gripped it in exactly the way the martial-arts instructor at the academy had taught her.

Then she squeezed.

"Like this?" she asked.

His eyes widened. And she tightened her grip on his throat.

His eyes bulged. And still she squeezed.

"Amelia," said Marc. "Stop. You'll kill him."

"Nothing to lose," she snarled. And squeezed until she felt his larynx begin to collapse. "I want the new stuff. I came all the way back for it. And if I can't get it, I'll take something else. Just." She squeezed. "For." Tighter. "Fun." Still.

And saw terror in his eyes.

Everyone stepped away, including Marc, while the dealer made a gurgling noise.

"I beg your pardon. What did you say?" she asked. And went through his pockets with her free hand as his eyes began rolling to the back of his head.

She found packets of pills. Packets of powder.

None of it was what she was looking for. She put the packets in her pocket.

Then released him.

He coughed and sputtered, then lunged at her. Amelia stepped aside, pushing him face-first into the wall and pinning him there.

"I'm not a little girl, shithead. I'm a fucking bitch," she hissed into his filthy ear. "But you know what else I am, you pathetic piece of *merde*?"

She twisted his head so that he could see her.

"I'm the one-eyed man. Tell that to your supplier. Tell him to watch out."

She gave him one last shove, turned around, and left. Marc scurrying behind her.

"What was that supposed to mean?" he asked. "What did you just do? They'll kill you."

"Maybe. Maybe not. I don't actually care." She handed him most of the packets. "One for you. Sell the rest."

"What about you?" He slipped through the snowy street, trying to catch up with her. His arms wrapped around his chest, his coat too thin to keep him warm on this bitter night.

"I have better things to find," she said.

The next morning she woke up in Marc's room, in Marc's bed. With Marc staring at her.

"Jesus, girl, what did you get up to last night? When I left you, you were looking for the new shit. Did you find it?"

She shook her head. "How'd I get here?"

"I carried you. Found you in an alley. I thought for sure you were dead. But you were just passed out. What did you take?"

She rubbed her hand over her face, feeling the grit of dried sleep, or tears, down her cheeks.

"I don't know."

Amelia had been stoned before. Lots of times. But never like this. Her head felt like it was splitting open, and she struggled for breath.

She tried to remember what had happened the night before. But all she saw were flashes that twisted and tilted in her memory. Turning her stomach until she thought she'd puke.

There was one that kept repeating.

A little girl. She was six or seven years old. Bright red Canadiens tuque on her head. She was wearing moose mittens and holding out a baggie of dope.

The child was swaying on her feet. Staring ahead of her.

But Amelia knew it wasn't so much a memory as a hallucination. Brought on by the shitface dealer calling her a little girl.

"You made quite an impression," Marc said, getting into bed beside her and pulling up the covers. "Everyone wants to know who you are."

"What did you tell them?"

Putting his arm around her, Marc hugged her to his bony chest. Speaking into her dirty hair, his voice muffled, he said, "I told them, Sweet Pea, that you're the one-eyed man."

CHAPTER 17

Armand strained to reach the hand. And the body attached to it.

"What is it?" shouted Myrna.

Pinned behind him, she couldn't see what he was doing, or why. But she could feel his almost frantic movements.

She tried to open her eyes, but the filth in the air kept forcing them closed. Billy, facing her, also had his eyes screwed shut. And his hands tightly clasped hers.

But Armand kept his eyes open, focused on the hand. Hoping, hoping to see movement as he stretched his arm out toward it.

He leaned as far forward as he could. But couldn't. Quite. Reach.

"What?" asked Benedict. "What's happening?"

"There's someone buried with us. I see a hand."

Benedict started to cough, and Armand eased up. Realizing he was pressing himself too hard against Benedict. Hurting the living to get to someone who was almost certainly dead.

They heard shouting and digging above them.

Still Armand reached out. In an unconscious imitation of *The Creation of Adam*. Two fingers, almost touching. But where Michelangelo had depicted the beginning of life, Armand knew this was the end. For someone.

"Who is it?" Armand asked.

Jean-Guy closed the door behind him and sat on the bench of the ambulance.

143

Armand was the last, by his choice, to be looked at by the medics. Benedict had been taken to the hospital for scans, given the injury to his head. After being checked out, Myrna and Billy were told it would be best to also go to the BMP Hospital, but both refused.

"All I want is to go home," said Myrna. "Have a bath. See my friends."

Jean-Guy sat across from Armand, who, despite having his eyes rinsed out several times by the paramedics, blinked against the irritation of the tiny bits of grit still in them.

His face was smeared with grime and sweat and water from the rinsing. But no blood.

Jean-Guy barely dared believe it. Not only was Gamache alive. They all were. Saved by a sturdy doorway.

"And Benedict," said Armand, coughing a little and using a Kleenex to wipe the filthy saliva from his mouth. "He pulled us into that doorway. And then protected me."

He could still feel the rubble hitting his arms, his legs. Crushing into him, into them, from all sides. His chest constricting, his breathing difficult.

What he could also feel, though not see, was Benedict. Using his own body to protect Armand.

And he could hear sobbing that died to whimpering.

The boy was terrified. Knowing he was about to die. And yet he'd chosen, as what might have been his last act, to try to save a near stranger, almost certainly at the cost of his own life.

Jean-Guy was nodding, agreeing.

He'd been just about the first one to them. Breaking free of the hands holding him back, he'd scrambled up the pile, slipping and stumbling on the snow and loose debris.

And then he heard them. Calling, crying out for help. Billy, Myrna, Benedict. But the one voice he was frantic to hear was silent. Panic had set in, and he began to dig with his hands. Throwing aside rubble he normally would never be able to shift.

Until the leather of his gloves was ripped away. Until he'd found them.

First Billy, then Myrna, then Benedict. And finally another face turned to him, squinting in the sunlight.

And the voice, rasping. "Jean-Guy, there's someone else."

While a rescue team, with dogs, dug out the body, Jean-Guy had helped free the others.

Myrna had some bruising on her legs, and Billy had a sprained ankle. Benedict had the blow to his head, and possibly other injuries from the original collapse and his night in the cold.

And Armand came away virtually unscathed.

Their heavy boots and heavy coats, thick tuques and mitts had, for the most part, protected them. Along with the doorway. And Benedict.

Armand blinked again, trying to bring Jean-Guy, sitting a couple feet from him in the ambulance, into focus. It felt like someone had smeared pebble-infused Vaseline into his eyes. Everything was opaque. The grit near blinding.

Like the others, he refused the offer of the hospital and, like the others, only wanted to go home.

But while Billy and Myrna had been driven back to Three Pines, Armand stayed. Needing to hear about the other one.

"They've just uncovered the body," said Jean-Guy.

He held out a wallet.

Armand opened it and saw the driver's license but couldn't read it. He shut his eyes tight to clear his sight, but still the words, the face, were blurred.

He handed it back to Jean-Guy. "Can you read it for me?"

Myrna slipped deeper into the tub, until the hot water was at her chin and the suds were piled so high she couldn't see over them.

"Oh God," she whispered as the chill and terror subsided.

What the warm bath couldn't do, the scent of lavender, the dark chocolate brownie, and the huge glass of red wine did.

Outside her bathroom door, she heard Bach. Concerto for Two Violins. And below that, unintelligible but recognizable, the murmured voice of Clara and very, very softly another sound.

"Fuck, fuck, fuck."

She closed her eyes.

Billy Williams rarely had baths and had never, ever had a bubble bath.

It wasn't that he considered them unmanly, he just never considered them.

But Madame Gamache had invited him in, to get clean and warm. And to stay for a meal. He was cold and hungry and about to decline when he smelled the scent of roses and followed her down the hall, limping, to the bedroom and the large bathroom attached. The tub was full, and high with foam from bubbles that smelled like his grandmother's rose garden.

It was too inviting to decline.

"I'll leave you to it," she said. "I'm going over to see how Myrna is doing."

"Say—" began Billy, then stopped. Considering. "Say hi from me."

"I will. There're clean clothes on the bed and stew warming in the oven."

When Madame Gamache had gone, he stepped into the bath, then sat. Sliding deep into the hot water. Feeling his taut muscles loosen as the water, and suds, rose over his aching body.

On a table beside the bath, he found a beer, his favorite kind. And a huge slice of pie. His favorite kind.

Lemon meringue.

Billy closed his eyes and sighed.

Amelia Choquet stood in the shower. Weak still. Bleary.

She'd wanted to take a bath. Long and hot. But Marc's bathroom was so disgusting, with a ring of dirt around the tub, stains in the toilet. Hair, both long and stringy and short and curly, clogging the drains. She wanted to spend as little time in there as possible.

She closed her eyes and felt the warm water cascade over her throbbing head. With the cracked, cheap soap, she washed her body and her hair. And for a moment felt almost human. She imagined that when she opened her eyes, she'd be in the clean, bright shower rooms of the academy.

Amelia held on to the fantasy as long as she could. Then opened her eyes and started scrubbing. And scrubbing.

It was then she noticed something written on her left forearm. A new tattoo, among all the others.

She took a closer look. No. It wasn't a tattoo. It was done in Magic Marker.

David.

That's all it said. Just, David. And a number: 14.

It wasn't her writing. Someone else had put it there.

She scrubbed harder. Until her arm was almost raw.

But the name wouldn't go away.

David. 14.

CHAPTER 18

———

Jean-Guy Beauvoir hung up the phone in the kitchen, then asked his father-in-law if he could use the one in the study.

"Of course."

Armand watched him go, then turned back to the others in the room.

Reine-Marie. Billy. Annie.

Benedict.

Armand and Jean-Guy had gone straight to the hospital and found him in triage. Bruised. Ravenous. With a bandage on his head, at his hairline.

"He's one lucky fellow," said the doctor. "No fractures or internal bleeding, not even a concussion. Your son?" the doctor asked. Jean-Guy. Who gave the young doctor a filthy look.

"No, he's not my son," he snapped, and saw Armand smile. "He's his grandson."

"That's not completely true," said Armand, but he did not completely deny it either.

The doctor looked at the two men, disheveled, dirty. Then at Benedict. Dirty. Disheveled. And didn't see the need to argue. "Well, he's all yours."

They'd taken Benedict home then. To the Gamache home.

Now, all showered and in warm clothes, they'd joined the others in a meal of beef stew and warm apple crisp with thick cream. Comfort foods that rarely failed in their one great task.

It was now midafternoon, and they sat warming themselves by the woodstove in the kitchen.

They'd asked, of course, about the body. The dead man. Wanting to know who he was. But Jean-Guy had explained that he couldn't tell them until the family had been notified.

That had been the call.

When Jean-Guy returned a few minutes later, he took a chair beside Annie, and after a brief glance at Armand he said, "The dead man is Anthony Baumgartner."

"What?" said Benedict. "But we just saw him yesterday."

"Baumgartner?" said Reine-Marie. "A relative of the Baroness?"

"Her son," said Armand.

"Poor man," said Annie. "Did he have a family?"

"*Oui*," said Jean-Guy. "His ex-wife's been told, and she's going to tell their children. They're in their late teens."

"What was he doing there?" asked Reine-Marie.

"That's the question," said Jean-Guy. Though there were other questions arising from the call he'd just received. And made.

"You're sure you didn't see or hear him when you arrived last night?" Jean-Guy asked Benedict, who shook his head. "And you saw no one else?"

Again Benedict shook his head while Armand looked at his son-in-law with interest.

"I saw the car," said Benedict. "But only when Billy and I got my truck started. It was in the headlights. I knew it'd take a while for the truck to warm up, so I went into the house, to get out of the cold."

"And I left you there," said Billy. "I'm sorry."

"That's okay. Not your fault. I was just stupid. Should never have gone in."

"The house was unlocked?" asked Armand.

"Yes."

Armand wiped tears from his cheeks as his irritated eyes again overflowed, and then he tossed the sodden tissue into the woodstove.

The medic had told him not to rub his eyes. That the grit could scratch the corneas and cause permanent damage.

But his eyes were crying out to be rubbed, and it was near impossible not to do just that.

Seeing this, Reine-Marie reached out and held his one hand while he sat on the other.

"Mind if we join you?" came a voice from the living room, and in walked Myrna and Clara. "I'd heard you were sprung from the hospital." Myrna hugged Benedict. "You okay?"

Billy had jumped up and offered Myrna his seat, blocking Clara from taking it. Reine-Marie's eyes lit up, and she grinned at Armand.

"Just a bump," said Benedict.

"A bimp," said Clara. "You minkey."

Benedict stared at her, in much the same way Armand stared at Billy when he spoke.

"I don't think you've met," said Myrna. "This's Clara Morrow, a neighbor."

"Hello," said Benedict, enunciating clearly and speaking loudly.

"You've never seen *A Shot in the Dark*?" asked Clara. She turned to Myrna. "Another movie we need to see again."

"Good idea."

"Clouseau?" Clara asked Benedict, who continued to stare, tilting his head slightly as though that might help decode this unkempt person.

"'My hands are lethal weapons.'" Clara lifted her hands in a karate chop, trying another movie quote, but now Benedict just looked alarmed, and, taking a step back, he bimped into Armand.

"It's all right," said Armand with a smile. "She only uses them to paint."

"Finger painting?" asked Benedict. "I had an aunt who did that. Therapy. Not quite right in the head."

"Speaking of which, your head's okay?" asked Myrna, returning to the original question.

"They did a scan, and apparently I have a thick skull."

He said it with such earnestness that they couldn't help but laugh.

Benedict, not quite getting it at first, looked confused. Then smirked.

"But a big heart," said Reine-Marie, patting the blanket at his knee. "You saved their lives."

"They saved mine."

"It must've been cold in that house," said Armand. "No heat."

"It was."

"Good thing you were able to light that fire to keep warm," he said.

"But it scared the crap out of us," said Myrna. "We could smell it and thought the place was on fire. Like just collapsing wasn't bad enough."

"Can you tell us now?" asked Clara, accepting Armand's chair as he pulled another over from the kitchen table. "Do we know the name of the person who was buried?"

"I just told them," said Jean-Guy. "The dead man is Anthony Baumgartner."

Myrna's face opened in shock. "The Baroness's son? We just saw him yesterday afternoon. At his house."

Benedict had said the same thing. Most people did, Armand knew. It was as though seeing someone recently should be protection against sudden death.

He turned to Benedict. "You were telling us that when you went into the home, it was unlocked. But you didn't see any evidence of Monsieur Baumgartner?"

"No, none. I called hello, thinking someone must be there, with the car and all, but there was no answer. I started looking around, using the flashlight on my iPhone. Just wandering, really, waiting for my truck to heat up. But then I got to thinking about maybe trying to save the place, so I went in further, to take a closer look. That's when it happened."

The young man went quiet.

Armand and Jean-Guy, both with personal experience of trauma, recognized the signs.

"What happened?" asked Armand softly.

His therapists had taught him something he tried to pass along to all agents in the Sûreté. The need to talk about what had happened. The physical, but also the emotional wounds.

And now he coaxed it out of young Benedict. He of the thick skull and big heart.

Henri, lying between Armand and Benedict, rolled onto his back. His huge ears flopping flat on the floor like two small area rugs.

Benedict bent down and rubbed Henri's tummy. Not meeting anyone's eyes.

"I could hear the cracking," he told Henri, who was listening closely. "I thought it was the frost getting into the wood. It happens with old places. I wasn't afraid. At first. I thought I knew what it was. But then there was another, huger noise. I was in the kitchen. I could hear something, like a train coming, and the place started to shake."

His voice was rising, and Myrna reached over and held his hand. Not to stop him but to reassure him.

Benedict looked at Myrna, then over at Armand.

Though his own eyes were bleary, Armand could clearly see the boy's terror.

"I began to run for the door," Benedict continued. "But a beam fell, right in front of me. I just managed to stop in time. And then—" He faltered.

"Go on," said Armand gently.

"And then it just felt like explosions everywhere. I got confused and froze."

He looked around, his eyes wide, and settled on Jean-Guy, who was looking at the young man not with pity, or sympathy. Not even with understanding, though Jean-Guy understood.

His expression held one thing. Reassurance. That what Benedict felt then, now, how he reacted, what he did or did not do, was natural and normal.

Freeze. Run. Cry. Scream.

Jean-Guy had done all those things himself. And he was trained. This boy was a carpenter. A builder.

"I know," said Myrna. "I froze too. When the place started to fall down. It was—"

"I was alone."

Myrna's mouth, open with the next words prepared, remained open. And silent.

"I was alone," Benedict repeated, in a whisper now.

And there was the difference. The gulf. Between their horror and his. They'd also faced death, but together.

He'd been alone.

Benedict's lower lip trembled, his chin puckering with the effort to hold it in.

"I was so afraid," he whispered. "When I finally did move, I saw the doorway and prayed it was under a support beam. I jumped in and got down. And waited. Everything fell around me." As he spoke, he hunched his shoulders. "And then the crashing stopped, but I was trapped. I shouted and shouted, but there was nothing. And then it got really, really cold. And dark. I'd dropped my iPhone, so I couldn't call or text. I didn't have any light. And then it got real quiet."

He was hugging himself and staring into the fire.

"But you had matches," said Armand.

Benedict nodded. "I'd forgotten about them. I made a little pile of wood. It was so old and dry that it burned easily. Every once in a while, there'd be more shifting, but I kinda got used to it, and once I had the fire, I felt better. I talked to myself. Telling myself how well I was doing. How great everything was. How smart I was. How lucky I was. And that someone would come find me." He looked at Billy. At Myrna. At Armand. "And you did."

"You never heard another sound?" asked Jean-Guy. "A human sound?"

"No. Not until you came."

They nodded, thinking. Imagining. Remembering.

And in at least one case, wondering.

"Why were you there?" Armand asked Benedict.

"To get my truck."

"Yes. But you promised not to drive it without snow tires. You gave me your word. So why did you?"

Benedict dropped his eyes from Armand. "I'm sorry." He heaved a sigh. "It sounds so stupid now, but after a couple of beers it seemed such a good idea. It's pathetic, I know, but there're two things I really care about. My girlfriend and my truck. I miss her. And I was worried about it. When Billy here offered me a lift, I took it."

He raised his eyes to Armand.

"I was going to call you in the morning. Tell you where I was. I'm sorry. I really am."

It was exactly the kind of reckless behavior a cop, and the father of a son, recognized. Armand nodded but kept his eyes on Benedict. Armand did not find it difficult to believe that this young man might have lapses in judgment. Witness the hair and sweater, the business card. Nor that he could be reckless. Witness trying to navigate a brutal Québec winter without snow tires.

But he found it difficult to believe that Benedict broke promises. And especially one he knew was being taken seriously.

And yet he had.

Which, Armand knew, meant he'd been wrong about the young man. In that. But in other things too?

The sun was setting, and Annie quietly got up to turn on some lights.

"Could anyone else use a drink?" she asked.

"Yes, please," said Myrna, getting up.

"I'll help," said Clara.

"Can we talk?" Jean-Guy asked Armand. "In your study?"

Once there, Jean-Guy closed the door.

"There's more, *patron*. Something I can't tell the others yet," he said. "The medical examiner doesn't think Anthony Baumgartner died in the collapse of the house."

"Then how?"

"His skull was crushed. There was concrete and plaster dust on the wound, but none actually embedded there."

"Internal bleeding?"

"None."

"Lungs?"

"Clear."

Gamache gave a curt nod and waved Beauvoir to a chair, sitting down himself.

"He was dead before the place collapsed," said Gamache, grasping the implication immediately. "Could it have been a heart attack or a stroke?"

"Dr. Harris considered both and doesn't think so," said Beauvoir. "She's ready to say the cause of death was the wound on the head, before the house came down."

"That's the phone call you made."

"*Oui*. I've classified it as a homicide and assigned Inspector Dufresne to the case. I'll be leading the investigation."

"Good," said Gamache.

"What can you tell me about your meeting with Baumgartner yesterday?"

Gamache thought. He'd already told Jean-Guy about it, and the will, but not in any detail. It had just been an odd event. He'd not seen it as a precursor to murder.

But now he reconsidered.

He described the gathering, the home, the others present. Their reactions to the will.

"So he questioned why you were a liquidator?" said Beauvoir.

"Yes. He'd thought he and his brother and sister were. They'd been led to believe that by their mother."

"Something must've happened, then, something must've changed, for her to take them off."

"But she still left everything to them," said Gamache. "If there'd been a falling-out, you'd think she wouldn't just take them off as liquidators but remove them completely."

Beauvoir was nodding. Thinking.

"Anything else strike you as strange, *patron*?"

Had it? Not at the time, but now? In retrospect?

He could appreciate how easy it was, how tempting, for people to overinterpret things.

Glances. Tones. Flare-ups. At the time they'd been guests and didn't realize that they were also witnesses.

He tried now to be accurate. Had something been said or done that had led, just hours later, to the death of Anthony Baumgartner?

It was the question he'd always asked himself when kneeling beside a body.

Why is this person dead?

And he asked himself that now. Why was Anthony Baumgartner dead? What had happened?

"It does seem too much of a coincidence," he admitted. "That the will is read and a few hours later one of them is murdered. But for the life of me, I can't remember anything happening at that meeting that could've sparked it. When we left, though, Hugo and the notary were still there with Anthony. Something might've happened after I left."

"What do you make of the will, *patron*?"

"I think from our perspective it was unexpected and even unhinged, but I have to say, her children, including Anthony, didn't seem at all surprised by it. They'd have been more surprised if she hadn't left all that money and property."

"Right," said Beauvoir, getting up. "It begins. We'll find out all we can about the Baumgartners."

"Including the Baroness," said Gamache. "I can't help but think if she were still alive, her son would be too."

He rose and went to the door but returned to his desk when the phone rang.

"*Oui, allô.*"

Gamache waved Beauvoir to a chair but remained standing himself. Jean-Guy saw Gamache's expression change.

"No, you did the right thing. She's still in there?" He listened, sitting slowly back down. "Tell me again what happened. . . . I see. And you're sure that's what she said?"

There was a pause during which Beauvoir could see Gamache's lips thin and whiten.

"Keep on it. . . . No, no. Do nothing. . . . Of course I know it's illegal," he snapped, then reined himself in. Taking a deep breath. When he spoke again, his voice was even. "Use your judgment, but understand that you're there simply as observers. Do not interfere."

When he hung up, Jean-Guy asked, "That was about Cadet Choquet?"

Gamache had told him what had happened the day before at the academy, and he knew the Chief was having Choquet followed.

"Former cadet," said Gamache, but he nodded. "*Oui.*"

"She's on the streets?"

"*Oui.*"

The Chief Superintendent seemed reluctant to speak. Not because he didn't want Beauvoir to know what was happening but because he himself seemed unsure.

"Her friend found her passed out in an alley and took her back to his place."

"*Merde,*" said Beauvoir, shaking his head. "Stupid, stupid girl." Then he looked more closely at Gamache. "But really, you can't be surprised, *patron.*"

He stopped just short of saying, *I told you so.*

Beauvoir had been warning Gamache about the young cadet since she'd been admitted to the academy by Gamache himself.

This was the one great divide between them. This was the Chief's weak spot. His soft spot.

Gamache believed people could change. For the worse, yes. But also for the better.

But Jean-Guy Beauvoir knew better. People did not, in his experience, fundamentally change. All that changed was their ability to better hide their worst thoughts. To put on the civilized face. But behind the smiles and polite conversation, unseen in the gloom, the rot grew and grew, and when the time was right, when the conditions were right, those terrible thoughts turned into horrific actions.

"What're you going to do?" asked Beauvoir. When Gamache didn't answer, Jean-Guy studied his boss and mentor. And got it.

"You're following her. Not to protect her but to see if she finds the opioids."

"*Oui.*"

Not so soft after all, Beauvoir thought, and tried not to let his shock show.

"The Montréal police have assigned two undercover agents to monitor her and report to me," said Gamache.

"You'd sacrifice her?"

"I'd sacrifice myself if I could," said Gamache. "But I'm not the one, the only one, who can lead us to the shipment."

Jean-Guy tried to keep his civilized face in place, but still, he suspected his feelings showed through.

Chief Superintendent Gamache had asked great sacrifices of his people before. Had placed himself in danger, many times.

But it had always been with knowledge and consent. They knew what they were in for.

This was different. Very different. The man in front of Beauvoir was using a troubled young cadet, without her consent. Placing her in danger. Without her consent.

It showed Beauvoir two things.

Just how desperate the Chief was to stop those drugs from hitting the streets.

And just how far he was willing to go to do it. But Jean-Guy could see something else.

The toll it was taking on this decent man.

Beauvoir wondered if he himself would be able to do something so horrific.

"David?" said the junkie. "No, no David."

Amelia pressed on. She didn't even know if this David was French or English. Was she looking for Day-vid. Or Dah-veed?

It seemed a small point, but in the underbelly of this world small points mattered. Like the tiny tear of the skin a needle made. Yes, this was a universe of small points. And big pricks.

She was pretty sure this David had tagged her because she was asking questions about the new shit. It was a warning. That he could get that close.

But Amelia wasn't going to be scared off.

In fact, just the opposite. She knew he'd made a mistake. Shown himself. And she now had a focus for the search.

Find David. Find the drug. And then her worries would be over. Then she'd show Gamache exactly what she was capable of.

Her feet, in running shoes, were wet through and caked in slush. Why hadn't she brought her boots when she left the academy? All she'd grabbed were her books.

She hadn't been back to the rooming house since leaving the day before, but she'd have to go back later that night. Marc needed his room. For business.

And she had her own business to do.

"I'm looking for David," she said to a prostitute.

"Unless you're looking for pussy, I can't help you, little man."

Amelia bristled, then realized that in her coat and tuque and jeans she did look a bit like a little man.

She trudged along rue Ste.-Catherine, a street named for the patron saint of illness. Peering into the dark alleyways, she saw the dregs, the detritus, the sick, the addicted, the whores, the near-dead and dying.

All kids. Most younger than herself. What had happened in the two years she'd been gone?

But she knew the answer. Opioids had happened. Fentanyl had happened. And worse was coming.

Amelia stared down a dark alley and thought she saw a child. In a bright red tuque. But it was just a hallucination, she was sure. An echo from the drugs she'd taken the night before.

Armand turned off all the lights in the house but didn't go to bed, though he was longing, after that horrible day, to crawl under the warm duvet and hold Reine-Marie close. In the curve of his body.

Instead he settled into an armchair in the living room, with a pillow and blankets.

Just down the dark hallway were the bedrooms where Billy and Benedict slept. Peacefully, he hoped.

But if one should wake up with night terrors, Armand needed to be there.

Clara turned off the lights in the loft above the bookstore. She'd made sure that Myrna was fast asleep and was about to leave when she paused at the top of the stairs and looked back.

And thought of all the times Myrna had stayed with her. After Peter. To be there when the nightmares began.

Clara put on the kettle, made herself a strong cup of Red Rose tea. And settled into the large armchair by the fireplace.

Armand sat up with a start. Some sound had awoken him, but as he listened, the house was silent.

And then it came again. A cry.

He threw off the blanket and walked swiftly down the hallway.

"Benedict?" he whispered, knocking on the young man's door and listening. There was the sound again. More like a whimper now.

Armand went in, and, pulling a chair up to the bed, he found Benedict's hand. And held it. Repeating, softly, over and over, that he was safe. And when that didn't work, he began to quietly sing. The first song that came to mind.

"'Edelweiss, Edelweiss . . .'" Until the boy stopped crying and his breathing relaxed. And he fell asleep.

In the next room, Billy Williams lay awake staring at the ceiling. In the darkness it seemed to be dropping, plunging toward him. He gripped the sides of the bed and repeated to himself it was just a hallucination.

I'm safe. I'm safe.

But he could barely breathe for the debris on his chest, and still the ceiling kept collapsing.

He heard a cry and felt his adrenaline spike. It was that very same sound he'd heard in the shrieking house. Inhuman.

And then he heard whispering. Murmuring. And then something else. Unintelligible but familiar.

His grip loosened, and his lids closed, and he fell asleep to someone softly singing.

Amelia pounded on the door to the landlady's room. It opened just enough for the ferret eyes to see who was there.

"What the fuck do you want?" the old woman demanded.

Her stained bathrobe was open, revealing more than Amelia wanted to see.

"I want my room. Someone else's in it."

"Yeah, someone who pays." The landlady's anger was replaced by satisfaction. "You had that room in exchange for cleaning. But you didn't, did you? You kicked over the bucket. I had to clean it up."

It was a lie, Amelia knew. She'd found the overturned bucket and mop still lying in the hallway outside her room.

The tiny eyes looked at Amelia through the crack in the door.

"Get out, before I call the cops," she said, and went to close the door, but Amelia's body stopped her.

"My things, give me my things, you filthy old slut."

"Don't have them."

"Where are they?"

"You feel that heat?" The old woman paused. Then smiled. "That's your stuff."

Amelia relaxed her pressure on the door as the landlady's words, and what they meant, hit her. In that moment the door banged shut and the dead bolt was pushed into place.

"You bitch," she screamed, and threw herself against the door. Over and over, until her voice was raw and her shoulder was so bruised she had to stop. Until she slid to the floor, exhausted.

She felt the carpet, crusty beneath her. She smelled the stale tobacco, and shit, and sweat, and piss. And she felt the warmth.

Her head dropped into her hands. And Amelia wept. For her life in ruins and her books in flames.

And then, the warmth too painful, she got up and walked back into the cold. In search of a drug so new, so powerful, it could take her away, far away, from there. Forever.

Reine-Marie found Armand nodding by the fire.

On seeing her, he roused and told her about Benedict. "I need to stay here."

"*Oui,*" she said, and, after adjusting the pillow and blankets, she pulled up a chair and sat beside him. Holding his hand and talking softly about Honoré. About their granddaughters in Paris. About Gracie and Henri.

Until he fell into a deep and peaceful sleep.

CHAPTER 19

⁓

The sun was streaming through the mullioned windows of the bistro, hitting the wide-plank floors, the comfortable chairs, the pine tables. The patrons.

But it didn't quite reach into the far corner, beside the large open fireplace, where Myrna, Benedict, and Armand sat with Lucien.

Armand had called the notary and asked him to meet them there and to bring some documents with him.

The notary listened, his face getting more and more slack as Myrna and Benedict related what had happened the day before.

"The house I was just in?" he asked when they'd finished. "Fell down?"

"Yes, we're feeling much better," said Myrna, responding to a question unasked. "Some bruising, but the bath last night helped. Thank you."

Lucien looked at her, puzzled.

They sat in wing chairs, their breakfasts and cafés au lait in front of them. Beside them the fire roared, fed by large maple logs.

"A body was found when the farmhouse fell," said Armand. "It was Anthony Baumgartner."

The notary's eyes widened. "Monsieur Baumgartner? He's dead?"

"*Oui.*"

"But we were just with him."

"He must've gone to the house after we left," said Myrna.

"But why?" asked Lucien.

"We don't know."

163

Gamache had decided not to tell them, yet, that Beauvoir was investigating it as a homicide. The longer that could be kept quiet, the fewer people who knew, the less guarded that people would be.

It would come out soon enough.

"Did Monsieur Baumgartner say anything to you after we left, about going to the house?" asked Gamache.

Lucien shook his head. "No, nothing. We just made small talk while I organized the papers. I didn't stay long, but it all seemed normal."

Both Myrna and Armand knew that Lucien might not be the best judge of what was normal human interaction. But even he would've noticed a fight breaking out.

"Do you know why they were replaced as liquidators in their mother's will?" Gamache asked.

"Not a clue," said Lucien. "And we don't really know that they were ever liquidators. They thought they were, but who knows?"

"Your father would've known," said Myrna. "And there must be an old will around."

"If there is, I don't know about it."

"Did you bring his papers with you?" Armand asked.

When he'd called the notary, Gamache had asked him to go through his father's files and bring anything relating to the Baumgartners. Now Lucien placed a neat pile of papers on the table.

"Your father wasn't the notary for Anthony Baumgartner, was he?" asked Gamache, putting on his reading glasses.

"No. Just for the mother."

"Have you read what's in there?" Gamache asked, pointing to the stack.

He blinked a few times and squinted a little, trying to get his still-blurry eyes to clear.

When he woke up that morning, he found that while his body was stiff and sore from the events in the collapsing house, his eyes were less irritated. But still the words in front of him refused to come into sharp focus, and he struggled to read.

"No," said Lucien. "I didn't have to. I've found what we're looking for."

"An old will?" asked Myrna.

"A very old will," said Lucien. "But not one belonging to Madame

Baumgartner. This's one I found when I did my own search. I believe I know why Bertha Baumgartner called herself 'Baroness.'"

Myrna turned in her chair to fully face him. Armand removed his reading glasses. And Benedict, after taking a huge bite of toasted buttered brioche, leaned forward.

Lucien paused, enjoying the moment.

"Oh for God's sake, just tell us," snapped Myrna.

The moment, it seemed, had passed.

"Fine. After our meeting with the family yesterday, and the extraordinary provisions of the will, I decided to try something. I did a will search under 'Kinderoth.' It took me a while, but I finally came on this."

He picked up a sheet of paper from the top of the pile and handed it to Myrna.

It was a printout of an old document, written in longhand with official-looking stamps all over it.

"This's in German," she said.

"Yes. I read a little," said Lucien. "It seems to be a case contesting the will of one Shlomo Kinderoth. The Baron Kinderoth."

Myrna's eyes widened, and she gave Armand a meaningful look, then handed him the paper.

He put his reading glasses back on and studied it, trying to focus, then handed it to Benedict. "Does the date at the top of that say 1885?"

"It does. This"—Lucien grabbed it from Benedict and held it up— "is a printout of the original filing in a court in Vienna in 1885. Seems Shlomo Kinderoth left everything to his two sons."

"Yes," said Myrna.

"Equally."

"*Oui*," said Armand.

"I'm not putting this well," said Lucien, and no one contradicted him. "He left everything to his twin sons. Both men inherited the title as well as his wealth, which was, according to the filing, vast. Estates in Switzerland. Homes in Vienna and Paris—"

"Wait," said Myrna, holding up her hand. "Are you saying he left the same thing to both?"

"Exactly."

"But how can he?"

"He can't. That's the thing," said Lucien, enjoying himself now.

"That's how all this started. I guess they didn't get along. They sued each other."

"And?" asked Benedict.

"And nothing. It was never resolved."

"What does that mean?" asked Benedict.

"You're not saying the will is still being contested," said Myrna. "That's a hundred and twenty years ago."

"One hundred and thirty-two," said Lucien. "And no, of course I'm not saying that. The Austrians are almost as efficient as the Germans. No, this would've been decided long ago. I just haven't found the judgment yet."

"But we can assume it wasn't in favor of Madame Baumgartner's side of the family," said Armand.

"Then why would she believe she was entitled to it?" asked Myrna.

But even as she asked that, and saw Armand's grim face, she knew the idiocy of her question.

Bertha Baumgartner clung to that belief because she wanted to. It served her purposes.

The Baroness lived in a fantasy world, where the fork in the road favored her. A world where she was both victim and heiress. A baroness cleaning woman. A walking Victorian melodrama.

How many clients had Myrna sat across from as they complained about having been "done wrong"? Whose grip on grievances was so tight it strangled reason. They'd give up sanity before giving up these injustices.

In some cases, in some people, it went on for years and years. The thorn planted firmly in their side. And while Dr. Landers had listened, guided, made suggestions on how to try to let their pain go, still they'd let it fester, until she'd finally realized some clients didn't want freedom from their resentments, they wanted validation.

Entitlement was, she knew, a terrible thing. It chained the person to their victimhood. It gobbled up all the air around it. Until the person lived in a vacuum, where nothing good could flourish.

And the tragedy was almost always compounded, Myrna knew. These people invariably passed it on from generation to generation. Magnified each time.

The sore point became their family legend, their myth, their legacy. What they lost became their most prized possession. Their inheritance.

Of course, if they lost, then someone else had won. And they had a focus for their wrath. It became a blood feud for the bloodline.

Myrna looked at Armand, who had taken back the document from Lucien and written something on it.

"So she thought her side of the family got screwed," said Benedict.

Myrna compressed her lips. All her psychology classes, her Ph.D., her years of study and work, and this young man put it more succinctly than she could.

Bertha thought her family had been screwed. For generations.

"What do you think, Armand?" Myrna asked.

"The sins I was told were mine from birth," he remembered Ruth's obscure poem, *"and the Guilt of an old inheritance."*

"There's a reason Anthony Baumgartner went into that farmhouse," he said.

"Maybe he just missed his mother," said Benedict.

Maybe, thought Gamache.

There was, after all, something precious in the house. The one thing that couldn't be stripped away.

The place was filled with memories.

He saw again the growth chart. And the photograph in Anthony's home, of the three children in the garden of flowers, beautiful and treacherous.

Armand Gamache knew that memories weren't just precious, they were powerful. Charged with emotions both beautiful and treacherous.

Who knew what lived on in that rotten old home?

Gamache studied the printout again. It was written in German, so he couldn't understand much. And he could barely read the writing anyway.

Is this what started it all? A crazy will written one hundred and thirty years ago. And another, equally crazy one, read two days ago?

"Where was Madame Baumgartner when she died?"

"In a seniors' home. The Maison Saint-Rémy," said the notary. "Why?"

"Cause of death?" Armand asked.

"Heart failure," said Lucien. "It's on her death certificate in your dossier. Why?" he asked again.

"But there was no autopsy?"

"Of course not. She was an elderly woman who died of natural causes."

"Armand?" asked Myrna, but he just gave her a quick smile.

"Do you mind if I take this?" He picked up the printout.

"I do," said Lucien. "I need it for my files."

"*Désolé*, but I shouldn't have put it in the form of a question," said Gamache, folding it up and putting it into his breast pocket. "I'm sure you can print out another copy."

He got up and turned to Myrna. "Is your bookstore open?"

"It's unlocked," she said. "Comes to the same thing. Help yourself."

Armand spent the next few minutes browsing the shelves of Myrna's New and Used Bookstore before he found what he wanted. Leaving money next to the till, he put the book into his coat pocket.

When he returned to the bistro, he saw Billy Williams heading to his truck.

"He shouldn't be driving," said Myrna, going to the door. "With his bad ankle."

She called to him, and, as Gamache watched, Billy turned, saw Myrna, and smiled.

"He's a nice man," said Armand. "A good man."

"A handy person to have around," she said. "That's for sure."

They watched as Billy approached the bistro. And while Armand couldn't understand a word Billy Williams said, he did understand the look on his face.

And he wondered if Myrna saw what he did.

CHAPTER 20

Jean-Guy Beauvoir stared down at the body of Anthony Baumgartner as the coroner went over the autopsy results.

Unlike Gamache, Beauvoir had not seen him in life, but still he could tell that Baumgartner had been a handsome, distinguished-looking man. There was about him, even now, an air of authority. Which was unusual in a corpse.

"An otherwise healthy fifty-two-year-old man," said Dr. Harris. "You can see the wound to the skull."

Both Gamache and Beauvoir leaned in, though it was perfectly obvious even from a distance.

"Any idea what did it?" asked Gamache, stepping back.

"I'd say, by the shape of it, a piece of wood. Something similar to a two-by-four, with a sharp edge, but bigger, heavier. It would've been swung like a bat." She mimicked a swing. "Hitting him on the side of the head, with enough force to do that sort of damage. Not as easy as you might think, to cave in a skull. What is it?"

Gamache was frowning.

"Are you sure it was done before the building collapsed?"

It was, of course, a vital question. One was accident. One was murder.

"Yes. I'm sure."

His eyes, still bloodshot and watery, watched her closely.

Dr. Harris sighed, and, stripping off her surgical gloves, she tossed them into the garbage can.

She knew Chief Superintendent Gamache and Inspector Beauvoir well. Well enough to call them Armand and Jean-Guy. Over drinks.

169

But over a body they were Chief Superintendent, Chief Inspector, and Doctor.

She didn't take offense at being pushed on this point. The Chief was a careful man, and nowhere was that care more necessary than in tracking down a killer.

And while she knew that Gamache was still on suspension, she'd continued to consider him head of the Sûreté, until someone forced her not to.

"Anthony Baumgartner had been dead at least half an hour before the place came down. I can tell by the condition of his organs and the lack of internal bleeding. Besides, he was hit on the side of the head. A building doesn't normally collapse sideways."

"I'm going to make a call," said Chief Inspector Beauvoir, pulling out his cell phone and stepping away.

"There were two collapses, is that right?" Dr. Harris asked Gamache.

"Yes. A partial one sometime in the night and then the final one yesterday afternoon."

"The one you were caught in," she said. "That revealed the body."

"*Oui.*"

He explained, briefly.

"Sit down," said Dr. Harris, indicating a stool.

"Why?"

"So I can flush your eyes out."

"I'm fine, they're getting better."

"Do you want to go blind?"

"Good God, no. Is that a possibility?"

She could see he was genuinely shocked.

"Remote, but who knows what material was in that building? The sooner you can get all the grit out, the better. It's possible it's scratching the cornea. Or worse, getting behind the eyeball."

He sat, and she leaned into his face, first taking a close look at his eyes, and then she brought the water up and squirted. He winced away as the water hit.

"Sorry, should have warned you it would sting."

When she'd finished, he grimaced, widening, then blinking his eyes.

"Don't rub," she warned, and took a good look in both eyes, finally clicking off the light on the instrument. "Better. Much better."

They didn't feel better. Now he could barely see, and his eyes were both irritated and painful. He sat on his hands.

"What did you say to him?" asked Beauvoir, returning from a call. "You've made him cry."

Dr. Harris laughed. "I told him the bistro had run out of croissants."

"Are you trying to kill the man?" asked Jean-Guy.

"Enough. I can still hear, you know," said Gamache. His sight was coming back and the irritation subsiding. "What did Inspector Dufresne say?"

"They're going over the wreckage, looking for the weapon," said Beauvoir. "And trying to work out where he was when he was killed."

"What do they think?" asked Gamache.

"Dufresne thinks probably in a second-floor bedroom. When the roof finally collapsed, it brought his body with it. That's what it looks like now."

Dr. Harris walked to the sink while Armand returned to the metal autopsy table. Clasping his hands behind his back, he stared down at Anthony Baumgartner.

So unlike his mother, who looked like an elderly British character actress playing a monarch in a comedy.

This man appeared to be the real thing. Even in death there was something almost noble about Anthony Baumgartner. Gamache wondered, in passing, who the title went to now. Caroline or Hugo?

Did primogeniture apply to fictional titles?

He picked up the white sheet and replaced it over Anthony Baumgartner's face.

And still the Chief Superintendent considered the sheet, and what was under it, for a long moment before he spoke.

"Do you think this was meant to look like an accident?"

"That seems pretty obvious," said Beauvoir. "Yes. We're supposed to think he was killed when the house fell down. And we might have, if Benedict hadn't been there and said there was no one else in there. No one living, anyway."

"True. But for it to look like an accident, the farmhouse had to fall down."

"Well, yes," said Dr. Harris, glancing over her shoulder from the sink.

But Beauvoir returned to the table, looking first at the Chief, then down at the white sheet.

"That's true," he said. Understanding what it was that Gamache meant.

It wasn't just a simple statement of fact. It was a vital element of the investigation.

Then Dr. Harris, drying her hands, turned around, and Jean-Guy could see that she also understood what Gamache was saying.

"How did the killer know the house would collapse?" asked the coroner.

"There's only one way," said Beauvoir.

"He had to make it fall," said Gamache.

"And there's only one person in the picture right now who might be able to do that," said Beauvoir.

Gamache stepped away from the body and put in a call.

After listening to Chief Superintendent Gamache, Isabelle Lacoste considered for a moment.

She'd agreed immediately to his request but now had to figure out just how this could be done.

Then she'd called a taxi. It had dropped her off, into a pile of snow and slush.

Lacoste walked carefully across the icy sidewalk. Her cane in hand. And stood at the entrance to the apartment building.

It was a low-rise, with windows that were so frosted up it would be, from the inside, impossible to see outside.

She tried the front door. It was unlocked.

Limping into the entrance, she had to make her way around a large pile of circulars on the floor. Clearly if there was a caretaker, he or she was taking the day off. Or the year.

Isabelle Lacoste checked again the information Chief Superintendent Gamache had texted her.

Benedict Pouliot. Apartment 3G.

After looking around for an elevator and realizing there was none, she stood in front of the stairs, took a deep breath, and began climbing.

After their meeting with the coroner, Jean-Guy dropped Gamache at a café on rue Ste.-Catherine.

"Bit scuzzy," he said, looking around. "You sure you want to wait here?"

"I used to come here as a young agent." Gamache looked around. "All I could afford. Even brought Reine-Marie here."

"On a date? Are you mad?" Beauvoir looked at the dregs slumped in booths. But the place itself seemed clean enough. The sort of diner where Mom and Dad and drug-dealer son could share a poutine together.

"I guess Reine-Marie likes the bad boys," said Armand, and Jean-Guy laughed.

"Yeah, they don't get much more brutal than you, *patron*. Now, you have everything you need?"

"I need you to leave," said Gamache.

And now Jean-Guy stood in front of the closed door in Sûreté head-quarters. A room he was fast becoming familiar with. And growing to hate.

He lifted his hand, but it opened before he could knock.

"Chief Inspector," said Marie Janvier.

"Inspector," he said.

"Thank you for coming." She stepped aside to let him in.

"Thank you for having me."

If she was going to pretend this was a social event, so could he.

"We have just a few more questions for you." She indicated the same chair he'd sat in last time.

The same people were at the same table, but now there was also an older man in a comfortable chair off to the side.

Beauvoir was prepared this time. He knew, despite the pleasant smiles, what it was they wanted from him.

Instead of taking his seat, he walked past the investigator, directly up to the quiet man in the corner.

"And who are you?" he asked.

The man stood up. He was not in uniform, but he held himself like an officer. Police or military. Senior.

He was slightly shorter than Beauvoir, middle-aged, with a trim body. There was an ease about him, and an alertness. The sort of attitude that came from years of being in charge, in difficult situations.

And this, it seemed, was a difficult situation.

"Francis Cournoyer. I'm with the Ministère de la Justice."

Beauvoir was surprised, even shaken. But tried not to show it. "Why're you here?"

"I think you know why, Chief Inspector."

"This has become political."

"This was always political. I expect your Chief Superintendent knows that. Knew that, even when he made the decision to let the drugs pass. But you don't need to look at me like that. I'm not the enemy. We all want the same thing."

"And what's that?"

"Justice."

"For whom?"

Francis Cournoyer laughed. "Now that's a good question. I serve the people of Québec."

"As do I."

"And the Chief Superintendent?"

Beauvoir couldn't contain his outrage. "After all he's done, you'd question that?"

"But his service needs to be seen in its totality. Yes, he's done a lot of good, but can you really say he's served the population well when he let loose what amounts to a plague?"

"To stop something worse."

"But how do we know it would've been worse?" asked Cournoyer. "All we do know is if that drug hits the streets, tens of thousands, maybe hundreds of thousands, will die. Either by the drug itself or the violence that comes with it. Is that justice?"

Even Beauvoir, not a political animal, could see that Francis Cournoyer was trying out the line that would be used on journalists. In talk shows and interviews.

To justify this assassination.

However apparently well-meaning the head of the Sûreté had been, he'd made a terrible blunder. And had to pay.

"What do you want from me?"

"You have a chance to limit the blowback, Chief Inspector. You were his second-in-command. This can mar the entire Sûreté, just when it's beginning to win back some credibility."

"You want me to say it was all his decision? All his doing?"

"You have a choice. Gamache is going to be blamed. There's no way around that. His ruin was inevitable, from the moment he made that decision. He knew it. And did it anyway. There's nothing you can do to stop that. You can't save him. That bullet has left the barrel. What you can do is stop the collateral damage to others."

"Including myself?"

Francis Cournoyer just shrugged.

"Including the Premier?"

Cournoyer's face grew grim.

"We've drawn up a statement, Chief Inspector. Take it with you if you like. Read it. Put it in your own words. But sign it. Do the right thing. Don't be blinded by your loyalty."

"You're kidding, right? You'd say that to me?" Beauvoir was trying to keep his voice down and his tone civil, but his anger was clawing its way out. "Releasing those drugs allowed us to break the largest drug rings working in North America. It was a Sûreté action that almost cost a senior Sûreté officer her life, and instead of thanking us, you treat me and the Chief like criminals?" Now he dropped his voice. "And I'm the blind one?"

"You have no idea what I see."

"Oh, I think I have an idea. We're a detail in your big picture, right?"

And he had the satisfaction of seeing, fleetingly, a moment of hesitation in Cournoyer's eyes. Of very slight surprise.

"It's nice you think we have a big picture," said Cournoyer, recovering. "But believe me, we're just bumbling along, responding to events and trying to do the right thing by our citizens."

Beauvoir didn't say anything, but he did know one thing. This Mr. Cournoyer did not bumble.

Gamache sat at the melamine table in the booth, sipping water and looking out the window.

Then he got a text.

"I'll be back," he said to the server, handing her a twenty. "Please hold the table for me."

"Oui, monsieur."

Pulling his tuque down over his ears and putting his gloves on, Gamache squinted into the bright, cold day. His feet crunching on the sidewalk, pedestrians hurried past him, in a rush to get where they were going.

But he was in no hurry. Up ahead and across the road, two people were also walking slowly. One tall, thin, gaunt even in the winter coat. The other shorter, fuller, more stable on her feet.

Amelia.

Gamache matched their pace for two blocks, and when they paused, he stepped into an alleyway. There, hunched into his parka, he watched, leaning against the cold bricks of the abandoned building.

He saw the dealers and addicts and prostitutes, going about their business in broad daylight. Knowing no cop would stop them.

This part of rue Ste.-Catherine wasn't so much an artery as an intestine.

He could see two scruffy men, in filthy clothing, going through garbage cans. Occasionally shoving each other. Fighting over cans and stale crusts.

Gamache watched, impressed.

The young officers were doing well. Taking this seriously. As they should. There would be few things in their careers more important than what they were doing at that moment. Though they didn't yet know it.

He'd had a text, a brief update, from one of them. Advising him where Amelia was. But they had no idea where he was. No idea that the head of the Sûreté had joined them and was also watching the former cadet.

Gamache stepped back further into the shadows, as Amelia and her friend approached a dealer. Both men looked frail, especially compared to Amelia.

The one-eyed man, thought Gamache.

Then Amelia did something odd. She shoved the sleeve of her left arm up to her elbow and held it out to the dealer, who shook his head.

Amelia said something, appearing to argue, before turning her back on the dealer and walking away. Her friend hurrying to catch up.

"Twenty bucks for a blow job." Gamache heard the male voice behind him.

Ignoring it, he continued to watch until he felt a poke in his back.

"I'm speaking to you, Grandpa. You want a blow job or not?"

Gamache turned and saw a man younger than his own son. Tattoos over his ravaged face. He must have been handsome once, thought Gamache. He must've been young, once.

"No thank you," he said, and turned to watch the exchange across the street.

"Then fuck off."

Gamache felt two fists hit his back with such force he was propelled out of the alley and across the icy sidewalk. Putting out both hands just in time, he thudded against a parked car, narrowly missing skidding onto the street. And into oncoming traffic.

A driver leaned on his horn and gave him the finger as he passed.

"You okay?"

Gamache felt a thin hand, like a skeleton's, on his arm and turned to look into a cavernous face. The cheeks were so sunken the thin skin barely stretched across the bones. And the eyes, with dark circles, were dilated. But kind.

Gamache looked across the road. His eyes sweeping over and past the couple a block away now.

Amelia had glanced back at the sound of the horn, but Gamache had already turned away and was looking at the person who held his arm.

"Do you need help?" asked the soft voice.

"*Non, non.* I'm fine. *Merci.*"

She looked behind her, shouting into the alley. "You fucking asshole. You might've killed him."

"Fucking tranny" came the reply out of the dark. "Get off my block."

The woman turned back to Gamache. They were about the same height, and it was clear she had once been robust but was withered, whittled down. She wore a short leather skirt and a pink, frilly coat. Her makeup was carefully, skillfully, applied, but couldn't hide the sores on her face.

"You sure you're okay?" she asked. "It isn't safe here, you know."

"You're very kind, thank you," he said, reaching into his pocket.

"Don't." She laid the same skeleton hand on his arm.

Gamache brought out a notebook and pen and wrote down his personal number.

"If you ever need help." He handed it to her, along with his gloves. "My name's Armand."

"Anita Facial," she said, shaking his hand and taking what he offered.

Amelia continued walking with Marc. She'd slept in the hallway outside his tiny apartment the night before and tried not to hear what was going on inside.

And now they were off again. He to find another score. She to find David.

A car horn had blasted just behind them, and she'd turned in time to see a prostitute holding the arm of a man who'd almost wandered into traffic.

She watched for a moment as the man gave the prostitute what must have been money for services. Some things never changed.

Amelia continued trudging down rue Ste.-Catherine. She bent her head into the wind and narrowed her eyes and repeated, as she had the night before, the familiar poems and favorite phrases seared into her memory. She went through them, her personal rosary. Over and over. Round and around. Until the bitter day faded. Until the addicts and whores and trannies faded and she was left with the warmth of the words from books now ash.

Gamache walked back to the café.

He knew it was probably unwise to have come here, but he wanted to make sure Amelia was indeed on the streets and was doing what he expected.

Looking for the carfentanil.

He was under no illusion about what would happen if she failed. If he failed.

Fentanyl, he knew, was a hundred times stronger than heroin. And carfentanil was a hundred times stronger than any fentanyl.

It would be like taking a flamethrower to every kid on the streets.

As he walked slowly back, he thought about what Beauvoir had said. That no one was more brutal than him. It was said in jest, but it was also, Gamache knew, true.

Armand felt a slight pain in his back where the young male prostitute had hit him from behind. There were two spots, side by side, that throbbed. If he were sprouting wings, that's where they'd be.

But Armand Gamache knew with certainty that he was no angel. Though he did wonder if there was ever another war in heaven, on which side he'd be placed.

After sliding back into the booth and ordering coffee and a sandwich, Armand put on his reading glasses and opened the book he'd bought that morning at Myrna's bookshop.

Erasmus's *Adagia*. His collection of proverbs and sayings.

The print was small, and Armand's eyes were still blurry, but he knew the book well and now read the familiar entries.

> *One swallow doesn't make a summer.*
> *A necessary evil.*
> *Between a rock and a hard place.*
> *A rare bird.*

And then he found the one he'd been looking for.

In the kingdom of the blind, Amelia recited to herself as she trudged along—

—*the one-eyed man is king*, Gamache read.

"Chief Inspector?"

Beauvoir turned and saw Francis Cournoyer walking down the corridor after him.

"A word, please."

Jean-Guy had been interrogated for an hour and finally been allowed to leave. But he hadn't made it very far down the hallway before Cournoyer caught up with him.

The Ministère de la Justice man looked around, then pulled Beauvoir into the washroom and locked the door.

"You forgot this." He held out a manila file folder.

Beauvoir looked at it. It contained the statement.

"I didn't forget it. I'm not signing. Ever."

"It doesn't say anything we don't already know," said Cournoyer.

"But signing it would say a lot about me, wouldn't it?" said Beauvoir. "Drop it. Drop this whole thing. Do what's right."

Cournoyer smiled. "Is it so clear to you, always? What's right? It isn't to me. And it isn't to Gamache."

"That's a lie. He did what was right."

"Then why do so many decent people think it was wrong? Not just them"—he jerked his head toward the interview room—"but others. Good people, yourself included, disagreed with his decision."

He looked closely at Beauvoir.

"You're surprised I know that? By the Chief Superintendent's own testimony, you pleaded with him to stop the shipment of opioids. Every one of the agents in the inner circle begged him to stop it. He admits that. But it didn't stop him. He let it onto the streets, to potentially kill thousands."

"It hasn't hit the streets yet, and he's gotten most of it back."

"But not all. And it will hit the streets, any day now. Any minute now. Every young death will be laid at his feet."

"You think he doesn't know that? Isn't that bad enough for him? You have to make it a public lynching? It's disgusting. You're disgusting. I won't have anything to do with it."

"You'll change your mind. Before this's over, you'll sign."

"I won't. What's your endgame in all of this? It can't be just protecting politicians."

Cournoyer unlocked the bathroom door, and then, looking back at Beauvoir, he seemed to make up his mind.

"Ask Gamache."

"What?"

"Ask him. He knows far more than he's telling you."

Cournoyer tossed the file, with the statement, onto the floor and left. Jean-Guy stared at it. Then picked it up.

CHAPTER 21

⌒

"Your Benedict . . . Pouliot does not live in 3G, as it turns out," said Isabelle Lacoste, picking up the burger with both hands and taking an almighty bite.

"But he does live in the building?" asked Gamache. "With his girlfriend?"

He had to wait while Isabelle chewed and chewed.

Beauvoir, who'd just joined them in the diner on rue Ste.-Catherine, waved at the server. "I'll have one of those too, please, and a hot chocolate."

It was difficult for a grown man to order a hot chocolate with authority, but he tried.

Armand smiled. But his amusement faded on catching the look Beauvoir gave him.

And Armand felt a slight chill, as though a locked door had opened, just a little.

"*Oui*," said Lacoste, finally swallowing. It had been a while since she'd been this hungry. "Well, sort of. They used to live in . . . 3G, but she moved out a month or so ago, and he moved into a smaller apartment. Same building. Did you know he's the . . . caretaker?"

She went to take another bite, but Gamache put his hand on her arm to stop her.

"I didn't know that. So he has no girlfriend?"

"Not anymore. Not that the neighbors know. I spoke to half a dozen of them. They all said pretty much the same thing. They'd lived together for a couple of years. The parting seemed . . . amicable."

She took another bite. The place might look like a dive, but the burger was freshly made, perfectly charbroiled, and delicious.

She did not mention that she'd hauled herself all the way up three flights of stairs, pausing at every second step to catch her breath. Only to discover that someone else now lived in 3G and the apartment she was looking for was actually just off the lobby.

"Fuck. Fuck. Fuck," she'd mumbled with each careful step down.

"What do they think of Benedict?" Beauvoir asked.

"They said he's polite. Nice. Trustworthy. There're a lot of older people in the building, and they seem to have adopted Benedict."

"He has that effect on people," said Gamache. "He's a good handyman?"

"Yes," said Lacoste. "According to the other tenants, he seems to know . . . what he's doing. But he hasn't been around for a couple of days."

This description of Benedict was far from conclusive. A handyman could fix a leaking faucet. He could not, necessarily, make a building collapse. At will.

Although a carpenter might. A builder. And that was Benedict's other job.

"But if Benedict killed Anthony Baumgartner," said Beauvoir, "he messed up. His plan couldn't possibly have been to get trapped himself."

"Probably not," said Gamache.

"What do you mean 'probably'?" snapped Beauvoir. "It's obvious."

Both Lacoste and Gamache stared at him in surprise.

"Is something bothering you, Jean-Guy?"

Beauvoir took a deep breath. "I'm sorry. I'm just hungry and tired."

His sponsor in AA had warned him about H.A.L.T. Hungry, angry, lonely, and tired were triggers.

He'd readily admit to hungry and tired. And the meeting had angered him. But it was the lonely that was surprising and upsetting Beauvoir. Cournoyer's final comment had left him feeling very alone.

Ask Gamache.

"It wasn't too much for you, Isabelle?" Gamache asked. "Going to the apartment building?"

"Are you kidding, *patron*? The best . . . therapy I've had in months."

She didn't tell them that she'd slipped and fallen into a snowbank and had struggled to get back onto her feet. Then it had taken another ten minutes to flag down a taxi.

She'd arrived at the restaurant frozen through and bushed.

But it was the most fun she'd had in months. Since the shooting.

She'd been afraid she'd be sidelined forever. Treated by well-meaning colleagues as a charity case. Someone to be patronized, coddled, pitied. And finally ignored.

But Gamache had done none of those things. Instead he'd trusted her with this task, and she'd proven to herself and him that she could do it.

"I've arranged to meet Baumgartner's brother, sister, and ex-wife at his home." Beauvoir looked at his watch. "At three o'clock. I'd like you there if possible, *patron*."

"*Oui. Absolument*," said Gamache. "They know he's dead, of course. But do they know he was murdered?"

"Not yet."

Though it was possible one of them knew perfectly well.

After Gamache headed to the archives to look up some documents, Lacoste was left alone with Beauvoir.

"Okay, spill," she said. "What's wrong?"

"Nothing."

"Oh for Christ's sake, don't make me drag it out of you. You're angry at the Chief about something. What is it?"

He told her about the conversation with the man from the Ministère de la Justice.

As he described what had happened, it all sounded ludicrous. And it would seem silly if he hadn't seen the look on Francis Cournoyer's face.

What's your endgame? Beauvoir had asked, the scent of disinfectant heavy in the air.

Ask Gamache.

With those two words, Cournoyer had thrown a bomb into Beauvoir's world. Though it had been, really, more of a crumble than an explosion. As he'd stood there in the men's toilet. Trying to grasp what was being said.

Cournoyer had more or less said that the person at the center of it all wasn't some vindictive politician. Wasn't some shadowy government operative.

It was Gamache. He wasn't the target, he was the sharpshooter. He wasn't the victim, he was the perpetrator. And he knew perfectly well what was happening. Why. And where it was leading.

And he was keeping Beauvoir in the dark.

And all of this—the investigation, the sneaking around, the threats—were meant to confuse, to dazzle. To misdirect. While something else was happening.

That's what Francis Cournoyer had said. With those two words.

Ask Gamache.

Jean-Guy could feel a headache coming on. The distant throbbing at the base of his skull. Like heartbeats at the birth of dark thoughts.

"But it doesn't mean that the Chief knows anything," said Lacoste. "This Cournoyer man might've been messing with you. Probably not his first mindfuck in a public washroom."

And despite himself Beauvoir snorted. Then heaved a heavy sigh.

He wanted to agree with her. But she hadn't been there. Hadn't seen Cournoyer's triumph as he'd said it.

"Gamache knows way more than he's saying," said Jean-Guy.

"Isn't that a good thing?" asked Isabelle. "You're just pissed off that he didn't tell you."

"Just?" demanded Beauvoir. "Just? I'm being grilled. My career possibly ruined. And he knows why all this is happening, and he's not telling me?" Jean-Guy's voice rose as he wound himself up. "Yes, I'm fucking angry."

There was silence for a long moment.

"You do know," she said, leaning across the table toward him, her voice so quiet he had to also lean in, "that he's the head of the entire Sûreté? Of course he knows more than you. Or me. Or anyone else in the force. He'd better. He's in charge. He's had to navigate these waters for years. So yes he knows more, sees more, than you, or me. And thank God he does."

"He's keeping secrets."

"And that surprises you, Jean-Guy?"

"He's playing me."

"Or maybe he's protecting you. Have you thought of that? Can't you see it?"

"Of course I can't see it," snapped Beauvoir. "He's keeping me in the dark. Letting me just waltz into these interrogations like an idiot. I'm tired, Isabelle. Just . . . tired."

And now he looked it. With an index finger, he pushed a fry around on his plate. Then looked up at her. And sighed. "You know?"

She nodded.

"I'm tired of playing catch-up," Jean-Guy said. "Of wondering what monster is around the next corner. Not the murderers. Them I can handle. It's the other stuff. The political games that aren't games at all." He shook his head, then looked down and spoke quietly. "I'm not good at it."

"You don't have to be. He is." She smiled then. "And you're far better at it than you let on. I know that. He knows that."

"But he's better."

"Monsieur Gamache is twenty years older than you. He's been at it a lot longer, at a much higher level. But you're up there now. He trusts you. And, more than that, he cares very deeply about you. For you. If you don't know that by now, you never will."

She flagged down the server again.

"I think we need some tea, don't you?"

She smiled at Beauvoir, who couldn't help but smile back.

Tea.

The Anglos in Three Pines were always pressing tea on each other in times of stress. Even Ruth. Though her "tea," while looking like it, was actually scotch.

He'd thought it vile at first. The tea. But then, somewhere along the line, he found he looked for it. Hoped they'd offer it. And drank it with pleasure, though he didn't show it.

He found now that just the aroma of Red Rose calmed him. He didn't even have to drink it.

The waitress returned, and the scent of the tea enveloped him. Strong. Fragrant. Calming. And yet Jean-Guy could still feel the throbbing radiating from the base of his skull, until it covered his head like a membrane that kept tightening.

He had to think. To be clear. To try to see what was really happening and not what others wanted him to see.

But all that kept coming to mind was Matthew 10:36.

His first day on the job, Chief Inspector Gamache had called him into his office.

The two men were alone, for the first time. And Agent Beauvoir took in two things immediately.

The sense of calm that came from the man behind the desk. It was unusual. Most senior officers Beauvoir knew gave off a "fuck you" energy. Something Agent Beauvoir had learned to copy.

The other thing he noticed was the look in the Chief Inspector's eyes.

Smart, bright. Thoughtful. None of that was particularly unusual in a senior Sûreté officer. But it was something else, in those eyes, that had taken Agent Beauvoir by surprise.

Kindness. Clear enough for a rattled young man to see.

"Have a seat," the Chief had said. And had proceeded to outline, quickly, clearly, what would be expected of Jean-Guy Beauvoir. It amounted to a code of conduct. It started with the four statements that lead to wisdom: I don't know. I need help. I was wrong. I'm sorry. And ended with him saying, simply, "Matthew 10:36."

"You can take all of what I've said to heart," the Chief had said, leading the young agent to the door. "Or none. It's your choice. As are the consequences, of course."

Jean-Guy Beauvoir was used to being told what to do. Ordered around. By his father. His teachers. His superiors.

The concept of choice was new. And more than a little baffling. As was the Chief's habit of tossing what appeared to be random quotes into conversations.

It wasn't until a few years later, and many experiences with the Chief in horrific investigations, that Agent Beauvoir had looked it up.

Matthew 10:36.

Jean-Guy had expected some inspirational biblical saying. From St. Francis, perhaps. Or something from one of those long letters to those poor, and almost certainly illiterate, Corinthians.

stead what he read struck dread into his heart.

a man's foes shall be they of his own household.

188

Far from inspirational, it was a harsh warning in a gentle voice. A whisper out of the darkness.

Be careful.

"I'm tired, Isabelle. Tired of all this." He waved his hand, to indicate not the dingy diner but a world that couldn't be seen. The world of suspicions. Of constant questioning. Of ground shifting.

He just wanted to rest. No, he wanted more than that. He wanted to curl up on his own sofa, in front of the fireplace. With Annie and Honoré in his arms.

And he wanted it all to go away.

He drove her home. At the door she hugged him and whispered, "Be careful."

It was so close to what he'd been privately thinking a few minutes earlier that he felt the hairs go up on the back of his neck.

"I've got Cournoyer's number now," he said. "Not to worry."

"Not of Cournoyer."

"Gamache," said Beauvoir.

"No. You."

As he drove back through Montréal, to pick up Gamache, he could smell a familiar, very, very faint scent. Of rose water and sandalwood.

And he could see, again, those kind eyes. Intelligent. Thoughtful. Trying to communicate something to a hardheaded young agent who was radiating "fuck you."

He watched as pedestrians leaped away from the wall of slush splashed up by cars. As elderly men and women clung to each other to keep from falling. As people, neutered by the bitter cold, scuttled from shops.

And Jean-Guy imagined walking along the Seine with his family. Taking them to the galleries and cathedrals and parks of Paris. Weekend trips to Provence. To the Riviera. Where sun gleamed off the Mediterranean and not off snow.

CHAPTER 22

⁓

"Ruth, what're you doing?" asked Myrna.

Clara and Gabri stopped tapping on their computers and looked up from their screens.

All four had driven in to Cowansville and now sat in the computer room of the local library, each at a laptop around the large conference table.

They'd come in not for the computers but for the high-speed connection.

Ruth had joined them when she found out where they were going.

Now the elderly poet sat at her laptop, fingers moving swiftly and noisily over the keys as she pounded rather than tapped. A look of satisfaction on her face that would have frightened Genghis Khan.

"Nothing," said Ruth.

Far from being computer-illiterate, Ruth in her early eighties had embraced the Internet.

"As a way," Gabri had guessed, "of spreading her empire."

If there really was a darknet, Ruth Zardo would find it. Conquer it. Become its empress.

"Queen of the Trolls," Gabri had said, and Ruth had not contradicted him.

Though they knew for whom she trolled. Not schoolchildren. Not people who were scorned for being different.

She trolled people who trolled them.

She attacked the attackers.

"Madame Zardo," the librarian had said, practically bowing when Ruth limped in. Elderly, unsteady. Stooped.

But when she sat at the table, behind "her" laptop, she was nimble. Strong. Unyielding. Relentless. No bully could hide. Ruth's hat was so black it was white.

The library was in the process of renaming this room: A F.I.N.E. Place.

"What's she doing?" Clara whispered to Gabri.

"I have no idea," he said.

"Anything?" Myrna asked, and Clara turned her laptop around.

Both Gabri and Myrna took a look.

Clara was in the Austrian registry of births, deaths, and marriages. With a worldwide interest in ancestry, these records were being made available online.

She was following the Baumgartner family, root and branch. Back in time.

To where it grafted onto the Kinderoths.

And then she followed them. To see where, and if, they became the Rothschilds.

"It's interesting, but I'm getting a bit lost. Who's related to whom, and then names change not just with marriage but to avoid discrimination. Obviously Jewish names become Christian. In fact, not only do the names change, but lots of them actually converted. But you see here?"

She pointed to one old document. A name changed from Rosenstein to Rose. But a Star of David remained above Rose. And followed it, through the generations.

And then it stopped. And there was just blank space. Except for the notation "10.11.38."

"What does that mean?" asked Gabri.

Myrna sat silent. Staring. She knew but couldn't say it. She was looking at the names. The ages.

Helga, Hans, Ingrid, Horst Rose. All born in the 1920s. With stars beside their names.

And then the simple notation. 10.11.38.

And then nothing.

"It's a date," Myrna finally said.

Ruth leaned over and looked. Then returned to her computer.

"Kristallnacht," she said, tapping even harder. "November tenth, 1938. When good, decent people revealed themselves for who they really were and turned on their neighbors. The Jews."

"Kristallnacht," said Myrna. "Because of all the broken glass."

"More than glass was broken that night," said Ruth. "It was particularly brutal in Austria."

She spoke as though she'd been there, and while her face was blank and her voice flat, her fingers pounded the keys even harder. In pursuit.

"The Baumgartners?" asked Myrna. "The Baroness's family?"

"Looks like they got out before the Holocaust," said Clara. "I'm trying to track them. Interesting thing is, they aren't called Baron and Baroness."

"So maybe they lost the case?" said Myrna.

"Seems obvious they must have," said Gabri.

"Shlomo Kinderoth left his fortune to both his sons," said Myrna. "You've found the part of the family that became the Baumgartners. How about the other branch?"

Clara spent some moments clicking through. "It's going to take time, but so far I can't find any more references to Baron or Baroness Kinderoth."

"You don't think—" Gabri began.

10.11.38.

"I don't know," said Clara.

"Any luck with the will?" Myrna asked Gabri.

"I have no idea," he said. "I got into the archives, but they're in German. I can't read them."

"I hadn't thought of that," said Myrna.

Armand Gamache sat in the quiet back room of the National Archives. The records he was looking for weren't Canadian. Or Québécois.

He'd used his pass code to get into Interpol. Then over to the Austrian records. The ones he had access to were more detailed than those available to the public.

But he quickly ran up against the same problem Gabri was having.

He could read the names. Baumgartner. Kinderoth. But he couldn't understand the court judgments.

What he did understand was that there were judgments. Plural. Lots of them. From 1887. Then 1892. Then another. And another. All involving Baumgartners and Kinderoths.

Against each other.

They stopped for a few years. And then started up again. Like trench warfare, only pausing to retrench. And then the combatants went at it again. More fiercely each time, he guessed. Such was human nature.

While he could understand the larger issues, the fact this was a case that was tried over and over again, he couldn't get the details. And it was the details that interested him. Though it was far from clear that they'd lead him to whoever had killed Anthony Baumgartner, 132 years after the death of Shlomo, the Baron Kinderoth.

Gamache knew he needed help. He did another search, and then, after finding what he was looking for, he got up and paced.

He was alone in the room, so no one saw him muttering. Gesturing. Finally, after a few minutes, he pulled out his phone and placed a call.

"*Guten Tag*," he said, and asked for the Kontrollinspektor.

"*Am pursuing powerful informations about a resolve.*"

The voice at the other end of the line was deep, calm, apparently intelligent. And yet Kontrollinspektor Gund couldn't help feeling he was dealing with a lunatic.

"And you are who again?" he asked.

The call had been put through to him by his subordinates. Who enjoyed playing jokes like this in the middle of a long shift, in the middle of the night. It was far from clear this was even a real call and not one of his own agents seeing how far they could push him.

"*I be Armand Gamache, Head Chief of that Sûreté du Québec.*"

"In Canada?"

"*That is the direction*" came the voice, sounding relieved. "Canada."

Gamache rolled his eyes. He knew he was making a balls-up of this.

He'd asked, at least he thought he'd asked, for a senior officer who spoke French. Or English. And had been put through to someone who clearly spoke neither.

It might've been the receptionist's idea of a joke, though the Austrians, renowned for many things, were not famous for their hilarity.

Before calling he'd practiced, dragging up from the mists of time whatever German his grandmother had taught him.

He'd sit at the kitchen table, and she'd chat away, in French. And then in German. With a smattering of Yiddish. Of course, as a child, Armand hadn't made the distinction.

As he paced the small room in the National Archives, he mumbled to himself. Repeating the words and phrases as they surfaced. Trying to cobble together an intelligible sentence or two. As he paced, and muttered, the scent of fresh baking became more and more pronounced. Wafting to the surface along with the words. And images.

He could smell, more and more clearly, the madeleines his grandmother had made every Friday.

She'd give him one fresh from the oven, but not before dribbling a spoonful of cod liver oil over the top and letting it soak in. So that when Armand took a bite, it was both delicious and vile. Comforting and gagging. It was like being hugged and shoved at the same time.

"*Sehr gut, meyn tayer.*"

"Very good, my darling," she'd say in Yiddish, and hug him to her so that his eyes came within inches of the tattoo on her left forearm.

"I'm investigating a murder, and a will is part of it," said Gamache into the phone. Or at least thought he was saying. "I need to find out how an estate was settled. It's an old case."

"*Me inspecting a dead murder body, and a resolve is . . .*"

There was a pause as Gund's subordinate at the other end pretended to search for a word. One that, Gund was sure, would be ridiculous.

"*. . . measure. No, that's not right. Is a . . .*"

Gund almost hung up. Enough was enough. And yet he was curious. And not completely convinced anymore that this was a bored agent playing a joke.

As the man on the other end struggled with what he was trying to say—

"... *amount*. No. *Quantity?* ..."

Gund turned to his computer and put in "Sûreté du Québec. Gamache."

"... *part*. That's it. *A resolve be part of it.* But resolve might be quite not right. *Oy gevalt.* What's the word?"

Gund read, raising his brows, then looked at the phone and tried to reconcile what he was reading with what he was hearing. Now the deep voice was saying, "*Force. Nein.* I almost have it. Will. That's it. *Gott im Himmel. Danke.*" There was a sigh. "*Will. A will be part of it.*"

"Chief Superintendent Gamache," said Gund. "If I understand correctly, you would like me to look into a decision about a will?"

He spoke slowly. Clearly.

"*Ja, ja. That is correctly. It is an elderly event.*"

Gamache winced, as much from the scent of cod-infused cakes now surrounding him as the stream of near nonsense coming out of his mouth.

"An old case," said Kontrollinspektor Gund.

"*Ja.*"

"Can you give me the name of the deceased and the date of the will?"

Gamache did, reading from the printout in front of him.

He also gave Gund his personal email address.

"I'll get back to you as soon as I have the information. It's a murder case, you say?"

"*Ja. Danke schön.*"

"*Bitte schön.*"

As Gamache hung up he felt that conversation had gone both well and badly. Was comforting and nauseating. Successful and humiliating. And almost certainly not German.

"Such a *tuches.*"

CHAPTER 23

Inspector Dufresne had already arrived with the homicide team. Their vehicles were parked discreetly along the road, waiting for Chief Inspector Beauvoir's signal to join him.

At Beauvoir's knock the door to Anthony Baumgartner's home opened and Anthony's sister, Caroline, stood there.

Tall. Elegant. The only evidence of grief were the circles under her eyes.

"Madame," said Beauvoir, introducing himself, though leaving out the department he headed. "I believe you know Monsieur Gamache."

Caroline had shaken Beauvoir's hand, but on seeing Gamache she stepped forward.

And hugged him.

It was quick and might have surprised her more than him.

When he'd been head of homicide, Gamache learned that people reacted to sudden death differently. The emotional could become restrained. Holding themselves back, for fear of what would happen if they cracked.

The restrained became emotional, not skilled at managing feelings.

The strong collapsed. The weak strengthened.

In grief people were themselves and not themselves.

Caroline hugged him.

Then led them both into the living room.

The place, Gamache knew, would soon be searched by those homicide agents waiting outside. Anthony Baumgartner's life would be laid as bare as his body now was.

Inspected. Dissected.

Pulled apart. As they, like the coroner, searched for the cause of death.

Dr. Harris's job was done. Anthony had died from a blow to the head. But theirs was just beginning.

Once they were in the living room, Hugo Baumgartner stepped forward and offered a hand but otherwise stood like a gnome in a garden. Concrete, mute, ugly. And yet, somehow, the dumpy little man dominated the elegant room.

"This is my sister-in-law, Adrienne Fournier," said Caroline. "Adrienne, this is Chief Inspector Beauvoir and Chief Superintendent Gamache."

They offered their condolences.

"*Merci*. It's terrible. I'm afraid I'm still struggling with it. I expect to see Tony come down the hall in his slippers." Then she smiled. "I can see you're a bit confused. Tony and I have been divorced for a few years but managed to remain friends. Probably should've just been friends all along."

"Probably?" asked Caroline.

Adrienne shot her a look but ignored the aside. "Though we have made great children."

She was of average height and well dressed. Over fifty, with hair dyed a rich brown, judicious makeup, and a trim figure. Her clothing was stylish without being showy.

"Before we begin," Beauvoir said after taking the chair Caroline had indicated, "I have some news for you. It's not good."

There was a snort from Hugo, who turned to Caroline when she gave him a look.

"What?" he said. "Like any news at this point could be good. It's all shit." He turned to Adrienne. "Sorry."

His former sister-in-law was regarding him with something close to amusement. Certainly affection.

"You're right, Hug. This is shit."

Caroline turned away. Distancing herself from them. Gamache couldn't help but see an iceberg breaking off from the mainland.

And drifting away.

Though he suspected that had actually happened long ago. Caroline might drift close but would always be separate. And vulnerable to currents and undertows. To the ebb and flow of opinions and judgments.

Probably since childhood.

Behind them he could see the photographs on the bookcase. And while it was too far away and his eyes still too blurry, he could make out the small silver frame and the vague suggestion of three grinning kids. Wet, sagging bathing suits. Tanned arms slung easily over one another's shoulders.

Caroline in the middle, bookended by her brothers.

Had she been happy then? Happy once?

Or had the cracks already begun to form? The cooling, the hardening. The distancing.

Was it in her nature, or had something happened?

And always, always, in the background of Gamache's thoughts, the main question.

Why was one of them dead?

"Your brother," Beauvoir said, looking first at Caroline, then to Hugo. Before moving his gaze to Adrienne. "Your former husband." She gave him a slight acknowledgment. "Wasn't killed in an accident. His death was deliberate."

He paused for a moment, then went on.

"He was murdered."

It was a short, sharp statement.

Both Beauvoir and Gamache knew that people's minds couldn't easily grasp the fact of murder. It was too big, too foreign. Too monstrous. Most just stared, as they stared at him now. As the word and its meaning sank in. Then sank further, from their heads to their hearts.

And there it would live forever.

Murder.

Caroline stiffened, and Hugo, after a pause in which his pudgy face opened in shock, reached out. And took his sister's hand.

In, it seemed to Gamache, an automatic, unscripted, instinctive act of mutual support.

Adrienne, sitting alone in a wing chair, closed her fingers over the arms of the chair. And pressed until her knuckles were as white as her face. She looked, Gamache thought, as though she might pass out.

Beauvoir got up and went to the kitchen, returning with glasses of water. But not before going to the front door and signaling Inspector Dufresne.

Gamache could hear the murmurs of voices in the front hall and the rustling as the Sûreté homicide team entered the house.

The postmortem had begun.

Hugo had abandoned his glass and gone to the bar.

"Screw water," he said, pouring three scotches. His hands trembled as he gave them to Caroline and Adrienne.

Adrienne took a great swig of the scotch, color returning to her face. Hugo downed his in a single shot. But Caroline simply took the glass and held it, as though she'd forgotten how to do everyday things. Like drink. And breathe.

"How?" she asked.

"Why?" asked Hugo.

"Are you sure?" Adrienne asked.

This last was the most natural of questions. Even though she knew the answer. Of course Chief Inspector Beauvoir was sure. He wouldn't have said it otherwise. But still, she had to ask.

And yet the other two had not.

They'd asked other natural questions. How? Why? But what the other two hadn't done was question the statement that someone had murdered their brother.

"We're sure," said Beauvoir. "Do you know of anyone who might want him dead?"

At that moment, on another continent, Kontrollinspektor Gund sat back in his chair.

It was getting on for midnight. A quiet evening in his precinct, and he'd had time to noodle around for the senior Québec cop.

He'd thought it would be a routine search into albeit a very old will.

An elderly event. He smiled as he remembered the epic struggle that poor man had had with the language.

But his smile faded as he read his screen. Then scrolled down.

Further. Further.

It was then he'd sat back and marveled.

"No life is blameless," Caroline began, her voice prim. "But I can't think that Anthony hurt anyone so badly they'd want him dead."

"It's not necessarily that he's hurt someone," Chief Inspector Beauvoir explained. "Motives can be"—he searched for the word—"complex. Your brother might have had something someone else wanted, badly. He might have stood in someone's way at work, for instance. Or have found something out."

Gamache sat quietly on the periphery of the circle and listened. And observed. Searching for some insight. Some reaction.

But all three were shaking their heads.

"Monsieur Baumgartner worked for Taylor and Ogilvy Investments," said Beauvoir. "As an investment adviser, I believe."

"That's correct," said Caroline.

"He invested people's money."

"He acted as a sort of money manager," Hugo clarified. "He'd design a portfolio, get the client's approval, and then others would do the actual trades."

"I see."

An agent, off to the side, was taking notes.

"We'll follow up, of course," said Beauvoir, "but was there anything at his work that was unusual? An unhappy client? A bad investment? Any suggestion of impropriety?"

"None," said Caroline.

"Was he good at his job?"

"Very," said Adrienne.

"I'm sorry to interrupt, but do you mind if I ask a question?" said Gamache.

"Please," said Beauvoir.

"Did any of you invest with him?"

They looked at each other, then shook their heads.

"Why not?"

"I did. A long time ago. But then it didn't seem a good idea to mix business with family," said Caroline.

Hugo was being uncharacteristically quiet, and Adrienne was sitting bolt upright.

"Madame?" Gamache turned to her.

"When we divorced, I moved my money over to another firm, of course."

"Even though you remained friends?"

"Well, that took a while."

"I see. And your children?"

"What about them?"

"I'm wondering if they have any investments, any money in trust or a college fund. That sort of thing."

"Yes, they each have an account."

"With their father?"

"No."

"That too was moved?"

"*Oui.*"

Beauvoir noticed that Madame Fournier's answers were getting more and more clipped. And there was not much more to be clipped before she'd lapse into silence altogether.

And, indeed, silence fell.

Where other investigators pressed and pushed during interrogations, especially when finding a weak spot, Gamache had taught his agents the power of silence.

It could be, often was, far more threatening than shouting. Though that too had its place. But not here. Not now.

Now silence filled the room.

Hugo fidgeted. Adrienne reddened.

And Caroline? She smiled.

Slight. Fleeting. But unmistakable.

Satisfaction.

Hugo made a noise, but Caroline shut him up with a small sound of her own. A quiet cross between clearing her throat and a hum.

It was as though brother and sister understood each other at a primal level, where grunts were enough.

Again the silence encroached. Enveloping them, so that even the young agent off in the corner fidgeted.

"What do you want from me?" Adrienne finally said.

"We want to know what you know," said Gamache. "That's all."

"Just tell them, Adrienne," said Hugo. "It was years ago, and they'll find out anyway. There's no shame."

"For you, maybe." Again there was silence as everyone stared at Anthony Baumgartner's ex-wife.

"My husband was having an affair with an assistant," she finally said. "I found out about it, and it ended our marriage. That's why I took not only my money but our children's money away from the company. From him."

"How long ago was this?" asked Beauvoir.

"Three years."

"Are they still together?"

"No. That ended."

"And the assistant's name?" asked Beauvoir.

"Does it matter?"

"It might. People hold grudges. Her name, please."

And again the slight smile from Caroline. Fleeting. Smug. Cruel.

"His name was Bernard."

Beauvoir raised his brows. "I see."

"Do you?" asked Adrienne. "I wonder what you see? The humiliation? The lies. The little ones and then that great shitty one that was our marriage? I loved a man who didn't, couldn't love me. Not in the same way. Never had, he admitted. Never would. We stood over there." She pointed to the fireplace. "That's where our marriage ended. Right there. When I confronted him and he admitted it. Didn't even try to soften the blow. He just seemed relieved. The bottom had fallen out of my life, and all he felt was relief. Nothing for me. Or the children. He just wanted out, he said. Out."

"Well, he didn't get all that far out, did he?" said Hugo.

"He never came out?" Beauvoir asked.

"No."

"And why not?"

Adrienne was on the verge of answering when she paused. Her shoulders, which had crept up to near her ears, slowly lowered.

She looked at Hugo, who gave her a small nod of support. Her eyes traveled past Caroline, not pausing, then stopped at Beauvoir.

"I don't really know. I never asked. I think, if I'm honest, I was just relieved he was being discreet. For the children's sake. Maybe," she added, "for myself too. I never stopped loving him, you know. I'd have remained with him, had he wanted. I never admitted that to anyone. I loved him, not because he was a straight man but because he was Tony."

She looked around. "I hate this room."

Gamache wondered if it was just the room she hated.

CHAPTER 24

—

"Excuse me," said Chief Inspector Beauvoir, ceding his place to Inspector Dufresne. "I'll leave you with the Inspector and Chief Superintendent Gamache."

He got up, and after nodding to his inspector he caught Gamache's eye.

Gamache, of course, knew exactly what Beauvoir was about to do. The same thing he'd done when he was head of homicide.

Beauvoir had listened to the family. Now it was time to meet the dead man. Or as close as he could come.

Beauvoir walked from room to room, looking in. Sometimes going in.

Agents were photographing. Taking samples. Opening drawers and closets.

They acknowledged him.

"Chief."

Beauvoir nodded back but was, for the most part, silent. Watching. Taking it in. Not monitoring their activity but absorbing the surroundings.

It was always an odd feeling, walking around a person's home uninvited. Seeing it as they'd left it in the morning. Not realizing they'd never return. Not realizing it was the day of their death.

There was something solid, comfortable, restful about this place. It was a home, not a trophy.

The colors were muted. A soft blue-gray for the walls. But there were touches that seemed almost playful.

A lime-green geometric print on the curtains in the master bedroom. Vintage Expo 67 posters were on the walls of the hallway.

Some clothes were tossed casually on a chair in the bedroom. There were balled-up tissues in the wastepaper basket. Some loose change sat on the chest of drawers, along with a framed photo of Baumgartner with his children. A boy and a girl.

On the bedside table, there was a nonfiction book about American politics and a copy of *L'actualité* newsmagazine.

Taking out a pen, Beauvoir pulled open the drawer. More magazines. Pens. Cough drops.

He closed the drawer and looked around for evidence of someone else living there. Or visiting. Overnight.

No one else's clothes, or toothbrush, seemed to be there.

If Baumgartner had a partner or a lover, there was no evidence.

Beauvoir walked down the hall and turned the corner into the room Baumgartner used as a study. And stopped dead.

He didn't know much about art. Did not recognize any artist. With one exception. And that exception was on the wall, over the fireplace in the study.

It was a Clara Morrow. And not just any "Clara," it was a copy of her painting of Ruth. But not just Ruth.

Clara had painted the demented old poet as the aging Virgin Mary. Forgotten.

Embittered.

A clawlike hand gripped a ragged blue shawl at her neck. Her face was filled with loathing. Rage. There was none of the tender young virgin about this grizzled old thing.

Ruth.

But. But. There. In her eyes. Was a glint, a gleam.

With all the brushstrokes. All the detail. All the color, the painting, finally came down to one tiny dot.

Ruth as the Virgin Mary saw something in the distance. Barely visible. Hardly there. More a suggestion.

In a bitter old woman's near-blind eyes, Clara Morrow had painted hope.

Beauvoir knew that most people who looked at the painting saw the despair. It was hard to miss. But what they did miss was the whole point of the painting. That one dot.

The few who got it, though, never forgot it. Dealers and collectors then went back and discovered more treasures in Clara's odd, sometimes fantastical, sometimes deceptively conventional portraits.

But it was Ruth who'd made her reputation and career. Ruth and a dot of light.

Beauvoir nodded to the portrait and heard the old poet snarl, "Numbnuts."

"You old hag," he murmured.

The agents, working in the study, looked at him, but he just gave them a curt nod to continue.

Chief Inspector Beauvoir walked around the room, trying not to get in anyone's way. He paused at the mantel, to look at the photographs.

Baumgartner with friends. With politicians. At business banquets. More photos of his children. One of Baumgartner and his now ex-wife. They looked good together. A confident and attractive couple. Then Jean-Guy picked up a small picture in a silver frame. It was black and white. This must have been his parents.

The father was slender, handsome, unsmiling. Severe. A tough man to please, Beauvoir guessed.

And his son took after him, at least in looks. In personality too? It didn't seem so, from the pictures. He was almost always smiling in them.

But then Anthony Baumgartner was good at hiding what he was really feeling. That much had been proven.

Beauvoir's attention shifted to the other person in the photograph. The Baroness.

She was, by just about any measure, ugly. No way around that. With a round body and sagging spaniel eyes and a complexion that even in the old photo looked blotched.

But she was smiling and had a look of near-permanent amusement about her. There was a gleam in her eyes too. And Beauvoir found himself smiling back.

The Baroness, despite all appearances, was far more attractive than her husband.

Though there was also a slight haughtiness, a suggestion of cunning, in that face.

Hugo Baumgartner obviously took after her.

And Caroline Baumgartner? More the father than the mother, though the Baroness's haughtiness was there. But what passed for cunning in the mother came out as cruelty in the daughter.

The photographs were interesting—revealing, even, in some ways—but what he was really interested in was on the desk. Baumgartner's laptop.

"Finished?" he asked the agent who'd been sitting at the desk, going over the papers.

"*Oui, patron.*"

He got up and relinquished the chair to the boss.

Beauvoir sat in front of the blank screen.

There were papers to the left of the computer. With numbers. And a few letters.

They weren't to Baumgartner but from him. Signed by him. Ready to be mailed out, presumably.

Beauvoir read one. It seemed a fairly standard explanation of investments and the state of the market.

The other papers looked like financial statements.

He opened the desk drawers. More paper. Stuffed in there.

"You've been over these?"

"*Oui.*"

Beauvoir pulled the papers out and began going through them. The mess in the drawers was in contrast to the neat desktop. Many people's lives were like that. The neat room and the messy closet. The well-ordered counters and the chaos in the cabinets.

But he also knew that, as homicide detectives, what they were looking for often lived in that gap, between the public and the private.

As they went through Baumgartner's life, that cavern, between public and private, would begin to narrow. Squeezing out whatever lived inside.

Now Beauvoir scanned each piece of paper, smoothing out the wrinkled ones and placing them to the right of the laptop.

He was looking for one specific thing.

When he'd finished, he turned to the laptop and considered it.

Baumgartner, like most people, almost certainly protected his devices with a security code. His iPhone had been found that afternoon in the wreckage of his mother's home. Smashed. But there were hopes some information could still be retrieved.

Beauvoir knew that almost everyone did four things, when faced with modern technology. First they created passwords. Then they forgot them.

Then, on being forced to create new ones, they simplified and went with only one, which opened everything. And then they wrote it down. And hid that paper somewhere.

That way they only had to remember the place, not the password.

Beauvoir grunted as he got onto his knees, then lay on the carpet, staring at the underside of the desk. Nothing. Rolling over, he got to his feet.

"Did you find anything that might be a code for the laptop?" he asked the team.

"Nothing," the lead agent said.

"Well," said another, "there was one thing. There's a piece of paper behind the painting of the crazy old lady."

Beauvoir felt his heart speed up as he walked over to take a look. Sure enough, there was a piece of paper Scotch-taped back there. With a number. And the words "Virgin Mary."

"Merde," he whispered.

Beauvoir had learned enough about paintings, and the art world, to know this was a numbered print of the Virgin Mary. And that was the number.

Sitting back down at the desk, his eyes settled once again on the papers Baumgartner had left beside his laptop.

Getting up, he walked down the hall to the master bedroom.

"Agent Cloutier? Would you join me, please?"

"D'accord, patron."

The woman, in her late forties, looked both relieved and worried to be called away by Chief Inspector Beauvoir.

"Hugo?" said Gamache.

"Yes?"

"You're being very quiet."

"I have nothing to add. My sister's doing a good job, as is Adrienne. I can't think of anyone who'd want to hurt Tony."

"What do you do for a living, monsieur?" Inspector Dufresne asked.

They'd already established that Caroline was a real-estate agent. Successful, she said. In the top five percent.

They'd later learn that was true. After a fashion. Top five percent in her company, in her area. Who specialized in condos. For young families.

Which put her in the bottom five percent of agents in Québec.

"I'm an investment dealer," said Hugo.

"The same as your brother?" Dufresne asked.

"Yes."

But Gamache had noticed the very slight hesitation and tucked it away.

"You worked together?"

"No. Different firms. I work for Horowitz Investments."

Gamache's expression didn't change, but he took this in.

This was the same firm he and Reine-Marie used for their investments. While Montréal based and founded by Monsieur Horowitz decades ago, it was now global, with offices in New York and Paris.

"And what do you do there, sir?" asked Dufresne.

"I'm a senior vice president. I have a portfolio of clients whose wealth I manage."

Hugo smiled, which, perversely, made him look even uglier. Like a jack-o'-lantern.

Without consciously realizing it, Gamache had put Hugo Baumgartner down as a bit of a rustic. If he worked at Horowitz Investments, it was in some support role, doing it affably, if somewhat lackadaisically.

Without ambition. Though perhaps not without resentment against a brother who'd fallen into a bucket of good luck at birth. While Oog had fallen into something else.

Gamache now smiled to himself. Humbled, yet again, by a mistake. How often had he warned agents against making assumptions? Leaping to conclusions.

And here he was, having done exactly that.

It never occurred to Gamache that this rough-hewn man might be a wealth manager, looking after tens of millions, perhaps hundreds of millions of dollars.

A phone call would have to be made.

But that was far down the list of things that occurred to the Chief Superintendent at that moment. Another question was forming, just as Beauvoir appeared down the hallway and caught his eye.

"A word?" Beauvoir mouthed.

Gamache was torn. He wanted, needed, to ask the question, but he also knew that Beauvoir would never interrupt unless it was important.

"*Excusez-moi*," said the Chief. He got up and nodded to Dufresne to continue.

"Find something?" Gamache asked as he accompanied Beauvoir down the hallway.

"I'll let Agent Cloutier explain."

Beauvoir's voice, while low, was excited.

Gamache turned the corner into the study and came face-to-face with maniacal Ruth. His brows rose, and then his gaze continued on, to the woman sitting at the desk.

She turned and immediately got up upon seeing Gamache.

"*Patron.*"

"Agent Cloutier." Gamache nodded. "Tell me what you have."

She was a fairly recent transfer from the financial division of the Sûreté. A bookkeeper. A bureaucrat. Not a field agent. Indeed, her accounting wasn't even forensic. She worked on the Sûreté's own budget.

But Chief Superintendent Gamache had been impressed with her, and after discussions with Chief Inspector Lacoste he'd arranged a temporary transfer to homicide. To see if it was a fit.

There was a whole division for financial crimes, but money, hidden or otherwise, was so often the motive for murder that Gamache felt it would help to have someone with financial expertise specifically assigned to homicide. And Lacoste had agreed.

Isabelle had been happy with Cloutier. Cloutier, though, had a very different reaction. Being called to a murder scene, or even being assigned to search a victim's home, was not simply foreign to her. She felt, at the age of forty-eight, as though she were experiencing an alien abduction.

She was not happy.

And even less so at this moment, as she faced the big boss. The head alien. Though he didn't look alien at all. But then, her whirring mind said, they so rarely did.

She had been grief-stricken, horrified by the raid that had so badly wounded her boss, Chief Inspector Lacoste.

She'd also been terrified at the thought that these things happened. That she herself could have been on that raid. Not realizing they'd have ordered the headquarters cat to arm up before they got to her.

But still. It was brought into stark relief that the Sûreté wasn't figures on a ledger. A matter of funding, or cutting, this department or that.

Lives were at stake. Lives were lost.

And she wanted nothing to do with taking or, worse still, giving a life.

She'd never met Chief Superintendent Gamache and had no idea he'd been behind her transfer and had been watching her progress, or lack thereof.

Gamache himself had had to admit that the transfer had not been a great success. It was clear she was unhappy, and a discontented agent never did her best work. Cloutier had been on the verge of being transferred back to the accounts department when the raid happened. And everything changed while, at the same time, staying the same.

The great Sûreté du Québec was in stasis until the leadership issue was resolved. For the moment Agent Cloutier was stuck. And Acting Chief Inspector Beauvoir was stuck with an agent who'd gnaw off her own arm if it would get her out of homicide and back into accounts.

But for now she was theirs. And there. In Baumgartner's home. Staring at the Chief Superintendent. Almost mute. But, sadly for her, not quite. A slight babbling was escaping her, an excruciatingly slow leak of lunacy.

Chief Superintendent Gamache saw this and tried to help, by guiding her.

"What did you find, Agent Cloutier? Was it in those papers?"

He pointed to the pile on the desk.

"Those and these." She pointed to the same stack of papers, confusing Gamache and herself. "Well, these are those, of course. Ha. Yes, well. Definitely something, but not definitive."

Inspector Beauvoir, watching this, sighed.

What he didn't know was that not that long ago Gamache himself had sounded almost exactly like Agent Cloutier, while on the phone to Vienna.

He might've sounded like an idiot, but Gamache knew he wasn't one. Just as he knew that Agent Cloutier wasn't.

"Is it to do with Anthony Baumgartner's personal finances?" Gamache threw her a lifeline.

He could see that the papers contained a lot of figures.

"Yes. No. I don't really know."

Now they all stared at one another, and Beauvoir thought maybe he should take away her gun. Not that she was likely to shoot anyone. Not on purpose. Really. Maybe.

Gamache smiled. "Let's sit."

He waved her to the comfortable chair behind the desk and dragged up two others for himself and Beauvoir.

"Now, Agent Cloutier, tell us what first caught your eye?"

"This." She picked up one of the papers before the laptop. "These look like financial statements, from Taylor and Ogilvy." Her voice was growing more confident. "I take it he worked for them?"

"*Oui.*"

"It's unusual, even unethical, for a money manager to bring home private and confidential papers," she said. "It's one thing to have them on a computer, which is protected by codes, but a printout? That anyone could read? I'm presuming Monsieur Baumgartner was senior enough to know that."

"Then why would he?" asked Gamache.

"I don't know for sure, of course," she said. "But there're two possible reasons. He was behind in his work and figured no one would notice or care. Or he was up to something."

"That something being . . . ?"

"Before I go into that, there's something else odd," she said. "About the papers."

She paused, letting her two *patrons* think about it.

"They're papers," said Beauvoir, getting there first. Getting it. "Wouldn't he be working directly on the laptop? On an electronic file?"

"You'd think so, yes. Assembling statements. Writing cover letters. Not working on hard copies."

"But I get my statements by mail," said Gamache. "Not emailed."

"Yes, for security most are still mailed out," she said. "Email can be hacked. But the mailing's the last step, normally done by an assistant. There's no reason for Monsieur Baumgartner to have the actual print-outs. And certainly not at home. They're of no use to him."

"No legitimate use," said Beauvoir.

"Exactly."

"So what's the illegitimate use?" Gamache asked.

"He'd have these statements here at home"—she looked toward the tidy pile on the desk beside the laptop—"because he didn't want any-one else to see them. And certainly not his assistant, who'd know immediately that something was up."

"And what was 'up'?" Beauvoir asked.

"Until I can get into his computer, I won't know for sure. But it's easy enough to see that they're addressed to different people and show portfolios in the millions. Transactions were done. Stocks bought and sold. These look like legitimate statements."

"But aren't?" said Gamache.

"They might be," she said. "But I'm not sure."

Chief Superintendent Gamache nodded. Financial crimes came under the Sûreté jurisdiction. Every year they uncovered a number of offenses. Some petty and downright stupid. Some close, but not quite crossing a line. A line Gamache had privately told the Premier should be changed.

Others, though, didn't so much cross the line as tunnel under it. Deep. Dark. Long-standing.

And when they were found, personal savings crumbled. Retirement funds disappeared. People were ruined. Often elderly people who could never recoup.

It was tragic and intentional. A fraud, a theft, committed not just over years but over lunches, dinners, weddings, bar mitzvahs, and chris-tenings. As the adviser. The accountant. The manager. Got closer and closer to the family. All the while stealing from them.

After all, who else could cheat you of everything except someone you never questioned?

Gamache stared at the papers, then at the blank screen. Then looked around the comfortable study.

Finally he got up.

"Call Taylor and Ogilvy," said Beauvoir, also getting to his feet, as did Agent Cloutier. "Find out what you can about Anthony Baumgartner. But be discreet."

"Yessir."

"And find out everything you can about Baumgartner's own finances. His accounts, hidden or otherwise."

"*Oui, patron.*" Her voice was crisp, efficient. Excited.

This she could do. And do well.

Gamache followed Beauvoir back to the living room.

When he'd been called away, Gamache had had one question he needed to ask. Now there were many.

CHAPTER 25

⁓

They stared at Chief Inspector Beauvoir as though he'd lost his mind.

As though, like Gamache earlier in the day, he'd lapsed into a language that did not actually exist.

"Tony?" said Adrienne. "Steal from clients?" She almost laughed. "Of course not."

She looked at Caroline and Hugo, who were also shaking their heads.

"You didn't know my brother," said Caroline. "He could never do such a thing. He volunteered at a hospice, for heaven's sake."

It was a non sequitur, though not altogether nonsense. Gamache knew the point she was trying to make.

Only a terrible person would steal from clients. Her brother did a beautiful thing by volunteering in a hospice. Hence he was not a terrible person.

It, of course, did not track. A shocking number of criminals were, in other areas of their lives, model citizens.

"Monsieur?" Beauvoir turned to Hugo Baumgartner.

Gamache was listening and watching. Paying close attention.

"I could believe it of myself before I could believe it of Tony," he said. "There's absolutely no way he'd do anything unethical, never mind criminal."

"Out of interest's sake." Beauvoir turned back to Caroline. "Before he came out, did you know he was gay?"

She shook her head, baffled by the change of topic.

Beauvoir looked at Adrienne and Hugo, who also shook their heads.

"Is it possible, then," he said quietly, "you don't know your brother as well as you thought?"

Caroline's cheeks reddened immediately, and Hugo looked, for the first time, angry.

"It's not the same thing," said Hugo. "One is nature and has no effect on character. The other is choice. People choose to break the law. They don't choose to be gay. Just because my brother was gay doesn't make him a criminal."

"I wasn't saying that, sir, and I suspect you know it," said Beauvoir, keeping his voice steady, though with a slight inflection of annoyance. "The point I was making is that your brother was very good at keeping secrets. He led two private lives, why not two professional ones? And would you even know?"

"Then why did you ask?" asked Adrienne.

But Gamache knew the answer to that. Beauvoir asked because he knew that the answer would tell them more about the family than about the victim.

Hugo glanced down the corridor. Then back at Beauvoir.

"You found something in his study, didn't you? Let me see. I can straighten you out. Explain anything that might look odd or incriminating."

Chief Inspector Beauvoir considered a moment, then said, "Come with me."

They all did. Caroline leading the pack.

"A moment, madame." Beauvoir stopped her from entering the study.

Going in first, he had a word with Agent Cloutier, who was on the phone. She nodded, then left the room.

Caroline and Hugo entered with Beauvoir, but Adrienne stopped at the doorway, not realizing, perhaps, that Gamache stood behind her.

This was Anthony Baumgartner's private space. His sanctuary. The well-worn leather chair in front of the fireplace had taken on his form. There was the laptop on his desk. The books on the shelves. The photos of private family moments and of business triumphs.

This room even looked like him. Elegant. Masculine. Comfortable. Slightly playful, with the orange shag rug.

Watching her sag, Gamache was struck by how much this woman

really did love this man. It was, he thought, the sort of intense love that could curve back on itself and turn to hate.

"Is this all you have?" asked Hugo, pointing to the papers beside the laptop.

"It is," said Beauvoir, not cowed by the tone.

"He was working on his clients' accounts," said Hugo. "That's all."

"At home?" asked Beauvoir.

"Well, it's unusual," admitted Hugo. "But you could just as easily conclude that he was hyper-responsible. Doing things for his clients in his own time. This isn't evidence of any crime. Just the opposite."

"Why paper?"

"Pardon?"

"If he was working on a client's statement, wouldn't he do it on the computer?"

"Some people prefer a printout," said Hugo. "Especially those of us who are older. I often have spreadsheets printed out. Easier to study them."

"Spreadsheets, yes," said Beauvoir. "But not a statement. Is that fair?"

Hugo shrugged. "We all have our systems. How you can look at these few pages and decide my brother was stealing, is . . . well, I have to say, unfair. He's the victim. Not the criminal."

"*Merci, monsieur*," said Beauvoir. "Now the laptop. Do you know his password?"

The Baumgartners looked at each other and shook their heads.

"The children's names?" suggested Adrienne.

"The house number?" said Caroline.

Without realizing it, Beauvoir suspected they'd just given away their own codes.

Once again Hugo was silent. But his eyes kept returning to the pile of statements.

"I have a question," said Gamache from the doorway, and he saw Adrienne startle at the sound of his voice behind her.

"Your accounts." He looked at Caroline. "Who has them now?"

It was the question he'd wanted to ask for a while, and now he watched her closely.

There was a long pause.

219

"They're with me, Chief Superintendent," said Hugo.

"Why did you really take your money from Anthony?" Gamache continued to look at Caroline. "You said it was because you didn't want to mix family and business. That obviously wasn't true."

"Hugo and I have always been closer," she said. "It felt natural."

"And that would make sense if you'd started with Hugo, but you didn't. Your money was first with Anthony, but something made you take it away from him. What was it?"

His voice was reasonable. Not betraying the fact he'd just cornered her.

"Anthony and I had a falling-out," she said.

"About what?"

"Does it matter?" asked Hugo.

"Do you know why she moved her money from your brother to you?" Gamache asked, turning his considerable attention to Hugo, who immediately regretted saying anything.

"It was her decision. I had nothing to do with it. And I certainly didn't poach her."

"That wasn't my question," said Gamache. Though it was an interesting answer.

"Sir?"

Agent Cloutier had returned. She was holding her phone to her palm, muffling any sound.

"Not now," said Beauvoir. "Wait for us in the living room."

"Yessir."

She left, holding the phone in front of her as though it might explode in her hands.

"Now." Beauvoir turned back to the Baumgartners. "Chief Superintendent Gamache asked you a question."

"I don't know why the account was transferred to me," said Hugo.

"You didn't ask?" asked Gamache. Then he turned to Caroline. "You didn't tell him?" He stared at her. "Of course you did. We're going to find out. Probably best we hear it from you."

"You tell him," Caroline said to Hugo. "You can explain it."

"Fine." Hugo took a deep breath. "It wasn't a falling-out. That's just what we told anyone who asked. Three years ago my brother had his license to trade suspended."

"Why?" asked Beauvoir.

"The man he'd been having the affair with was the assistant to a senior partner. That assistant stole money from some clients. Tony caught it and told the firm. The money was put back, the assistant fired, and Tony was kept on, but they suspended his license."

"Why? If he'd done nothing wrong?"

Beauvoir glanced at Gamache, who was quietly listening.

"Exactly, Inspector," said Adrienne. "Exactly what we thought. He'd done everything right, but still they came down on him."

"Why?" asked Beauvoir again.

Hugo was shaking his head and shrugged. He was slouched over and looked less like a garden gnome and more like a gargoyle.

"As with most things, it was political. Internal politics in his company. The partner didn't want to be accused of using bad judgment in hiring the assistant, so they shifted the blame to Tony. Said it was gross negligence. That he'd given the assistant information on clients that he shouldn't have."

"By having printouts at home?" suggested Beauvoir.

"I don't know. All I know is that they made an example of him."

"So he was punished?" asked Beauvoir.

"Yes. After that his career was pretty much over, at least internally. He'd never be promoted to partner. Tony stayed on the accounts, but the trades were done by someone else in the firm. He'd done nothing wrong, but still they suspended and humiliated him."

Again Beauvoir glanced quickly at Gamache, to see his reaction to this. Then away.

"And that's why you moved your accounts?" Beauvoir asked Caroline.

"I didn't want to, but Anthony insisted. He thought they were better with Hugo, who could both advise and trade."

"And were they?" Gamache asked. Seeing the blank look on Caroline's face, he clarified. "Better?"

"I think so," she said, glancing at Hugo.

"My brother knew the market well, Chief Superintendent. The truth is, while I'm good, Tony was better. It was shitty that his license to trade was pulled."

"Did he see it that way?" asked Beauvoir. "Did he hold a grudge?"

"No," said Hugo. "He was grateful to the partners for being discreet.

They could've made a public announcement. They could've fired him. I thought they were shits, but Tony was loyal."

"*Merci*," said Beauvoir. "Was your brother in a relationship right now?"

"Not that I know of," said Caroline.

"Do you know this Bernard's last name?"

They shook their heads.

"The less I knew about him the better," said Adrienne when Beauvoir turned to her.

"Is there anything we should know? Anyone you can think of who might've wanted Monsieur Baumgartner gone?"

They thought about that and again shook their heads.

"You stayed behind with your brother after the reading of the will," Gamache said to Hugo. "Is that right?"

"Yes. We often had dinner together. Two bachelors. I brought the wine and Tony cooked."

He lowered his eyes, perhaps, Gamache thought, the reality of his brother's death and all that had changed being brought home to him.

"What did you talk about?"

Hugo threw his mind back. In time it wasn't all that long ago, but measured in events, it was an eternity.

"We talked about Mom. About the Baroness. She was a one-off." Hugo gave his pumpkin grin. "We talked about how much we miss her."

"I do too," said Caroline.

But her voice spoke more about herself than of any affection for her mother. About a need to be included and, perhaps more crucial, a fear of being left out. Left behind.

"What time did you leave?" asked Beauvoir.

"It was an early dinner. I was home by eight," said Hugo.

"Did he mention wanting to go to your mother's house?"

"No, though we talked about whether it should be saved or not. You think that's why he went there?"

"Could be," said Beauvoir.

He handed them one of his cards with the standard request that they call should they think of anything.

Then he asked for their keys to the house.

They looked surprised. Then not surprised. And handed them over.

After the Baumgartners left, Beauvoir and Gamache joined Agent Cloutier in the living room.

"She hung up," said Cloutier. "But said I could call back when you were ready."

She made the call and handed the phone to Beauvoir.

"*Bonjour?* Madame Ogilvy? This is Chief Inspector Beauvoir. I'm the head of homicide for the Sûreté du Québec. Yes, it is about Anthony Baumgartner."

He explained briefly what she would soon see in the news anyway. Then asked the question.

"He had papers at home?" asked Madame Ogilvy. "Statements? Hard copies?"

"Yes. Can you think why?"

She paused before answering, "No."

"I think you can, madame. I'll let you consider the question a little longer. Can we meet tomorrow? I'll bring the statements and letters with me."

Before he hung up, Gamache touched his arm and whispered something.

"One more question," said Beauvoir. "Do you have any clients named Kinderoth?"

"We have thousands of clients, Chief Inspector."

"Can you look it up?"

"Our clients' names are confidential."

"We can get a court order."

"I don't mean to be difficult, but I'm afraid you're going to have to."

Beauvoir rolled his eyes but could tell there was no arguing. If and when it became known that she'd given out confidential information, Madame Ogilvy would have to prove it was forced from her.

Everyone covers their asses, Beauvoir knew.

"Seems there's a lot of that going around," said Beauvoir once they were back in the car.

"What's that?" asked his father-in-law.

"Suspending people who've done nothing wrong. Shifting blame."

There was a slight grunt of amusement beside him.

This was Jean-Guy's form of apology. For being abrupt with Gamache. For allowing the man from the Ministère de la Justice, Francis Cournoyer, to get into his head.

He now suspected that had been the whole purpose of the meeting. Everyone else, everything else, were all just props. Extras.

The quiet man in the corner was the lead. And Beauvoir was the audience.

He felt ashamed of himself for letting it happen. For even once believing that when Cournoyer had said, "Ask Gamache," it was anything other than, as Isabelle had put it, a mindfuck in a public toilet.

Gamache turned to him and smiled. "You do know that all the things I'm accused of doing, I did. I admitted it. Freely. But, unlike Monsieur Baumgartner, I'm not likely to keep my job."

Now it was Beauvoir's breath that hung in the air. Hung in the silence.

"What do you mean?"

"When this suspension is lifted, I won't be returning as Chief Superintendent."

"You can't know that."

"I do. There can't possibly be a head of the Sûreté who's broken the law."

Beauvoir stared straight ahead and let that sink in. The heater, on full blast, had melted the frost off the windshield, and although he put the car in gear, his foot remained on the brake.

"The fact Anthony Baumgartner kept his job," said Gamache, "doesn't mean he didn't do it. It's possible that young assistant took the fall for him. Not the other way around. Who are the partners more likely to protect? A young man barely starting out or a vice president of the company?"

"And you?"

"Me?"

"Is there more happening than you're telling me?" Beauvoir asked.

Ask Gamache. Despite himself, Beauvoir had just done as Cournoyer suggested.

"Where did that come from?" Gamache asked. "Is that what's been bothering you? Has someone said something?"

"Is there?"

"If there is, I'm as much in the dark as you. This is political. We both know that. But how high up it goes and what the purpose is, I don't know. What I do know is that it doesn't matter."

"Doesn't it?"

"No. All that matters is getting the drugs back. That's it. My punishment for releasing them goes far beyond anything a disciplinary committee can possibly do."

Jean-Guy could see that was true, and already happening. He could see the punishing weight of responsibility. Of guilt. Of fear.

He could sense the anxiety growing to near panic as the Chief struggled to find the last of the drugs.

It was evident in the lines at the mouth. Between the brows. The hands that even in casual conversation were clenched, as though in pain.

That bullet's left the barrel, Cournoyer had said. And now Beauvoir could see it had reached its target.

"We'll find it, *patron*."

"We have to."

It was said with cold determination, and Jean-Guy wondered at the lengths Gamache would go to to get the drugs back. But then he remembered their conversation. About Amelia Choquet. And he stopped wondering.

"Home?" Beauvoir asked, pointing the car in the direction of Three Pines.

"A home, for sure," said Gamache. "But not ours quite yet."

Half an hour later, they were at the Maison Saint-Rémy.

The head nurse greeted them and invited the Sûreté officers into her office.

"What can I help you with? You say you're with the police?"

She spoke English, and the two officers quickly switched languages. As they'd waited for her at the front desk, Beauvoir had picked up a brochure and noted that this was an English seniors' home. One of the few where services were primarily English.

Even those who were bilingual preferred, at the end of their lives, to live it out in the tongue they'd learned from their mothers.

"*Oui,*" said Beauvoir. "We'd like to know about the death of Bertha Baumgartner."

"The Duchess?"

"The Baroness," said Gamache.

"Why? Is something wrong?"

"We just need a few questions answered," said Beauvoir. "What did she die of?"

The head nurse turned to her computer and, after a moment, replied, "Heart failure." She took off her glasses and turned back to them. "Vague, I realize. It's almost always heart failure. Unless the family asks for an autopsy, that's what the doctor writes. The people here are elderly and frail. Their hearts just stop."

"Was it expected?" Beauvoir asked.

"Well, it's almost always expected, and yet a surprise. She wasn't sick. She just went to bed and didn't wake up. It's the way most of us hope to go."

"Did she have many visitors?"

"Her sons and daughter would come, but they work and it's difficult." Beauvoir heard what was unsaid. They did not visit often.

"They called her often, though," said the head nurse. "Unlike some here, Madame Baumgartner clearly had a family who cared. They just couldn't visit as often as they might have liked."

"And the day she died?"

"I'd have to look it up."

"Please do," said Gamache, and they followed her to the reception desk, where there was a sign-in book.

Flipping back, she came to the date. It was empty.

"Joseph?" she called to a middle-aged man, who went over. "These men are with the Sûreté. They're asking about Madame Baumgartner."

"The Countess?"

"The Baroness," said Beauvoir, barely believing he was defending the title. "You're at the front desk?"

"*Oui.*"

"Did she have many visitors?"

"*Non.* Her family every now and then. Mostly on weekends. And the young woman, of course. She always made it a point to see her."

"Young woman?" asked Beauvoir. "Do you have her name?"

"Yes, of course," said the nurse, walking back to her office. "She's the one we called when the Empress—"

"Baroness," said Gamache.

"—died. Yes, here it is." She was at her computer once again. "Katie Burke."

"Can you spell that, please?" asked Beauvoir, pulling out his notebook.

He couldn't see how the natural death of an elderly woman in what appeared to be a well-run and caring seniors' home could possibly have anything to do with her son's murder a month or more later. Still, he took down the information she gave him.

"Why did you call her when Madame Baumgartner died?" asked Gamache. "Is it that you couldn't reach the family?"

"We didn't try."

"Why not?"

"Because Mademoiselle Burke's name was at the top of the contact list. Ahead of her children."

CHAPTER 26

"So, numbnuts, where's your boss?"

"He's at home, babysitting Ray-Ray," said Jean-Guy, passing the salad bowl to Olivier, who was sitting next to him at Clara's long kitchen table.

The fact he'd actually begun answering to "numbnuts" was a little worrisome to Beauvoir, though he'd been called worse. By murderers. Psychopaths. Ruth.

"Babysitting? Just the job for a fourteen-year-old girl," said Ruth. "He's reached his level of competence, I see."

When Clara's invitation for dinner came, Beauvoir at first thought to beg off. He was tired, and it was dark and cold.

He'd assigned an inspector to find this Katie Burke, then settled down to read the reports that were coming in. He'd head back to Montréal and the office first thing in the morning. But for now all he wanted was to put his feet up and nod off by the fire.

But then Annie had whispered the magic words.

Coq au vin.

There was a wild rumor, racing through the Gamache home, that Olivier had made his famous casserole and was taking it to Clara's.

"Don't toy with me, madame."

"And for dessert? Salted," she whispered again, her breath fresh and warm, "caramel—"

"Nooo," he moaned.

"—and burnt-fig ice cream."

"Okay, I'm in," he said, getting up. "You coming?" he called into the study as he made his way to the front door.

When there was no answer, he backed up.

"Patron?"

Armand was peering at the computer, a book open beside it on the desk.

"What're you doing?"

"Trying to translate something, isn't that right, *mein Liebling*?"

He held Honoré on his knee as he read, consulted, blinked to clear his bleary eyes, and wrote longhand in a notebook.

"Coq au vin," said Reine-Marie, joining Jean-Guy at the door.

"Ahh, so the rumor is true," said Armand. "But we already have dinner plans, don't we?" He looked at his grandson. "Sweet potatoes. Yum. Maybe some avocado. Yum-yum. Some gray stuff that they say is meat." He looked up then. "You all head off, we'll be fine. Eh, *meyn tayer*."

"There you are," said Annie. Her coat already on, she came over and kissed her son. "Don't let him get into any mischief, now."

"You're talking to Honoré, aren't you?" said her father.

"I am."

"You sure you don't want to bring him to Clara's?" asked Reine-Marie.

"Non, merci," said Armand. "We have a full evening planned. Dinner. A bath. A movie. A book. Some all-star wrestling—"

"Were you planning on putting him to bed at any stage?" asked Jean-Guy.

"Eventually. Maybe."

"Dad," said Annie.

"Okay, but we will read a book, right?" he asked the boy. "And I'll recite 'The Wreck of the Hesperus': 'It was the schooner Hesperus, / That sailed the wintry sea—'"

"Dear God," said Jean-Guy. "Flee. *Sauve qui peut.*"

"What about Honoré?" asked Annie in mock terror.

"We can make more. Run, woman, run."

Armand rolled his eyes as Reine-Marie laughed and wondered what would happen if anyone ever called Armand's bluff and realized that all he knew of the dreadful poem were the opening lines.

"Work?" She nodded toward the computer.

"A bit."

"Want me to stay?" Jean-Guy asked.

"And miss coq au vin?"

"Ruth will be there. Sorta evens out."

"Myrna's made her whipped potatoes," said Reine-Marie.

"You're on your own," Jean-Guy said to Armand just as a rush of cold air hit them.

Annie, Reine-Marie, and Jean-Guy turned and shouted, "Close the door."

It was a chorus more familiar than the national anthem.

"Man, it's cold out there," they heard, along with foot stomping. "And this one," Armand could hear Benedict saying, "takes her sweet time doing her business."

Armand smiled. Benedict couldn't bring himself to say "poop" or even "pee." He knew the young man was referring to Gracie, and he sympathized. He'd spent many a cold night begging the little creature to do something, other than chase Henri.

Benedict had taken it upon himself, in exchange for room and board while he waited for his truck to return, to walk the dogs.

Armand felt this left them owing Benedict.

"I'll bring you back something," said Reine-Marie, kissing the top of Honoré's head before putting her hands on the side of Armand's face and kissing him on the lips and whispering, *"Meyn tayer."*

He smiled.

"Is that German?" she asked, glancing at the screen.

"It is. Taking me a while to read it."

"Your eyes still sore?" she asked, looking into them and seeing the bloodshot.

"My German is a little rusty," he said.

"Rusty. Is that German for 'nonexistent'?"

He laughed. "Just about."

She looked at the screen again. "It's long. Who's it from?"

"A police officer in Vienna."

She tied the scarf at her neck. "See you soon."

"Have fun."

He returned to his computer, leaning over Ray-Ray and smelling his fragrance as he read about a family ripping itself apart.

231

Jean-Guy looked at the tender pieces of chicken along with mushrooms and rich, fragrant gravy, next to the mountain of potatoes.

Whipped, Myrna insisted. Not just mashed.

He was so hungry he thought he might weep.

"So it's true, then," said Ruth. "The Baroness's son was murdered."

Jean-Guy had told Clara and Myrna as soon as they'd arrived for dinner, taking them aside quietly. And word had spread, of course, as others arrived at Clara's home.

"I thought you were lying," said Ruth to Myrna.

"Why would I lie about that?"

"Why do you say your library is a bookstore?" asked Ruth. "Lying is just natural to you."

"It is a bookstore," said Myrna, exasperated. "Don't think I don't see you taking books out under your coat."

"Oh, there's a lot you don't see," said Ruth.

"Like what?"

"Like Billy Williams."

"I see him. He shovels my walk and brushes off my car."

"Doesn't brush off my car," mumbled Clara, and catching Olivier's eye, they both grinned.

"What's that supposed to mean?" asked Myrna. "He's a nice man, that's all."

"Then why isn't he here?" asked Ruth.

"Here?" said Myrna, looking around. "Why would he be here? Does something need fixing?" she asked Clara.

"I'd have to say yes," said Ruth, and Rosa beside her nodded.

"Let's change the subject," said Reine-Marie.

"Well, if murder's out," said Ruth, "and the librarian here being prejudiced is something we're not allowed to talk about—"

"Prejudiced? I'm not—"

"I saw one of your paintings today," Jean-Guy leaped in, spouting the first thing that came into his head.

"You are prejudiced, you know," said Ruth. "You only see the surface and then pass judgment. Billy Williams is just a handyman."

"One of my paintings? Really?" asked Clara. "Where?"

232

"A print, actually," said Jean-Guy. "One of the numbered prints."

"And who's calling the kettle black?" demanded Myrna. "Did you see the Baroness as anything other than a cleaning woman? Did you even know her name?"

"Isn't it about time you proposed to Gabri?" Annie asked Olivier, jumping onto the conversational pile. "We're all waiting."

"You're waiting?" said Gabri. "If he waits much longer, I won't be able to fit into my going-away outfit."

"And there's your answer," said Olivier.

"You don't have to know someone's name to care about them," said Ruth.

"And you cared?" said Myrna. "Did you even know she'd died?"

"I saw your painting at Anthony Baumgartner's place," said Jean-Guy, raising his voice.

"The dead man?" asked Clara.

"Hey, I thought we weren't allowed to talk about murder," said Ruth. "That's not fair."

"We're not talking about murder," said Jean-Guy. "I'm talking about art."

"You?" Annie, Gabri, Olivier, Clara, Myrna, Ruth, and even Reine-Marie said. As one.

Rosa looked startled. But then ducks often did. And often for good reason.

"What?" said Jean-Guy. "I'm cultured."

"With a capital K," said Annie, patting his hand.

"That's right," he said. *"Merci."*

They laughed, then Myrna turned to Ruth.

"I'm sorry I snapped at you about the Baroness. But that's a terrible thing to say about someone. That they're prejudiced."

"Not 'they,'" said Ruth. "You. Just because you're a pot, that doesn't mean you can't—"

"I'm a what?"

"Which painting did he have?" asked Reine-Marie.

"The one of—" Jean-Guy jerked his head toward Ruth. "Not the original, of course."

"No, we have the good fortune of having the original here," said Reine-Marie.

"I meant not the original painting," said Jean-Guy.

"Did you?" said Reine-Marie, and she smiled.

"Oh that's right," said Clara. "I gave that print to the Baroness. I'd forgotten."

"Annie's not wrong, you know," said Gabri to Olivier. "You'd better pop the question soon if you want a dewy husband. I'm not going to be thirty-seven forever."

"Well, you have been thirty-seven for quite a while now," said Olivier.

"I guess she gave it to her son," said Clara. "It's just tragic. Do you have any idea who killed him? Oh, sorry, not dinner-table conversation."

Though it wouldn't be the first time a murder had been discussed around that table, by those people, in the flickering candlelight.

"Well, Ray-Ray," Armand murmured as he took his reading glasses off and wiped his hand over his weary eyes. "What do you make of that?"

They'd had dinner and a bath, and now they were on the sofa in the living room in front of the fireplace. Armand reading his rough translation of the Kontrollinspektor's email. Honoré, in his favorite bear pajamas, was lying in the crook of his grandfather's arm, with Henri on the sofa on one side and Gracie on the other.

Honoré knew exactly what to make of that. While not understanding the words that were spoken, he understood the deep, warm resonance coming from his grandfather's body. Each word radiating into him.

So that they were in tune.

And it was a nice tune.

He gripped the large hand holding him securely and felt a soft pat. And a kiss planted on his head.

And he smelled the familiar scent. Of Papa.

While Papa read about a reason for murder.

And then Armand put down his notebook and carried Honoré upstairs to bed, where he picked up *Winnie-the-Pooh*. And Honoré fell asleep listening to the adventures of Tigger and Roo and Piglet and Pooh. And Christopher Robin. In the Hundred Acre Wood.

"It still gives me goose bumps," said Reine-Marie, looking at the original oil painting in Clara's studio.

"Almost gave me a heart attack," said Jean-Guy. "When I saw Ruth in Baumgartner's home. Hovering above his fireplace."

"There must be a lot of these out there," said Reine-Marie. "It was your big success. Your breakout work."

"Nah, the gallery hardly sold any," said Clara, contemplating her masterwork. "Though they did print lots. People love looking at it. And then they like leaving. Really, who wants that"—she jerked her spoon, with ice cream on it, toward the easel—"in their home?"

"Apparently Anthony Baumgartner," said Jean-Guy.

All three looked at the rancid old woman in the painting, then leaned back and looked out the doorway of Clara's studio, into the kitchen, at the rancid old woman at the table.

Ruth was still arguing with Myrna. This time, it seemed, about how choux pastry should be made.

"And that's why they call them loafers," they heard the old woman say.

"Like a loaf of bread? Really?" said Benedict.

"No, not really," said Myrna. "It's c-h-o-u-x. Not shoe. Or loafer."

"Well, that doesn't make any sense."

They returned to the painting leaning against the wall of the studio.

"I wonder what it says about the dead man," said Reine-Marie. "That he was drawn to this particular painting."

"Besides that he had great taste in art?" asked Clara.

"But he wasn't drawn to it," said Jean-Guy. "His mother was. You said that she's the one who wanted it. Then she gave it to him."

"But he hung it," said Reine-Marie. "He didn't just put it away in the basement."

"True." Jean-Guy continued to stare at Ruth on canvas. "Do you think the Baroness understood what the painting's about? Not bitterness but hope."

They looked at him in undisguised—and fairly insulting, he felt—surprise. Annie came over and put her arm around his slightly thickening waist.

"We'll make an art aficionado of you yet," she said.

"Aficionado," he said. "That's a type of Italian ice cream, isn't it? I think what you meant to say is an art gelato."

"And I think you're in the wrong conversation," said Annie. "I believe the one you want is over there."

She pointed to the trio of Myrna, Ruth, and Benedict. Who were now discussing the difference between semaphore and petit four.

"No thank you," said Jean-Guy. "Besides, I already know all I need to about art. Chiaroscuro." He said the word triumphantly, as though opening the Olympic Games or launching a ship. "That's it. My one word of artspeak, but it impresses the pants off people."

"What was that word again?" asked Gabri from the freezer, where he was getting more ice cream.

"Please don't tell him," said Olivier.

"Are there any leftovers? I'd like to take some home to Armand," asked Reine-Marie, walking over to the kitchen.

Olivier pointed to a container on the island, filled with coq au vin and whipped potatoes. "All ready for you."

"*Merci, mon beau.*"

"So," Ruth was saying to Benedict, "if anyone offers you a semaphore, don't eat it."

"But a petit four?"

"You give that to me."

Benedict was nodding, and both Myrna and Rosa were staring, glassy-eyed, at them.

Jean-Guy tapped Benedict on the shoulder. "Come and help me do the dishes."

While Jean-Guy washed, Benedict dried.

"Why did you lie?" Beauvoir asked quietly.

"About what?" asked Benedict, taking a warm, wet glass.

"About your girlfriend."

"Oh. That."

"Tell me the truth," said Jean-Guy.

"Does it matter?" asked Benedict.

"This is a murder investigation. Everything matters. Especially lies."

"But the man who died has nothing to do with me."

"Do you really believe that?" asked Beauvoir. "You're a liquidator on a will in which he was a major heir. It was read just hours before he was murdered. His body was found in an abandoned home where you were also found. You were there when he was there."

He let those words sink in.

"But I didn't know that," said Benedict.

"And how do I know you're not lying now? Again?" He watched the young man's face. "And now you see why lies matter. The actual fib might not matter, but what it shows us is that what you say can't always be trusted. You can't always be trusted."

"But I can," he said, his cheeks a fluorescent red now. "I don't lie. Not normally. But I . . . I hate saying it out loud."

"What?"

"That she left me. That we broke up. It's too soon."

"It's been a couple of months."

"How do you know that?"

"I'm the acting head of homicide for the Sûreté du Québec," said Jean-Guy, handing a soapy plate to Benedict. "Do you really think we wouldn't ask questions about you?"

"Then you've gotta know my relationship has nothing to do with what happened."

"Doesn't it? You lied again to Monsieur Gamache when he asked why you went to the farmhouse last night. You said you missed your girl-friend and wanted to go home. But that wasn't true, was it?"

Benedict concentrated on the glass he was drying.

"It is true, sorta. You wouldn't know what it's like, to have your heart broken and then to be around people who're happy."

He looked at Jean-Guy.

"You. Your wife. Ray-Ray. Monsieur and Madame Gamache. You have what I want, what I wanted. And lost. I couldn't take it anymore. It hurt too much. I had to leave."

Benedict's eyes were wide. Pleading.

For what? Jean-Guy wondered. *Understanding? Forgiveness?*

No, he thought. *He wants what I wanted, when I was heartbroken. He wants me to stop poking the wound.*

"I understand," he said. "No more lies, right?"

"I promise."

Beauvoir turned to face the young man and stared him squarely in the eyes.

"Why do you think Madame Baumgartner put you on as a liquidator of her will?"

"I don't know."

"You must've thought about it. Come on, Benedict. Why would she do that? You must've known her."

"I didn't. I swear. I never met the woman. The Baroness. You can give me a lie detector. Do they still do lie detectors? I should ask Ruth."

Beauvoir sighed. "She's a lie manufacturer. She knows nothing about detecting them."

"But if you make something, wouldn't you normally recognize them?" asked Benedict.

It was, Jean-Guy had to admit, insightful. And true. Ruth was an expert in lies. It was the truth that sometimes eluded her. And, perhaps, eluded this pleasant young man.

Across the room, Clara was watching the conversation between Jean-Guy and Benedict.

"What're you thinking?" Reine-Marie asked her.

"That I'd like to paint that young man."

"Why?"

"There's something about him. He's both transparent and . . . what's the word?"

"Dense?" ventured Reine-Marie.

Clara laughed. "Well, yes. And yet . . ."

And yet, thought Reine-Marie, watching her houseguest. *And yet not.*

As they left, Ruth handed Jean-Guy a gift.

"A poetry book," she said. "One you might appreciate. But don't read it to my godson."

"Why not?" he asked, his eyes narrowing.

"You'll see."

"One of yours?" Annie asked, looking at the gift, wrapped in old newspaper.

"No."

"One of mine?" asked Myrna.

"None of your business," said Ruth.

"I bet it is my business," muttered Myrna as she put her boots on.

At the door the two women embraced and Myrna offered to walk Ruth home.

"We'll see her home," said Olivier.

Out of the darkness, just as she closed the door against the biting cold, Clara heard Gabri say, "Oh look. An ice floe. Come on, Ruth. It has your name on it."

"Fag."

"Hag."

And a sleepy, soft "Fuck, fuck, fuck" as the door closed.

Armand greeted them at the door.

"Have fun?"

"Ruth was there," said Jean-Guy.

Armand smiled. Understanding.

"You've probably already eaten," said Reine-Marie. "But in case you're still hungry."

She offered him the container.

"Oh you savior. I'm starving." Armand kissed his wife and took the container into the kitchen.

"Did you manage to translate the email?" Jean-Guy asked.

"Yes, I think so. At least the gist of it."

"Which was?"

Armand was about to tell him but could see that Annie was waiting for her husband to join her.

"I'll tell you in the morning. Do you mind if I drive into Montréal with you?"

It was meant to be a rhetorical question, but, to his surprise, Jean-Guy hesitated.

"I don't have to," said Armand. "I'm sure someone else—"

"*Non, non*, of course I'll drive you. It's just that I'm not coming back out, and I have an early meeting. We'll have to leave here early."

"I can drive you in, sir," said Benedict. He'd had his head in the fridge and now came out with pie. "If you don't mind my using your car. I really need fresh clothes and should check on the apartment building. Then I can drive you back out. My truck might be ready by then."

"That would be perfect," said Armand. "*Merci.*"

"Why're you going in?" asked Reine-Marie.

"I'm having lunch with Stephen Horowitz." He turned to Jean-Guy. "Horowitz Investments."

Jean-Guy nodded. Hugo Baumgartner's firm.

Annie and Jean-Guy said their good-nights, and Benedict took a huge slice of pie and a glass of milk to his room.

"Anthony Baumgartner must've been an interesting man," said Reine-Marie as the leftover coq au vin warmed up.

"Why do you say that?"

"Well, because Jean-Guy told us that he had Clara's painting in his study."

"Yes. Quite unexpected."

Armand thought about the email he'd spent the evening translating.

Like the painting, it was infused with bitterness. But there was also hope. Though a different kind from the one in Clara's painting.

This was hope of revenge. Of retribution. It reeked of greed. And delusion. And profound optimism that something horrible would happen to someone else.

And it had.

Hope itself wasn't necessarily kind. Or a good thing.

Armand wondered what Baumgartner saw when he stood in front of the painting and looked into the eyes of the Virgin.

Did he see redemption or permission to be bitter?

Maybe, in that face, he saw his own mother. Glaring down at him. In all her madness and delusion, disappointment and entitlement.

Maybe he saw what happens when false hope is spread over generations.

Maybe that's why he liked it.

Maybe he saw himself.

"You go to bed," he said to Reine-Marie. "I'll be along soon. Still have a little work to do."

"So late?"

"Well, Honoré wanted to watch the second *Terminator* movie, and then we visited the casino, so there wasn't much time to work."

"You're a silly, silly man," she said, kissing him. Her thumb traced the deep furrow of scar at his temple. "Don't be late."

She took her tea with her but left behind the delicate scent of chamomile and old garden roses, mingled with the rich, earthy aroma of coq au vin. Armand stood in the kitchen and closed his eyes. Then, opening them again, he headed to his study.

Henri and Gracie followed and curled up under the desk. Armand put in his password and saw that the photos and video he'd opened had finally downloaded.

Amelia and Marc had parted ways early.

It was dark now. The time when hungry people slipped out of tenements and rooming houses. On the hunt.

She'd gone from alley to back street, to parking lot, to abandoned building. Saying the same thing. Over and over.

"I'm looking for David."

A few times she thought she saw a flicker of interest, of recognition, but when pressed—"Where is he? How can I find him?"—the person turned away.

She'd attracted, though, a group of mostly young women. Some prostitutes. Some transsexuals. Most hard-core junkies. Who'd steal, suck, tug anything for a hit.

They came to her because she didn't ask anything of them. And she could fight. Had fought. And won.

They didn't know it was possible. To fight back.

But now they did.

Armand looked at the photos of Amelia taken just a few hours earlier.

They were shot from a distance.

He could see that in one of them she was making a gesture. Grabbing her forearm in what he assumed was a fairly common curse. He could imagine what was also coming out of her mouth.

He looked closer.

She was grubby. Hair unwashed. Clothes dirty. The lower part of her jeans was soaked in slush.

He tried but couldn't see her eyes. Her pupils.

Then he clicked on the video.

"You know, don't you, you shithead," she snarled. "Where's David?"

"Why do you want him?"

"None of your fucking business. Tell me or I'll break your arm."

The dealer turned away.

A semicircle of young women stood behind Amelia. They were barely more than girls.

"Don't you turn your goddamned back on me."

Amelia moved swiftly. Much quicker than the stoned dealer could react. She pushed him into the wall. Then, grabbing his arm, she twisted it behind his back. Jerking it up in a quick, practiced movement.

He let out a shriek that scattered those around. The onlookers scampering away.

The man, barely more than a boy, slid to the ground, weeping. His arm hung at a terrible angle. Useless.

"Next it's your leg. Then your neck," said Amelia.

She squatted beside him and slid the sleeve of her jacket up, exposing her forearm.

"David. Where's David?"

Armand moved this way and that, as though changing his vantage point would let him see better.

But her body was blocking it, and despite the fact there was sound in the recording, her back was to him and he couldn't hear very well.

He did see her get up, and with her foot she pushed the man over.

He heard him cry out. Then Amelia, and her gang, left the picture. The young men who'd stood with the dealer now turned away. And followed Amelia.

Armand narrowed his eyes and scowled. Then went back to the beginning of the video and watched again and again. Until something caught his attention.

He froze the frame. Then enlarged it. As he did, the image grew less and less defined. But still he zoomed in. Closer and closer.

And brought his face closer and closer to his screen, until his nose was almost touching it.

She wasn't just making a gesture with her forearm. That arm, he saw on closer inspection, was uncovered.

In minus twenty degrees, Amelia had shoved her jacket and sweater up so that her skin was exposed.

There were two reasons he could think of that someone might do that.

To shoot heroin, though she hadn't.

Or to show someone something.

And there was something there. Her tattoos. He'd seen them licking out from the cuffs of her uniform but had never seen the actual images. Now he could.

The needle work seemed fine, refined. No pictures. Just words, intertwined. All up and down her arm. Though he couldn't read what was written, he could see that some words, phrases, were in Latin. Some in Greek. In French and English.

Her body, it seemed, was a Rosetta stone. A way to unlock, decode, Amelia.

He wished he could read what was actually written there.

But one thing did stand out. Something scrawled boldly on her skin. More like graffiti than the fine etchings of the other words.

He looked closer. Then sat back hoping that, as with paintings, distance would give him perspective. It didn't.

He zoomed closer. Cursing his bleary vision.

D he could make out. At both ends. And then, with his finger, he traced the lines. Slowly. Having to back up when he realized he'd taken a wrong turn and was now deep into Latin or Greek.

V.

A.

DAVD.

"David," he whispered.

And beside the name some numbers. "One. Four," he mumbled.

He unfroze the image, and the now-familiar video rolled on. He watched as she once again used the move they'd taught her at the Sûreté Academy and dislocated the dealer's shoulder.

Then Amelia and her followers left the frame. Along with his friends. Her entourage was getting larger and larger and now included young men.

Her influence was growing.

It hadn't taken long. And he probably should have seen this coming, and maybe he had and just didn't want to admit it.

He'd not only released a deadly narcotic onto the streets of Québec. He'd released Amelia.

And she was doing what Amelia always did. She was taking over.

"What are you up to?" he whispered. "And who's David?"

The video continued to roll, but all that was left was the heap on the ground, like garbage.

And the whimpering.

Armand was about to turn it off when he noticed movement. A little girl in a bright red tuque. She walked out of the darkness and paused on the sidewalk. Alone. All alone. Then the girl turned and walked out of the frame. After Amelia.

He stared, his face pale. His mouth slightly open. Sickened to see a child alone on the streets.

He was so absorbed by what had just left the frame that he almost missed seeing what remained.

There was someone else, he now noticed. A man. On the very edge of the screen. He was leaning, almost casually, against the wall of the alley. His arms folded, he stared after Amelia. And appeared to be thinking. Then he made up his mind. Pushing off from the wall, he moved. But he didn't follow the others. Instead he stepped over the writhing dealer and walked in the opposite direction.

Armand wondered if he'd just met David.

CHAPTER 27

By midmorning, when Armand and Benedict left for Montréal, Jean-Guy was long gone.

And because Armand wasn't with him, he didn't see Jean-Guy stop in back of the building and look around before being buzzed inside.

The large conference room was empty when he arrived.

Jean-Guy sat but soon got up. Restless, he paced back and forth in front of the windows. Then around the table. Pausing to look at a familiar painting. A copy of a classic Jean Paul Lemieux.

Then he paced again, looking out the window at Montréal, slightly obscured by ice fog. Like a veil of gauze.

He gripped his hands behind his back and puffed out his cheeks before exhaling.

I have a family now, he told himself, *and need to put them first.*

Yes. That was why he was there. Not for himself. Not because he was a chickenshit. Or just a chicken. Or just a shit.

The door opened, and he turned around to see the now-familiar men and women who'd interviewed him. Who'd made the offer just a few days earlier.

He'd declined to accept. Which did not make them at all happy. Apparently not many said no.

He'd explained that he was loyal to the Chief Superintendent. And they'd explained the advantages, and distinct disadvantages, of refusing their offer.

He was being worn down. Acting Chief Inspector Beauvoir recognized the technique, even as he recognized it was working.

But sitting in bed the night before, Annie asleep beside him, he'd gone back over the papers. Reading. Rereading. Would it really be so bad if he signed? Could anyone really blame him?

Ironically, it was the sort of thing he'd normally discuss with the Chief. But could not. Not this time. Not this deal.

He had, of course, discussed it at length with Annie. The options. The consequences.

And now here he was. About to do something he'd never have thought possible.

After shaking hands, they all sat. In the awkward silence, while an assistant brought coffee, Jean-Guy pointed to the Lemieux.

"I like it."

"I'm glad," the woman said.

"A numbered print?" he asked.

"The original."

"Ah," he said. "Chiaroscuro."

A man next to her smiled. "I see you know your art. Yes. Not many realize that it's the play of light and dark, of subtleties and extremes—"

Beauvoir nodded and smiled. But all he could think of, for some reason, was ice cream.

When the coffee arrived, rich and strong, he took a long, restorative gulp. He was ready for them.

And they for him, it seemed.

The woman in charge pushed a small stack of papers across the table, with a pen lying on top of them.

"We're so glad you've changed your mind."

He picked up the pen and signed quickly. He couldn't afford to hesitate now. It was one of the early lessons in homicide from then–Chief Inspector Gamache.

Once an action has been entered, you cannot hesitate. Once committed, you cannot second-guess. Never look back.

This action, Beauvoir realized as he put the cap on the pen, had been entered months ago. When he and Gamache had been suspended. And the investigation had begun. When their own people had questioned not just their actions but their integrity, their commitment.

It had all led here. To this moment. In this room.

He pushed the document back across the table.

"Keep it," said the woman, when Beauvoir went to hand the pen back. "I'm glad you've decided to join us."

She was smiling, they were all smiling. She put out her hand, and after a brief hesitation he shook it.

It was the schooner Hesperus, the deep voice came to him. *That sailed the wintry sea.*

That's as far as it ever went, and Jean-Guy always laughed at the running joke. But now, as he looked out the window at the falling snow and felt the pen heavy in his breast pocket, he remembered the title.

And he wondered if, in his effort to get to safety, he wasn't fleeing from a wreck but causing it.

Benedict proved a careful, though tense, driver.

He gripped the wheel at the ten and two positions and sat bolt upright, his eyes never wandering from the snowy road.

Car after car passed them on the autoroute. But Armand was in no hurry and preferred safety to recklessness. He also knew that it was his presence that was making the boy extra cautious. Tense, even.

He'll relax soon enough, thought Gamache.

They talked about mundane things, like home ownership and Benedict's job as caretaker and what could go wrong with buildings. Large and small.

Armand told him about renovations they were considering to their home.

"I hope you don't mind my picking your brain," said Armand. "There're quite a few bedrooms, but when our son, Daniel, and his wife and two daughters come, along with Annie and Jean-Guy and their family . . . well, there won't be enough room."

"So you'd like an addition?"

They discussed possibilities. Benedict suggested going up instead of out and renovating the attic. And how to do it without making the whole place fall down.

"One collapsed house is more than enough," said Armand, and Benedict agreed.

Gamache tucked the information away. Not about renovations he had no plans to undertake but that Benedict did indeed know how to prevent a house from falling. And would therefore, presumably, also know how to bring one down.

Benedict dropped Armand off in downtown Montréal, at the quite splendid offices of Horowitz Investments, and promised to pick him up later.

It was snowing lightly. Prettily. Covering the grime of the city. At least for a little while.

Gamache watched Benedict drive around a corner, then hailed a cab and gave an address on rue Ste.-Catherine.

"Are you sure?" the driver asked, looking Armand up and down.

His fare was nicely dressed, in a good parka, with a white shirt and a tie just visible below the scarf.

"I'm sure. *Merci.*"

He leaned back in the seat, and as he did, his face settled into a grim expression.

"Wait for me, please," he said when they reached their destination.

"I won't wait long," the driver warned. Though he hadn't yet been paid, he was willing to leave rather than be carjacked, or beaten and robbed by junkies.

This was, every cabbie knew, a no-go area. Or, if you had to go, it was a place you didn't linger.

He locked the doors and kept the car in gear.

Still, he was curious and watched as his fare walked with more confidence than he should have had, then turned in to what the driver knew was an alley. Clogged with garbage cans and whores.

He waited a minute. Two. Then crept up until he was idling at the mouth of the alley.

The cabbie watched as his fare shook the hand of another tall person. But this one was emaciated. A prostitute. A transsexual.

He passed her money in a thick envelope. Oddly, the woman appeared to try to give it back, but his fare insisted. Then he turned and, on seeing the taxi, nodded.

The man walked back to the car with ease, with authority. And while the driver was tempted to leave him there, after whatever disgusting thing had just happened in the alley, he didn't.

Armand thanked the driver, then sat back in the seat and exhaled as he looked out the window. Scanning the icy streets for a little girl. A child. In a red hat.

But he felt confident his new friend, Anita Facial, would find her. And call him. And he'd go and get her.

He knew in coming here today he'd risked blowing the whole thing. Risked being seen. But there were lines, there were limits. And Armand Gamache was tired of crossing them. Of exceeding them. He was tired of the tyranny of the greater good.

He'd found a line, in the fleeting image of a little girl, that he would not cross.

"'It was the schooner Hesperus,'" he whispered, his breath creating a small circle of vapor on the window, "'That sailed the wintry sea.'"

He realized everyone suspected he only knew the opening lines of the epic poem. That was part of the joke. But the truth was, he knew it all. Every word. Every line. Including, of course, how it ended.

"'Christ save us all from a death like this,'" he quoted under his breath as he looked out the window.

Beauvoir grabbed a quick sandwich in his office as he read over reports of the Baumgartner murder. Updates on interviews. Background checks. Preliminary scene-of-crime evidence. Photographs.

He chaired the morning briefing with lead inspectors about other homicides they were investigating.

He then called Agent Cloutier into his office to get a report on her findings.

She balanced the papers on her knee, then knocked them off. Then her glasses fell off as she stooped to pick up the papers. Beauvoir went around the desk to help her.

"Let's sit over there," he said, taking a pile of papers to the table by the window. One he'd sat at hundreds of times, going over cases with Gamache.

"Tell me what you know," he said to her.

And she did.

"These"—she laid her hand on the statements found in Anthony Baumgartner's study—"are not legitimate. The numbers don't add up.

The transactions look good until you cross-check and realize the buy and sell figures are off."

"So what are they?"

"A play."

"A what?"

"They're like a theater production. An illusion. Something made to look real, but isn't. Monsieur Baumgartner must've known that these clients wouldn't look too closely. Most don't. And the fact is, you'd have to be an expert to figure it out, and even then it takes time."

"Was he stealing from them?"

The clarity, the simplicity of the question seemed to surprise her. She thought about it, then nodded. "Absolutely."

"Have you found the funds?"

"That'll take longer, sir. And a court order."

Beauvoir went to his desk and brought over a paper. It was the court order, allowing them full access to Baumgartner's finances. Another one granted access to the Taylor and Ogilvy client list.

He'd put that in his satchel, along with the copy of the statements Cloutier had given him.

"It would also help if we could get into his computer," he said.

"I'm working on it, *patron*."

The taxi let Armand off where it had picked him up. Outside the offices of Horowitz Investments. They were just down rue Sherbrooke from the Musée des Beaux-Arts and Holt Renfrew. On Montréal's Golden Mile, where glass towers were fronted by old Greystone mansions.

A cab ride, and a lifetime, away from where he'd just been. What separated them, Gamache knew, wasn't hard work but good fortune and blind luck. That picked some and not others. That introduced some to opioids and not others. Five years ago, two years, even a year ago, the futures of the ghastly figures on the street looked very different. And then someone introduced them to a painkiller. An opioid. And all the promise, all the good fortune of birth and affluence—of a loving family, of education—were no match for what came next.

Loved. Beaten. Cared for. Neglected. University graduate or drop-out. All ended up in the gutter. Thanks to the great leveler that was fentanyl.

What was on the streets now was not, Gamache knew, his doing. They were opioids. Killers. Hollowing out a generation. And so far the carfentanil he'd let through hadn't yet gone into circulation.

But it would, he knew. Soon. And if it was bad now, it was about to get incalculably worse.

He'd read a report recently that said an American state with the death penalty was considering using the drug to execute prisoners. It was swift and lethal and guaranteed to do the job.

He'd stared at that report, feeling the blood drain from his face. It wasn't telling him anything he didn't already know. But it did put a word to what he'd done. What he was.

The executioner.

"Armand."

Stephen Horowitz came out of his office, hand extended. His voice still lightly accented from his European upbringing.

All of ninety-three now, he was as vibrant as ever. And as rich as Croesus.

"You're looking well," said Armand, taking the firm hand and shaking it.

"As are you."

The sharp eyes traveled over Gamache before coming to rest on his face.

"Have you been crying?"

Armand laughed. "Seeing you always makes me emotional. You know that. But *non*. Just some irritation."

"That sounds more likely. Most people find me irritating."

Armand did not disagree.

"I've made reservations at the Ritz. Too pretentious, but I like seeing which of my clients are there and think they can afford it."

They walked the two blocks to the Ritz, with Horowitz taking Armand's arm every now and then, far beyond being bashful about any frailty.

He'd been Armand's parents' financial adviser. In fact, Armand's father had helped set Horowitz up in business when he'd been a young refugee after the war. One of the displaced people who never forgot how that felt. Nor, seventy years later, had Stephen Horowitz forgotten that act of kindness.

There was now a shockingly generous account, in Annie's and Daniel's names, with Horowitz Investments. One Gamache himself didn't even know about.

Horowitz had left instructions in his will, and only then would the Gamaches find out.

"I hear you're still suspended," said Stephen, allowing a liveried waiter to flap open the linen napkin before laying it on his lap. "*Merci.*"

"I am," he said in response to Stephen's question.

Sparkling water with lime was on the table waiting for them, along with two scotches and two plates of oysters.

"*Merci,*" said Armand as the napkin was laid on his lap.

"Stupid of them." The elderly man shook his head. "Would you like me to make a call?"

"To whom?" asked Armand. "Or do I want to know?"

"Probably not."

"You've already made one call, I know. Thank you for that."

"You're my godson," said Stephen. "I do what I can."

Armand watched him prepare his oysters. With precision. Knowing exactly how he liked them.

Stephen Horowitz was as close as Armand came to having a father. The investment dealer had been disappointed when the young man had chosen the law over finance, though Stephen had his own three children to leave the business to.

Armand's relationship with Stephen was divorced, as far as Armand knew, from money. It was about other forms of support.

"See that man over there?" Stephen was now engaged in his favorite thing. Passing judgment. "Runs a steel company. A complete dickhead. My people have just discovered that he's planning on giving himself a hundred-million-dollar bonus this fiscal year. Excuse me."

To Armand's alarm, though no real surprise, Stephen got up and walked over to the man, said something that made the man turn purple, then returned to the table, grinning all the way.

"What did you say to him?" Armand asked.

"I told him that I was dumping all the shares Horowitz Investments holds in his company. I gave the order just before we left. Look."

And as Armand watched, the man pulled out his iPhone, punched some numbers, and stared. Pale now. As he saw his shares tumble.

"When the stock reaches a low, I've told my people to buy it. All," said Stephen.

"You've bought the company?" asked Armand.

"Controlling interest. He'll see that in a few minutes too."

"You'll be his boss."

"Not for long."

Stephen raised his hand, and the maître d' hurried over, bent down, nodded, then left. Armand raised his brows and waited for an explanation.

"I told Pierre that I'd pay for that table. The man won't be able to afford it after this, and I don't want the restaurant stuck with a bad debt."

"You're very thoughtful," said Armand, and he watched as Stephen smiled broadly. "Did you know he'd be here when you booked?"

"It's Wednesday. He's always here Wednesday."

"So that's a yes."

"Yes."

Wheels within wheels, thought Armand as their lunch arrived. And most of the wheels were running over some poor sod who got in Stephen's way. Or did something he didn't approve of.

"Have you ever heard of Ruth Zardo?" Armand asked, cutting into his sea bass on a bed of pureed cauliflower with braised lentils and garnished with grilled asparagus and grapefruit wedges.

"The poet? Yes, of course." He lowered his knife and fork and looked into the distance, recalling the words: "'Who hurt you once so far beyond repair / That you would greet each overture with curling lip.'"

"That's the one."

"Why do you ask?"

"I just thought you two might get along."

Stephen went back to his food. "Are you hurt, Armand?" He spoke into his Dover sole.

"Not beyond repair, no."

Stephen looked up then. His eyes clear and searching. "I don't mean physically. Those wounds heal. I mean by the Sûreté investigation. By this suspension that seems to be going on a long time."

"There're things you don't know, Stephen."

"True. But I know you. It would be a terrible shame to lose you as head of the Sûreté."

"*Merci.*"

"Are you sure I can't put in a call?"

"Don't you dare," said Armand, pointing his knife at the elderly man in mock threat.

Stephen laughed and nodded. "Fine. Now, why did you want to see me?"

"It's delicate."

"Let me guess. It's about Hugo Baumgartner."

"Well, so much for delicate."

"His brother was just killed, so it wasn't hard to guess. Murdered, according to the news. But you can't be involved in the investigation. You are, as we've established—"

"Suspended. *Oui.* But I'm a liquidator on his mother's will and came at it in a roundabout way."

He explained about the will, and Horowitz listened carefully before thinking it over and finally saying, "That's some weird shit."

Armand laughed. "Your considered opinion. Well, you're not wrong. But I want to ask you about Hugo Baumgartner. He's one of your senior vice presidents."

"He is. Ugly as original sin. Vile to look at. Really quite disgusting. But, like many ugly people, who look like villains, he has to make up for it by being obviously decent. If I didn't have three children capable of taking over the company, I'd consider him."

"He's that good?"

"He is. He's as good as his dead brother was bad."

"So you know about that."

"I do. Hugo didn't tell me. He's protective of his brother. But word on the street—"

"Does everyone know?"

"If they don't, they're dumber than I thought. Why else would a

254

senior VP at Taylor and Ogilvy have his license suspended? That's a serious move. Not done lightly."

"Hugo says his brother was railroaded, made an example of. That it was the assistant who actually stole the money."

"Yeah, yeah," said Stephen, gesturing with his knife and fork. "Blah, blah. What else's he going to say?" The elderly man leaned toward Armand. "Who's more likely to know how to steal money from a client's account and be able to cover it up for months? The VP or the assistant? Who's more likely to have access? And who's more likely to be fired? I'll give you a hint—the answer to the last question is different from the first two."

Armand nodded. He'd gotten that far himself. "What can you tell me about Taylor and Ogilvy?"

"They're a relatively new firm. Been around for about thirty years, though they like to give the impression they were created by royal charter in the 1800s."

"Victoria banked with them?" asked Armand.

"Something like that. Magnificent offices, clearly meant to impress."

"And yet?"

"I'm always suspicious of anyone who feels they need to impress with surroundings rather than track record."

"You're suspicious of everyone," Armand pointed out. "Hardly telling."

"True," admitted Horowitz with a smile.

"You think they're hiding something?" Armand asked. "Are they legitimate?"

"Oh yes. Just sail a little close to the edge."

"You do know that the earth is round."

"The earth might be, but human nature isn't. It has caverns and abysses and all sorts of traps."

"Taylor and Ogilvy exists on the edge of one such trap?"

"If they employ humans, then yes."

"You employ humans," Armand pointed out.

"But I watch over them," said Stephen. "And I'm immortal."

"And infallible."

"Now you're getting it."

"Hugo Baumgartner," said Armand. "He's about as human as they come. Can he be trusted?"

"As far as I know. But you're not asking me to transfer your account to him, are you?" He watched his godson. "No. You're not sure about him, are you, Armand?"

"Dessert?" asked Armand when the waiter took their plates.

Stephen smiled and accepted the dessert menu. After they'd ordered warm apple tarts, tea ice cream, and coffee, Stephen spoke again.

"It's the will that interests me. I've known families torn apart by them. Expectations. Those're corrosive. Combined with greed or desperation, it can get pretty nasty. Go on for years."

"Generations," said Armand.

"Do they really believe that a title and all those possessions belong to them?"

"They say not, but—"

"What's bred in the bone," said Stephen. "Sometimes we think we haven't bought into someone else's craziness until it's tested. They're Jewish, aren't they?"

"Yes. Does it matter?"

"It might. From Austria? Vienna?"

"*Oui.*"

Stephen was nodding.

"You have an idea?"

"Nothing as good as an idea. More like a vague thought. I just wonder if the old woman—the Baroness, you call her?—if she might've been right after all, without realizing it. Let me do some research." He waved for the bill. "That's what you wanted, wasn't it? For me to do some digging."

"I wanted your company," said Armand. "And a delicious meal."

"You got a nice meal, and I just got fed bullshit." He shoved the silver salver across the linen tablecloth. "Here. You can pay."

Armand smiled and shook his head. It had always been his intention to pay. He always did. And now, it seemed, he was also, thanks to Stephen, paying for the meals of four people he didn't even know.

"Let's hope my suspension is over soon," said Armand, laying down his credit card.

"Why? So you can pay for this? Don't worry, you can afford it."

"No." He nodded toward the steel magnate, who, ruined over his meal of veal sweetbreads, glared at Stephen as he left. "So I can solve your murder."

The old man laughed.

CHAPTER 28

～

Jean-Guy looked around the waiting room of Taylor and Ogilvy.

He was on the forty-fifth floor, but you'd never know it. There was oak paneling, and oil paintings, and even a bookcase with leather volumes, as though to say if your investment adviser could read, he was sure not to screw you.

Jean-Guy expected, when he looked out the window, to see the magnificent garden of an estate, and not Montréal from the air.

Illusion.

What was it Agent Cloutier had said?

A play. A set. Something that looked like one thing but was actually another. This place was made up to look like a solid, conservative, trustworthy firm. But was it something else?

He peered at the paintings, then got up to look at one in particular.

A numbered print.

Not exactly a fake, but not the real thing either.

"Do you like it?" a woman's voice behind him asked.

He turned around, expecting it was the receptionist who'd spoken, only to find a very elegant and surprisingly young woman standing at the open door.

"I do," said Beauvoir. "I'm here to see Madame Ogilvy."

"Bernice, please." She extended her hand. "Have I heard correctly? Tony was murdered?"

"I'm afraid it looks that way."

Her eyes narrowed in a wince, absorbing the words. "Jesus. I'll do whatever I can to help."

"*Merci.*"

She turned, and he followed her down the hushed corridor. Taking in the offices on either side, where brokers, mostly men, sat speaking on telephones or tapping on laptops.

The hallway was paneled in wood and art.

"Nice paintings," he said.

"Thank you. Most are prints, but we do have some originals," she assured him. "Some awful things my grandfather bought, thinking they were good investments. They were not. We hide those in the offices of the partners, as a reminder."

"Of what?"

"Of what happens when we think we know about something when we do not." She stopped then and smiled at him. "You must run into the same danger in your profession, Chief Inspector. Only your mistakes can cost lives."

"As can yours."

Her smile faded. "I'm aware of that."

She turned and continued her chat about the art. It was, he could tell, rehearsed. A patter she repeated for everyone. To put them at their ease.

"We specialize in Canadian art. Québec, wherever possible."

"But not always originals."

"No. The originals are often not available, so we buy numbered prints. But only the low numbers."

He laughed, then realized she was serious. "Why's that?"

"Well, because they're more valuable. Everything's an investment, Chief Inspector."

"Everything?"

"Everything. And I don't just mean in business. As humans, we invest not just money. We spend time. We spend effort. There's a reason it's put like that. Life's short, and time is precious and limited. We need to pick and choose where we put it."

"For maximum return?"

"Exactly. I know it sounds calculating, but think about your own life. You don't want to waste your time with people you don't like or doing something you don't find fulfilling."

Beauvoir felt there should be some clever response, but all that came to mind was to say, *That's bullshit*.

A few years ago, he might've. But then a few years ago he wasn't the Chief Inspector.

"What're you thinking?" she asked.

"I'm thinking that's bullshit."

Oh well, if life really is short, might as well be himself.

She stopped and looked at him. "Why do you say that?"

He looked around before his attention returned to her. "It's the sort of thing someone who works here would say. I'm not saying you don't believe it. I'm saying most people don't have the luxury to pick and choose. They're just trying to make it through the day. Taking whatever shitty job they can. Trying to hold the family together. Maybe in a shitty marriage with kids who're out of control. You live in a world of choice, Madame Ogilvy. Most don't have investments. They have lives. And they're just trying to get by."

"A zero-sum game?" she asked. "That's bullshit. And patronizing. People might not be able to choose to work here, or live in a mansion, but they still have choices. And investments of time if not money."

They stared at each other, the strain obvious. Beauvoir didn't care. He preferred it like this. Pushing people. Seeing what they're really like underneath.

He found it interesting that when he'd become crass, she'd changed. Used exactly the same language. The difference was, it was natural to him. Not to her.

Here was a chameleon. Who adapted to situations, and people.

It was a useful skill. Both a defense and an offense. It was designed to lower people's guards. *I'm just like you*, she was saying. *And you're "one of us."*

It was a subtle and powerful message. One that put people at ease and let her into their confidence.

Elegant and refined when called for. Foulmouthed when called for.

Demure. Scrappy. Crass. Classy.

All things. And nothing. Except calculating.

One of the many things he loved about Annie was that, while adaptable, she was always herself. Genuine.

This woman was not.

Still, this was going to be, if he was smart, a good investment of his time.

"Do you have any Clara Morrows?" he asked as they turned a corner.

"No. I tried to buy one of her Three Graces, but there were no prints left. Only the one of that old woman. Scared the *merde* out of me."

"You should see the original," said Beauvoir. "Better than an enema."

She laughed and showed him into her office.

It was like walking from the past into the future or, at least, a very glossy present day. It was a corner office, of floor-to-ceiling glass. There, before him, spread Montréal. Magnificent. In one direction he could see the Jacques Cartier Bridge across the St. Lawrence River. In the other, Mount Royal, with its massive cross. And in between, office towers. Bold, gleaming, audacious. Montréal. Set for the future with roots deep in history. It never failed to thrill him. And the ice fog only made it more otherworldly.

Her desk was wood. But sleek and simple. An age-old material with a modern design. There was a sofa, some chairs, and the art, like everything else, was contemporary.

"No one you'd know," she said as he scanned the walls. "Students mostly. We fund a scholarship for young artists to study at the Musée d'art contemporain. What I ask in return is one of their works."

"In the hopes one day it'll be worth something?" he asked.

"There's always that, Chief Inspector. But mostly I hope they do what they love."

"And do you?" he asked, sitting down.

"As a matter of fact, I do. Born to it, I suppose. Investing, finance, the market. Both my parents are in investing."

"Your father's the CEO and your mother's the chair of the board."

"You've done your homework."

He felt himself getting prickly. It was such a condescending thing to say.

"Not difficult. A simple Google search. Is that how you got your job?"

Two can be insulting.

"Well, it's not a coincidence my name is Ogilvy. But I earned this office. Believe me. Investing not only comes naturally, it fascinates me."

"How so?"

"The chance to make a real difference in people's lives. To secure their retirement. Their children's educations. Their first home. What could be better?"

The truth, thought Beauvoir. That could be better. This was, like the patter down the hallway, a practiced speech. More oak paneling. More fake originals.

"And you?" she asked.

"Me?"

"Do you love what you do?"

"Of course."

But the question surprised him. He'd never really thought about it. Did he love it?

He certainly hadn't stood over corpses, hunted killers all these years for the money or glamour. Then why had he? Was it possible he did love it?

Beauvoir brought the warrant from his satchel and placed it on the desk.

Madame Ogilvy didn't bother to look at it. "I also did some research. In answer to your question yesterday, we don't have any clients named Kinderoth. Now. But we did. Both have died. One five years ago and one last year. They were elderly and in ill health."

"Did Anthony Baumgartner look after their finances?"

"No. They were with another adviser, and, frankly, it was such a small account that when it was divided among the heirs there was hardly anything left. Though I understand the will was a little strange."

Beauvoir felt that frisson that came with an unexpected find.

"How so?" his voice betrayed none of his excitement.

"I can't remember the exact details, but it seems they left far more than they actually had. We talked to the adviser, of course, about why they thought they had what amounted to a fortune, but he was as baffled as anyone. We did our own investigation, and there was absolutely nothing wrong with our accounts."

"Do you know if there was an aristocratic title involved?" He asked this as though it were a perfectly natural question. And braced for ridicule.

But she wasn't laughing. She was looking at him with genuine surprise.

"How did you know that? As a matter of fact, there was. We think they must've been suffering from dementia, or some sort of collective delusion. Monsieur Kinderoth was a taxi driver and Madame Kinderoth had raised the children. They had a very modest house in East End Montréal and a small retirement income. And yet in their will they left millions, and a title."

"Baron?"

"And Baroness, yes. Apparently that's what they called themselves."

Beauvoir could feel his heart speeding up and his senses sharpening, as they always did when he was closing in on something. Or, really, had fallen face-first into it.

But his voice remained neutral. His own oak paneling. His veneer in place.

"Do you have the address of their children?"

"I thought you might ask. They had two daughters, both living in Toronto. Both married. What does this have to do with Tony Baumgartner's death? As I said, they weren't his clients."

Her hand rested on a slim manila folder.

"I'm afraid I can't tell you that."

He saw a flash of annoyance, quickly there and rapidly hidden. Here was someone not used to hearing no. And someone who clearly thrived on information. No surprise there. You didn't land in this office by being ignorant.

And you weren't the acting head of homicide for the Sûreté by handing out information.

He extended his hand, and she gave him the folder.

"*Merci.* No relatives living in Québec?"

"Not that I know of."

He nodded. They'd done searches from the government databases for Baumgartners and Kinderoths. Both, fortunately, unusual names.

While there were a few Baumgartners scattered around, perhaps distant cousins or not related at all—agents were checking—there were no more Kinderoths in Québec.

Jean-Guy's mind was working quickly, to absorb this news of another strange will. One, he suspected, that left exactly what the Baroness Baumgartner had left. He'd have agents check. The Kinderoth will would be in the public domain by now.

"Thank you." He held up the file before tucking it into his satchel. "Now, the main reason I came here is to ask you about Anthony Baumgartner."

"Exactly," she said, and leaned forward in her chair. "How can I help?"

"What was he like?"

"He was a brilliant analyst. He understood—"

"We'll get to that in a moment. I'd like to hear what he was like as a person."

Beauvoir's technique was very different from Gamache's. The Chief wanted to remain quiet. To listen. To put people at their ease. Draw them out and have them almost forget this was an interrogation. He used silence. And calm. Reassuring smiles.

While Beauvoir could see the benefits and the results of that, his own approach was to get in their faces. Keep them off balance so that they'd erupt.

He asked a lot of questions. Interrupted answers. Let them know who was in charge. And kept turning up the pressure.

"As a person?" Bernice Ogilvy asked.

"You know. A human being. Not an investment."

He saw her color. "I understand. He was nice—"

"You can do better than that. Did you like him?"

"Like him?"

"It's a feeling," he said. "How did you feel about Anthony Baumgartner?"

"He was nice—"

"Puppies are nice. What was he? How did you feel about him?"

"I liked him," she snapped. "A lot."

"A lot?"

"Not like that."

"Then how?"

"He was nice—"

"Come on. What was he to you?"

"An employee."

"More than that?"

"Of course not."

"Did you know he was gay?"

"Only when he told me."

"Is that true?"

"Yes. It didn't matter. He was—"

"Nice?"

"More. He was like a father."

It came out almost as a shout. Defiantly. Challenging Beauvoir to challenge her.

He did not. He had what he wanted.

"To you?"

"To everyone. All of us. Even the older men, they looked up to him."

She regarded him, expecting another interruption. But Beauvoir had learned from Gamache when to keep his mouth shut. And listen.

"He never forgot a birthday or an important anniversary," she said. "And not just of the partners but everyone. Assistants, cleaners. He was that sort of man."

A good man, thought Beauvoir. Or just good at appearances.

"When I came into the firm, I used my mother's maiden name. I didn't want anyone to know who I was. I started as Tony's assistant. He was patient and kind. Taught me more about the market in six months than I'd learned in four years at university. How to read trends. What to look for. To not just study the annual reports but to get to know the leadership of companies. He was brilliant."

"And what happened when he found out who you really were?"

She raised her brows and compressed her lips.

"He wasn't happy. He took me out for drinks, and I thought he'd be pleased. He'd mentored someone who'd one day have—" She raised her hands to indicate the corner office.

"But he wasn't," she said. "He told me that this was a business built on relationships and trust. Not on tricks. Not on games. He wished I'd been honest with him. And that it didn't speak highly of him, or of me, that I felt I needed to pretend. That I didn't trust him. He didn't say it, but I could see I'd disappointed him. It was awful."

And I bet you've spent the last few years trying to make it up to him,

266

thought Beauvoir. Was Baumgartner that clever? To play her like that. To talk about trust when he himself was violating it?

Beauvoir reached into his satchel and placed the statements on her desk.

"I've had an agent working on these. I suspect you'll come to the same conclusion."

Madame Ogilvy put on glasses and picked up the statements, without comment. A minute. Two. Five went by. Jean-Guy got up and wandered the office, examining the walls and the art. Glancing at her every now and then.

His iPhone buzzed, and he looked at the text. It was from Gamache, asking if he could meet him over at Isabelle Lacoste's place in an hour.

He sent back a quick reply. Absolutely.

Finally Madame Ogilvy put down the statements. Her face was bland. Almost blank. Though he saw her fingers tremble, just before she closed them into fists.

"You were right to be concerned, Chief Inspector." Her voice now held none of the emotion of before. It was clipped. Controlled. "I'm glad you brought these to me."

"Are you?" he asked, sitting back down.

Her smile was thin. Her eyes cold. This was not a young woman. This was the senior partner in a multibillion-dollar investment firm. Who didn't get the job because she was the CEO's daughter but because she could do just this.

Absorb information quickly. Break it down. See the implications and options. And not hide from reality, no matter how unpleasant. They were skills that would have served her well in any business. Including his.

"I am," she said. "It would come out eventually. Better we have a chance to manage the situation."

At least she was being honest about that, thought Beauvoir. But he wasn't fooled by her sangfroid. Agent Cloutier had made it clear that embezzlement on this scale, for what appeared to be a long time, would probably need the collusion of someone very senior.

They were far from sure Anthony Baumgartner had been in it alone.

In fact, Beauvoir had begun to formulate a theory.

That Baumgartner was corrupt, that much seemed obvious, but he was also a tool. He'd set up the shell, directed the play, to use Cloutier's analogy. But someone else wrote the script.

Who better than the CEO's daughter? Baumgartner's former protégée?

Had the story she'd just told him been more bullshit? Beauvoir wondered. About disappointing Baumgartner? About him not knowing who she was? About his decency?

Had he in fact taught her things she didn't learn in business school? Like how to steal from clients?

Who, after all, was in a better position to hide what was happening? And to protect him if caught. As he had been.

Instead of firing his ass, they'd fired the assistant.

And then there was the question of where the money went.

Anthony Baumgartner's lifestyle showed none of the fruits of this labor. He lived in the same home he'd been in for years. Drove a nice, though midrange, vehicle. Had not gone on any luxury vacations.

It was a rare person who was greedy enough to steal clients' money and then disciplined enough not to spend it.

Unless the lion's share was going somewhere else. To someone else.

"And how do you manage this situation?" he asked.

"Well, the first thing I do," she said, reaching for the phone, "is call the regulatory commission and report this."

"We've already done that."

"I see. I'll call as well, later." She put down the phone, slightly miffed. "We will, of course, replace any money taken from clients."

"Stolen."

"Yes."

"Bit awkward, isn't it?" he said. "This isn't the first time Anthony Baumgartner embezzled from clients."

"You're talking about what happened a few years ago," she said. "That wasn't him. Not directly. It was the assistant of one of the senior partners."

"You?"

"No."

"They were having an affair, I believe," said Beauvoir.

"That's true. The assistant apparently used Tony to get at his access codes and was siphoning money from various accounts. He was bound

268

to be caught. Not very smart, really. But he did get away with quite a bit before it was discovered."

"Who caught him?"

"Tony. He came to us immediately, and we acted."

"By firing the assistant."

"Yes."

"And not Monsieur Baumgartner."

"He'd been foolish, trusted someone he shouldn't have. But his actions weren't criminal."

"And yet you suspended his license."

"There had to be a consequence. Other brokers had to see that if you're tainted in any way, there will be a punishment."

"And his clients?"

"What about them?"

"Were they told?"

"No. We decided not to. The money was replaced, and it was decided Tony would work with another broker, who'd put in the tickets and do the actual transactions. But Tony would continue to manage the portfolios. Make the decisions. It wasn't necessary for this to be spread on the street."

"The street?"

"Our language. It means the financial community."

The street.

Beauvoir was beginning to appreciate that the only thing that separated this "street" from rue Ste.-Catherine was a thin veneer of gentility. But once that was peeled away, what was revealed was just as brutal, just as dirty, just as dangerous.

"Baumgartner was fine with the new arrangement?"

"He understood. Look, he didn't have to come to us. He probably could've figured out how to cover it up. But instead he sat right where you're sitting and told me everything. About the affair. About finding out Bernard had stolen his access codes for the accounts. He offered to quit."

"But you didn't take him up on it?"

"No."

"Why not?"

"I've already told you."

"You know as well as I do that you could've fired him. And given what's happened, perhaps even should have." He looked at the statements. "I want the truth."

She took a deep breath and continued to hold his eyes.

"He was the best financial adviser we had. Brilliant. I am, after all is said and done, my father's daughter, Chief Inspector. I know talent, and I want to keep it. Tony Baumgartner was that. And so we chose a middle ground. Suspending his license to trade but allowing him to continue managing portfolios."

"So if he could no longer trade, how did he manage to steal all that money?" Beauvoir pointed to the papers on her desk.

"No, no, these are all fake. There were never any trades. That's the whole thing. He made it look like there were, but it's all gobbledygook. If a client actually bothered to read this"—she put her splayed hand on the paper—"what they'd see are numbers that are both impressive and mind-numbingly boring. No one, other than another financial wonk, would bother to study these."

"So where did the money go?"

She shook her head and took a deep breath. "I don't know. But it looks like millions. Tens of millions."

"More," said Beauvoir, and, after a small hesitation, she also nodded.

"Depending on how long this's been going on, yes. It'll take us a while to work it all out."

"But wouldn't people, his clients, realize? When there was no actual money in the account?"

"How?"

"When they asked for it."

"But people don't," she said. "They give it to their investment dealer, and at best they cash in the dividends or take the profits. But the capital remains in the account. Weren't you ever told by your parents never to touch the capital?"

"No. I was told not to touch my brother's bike."

She smiled. "Point taken. But a truism in investing is that people take the profits, the dividends, but leave the capital."

"Is this a Ponzi scheme, then?" he asked.

"Not quite, but similar. This's even harder to find, since he's made it look like these clients were investing through Taylor and Ogilvy, but

270

they weren't. He's used our letterhead, our statement format. Our address. Everything. Except our accounts. The money just went into Tony's personal account."

"Where?"

"I have no idea."

"So you wouldn't know it was happening?"

"Not at all. Our auditors would never catch it, because it's not there to catch."

Beauvoir was beginning to see the genius of this. The simplicity.

"So he had two sets of clients? There were the ones whose accounts he was legitimately working on, and then there were those he kept at home. The ones he was stealing from."

"That's what it looks like."

"We'll need to know if any of these clients also have legitimate accounts with Taylor and Ogilvy."

"Of course. May I keep these?" She looked down at the offending statements.

"Yes."

"You'll be questioning them?"

"Yes," he said again.

She nodded. Like mad Ruth in Clara's painting, Bernice Ogilvy could see just the hint of something on the horizon. Far off, but approaching. And gathering speed. Something that had been there a very long time. Waiting. Inevitable.

But where Ruth saw the end of despair, Madame Ogilvy saw the beginning of it.

Once this got out, and it would, no one would trust Taylor and Ogilvy again. It might be unfair, but such was life, when everything depended on something as fragile as trust. And human nature. And a thin oak veneer.

"Is this why Tony was killed?" Madame Ogilvy asked.

"Possibly. We'll need to interview everyone. Are you really so surprised that Monsieur Baumgartner was stealing?"

"I don't know anymore." She'd been so sure of herself, so in control of the room and her emotions. But now a crack appeared.

"Is it possible he was behind the original embezzlement, and not the assistant?"

She nodded, slowly. Thinking. "It's possible."

"It might've been a test run," said Beauvoir. "And he learned from it."

Now she was shaking her head. "I can't believe it."

"That he did it?"

"That, yes. But also that I didn't see it. When I looked at Tony all I saw was a good, decent man."

"That's why it's called a 'confidence game,'" said Beauvoir. "It depends on confidence."

"Suppose it isn't true?" she asked.

"It's true."

"But just suppose, for a moment, that it isn't. That Tony was telling the truth about the assistant and that he didn't do this." She laid her hand on the statements.

Beauvoir was silent. Not wanting to feed this delusion.

It was one of the many tragedies of a murder. That there was an inquiry, into the life of the dead person. And it often revealed things people wished they'd never known. Often things unrelated to the murder. But exposed nonetheless.

And when this happened, friends and family refused to believe it. The affair. The theft. The unsavory acquaintances. The pornography on the computer. The questionable emails.

It got messy. Emotional. Sometimes even violent, as they defended the honor of the dead. And their own delusions.

"Thank you for your time," he said, getting up and walking to the door. "An agent Cloutier will be in touch, probably later today."

She colored. Not used to having her statements ignored. "You asked for Bernard's name and address? My assistant will give it to you as you leave."

"*Merci.* You'll cooperate?"

"Of course, Chief Inspector."

She might as well cooperate, he thought. The damage was done. The deed was done. No amount of hiding, of wishful thinking, of lying, would stop, or even slow down, what was hurtling over the horizon.

Driving through Montréal, on his way to Lacoste's home, he thought about Madame Ogilvy's final question.

Suppose Anthony Baumgartner wasn't stealing clients' money.

That would mean someone else was.

Anthony Baumgartner's name was on the statements. His signature was on the cover letters.

Beauvoir edged forward, through the snow-clogged, car-clogged streets.

It would have to be someone close to Baumgartner. Who knew the system. Who knew his clients. Who had access to his files and the letterhead. Who knew the man well.

Someone in Taylor and Ogilvy.

Now Beauvoir was seriously considering the question.

Suppose Anthony Baumgartner hadn't done anything wrong. Hadn't been stealing. Suppose those statements were in his study, overseen by mad Ruth, because he'd found out that someone else was. And he was poring over them, to figure out who at the company was stealing millions of dollars from clients.

Suppose, Jean-Guy thought as he turned in to Lacoste's narrow street and looked for a parking spot amid the piles of snow still waiting to be cleared, suppose Anthony Baumgartner was exactly what Madame Ogilvy had described.

A good, decent man. An honorable man. Who'd offered to resign when someone else had done wrong. Who understood the value, and fragility, of trust.

What would a man like that do if he discovered corruption on that scale, or any?

He'd confront the person. Demand an explanation. Threaten exposure.

And what would that person do?

"Kill Anthony Baumgartner," mumbled Beauvoir, backing carefully into a spot.

CHAPTER 29

"And what do you want from me?" asked Lucien as he looked at the two women in his office.

"I'd like to know why you said you'd never met the Baroness," said Myrna, "when you had."

She laid his father's agenda on the desk.

Beside her, Clara tried not to fidget. All around them were towers of boxes. Each the same height. Six feet. Placed, it seemed, consciously, strategically, around the office. Like an obstacle course, she thought.

Though there was something else vaguely familiar about them. Were they meant to resemble those ancient rock formations? Like Stonehenge. Or the mysterious heads on Easter Island.

The boxes—files, she saw—were stacked one on top of the other and seemed far from secure. Why not just pile them along a wall, like any sensible person would?

But she could tell that Lucien Mercier was far from sensible. Rational, yes. In the extreme. But "sensible" demanded the person also be sensitive. In order to make good, sensible decisions.

This man was not.

Clara was all for creativity. But the precarious files looming around them were not works of art. They were, she felt, projections of something innate to Lucien. Something intimate, private. Unhappy.

It sounded almost silly to put it that way. Too simplistic. But how razor-sharp was that simple word? Unhappy.

"In fact," Myrna went on, "you'd been at her house, with your father. You were there when the will was discussed. It's in his notes."

Lucien remained unmoving, except for his eyes. Which moved freely, from woman to woman. They flickered to a stack of boxes behind them. Then back.

He was like, Clara thought, a child who thinks that if his body is immobile, no one will notice his eyes moving. Or if he closes his eyes and sees no one, then he himself becomes invisible.

It was, she knew, a highly egocentric state. One most children grew out of.

Clara was watching him closely. Openly.

She was there at Myrna's request. Her friend wanted a witness. Not because she was afraid of this reedy little man but because, after reading his father's papers, Myrna realized the son could not be trusted. That he could say one thing to her, then change his story later.

"But you have to pay attention," Myrna had warned Clara in the car driving over. "Promise me you will."

"What did you say?"

"Come on, I'm serious. I know you. You look like you're following a conversation, nodding and smiling, but in fact you're trying to work out some issue with your latest painting."

Myrna was, of course, right. As they drove over to the notary's office, Clara had been letting her mind wander. Freeing it up. To see what her subconscious might do with Benedict. He of the silly haircut and goofy grin. And happy eyes.

She wondered if she might paint him as a sort of cartoon character. All bright colors and pastel outlines in bold strokes.

But now that she was in this office, all thought of the shiny young man was banished as she sat in the shadows of the boxes and watched Lucien.

And considered how she might paint him.

"I didn't lie," said Lucien. "I just hadn't remembered. I meet a lot of people."

"Why did you go there with your father? Why did he take you there?"

"He was a cautious man. He always wanted a witness when meeting with elderly clients. A second opinion."

"About what?"

"If the person was competent."

"And was the Baroness?"

"Of course. Otherwise he'd never have allowed her to do that will."

Charcoal, thought Clara. That's what she'd use.

Bright crayons for Benedict and the charred remains of something once living for this man.

"Why can't I find David?" asked Amelia.

Marc shrugged.

He'd given it absolutely no thought. What was left of his mind was taken up with only one thing, the search for more dope. He was like a Neanderthal, completely driven by survival.

Though he recognized that while he was focused on one hit, the next hit, Amelia was looking at the mother lode. At having more shit than they knew what to do with, except use and sell. To get high and get rich.

But still, he couldn't get past worrying. About the next hit.

Amelia was standing in his kitchenette, making peanut-butter sandwiches with the loaf they'd stolen from the convenience store. It was stale and beginning to mold. The fresh loaves had been lifted by others, earlier in the day.

She'd have to remember that.

"Here."

She handed one to Marc, who looked at it with disgust. It was all he'd eaten for months. Peanut fucking butter. The very smell turned his stomach.

Taking a bite, he grimaced. It tasted like despair.

"He's out there somewhere," she said, walking to the window. "But if he has the new shit, why isn't he selling it? What's he waiting for?"

Marc joined her at the window. The sandwich hanging loose in his thin hand.

For just a moment, he allowed himself the aroma of pancakes and bacon on a Saturday morning.

Then he locked it away again. In the private room he was saving. He'd crawl into it, and curl into a tiny ball, and close his eyes. And sit at his mother's table. Eating pancakes, and bacon, and maple syrup. Forever.

He stared down at the junkies and trannies and whores gathered out there. Waiting for Amelia. To do what?

They only wanted one thing. He only wanted one thing. For the pain to stop.

"This David doesn't want to be found," said Amelia.

And for good reason, she knew. If they were looking for the carfentanil, others would be too. And he wouldn't have it in his pocket. He'd have to have a whole operation.

"Like a factory," she said out loud, though she knew she was still just talking to herself. "Right? 'Cause he'd have to cut it. Package it. Prepare it for the streets. Thousands and thousands of hits. He'd need space. And time. He'd know that once it hit the streets, all hell was going to break loose. Between the cops, the mob, the bikers. Every piece of shit within thousands of miles will come to Montréal, looking for it. Looking for him. Right?"

Marc's sandwich hit the floor with a soft thud. But he remained standing. Swaying slightly. Like a cow asleep on its feet. Not aware it was in the abattoir.

"So he'd have to sell as much as he could, as fast as he could, then get the hell gone," said Amelia. "That's why it's not out yet. David doesn't want to sell it until he can sell it all. It must be in some basement. Some drug factory."

This David had marked her. To warn her off. Thinking she was just some newcomer junkie, making inquiries.

She might not know who David was, but he clearly had no idea who she was. And what she was capable of.

CHAPTER 30

⁓

Chief Superintendent Gamache was already there when Jean-Guy arrived at Isabelle Lacoste's home.

He joined them at the kitchen table.

They looked at each other, and then, in unison, all three said, "Tell me what you know."

"You first, Jean-Guy," said Gamache, smiling at his son-in-law and naturally taking charge.

Beauvoir told them quickly, succinctly, about his meeting with Bernice Ogilvy. And his thoughts as he drove over to meet them.

"Do you think it's . . . possible Baumgartner knew nothing about it?" asked Lacoste. "That someone else was stealing the client's . . . money and using his name?"

"And Baumgartner was killed because he found out?" said Beauvoir. "Follow the money. One of the first rules of homicide."

He looked at the Chief Superintendent. They'd spent much of their apprenticeship as agents watching Gamache break not the law but the so-called rules of homicide investigation. Which was why, as Beauvoir and Lacoste knew, his department had a near-perfect record of finding killers.

"Murderers haven't read the rule book," he'd told them. "And while money's important, there are other forms of currency. And poverty. A moral and emotional bankruptcy. Just as a rape isn't about sex, a murder is rarely about money, even when money's involved. It's about power. And fear. It's about revenge. And rage. It's about feelings, not a bank balance. Follow the money, certainly. But I can guarantee when you find it, it'll stink of some emotion gone putrid."

"Go on," Gamache now said to Beauvoir.

"It would sure be a good reason to kill Baumgartner," said Beauvoir. "Whoever was stealing from the clients was facing not just ruin but prison if Baumgartner exposed him."

"In killing Baumgartner he kept his wealth and freedom," said Lacoste. "Pretty good motive, I agree."

"And now," said Gamache, "pick it apart. What's wrong with that theory?"

Far from being annoyed at this challenge, Beauvoir found it one of his favorite things to do. He was very good at finding fault, even with his own theories. And this was far from a theory he owned or, as Madame Ogilvy would say, was invested in. It simply interested him.

"Okay," said Beauvoir. "If he wasn't stealing from his clients, then what were the statements doing in Baumgartner's study?"

"He'd just discovered what was happening," said Lacoste, taking on the devil's-advocate role, to Beauvoir's delight. "He was shocked and angry and needed to study them to make absolutely sure before accusing anyone."

"But how would he know, just from those papers, who was doing it? They only have his name on them."

"He's a smart man," said Lacoste. "He knows Taylor and Ogilvy and who was likely to be able to do it."

It was a weak argument, they recognized. One the devil would probably lose in court. But possible.

"And who would that be?" Gamache asked. It was unusual for him to interrupt this part of the process. He preferred to listen and absorb.

This showed he thought they just might be onto something.

"The broker doing the trades for him," suggested Beauvoir. "I'm having him brought in for questioning."

"And?"

"The obvious," said Jean-Guy. "Bernice Ogilvy."

"What did you make of her?" Gamache asked.

"She's young, bright. Got there because of her family, of course, but she has the skills and temperament to keep the job. She's smart. Ambitious. Adaptable."

"Greedy?" asked Gamache.

Beauvoir thought about that. "Entitled, maybe. I think she'd do just about anything to protect what's hers."

"Would she steal from clients and blame her former mentor?" asked Gamache.

Jean-Guy Beauvoir found himself coloring slightly at the mention of betraying a former mentor. And he wondered, fleetingly, whether Gamache could possibly know about the meeting that morning. And the paper he'd signed.

"She understood very quickly how it could be done," said Beauvoir. "Maybe too quickly. And she strikes me as the sort who thinks she's smarter than those around her."

"Probably . . . because she is," said Lacoste. "Besides, who really believes they're going to get caught? Madame Ogilvy knows the . . . business and knows how to get around any scrutiny."

"Just set up fake accounts," said Gamache. "It's so simple. No one at Taylor and Ogilvy would see them. And the clients would have no idea. They'd continue to get what looked like real statements, with real transactions. They'd have dividends and profits deposited in their accounts. All would look perfectly normal."

"Except she'd be putting the capital, their initial investment, into her own account," said Beauvoir. "And paying out generous so-called dividends to keep clients from asking any questions."

"Could they have been in it together?" Lacoste asked. "Ogilvy and Baumgartner?"

"Agent Cloutier suspects there'd have been two of them," said Beauvoir. "And don't forget, Baumgartner himself wasn't exactly splashing money around. He lived in the same house. Drove a decent but sensible car. Why would he steal and not spend the money?"

"Retirement," said Lacoste. "Squirreling it away in some offshore account. Then one day he disappears."

As Gamache listened, a series of photos in Baumgartner's home came to mind. Of Baumgartner and his children. Happy. Radiant, in fact. Was this the face of a man willing to turn his back and never see them again? Disappear to some Caribbean refuge? For what? A power boat and marble bathrooms?

"*Désolé*," said Gamache. "I've taken you off course. Back to the arguments. You were making the case for Anthony Baumgartner's finding out about the embezzlement and confronting whoever was doing it."

"Right," said Beauvoir, refocusing. "So he stumbles on what's happening. Maybe one of the so-called clients calls him or he runs into them at a party, and they ask about their account. An account he knows nothing about. Baumgartner does some digging, finds the fake statements, and brings the evidence home. He pores over them, then arranges to meet the person he suspects was—"

"Why?" Lacoste interrupted.

"Why what?"

"Why not just go to his manager?"

"Maybe the manager's the one who's doing it?" said Beauvoir.

"Then why not go to the industry regulator?" asked Lacoste.

"Because he's not sure," said Beauvoir, feeling his way along more slowly now. "Or he is sure and doesn't want to believe it. He wants to give this person a chance to explain or clear themselves. Or maybe he doesn't realize he's talking to the guilty party."

Gamache shifted in his chair and tilted his head.

This was interesting.

"Maybe he asked to meet someone he thinks will be an ally," said Beauvoir, gaining more confidence in this unexpected theory. "To show them the evidence and ask what they think."

"And the person kills him?" asked Lacoste. "Bit of an . . . overreaction. Can't the person just muddy the waters or send B- . . . Baumgartner off in the wrong direction? They must know that if they kill Baumgartner then the cops, aka us, will definitely be involved, and asking questions."

"Why?" asked Beauvoir, turning the tables on her.

"Why ask questions? It's kinda how we . . . solve murders, isn't it?" asked Lacoste.

Armand Gamache was watching this. Two smart young investigators, hashing out the most vile of crimes. His investigators. His protégés. Now more than capable of running whole departments on their own.

He missed this. Not simply sitting around kitchen tables trying to solve a murder. But doing it with these two. With Jean-Guy and Isabelle. Going at it like siblings.

"I know you prefer to just arrest the first person you meet in an . . . investigation," said Isabelle. "But the rest of us actually investigate."

"*Merci,*" said Beauvoir, smiling thinly and recognizing the patronizing tone as a ruse, an attempt by Isabelle to get under his skin. It worked more often than he was willing to show.

"But I meant why would we ask about an embezzlement?"

"Because"—now she sounded patient in the extreme—"the investigation would uncover it."

"But would it? I hope so, but it's far from a given, especially if Baumgartner had nothing to do with it," said Beauvoir. "Look, suppose Baumgartner was inadvertently meeting with the person who was actually responsible for the embezzlement—wouldn't he take along his evidence? Even if he was meeting with someone he suspected, he'd take it along. As proof."

"Right," said Lacoste, her voice guarded. Trying to see where this was going. "So?"

But Gamache could see and was smiling slightly.

"So that person would know two things," said Jean-Guy. "That there was nothing linking Baumgartner to the thefts. On his computer or files or anywhere. So any investigation into his death would reveal exactly nothing. And the killer would reasonably expect that whatever papers Baumgartner had with him were probably his only copies. Might even have asked, to make sure they were."

"So he'd kill Baumgartner and destroy the evidence," said Lacoste, forgetting to argue.

"Exactly."

Gamache waited to see if either of them would spot the flaw in that argument. He waited.

And waited.

"If those were his only proof," said Jean-Guy, "why were the statements found in his study?"

And there it was, thought Gamache. The problem.

If Baumgartner was meeting someone to either confide suspicions or confront them about the embezzlement, he'd take proof. And the person, after killing Baumgartner, would take that proof and burn it.

So why were there copies of the incriminating statements next to his computer?

And there was another problem with this theory.

"Why the farmhouse?" asked Lacoste.

Yes, thought Gamache. Why meet at the farmhouse?

"Familiar ground," suggested Beauvoir. "Maybe he was going to be there anyway, a final look around before it was torn down. Maybe the reading of the will brought up childhood memories and he wanted to visit. Convenience, coupled with the need to be in what he, even unconsciously, considered a safe place."

"At night? Without electricity or heat?" asked Lacoste.

Beauvoir nodded. Hugo had said they'd had dinner together. He'd left early, but still, it would have been dark.

"And why was he upstairs?" asked Lacoste.

"Looking around," said Beauvoir. "In his childhood bedroom."

It was credible, though hanging on to believability by a thread.

"Don't forget," said Beauvoir, "Baumgartner didn't expect to be killed. Either he thought he was meeting a friend, someone who'd help him, or he thought he'd be confronting someone. That it would be a shitty conversation. But he clearly didn't see this person as any physical threat. Or he'd never have agreed to meet him—"

"Or her," said Lacoste.

"—there."

"There's another problem," said Lacoste. "The convenience of the building falling down."

"But was it convenient?" asked Beauvoir. "It meant Baumgartner's body was found, maybe sooner than the killer expected. If it hadn't fallen, it's possible his body wouldn't have been found for a long time."

"I guess it's also possible Baumgartner didn't arrange to meet this person at the farmhouse," said Lacoste. "Maybe he was followed there and killed."

"What do you mean?" asked Beauvoir.

"Suppose Baumgartner got in touch with the person he suspected and arranged to . . . meet them the next day, at the office. The person, knowing they were in trouble, drives over to Anthony Baumgartner's . . . home, maybe to kill him there, but then sees him leaving. He follows him to the abandoned house and kills him there."

"Bit convenient for the killer, *non?*" asked Beauvoir.

"But it fits, and it explains the timing, with the will," said Lacoste, warming to her just-discovered theory. She turned to Gamache. "You and Myrna and Benedict read them their mother's will. While . . . ridiculous, it was very much the Baroness. It stirs feelings of childhood, and Anthony decides to drive out and see the old . . . place before it's torn down or sold."

Beauvoir snorted, but Gamache tilted his head. He drove, every now and then, past the house he grew up in. And after Reine-Marie's mother died and before they sold the family home, she'd wanted one last walk around.

What Lacoste was describing was emotionally valid. Though Beauvoir was also right. It did seem a bit too convenient for the murderer. That Baumgartner would just happen to be in a remote farmhouse, designed for quiet murder.

"*Bon*," he said. "Let's move on to the more likely theory. That Anthony Baumgartner not only knew about the money being stolen but was responsible. Who killed him then?"

"One of his targets," said Beauvoir. "Someone who found out."

"But why kill him? Why not just tell someone at his company or, better still, go to the police?" asked Lacoste.

"Because the company had been told once and nothing happened to him," said Beauvoir. "A slap on the wrist. Why trust Taylor and Ogilvy to do something this time, when they did nothing last time?"

"Okay, but my question stands," said Lacoste. "Why not go to the police or a lawyer? Why not sue his . . . ass? Why confront Baumgartner?"

"Because they weren't sure," said Beauvoir. "Most people can't believe someone they trust is stealing. They'd ask first, and if they didn't like the answer, then they'd take the next step."

"Right," said Lacoste. "A lawyer or the police. Plan B surely isn't to kill the guy. But you're saying that's what . . . happened. What would that achieve?"

"It was a bang on the head," said Beauvoir. "Has the makings of a sudden rage, not something planned out. As much as Baumgartner didn't expect to be killed, I'm betting whoever did this didn't expect to kill."

Gamache was listening. But there remained one big problem with that theory. A familiar one.

"Why the farmhouse?" Lacoste asked. "Would Baumgartner really agree to meet a client, someone he was stealing from, there? Even if he didn't know . . . what it was about, that's a long way to go. Out in the middle of nowhere. And a pretty personal space. I just don't buy it."

Gamache was listening to this and thinking that it wasn't so easy to find a place to kill someone. Even in rural Québec. A forest would make sense, but how do you lure a client, who's already suspicious, into the woods?

"Come on," said Lacoste, following the same line of thought. "Would the client really agree to meet in an isolated, abandoned home? I wouldn't."

"Why not?" Beauvoir turned to Gamache. "You did. When you got the letter from the notary."

Gamache gave a short laugh. "True, but I wasn't going there to confront someone. And I didn't realize it was abandoned until I got there."

"And there you have it," said Beauvoir. "The client who's being screwed wouldn't know either. He'd gone that far, and I'm sure Baumgartner explained it was his mother's house. It sounded okay. Safe."

It was possible, thought Gamache. But far from probable. Though it did explain why those statements were still in Baumgartner's study. He was doing the stealing. And the killing. And he expected to be home.

"So," said Lacoste. "We have two theories. That Anthony Baumgartner was doing the stealing and that he wasn't."

"Doesn't feel like progress to me," admitted Beauvoir.

"Let's move from theories to facts," said Gamache.

"*D'accord*," said Beauvoir, putting a slip of paper on the kitchen table. "I have information on the assistant who was fired. His name's Bernard Shaeffer. Taylor and Ogilvy had his address from when he worked for them, but nothing since."

"Bernard Shaeffer," repeated Lacoste. She took the paper and entered his name in her laptop. "His address is the same," she said, reading from the government files. "Looks like he's now working for the . . . Caisse Populaire du Québec."

She looked over the screen of her laptop at her colleagues. Her brows rose.

"A bank?" asked Jean-Guy. "The Caisse hired him after what he did at Taylor and Ogilvy?"

"Let me make a quick call," said Gamache, picking up his iPhone.

He dialed, waited, then gave his name and asked for Jeanne Halstrom. The president of the Caisse Populaire. After inquiring about her family, he asked a few other questions, listened, thanked her, then hung up.

"Bernard Shaeffer was hired as a financial adviser eighteen months ago. He had Anthony Baumgartner down as a reference. According to the personnel file, Monsieur Baumgartner vouched for him and said he'd been an outstanding employee. They'll start an investigation into Shaeffer's activities, including if he's set up any unusually large accounts in his or Baumgartner's name. We'll need a warrant, but she'll get things started."

"We might've just found out where the client's money went," said Beauvoir. "Looks like Baumgartner didn't break off contact with Bernard. Just the opposite."

"He wouldn't be so stupid as to have the accounts in his own name, would he?" asked Isabelle.

"We'll find out," said Gamache. "Even if it's offshore, the Caisse can probably track Shaeffer's activity."

"And I'll go visit young Monsieur Shaeffer right after this." Beauvoir thought for a moment. "Better still, I'll have Agent Cloutier bring him in for questioning."

He made a call, then hung up. "She's on her way."

"Good," said Isabelle. "She's found her . . . footing?"

"Yes. Finally. But she's frustrated about not being able to get into Baumgartner's laptop and get at his personal files. We all are. We're still trying, of course. Put in the names of his children, and his mother. And father. All the obvious ones."

"Maybe it's not a name," said Gamache, "but a number."

"We've tried the children's birth dates. His birthday. But you asked for facts, *patron*. There is something else I found out from Bernice Ogilvy," said Beauvoir. "Not about Baumgartner this time. It's about

287

Kinderoth. An elderly couple by that name had an account at Taylor and Ogilvy."

There was a beat while they took that in.

"With Baumgartner?" asked Lacoste.

"*Non.*"

She deflated a bit. It was probably too much to ask.

But Gamache was leaning forward. He knew Jean-Guy well. Very well. And he could see this wasn't some aside. This was, perhaps, the main course.

"Go on," he said.

And Beauvoir told them what Madame Ogilvy had said about the Kinderoths. And their will.

Beauvoir watched for their reaction and wasn't disappointed. Gamache smiled, and Lacoste was almost throbbing with excitement.

The three sat around the kitchen table, as they'd sat around so many tables, across Québec, across the years. Sipping strong teas and coffees and discussing terrible crimes.

So much had changed over time, but the core remained the same.

Beauvoir thought about the question Bernice Ogilvy had asked. Did he love his job? The answer, he knew for certain, was yes. And it wasn't just his job he loved.

Chief Superintendent Gamache sat back, a look of extreme concentration on his face. Then he brought a notebook out of his breast pocket.

"This came in last night," he said. "From Kontrollinspektor Gund in Vienna. I'd asked him to look up that original will."

"The one going back a hundred years," said Isabelle.

"A hundred and thirty. Baron Kinderoth, Shlomo, had two sons, twins," Gamache reminded them. "He left them each the entirety of his estate. We'll probably never know why he did it, but we can see the effect it had. It clearly caused hurt and confusion. Who inherited? I asked the Kontrollinspektor if he could do some searching through their records. This's what he sent back."

He put on his glasses while Beauvoir and Lacoste leaned closer.

"I won't read it verbatim," said Gamache. "My translation is pretty bad, but I think I got the gist of it. I've sent it on to an acquaintance who does speak German, but in the meantime this'll have to do. Both sons took it to court, of course, and after a few years it was decided in favor of one son, the one deemed the firstborn of the twins. By then both men had themselves died, and the heirs of the other son contested the decision. Because of the complexity and confusion over who was really firstborn, the case lingered. It took another few years to be heard and another few years for a decision. This time it was in favor of the supposed younger son. He worked in the family firm, and the first seems to have been, in the words of the court, a rotter."

"How long out from Shlomo Kinderoth's death did this happen?" asked Lacoste.

"That decision for the younger son, and now his heirs, was thirty years after Shlomo's death. Again the family of the older son contested the decision."

"And the money?" asked Beauvoir.

"It remained in trust," said Gamache. "Growing, but not dispersed."

Lacoste did a quick calculation. "Thirty years. That would put that decision around 1915."

"Exactly," said Gamache. "World War One. According to records the Kontrollinspektor found, much of the family was killed, at least the young men. Austria was in turmoil. It wasn't until the 1930s that the family took another run at it. By then the descendants of one of the sons had become Baumgartners, through marriage. And had since moved to Canada. Montréal. The Kinderoths stayed in Austria."

"Oh dear," said Lacoste.

"*Oui*," said Gamache. "All I have are the court records. That's all I asked for, and I'm not sure if more detailed accounts are possible, but it does seem that at least one Kinderoth survived the Nazis and came to Montréal after the war. There might be others still in Europe somewhere. Kontrollinspektor Gund is looking."

"Why Canada?" asked Beauvoir.

"Not just Canada," Lacoste pointed out, "but Montréal."

"Where the Baumgartners had settled," said Gamache. "It cannot be a coincidence."

"Were they looking for family?" asked Lacoste. "After what happened, maybe distant and even unpleasant family was better than none. It might be instinctive."

"It's possible," said Gamache. "But I think by then their instincts had warped and something else motivated them. Shortly after the war

289

ended, another petition was filed in the Austrian courts. For the Kinderoth fortune."

"My God," said Lacoste. "Don't they ever give up?"

"Was there even a fortune left?" asked Beauvoir.

"I doubt it," said Gamache, "but they wouldn't know that. I think they were still going on family lore."

"Or maybe they knew something the authorities didn't," said Lacoste. "Some Jewish families managed to convert their money into art, or jewelry, or gold, didn't they? And then hid it or smuggled it out of the country."

"Yes," said Gamache. "But neither the Kinderoths nor the Baumgartners could get at the money. It was held in trust. And the Nazi regime would've confiscated it. Stolen it."

"So they've been fighting over nothing?" asked Beauvoir. "All these years?"

"Nothing tangible anyway," said Gamache. "But who knows? It was there once, so I suppose there's a possibility—"

He left it hanging.

"And now?" asked Lacoste, looking down at the notebook and the careful writing there.

"And now, according to Kontrollinspektor Gund, a final decision is about to come down in the Austrian courts."

"When?" asked Beauvoir.

"Anytime now. According to Gund, it's been expected for a year or so, but there's a backlog, of course, of lawsuits dating from the war. They're getting through them slowly."

"This slowly?" asked Beauvoir. "Most of the people who brought them would be long dead."

"Their descendants would benefit," said Gamache. "And the Austrians want to be very careful. To be as fair as possible, especially about anything to do with the Jewish population and what was stolen. They can't, of course, undo the Holocaust, but they can try to make reparations."

"Why don't the Kinderoths and Baumgartners just decide to divide it equally?" asked Lacoste. "This would've been settled generations ago."

"Maybe you want to suggest it to them," said Jean-Guy, and he got a glare from Isabelle.

"Up until now it's been unpleasant but civil," said Isabelle. "Do we really think Anthony Baumgartner's death—"

"And maybe his mother's," said Beauvoir. "She died suddenly and then was cremated."

"*Oui*," said Lacoste. "Okay. Maybe the Baroness too. But do we really think they were murdered because of a century-old will?"

"One that was about to be settled," said Gamache.

"And contested again," said Beauvoir.

"*Non.* The courts have said they won't tolerate another appeal. They have too many old cases to go through to keep retrying the same one."

"So whoever wins could inherit a fortune," said Lacoste.

"Real or imagined," said Gamache. And this seemed, he thought, a family rich in imagination. Clinging on to the myth of aristocracy and power and wealth, even as they drove cabs and cleaned toilets.

Beauvoir shook his head.

Why kill Anthony Baumgartner now? Did they think Caroline and Hugo had murdered their brother for a larger stake in a fictional inheritance?

He'd met these people. They seemed intelligent. And no intelligent person would believe in the fairy tale of an old fortune that had somehow survived wars and pogroms and the Holocaust to come to them now.

And suppose the other arm of the family won? The Kinderoths? What then? A fratricide for nothing?

The three of them stared into space. Thinking. Trying to see through the tangle of time and motives.

Gamache looked at his watch. He was meeting Benedict in downtown Montréal in twenty minutes. He'd have to be leaving soon to make the rendezvous.

"And there's still the issue of the liquidators of Madame Baumgartner's will," he said.

"Very suspicious lot," Beauvoir said to Lacoste, who nodded agreement.

Gamache smiled patiently. "We don't know why Myrna and I were on it, but we at least have some connection through Three Pines, where the Baroness worked. But are we any closer to knowing why Benedict was a liquidator?"

"Not at all," said Lacoste, who'd been charged with finding out. "There seems absolutely no connection. He never worked in the area. He never met her. How Madame Baumgartner even knew he existed, never mind trusted him enough to put him on the will, is a mystery."

"Dead end?" asked Beauvoir, needling her.

"Never," said Lacoste. "There's a reason, and I'll find it. I plan on speaking with his ex. This Katie might know something or remember something he'd forgotten. I've never met him, but by your description Benedict does seem pretty scatterbrained."

Once again Armand felt the body of the young man on his back. As Benedict protected him from falling debris.

And then, when the worst was over and he could straighten up, Armand had looked, through grit-clogged eyes, at the young man in the silly hat. With blood streaming down his face. From a chunk of concrete that would almost certainly, Armand knew, have struck him.

It was an act of extreme selflessness. And instinct. It spoke of Benedict's good heart, though it was no use denying that his brain was perhaps not the sharpest.

Gamache got up. "I've got to go meet him. He's giving me a lift back to Three Pines. I'm probably late already."

"Can I drive you over?" Jean-Guy asked as they walked to the front door.

"If you don't mind."

Beauvoir went down the outside stairs to start the car.

Gamache thanked Isabelle. And she thanked him.

"What for?" he asked.

"For this. For not leaving me behind."

"Never." He kissed her on both cheeks, then walked carefully down the flight of icy steps. But at the bottom he stopped. Dead.

Then, as Beauvoir watched from the warming car, Armand turned and raced back up the stairs, taking them two at a time. Shouting to Isabelle.

Beauvoir got out of the car and was halfway up the stairs himself when Gamache emerged from Isabelle's home.

"What is it? What's happened?" Jean-Guy asked.

"What was the name," Gamache asked, his voice brusque, "of the young woman who was at the top of the contact list for Madame Baumgartner?"

As he spoke, he came down the stairs quickly, faster than he probably should have.

"In the seniors' home?" asked Beauvoir. "I can't remember."

"Can you find it?"

"I can find my notes."

"Great," said Gamache as he got into the passenger seat. "Give them to me, please."

Beauvoir handed them over, then drove as Gamache turned on the reading light and scanned, not even bothering to put on his glasses. After a couple minutes, he lowered the notes, wiped his eyes, and stared out the windshield.

"Katie Burke," he said.

"Yes, that's it," said Beauvoir. He glanced over at Gamache. "What is it?"

Something had happened.

"I asked Isabelle for the full name of Benedict's girlfriend—"

"Katie Burke," guessed Beauvoir, and he saw Gamache nod. "Holy shit," exhaled Beauvoir. "Benedict's girlfriend not only knew the Baroness but was her first contact?"

He was elated, but as he shot a look at Gamache, he could see that far from being triumphant at finding this unexpected connection, Gamache was subdued.

There was silence as they drove through the now-dark streets of the city, and both men considered what this might mean.

When he pulled over to drop Gamache off, Beauvoir said, "Benedict lied."

"Yes."

"Do you want me there when you speak with him, *patron*?"

"No, that's not necessary. You have a lot to do. Isabelle said she'd find out all she can about Katie Burke and report back to you."

"Well, at least we now know how Benedict got onto Madame Baumgartner's will," said Beauvoir. "But we don't know why."

"We will," said Gamache, his voice clipped.

It was going to be, Beauvoir thought, a very long drive back to Three Pines, for both Gamache and the young man.

It was never a good idea to lie to the Chief.

Jean-Guy headed off for his interview with Bernard Shaeffer, who even now was waiting in an interview room at Sûreté headquarters.

Gamache stood on the sidewalk, scanning for Benedict. The warmth of the drive over slid off him as the biting cold seeped up the cuffs of his sleeves and down his collar and settled against the exposed skin of his face.

But he felt none of that. He was staring ahead. Thinking. Trying to bridge the chasm between what he knew and what he felt.

"Chief Superintendent" came a familiar voice, and Gamache turned to see Hugo Baumgartner approaching. "You look deep in thought," said the ugly little man.

A thick winter coat, a tuque, and cheeks ruddy with cold did nothing to improve Baumgartner's appearance.

But his eyes were bright and his deep voice warm.

"I was."

"Can I help you with anything?"

"No, I'm just waiting for my lift, *merci*."

"Would you like to wait inside?" Hugo waved behind him, toward the office building he'd just come from. The head office of Horowitz Investments.

"No, I'm fine. Thank you."

But Hugo didn't leave. He stood beside Gamache, shifting from cold foot to cold foot. And thumping his gloved hands together. He looked like a lug, a pug, a failed boxer who made a living being beaten up by his betters in practice rounds.

Gamache turned to him. Clearly Hugo had something to say.

"I hear you had lunch with Mr. Horowitz."

"I did," said Gamache. "How'd you know about that?"

"Ahh, the street. Everyone knows everything. For instance, I know that during lunch Stephen approached that moron Filatreau and told him he was dumping his stock."

"True. Do you know what Monsieur Filatreau had for lunch?"

It was meant as a joke, but Hugo answered, "Sweetbreads. And you had sea bass."

Gamache's smile faded, and he nodded. The street, it seemed, was well informed.

"What else do you know, Monsieur Baumgartner?"

"I know you asked about my brother and that Stephen said he was a crook. Mr. Horowitz is a financial genius and a good judge of character. But he isn't always right. He likes to imagine the worst in people. His worldview is that everyone's a crook. Or about to be."

"He spoke highly of you."

"Well, maybe I have him fooled," said Hugo. "My brother was a good man. He wouldn't steal. Word's spreading that that's why he was killed. You have to find out who did this, please. It's bad enough what happened. Anthony's reputation can't be ruined too."

"What do you know about the will?"

"My mother's? Just what you do. That she believed the hokum about some long-lost family fortune that was really ours. It was amusing to us as kids but grew tiresome."

"And yet when we were reading the will, and your brother and sister seemed embarrassed by it, you defended your mother."

"Her, yes, but not the will."

"As I remember, you did defend it, saying you thought maybe she was right."

Hugo looked around and again shifted from foot to foot. "I loved my mother and hated when anyone mocked her. Even Tony and Caroline."

"You're a loyal man."

"Is that such a bad thing?"

"Not at all. I admire it. But loyalty can blind us to the truth about people. Though, as it turns out, your mother might've actually been right."

"What do you mean?"

Hugo had stopped shifting and stared at Gamache.

"I think you know exactly what I mean, monsieur. Think about it, and call me when you decide you do know."

He gave Hugo a card.

Just then Gamache saw Benedict draw up in his Volvo. It was rush hour and dark, and it didn't take long for other cars to start honking at Benedict, who was gesturing at Gamache to hurry.

"There's one more thing," said Gamache. "Who's Katie Burke?"

"Who?"

"It's cold, and my ride is about to be murdered by other drivers, so just tell me. You know I know."

"Then why ask?"

"To see just how truthful you decide to be. So far you're not doing well."

"I've told you the truth about my brother."

"Did you?"

There was a pause, and all they could hear were more horns joining in, a veritable shriek of rage from rue Sherbrooke. Directed at Benedict.

"Who is Katie Burke, Monsieur Baumgartner?"

"She used to visit the Baroness in the nursing home."

"Why?"

"I don't know. But Mom liked her, and it sort of relieved us of some responsibility, I'm ashamed to say."

"She was at the top of your mother's contact list."

"Was she?"

"You didn't know?"

By now Benedict had lowered the window of the Volvo and was pleading with Armand to get in.

Hugo shook his head. "Does it matter?"

"Would I ask if it didn't?" Armand gestured toward the card in Hugo's gloved hand. "Your mother's will, Monsieur Baumgartner. Give me a call when you decide to tell the whole story. Don't wait too long."

He walked to the car and waved at the line of cars behind Benedict. More than one driver raised a finger in return.

"Thank God," said Benedict, exhaling and pulling into traffic. "Who was that? Looked like you were speaking with something from *Lord of the Rings*."

"Hugo Baumgartner."

"Oh right. I didn't recognize him."

Armand buckled up, and as they headed over the Champlain Bridge, he found himself humming under his breath.

"'Edelweiss, Edelweiss . . .'"

CHAPTER 31

—◡—

Bernard Shaeffer sat in the spartan interview room at Sûreté headquarters. Looking around. Crossing and recrossing his legs. Trying to get comfortable on a metal chair that would never allow it.

Chief Inspector Beauvoir looked through the two-way mirror.

"Did he say anything on the ride over?"

"*Non, patron*," said Cloutier. "Only asked if this was anything to do with the death of Anthony Baumgartner."

"And what did you say?"

"Nothing. Here's his iPhone."

She handed Beauvoir the device. It was now the first thing they did with suspects. Relieve them of their devices, so they couldn't contact anyone or delete anything.

Monsieur Shaeffer was not what Beauvoir expected. He'd been prepared for a young buck. Someone sharp. Attractive.

Not this average-looking, nervous young guy wearing a good but not exceptional suit.

Though, Beauvoir dropped his eyes and noticed Shaeffer's shoes. Pointy and on point. Completely of the moment.

Fashionable and expensive.

Jean-Guy knew. He too tried to be fashionable but could not afford this level of expense.

While suggestive, it was far from definitive. Some people bought expensive cars. Some spent their money on vacations. And some single young men spent their money on clothes.

It did not mean Shaeffer was living beyond his means. Or was a thief.

"Right," said Beauvoir. "Come with me."

Cloutier followed him into the interview room, where Beauvoir introduced himself.

"My name's Jean-Guy Beauvoir. I'm the acting head of homicide. You've met Agent Cloutier."

This was said for both Shaeffer and the recording.

They took seats, Beauvoir across from the young man.

"Thank you for coming in. We just have a few questions for you."

"About Tony?"

"Mostly, yes." Beauvoir's tone was friendly. "Tell us about your relationship with him."

"We worked in the same office. Taylor and Ogilvy. This was a few years ago. I was an assistant, and Monsieur Baumgartner was a senior vice president."

Shaeffer was watching Beauvoir closely and seemed to come to a decision.

"We had an affair. And then I was fired."

"Why?"

He'd made it sound as though it was because of the affair.

"You might as well tell us, Bernard." Beauvoir smiled encouragingly. "You must know we've already visited Taylor and Ogilvy."

"I was accused of stealing from clients' accounts. But I didn't do it."

"Then why would they fire you?"

"They had to blame someone, didn't they?"

"If you weren't doing it, who was?"

Shaeffer hesitated.

"Come on, Bernard. The truth. It's all right. Just tell us."

"Monsieur Baumgartner."

"Anthony Baumgartner?"

"Yes."

"But if he was stealing, why would he go to Madame Ogilvy and tell her about it?"

"He thought they were going to find out, so he went and blamed me."

"His lover."

Shaeffer nodded.

"What did you do?"

"What could I do?"

300

"I don't know. Tell the truth?"

Shaeffer laughed. "Right. Me against a senior vice president. Let's guess who they'd believe."

"So you just left?" asked Beauvoir, and when Shaeffer nodded, Jean-Guy stared at him for a long moment. "Then why did you put Anthony Baumgartner down as a reference at the Caisse Pop?"

Shaeffer reddened. Clearly they knew far more than he realized.

"Tony told me if I kept quiet, he'd find me a job at the Caisse and vouch for me."

"So you accepted?"

"What choice did I have? If I refused, I'd be thrown out on my ass anyway. I was pretty well screwed."

An agent walked into the interview room and whispered in Beauvoir's ear, then left.

"So," said Beauvoir, "you're saying Anthony Baumgartner was stealing and you were completely innocent?"

Shaeffer straightened up. "Well, okay, I knew what he was doing. But I wasn't involved."

"He told you?"

"He'd had too much to drink. He was relaxed, and he talked too much. He knew I wouldn't tell anyone."

"Why wouldn't you?"

"Because I cared for him. A lot."

"And?" said Beauvoir.

There was silence again as Shaeffer fidgeted. "And he said if I told anyone, he'd say it was me, not him."

"Which he did anyway."

"Yes."

Beauvoir studied the unremarkable young man.

"Were you ever in his home?"

"Once. He wanted help putting up a picture his mother had given him. I think it might've been of her. She looked kinda crazy. Anyway, we hung it above the fireplace in his study and then had a few drinks. He asked for help setting up his new laptop, so we had a few more drinks, then fiddled with the computer for a while and got sorta giddy—"

"Did you get the laptop working?" said Beauvoir.

"Yes."

"And did he put in a security code?"

"Yes. I remember because it took him a while to come up with one. He said he was running out of ideas for new codes."

"And do you remember the code?"

The question was asked casually, but the room crackled with the tension between the Sûreté officers.

"No idea. He didn't tell me."

"Did he hint? Say anything?" prodded Beauvoir.

Shaeffer thought. "If he did, I can't remember."

"Did you sneak a peek? Look over his shoulder when he entered it?"

"Of course not."

"'Of course'? Come on, Bernard. We all do it. Just out of curiosity. Did you watch while he put it in?"

"No."

"Then what did you do?"

"Huh?"

"In the study, while Monsieur Baumgartner put in his password, what did you do?"

"I stared at the picture. I don't know why anyone in their right mind would have that thing in their home."

Beauvoir considered. It could be true. That painting of Ruth was as riveting as it was revolting. As Clara herself said, it was hard to look away.

But this was a sharp young man, and given a choice between finding out the password to a laptop and looking at the picture of a mad old woman, Beauvoir was pretty sure he knew which one Bernard Shaeffer would choose.

"What happened next?" Beauvoir asked.

"We got drunk and had sex."

"For the first time?"

"Yes. We'd been sorta feeling each other out, but I wasn't sure he was gay. But he kept sending these signals, and then—"

"What was he like?" asked Beauvoir.

"As a lover?"

"As a man."

Shaeffer considered the question. "Kind. Smart. Decent. I thought."

"Until he blamed you for stealing and got you fired."

"Yes."

"When he got you the job at the bank, did he ask for any favors?"

"Like what?"

Beauvoir stared at him for a moment, then stood up.

"I'll let you think about that. Excuse me."

Beauvoir nodded to Agent Cloutier, and they went out, leaving Shaeffer to stare at the slowly closing door. Then at the blank wall across from him.

The ice fog that looked pretty when stuck like crystals to branches was a lot less attractive when it settled onto the roads. And then was covered by the soft snow falling.

Benedict and Gamache made small talk, as Benedict drove carefully back to Three Pines, watching for black ice on the highway.

They talked about their day. About the weather.

Benedict asked about Gamache's eyes.

"Better, thank you. I'm seeing much more clearly."

They'd lapsed into what appeared to be companionable silence.

But appearances deceived.

Once again Chief Inspector Beauvoir introduced himself and Agent Cloutier, then sat down in the interview room.

"You are Louis Lamontagne?"

"I am."

"And you work for Taylor and Ogilvy as a broker?"

"I do."

He was forty-five, maybe slightly older, thought Beauvoir. Plump but not heavy. Just a little soft. "Comfortable" was the word that came to mind. His hair was trimmed and graying.

He looked upright. Intelligent. Conservative in every way. If "trustworthy" had a poster child, it would be the man across the table, thought Beauvoir.

And he wondered if he was looking at another numbered print. Close, but not the real thing.

"You did Anthony Baumgartner's trades for him, I understand."

"Yes."

"How does that work?"

"Well, Tony was a wealth manager, so he created portfolios for his clients. Given their age, their needs, their tolerance for risk, he'd decide which vehicles to put them into. Then he'd ask me to do the actual buying and selling."

"And that was fine with you?"

"Absolutely. More than fine. He was a brilliant investment adviser. To be honest, if he bought a stock, I'd often put my own clients into it. He had a knack for seeing how apparently unconnected elements came together and could affect the market. It's a terrible loss. A really sad thing to happen to a fine man. Do you have any ideas who did it?"

"We're hoping you can help."

"Anything."

Beauvoir slid the statements across the table and watched as Monsieur Lamontagne picked them up.

After a minute or so, Beauvoir saw his brows rise, then draw together in concentration and consternation. His blue eyes blinked behind his glasses, and his head leaned to one side. Just a little. Perplexed.

"None of these people are on Tony's client list. I didn't do any of these trades." He looked at Beauvoir over the papers. "I don't understand."

"I think you do."

Lamontagne went back to the statements, going from one to another and rereading the cover letter.

"I can guess," he said, finally putting them back down on the table. "But I can't explain."

"Try."

Louis Lamontagne held Beauvoir's eyes, in a look that was smart, assessing.

"I think you already know," the broker said.

Beauvoir held the gaze but said nothing and saw Lamontagne's eyes open in surprise.

"You think I had something to do with this."

"What is 'this,' monsieur?" asked Beauvoir.

Watching closely, Agent Cloutier took mental notes. On what the

Chief Inspector was saying and not saying. How to imply. How intimating became intimidating. It was subtle, and all the more powerful for it.

In her previous assignment, in the accounting department, she never ended up in interview rooms.

This she found fascinating.

It took nerves, she saw. And intense concentration, while appearing to be completely relaxed. Her instinct was to come out with things. To show how much she knew. Now she could see the value of saying very little. And letting the other person come to their own conclusions about how much was known. Let their fears take hold and take control.

"'This,'" said the broker, "is a scam. Someone set up a shell and made it appear to be Taylor and Ogilvy business."

"Someone?"

"I know you want me to say it was Tony, but it could've been anyone."

"Including yourself?" It was said casually, with a touch of humor.

Lamontagne smiled, but his color betrayed him. "I supposed I could have, but I didn't."

Beauvoir waited.

"All right, I admit, it looks like it was Tony. His name's on the statement and the cover letter."

"With Taylor and Ogilvy letterhead," said Beauvoir. "The clients would think their money was being managed through the company, but in fact he was stealing it and paying out generous dividends to keep them from asking questions."

Lamontagne nodded, staring at Beauvoir. "Yes. Exactly." He picked up the paper again. "Tony must've chosen people he knew weren't plugged into the market. Who almost certainly never read the business pages or the statements."

"Does this surprise you?" asked Beauvoir.

Lamontagne shifted in his chair.

"I'd have to say it does."

"But you've heard the rumors about Monsieur Baumgartner."

"I know his license to trade was pulled. That's why I was asked to do his trading for him. That's a serious penalty. I'd heard it's because

305

he was involved in something with clients' money. But not directly. Apparently it was an assistant who did it, and Tony was the one who blew the whistle. And took some of the blame. The street loves a rumor, and a scandal, and especially loves a fall from a great height, even if it's unfair. Especially if it's unfair."

"You make the street sound like it's a machine," said Beauvoir. "And not brokers like yourself."

"I wasn't involved in those rumors."

"But did you do anything to stop them?"

"I didn't feed them."

It wasn't the same as stopping them. As defending Tony Baumgartner.

"Did you think there was truth to the rumors?" asked Beauvoir.

"I saw no reason to believe them," said Lamontagne.

"Did you see any reason not to believe them?"

"This business is made up of more than its fair share of wide boys." When Beauvoir looked puzzled, he explained. "Mostly young men desperate to make a killing. Make a mark. They throw money around, they talk loud. They have all sorts of theories about investing that sound good but are bullshit. They genuinely think they're brilliant. And their confidence convinces clients to invest with them. They're snake-oil salesmen, and most don't even realize they have no idea what they're doing."

"And Anthony Baumgartner was one of them?"

"No, that's what I'm saying. He wasn't. And from what I saw, he didn't tolerate it. That's why he turned that young fellow in. He must've known there'd be blowback and some of the shit would land on him. And it did. More than he probably realized."

"So how do you explain this?"

Beauvoir placed his index finger on the statement.

Lamontagne stared at it and sighed. "He was in his mid-fifties. He'd been screwed over by the company. A company he'd helped build. By a woman he'd mentored. He'd been made an example of. Humiliated. It's possible he saw a bleak future and decided to hell with it. If that's what came of decency, maybe it was time to be indecent."

Beauvoir saw another set of documents, pushed toward him. Across a sleek boardroom table. And he saw himself signing. Was he so very different from Anthony Baumgartner? Disillusioned. And now indecent.

"But if that was the case," Lamontagne went on, "I never saw it. In all the trades I did for him, he was smart and fair. Often brilliant and prescient. He made his clients a lot of money."

"You're of course talking about the clients he wasn't stealing from," said Beauvoir.

The broker hesitated, then nodded. "Yes. I honestly thought he was one of the good guys." He smiled. It was more wistful than amused. "There's a book we're all told to read when we first get into the business. Tony gave me his copy as a thank-you gift when I agreed to use my license to do his trades. It's called *Extraordinary Popular Delusions and The Madness of Crowds*. I guess we're all deluded at times."

"Could Monsieur Baumgartner have set that up"—Beauvoir pointed to the statements—"by himself, or would he need help?"

"No, he could do it himself. It would take organization, but I suspect he started small, then grew it. All he'd need is a hidden account and to choose his targets wisely."

"People who wouldn't see," said Beauvoir.

"People who wouldn't question, Chief Inspector. And there are a lot of those."

Lamontagne looked at the statement on the table. A few slender sheets of paper, but, like Madame Ogilvy that afternoon, the broker could see what they meant.

Ruin.

This scandal would kill Taylor and Ogilvy. And throw them all out of work. And maybe Anthony Baumgartner would, in death, have his revenge.

Beauvoir thanked Monsieur Lamontagne and made his way back along the corridor to the interview room where Bernard Shaeffer waited.

Delusion and madness, he thought as he reentered the room. There was a lot of both in this case.

It was close. Amelia could feel it.

Even those around her, the junkies, the whores, the trannies who'd been drawn to her, could feel it. They couldn't feel their fingers and toes. Their faces were numb and ravaged.

They'd lost all compassion. All good sense. Even their anger and despair were gone. They'd lost their families, and they'd lost their minds.

But this they could feel.

Something big was coming.

It didn't yet even have a street name. Whoever controlled it would get naming rights. For now it was just "it." Or "the new shit." And that seemed to only add to the excitement, the mystique.

Amelia knew what "it" was.

Carfentanil.

She also knew that whoever had it, whoever controlled the carfentanil, would win. And Amelia was determined to win.

But time was short. Once it hit the street, it was out of her hands.

Amelia stood at the window, but the view was obscured by thick frost and grime, so that all she saw were blurry streetlights.

Though she couldn't see them, she knew they were out there. Waiting for her.

The junkies and whores and trannies. Who'd turned to her for protection. Because she had muscle on her bones and a brain not completely fried. And she could see around corners. What was hiding. What was waiting. What was coming.

They slept in the corridor outside Marc's room, armed with guns and knives, and some had clubs, and waited for her to come out. And lead them.

Their eyes glowed in ways their mothers would never recognize.

They had nothing to lose and one thing to find. It.

Out there somewhere, in the hollowed-out core of Montréal, there was a factory cutting and recutting the drug. And this David knew where it was.

If she wanted to find it, she'd have to first find him.

"So, Sweet Pea," said Marc as they prepared to leave. "What're you going to call it?"

"What?"

They'd stepped out of his room, and Amelia saw, up and down the dingy hallway, skeletons struggling to stand on pin legs. On feet clad in boots stolen from corpses of friends who'd OD'd.

Bodies. Pale. Frozen. Picked up by dark vans and taken to lie on autopsy tables, then in drawers. Unnamed. Unclaimed. By mothers and fathers, sisters and brothers, who'd spend the rest of their lives wondering whatever became of their bright-eyed child.

"It. The shit," said Marc. "Ha. It rhymes. It the shit."

Amelia had to smile. She thought her favorite poet, Ruth Zardo, would like that little morsel. It the shit.

"When you find it, you'll have naming rights," said Marc. His eyes were unfocused and his words indistinct. Mumbled. His lips and tongue no longer able to work properly. He shuffled and muttered like an old man after a stroke. He put his arm around her shoulders. "Dragon. Wicked. Suicide. Something terrifying. Kids like that."

She felt, even through his winter coat, his bones.

There was hardly anything to him anymore. He was being eaten alive. Consumed from the inside out. They all were.

Except Amelia. At least not so that it was visible. But still she wondered if her mother would recognize her anymore. Or claim her as her own.

Beauvoir took his seat across from Bernard Shaeffer and smiled.

"Tell me."

"What?"

"No more games," said Beauvoir, his tone cold but calm. "Baumgartner set you up at the Caisse Populaire, a bank, for a reason. Now I want that reason."

"I don't—"

"Tell me."

"There's—"

"Tell me," Beauvoir snapped. "Where do you think I was just now?"

Shaeffer looked from Beauvoir to Agent Cloutier, his eyes wide. He clearly hadn't given it any thought. Now he did.

"I don't know—"

"I was next door, in another interview room." Beauvoir glared at him. "Asking questions and getting answers. Now I'm giving you a chance. Answer the question. What did Baumgartner want from you?"

There was silence.

"Now," shouted Beauvoir, bringing his open hand down on the table with such force that Shaeffer nearly jumped out of his skin. As did Agent Cloutier, who dropped her pen on the floor and had to quickly bend to scoop it up.

"An account," said Shaeffer. "Okay? He wanted me to set up an off-shore account. And put the money he sent into it."

"For both of you?"

"No. Just under the name Anthony Baumgartner."

"He used his own name?"

The question seemed to surprise Shaeffer. "Of course. Why not?"

"Easy to trace."

"He didn't expect to be caught."

"How much is in it?"

"I'd have to check, but I think it's somewhere around eight million," said Shaeffer.

"And how much did you take for yourself?"

"Nothing."

"Oh for Christ's sake," said Beauvoir. "How stupid are you? You know we'll find out." He turned to Agent Cloutier. "She's in charge of forensic accounting for the entire Sûreté. Nothing gets past her. She's brought down business leaders, politicians, mob heads. She'll bring you down too. Before breakfast. So save us the trouble."

Shaeffer looked at Cloutier, who now wished she hadn't stuck the pen in her mouth and chewed it.

"Okay," he said. "Maybe a little. But don't tell him."

"That I can promise," said Beauvoir.

Shaeffer shook his head. "Sorry. I forgot he's dead."

Beauvoir hadn't missed the tone of Shaeffer's voice when he'd, just for a moment, forgotten that Baumgartner was dead.

He was afraid of him, thought Beauvoir. Genuinely afraid. In fact, Jean-Guy thought as he got to his feet, that might've been the most genuine moment in this whole interview.

"Give Agent Cloutier the information on the account, please."

"I can go?"

"We'll see."

They were getting closer, thought Beauvoir as he walked toward his office. Closer to embezzlement, if not murder. But he knew Gamache was right. When they found the money, it would be infused with delusion. With madness. With the stink of emotions rotten enough to lead to murder.

Amelia could hear the footsteps of the junkies and whores and trannies following them as she and Marc walked down the concrete stairs. Marc gripping Amelia's hand for support.

The air got colder and colder the closer they got to the front door.

Amelia braced for the frigid blast as soon as the door opened, but still it took her breath away and made her eyes water.

"Oh, fuck," she heard Marc say, coughing and choking on the air.

Through watery eyes Amelia saw a little girl in a red hat with the Montréal Canadiens logo. She stood alone, at the mouth of an alley.

Amelia could just see, poking out of the darkness, a pair of legs. On the ground. In ripped fishnets. The rest of the body was in darkness. But Amelia had no doubt. It was a body.

She caught the eyes of the girl, who looked to be five or six years old.

Amelia took a step toward the girl but was stopped by a single word.

"David."

A skinny black kid had come up to her. No more than fifteen, she thought. He was staring at her with eyes far too big for his head.

"What about him?" she said, and felt, more than saw, the junkies and whores and trannies form a semicircle behind her.

"I'd heard you want him. I know where he is. For a tab I'll tell you."

"Yeah, right. Get outta my way, shithead," she said, and shoved past him, heading across the street. To the girl, who was still standing there. Staring.

"David," he repeated, and pushed the sleeve of his thin coat up. To expose his forearm. "Look."

And there, written in Magic Marker, was the same word she'd found on her own arm. The word that was still there. Indelible.

David.

Like a calling card.

And beside the name there was a number: 13. No. It was 1/3.

She pushed up the sleeve of her jacket and took a closer look at her forearm. "David," it said. And the number. Not 14 but 1/4.

Amelia stared at it and felt her heart beating in her throat. "Where is he?"

"I have to show you. Now. Before he leaves." He put out his hand.

"Give him one," said Amelia, and Marc handed over a single pill. "You'll get another when we get to meet David."

The kid pocketed the currency and without another word turned and walked down the dark street.

Amelia looked behind her. To the mouth of the alley. But the little girl was gone.

"Almost there," Marc whispered as they followed. "Come up with a name yet?"

"Sweet Pea," she said. "You started calling me that when I was five years old."

"That's what you're going to name the shit? Sweet Pea?"

"No. I'm going to call it Gamache."

"After the head of the Sûreté? The guy who got you into the academy?"

"The guy who got me kicked out. The genius who gave us the shit. He deserves to have it named after him. To know that the last thing tens of thousands of kids will say will be his name. It'll become synonymous with death. Gamache."

"You hate him that much?"

"He ruined me," said Amelia. "Now it's his turn."

CHAPTER 32

———

"Oh look," said Benedict. "I think my truck's back."

They'd crested the hill leading down into Three Pines. There were lights at the windows of the homes, and in the bistro they could see figures moving about.

The headlights of Gamache's car caught the swirl of snow as it fell, and where the beams hit the surrounding forest, the trees were alternately dark and bright as snow rested on the branches.

Armand knew there'd be fires lit in each of the homes, including his own. But before he could join Reine-Marie in front of it, there was something that had to be done.

Benedict pulled up behind his truck, and, getting out, he went to inspect the tires.

"They're very good," he said. "The best. Are you sure I can't pay for them?"

"I'm sure," said Armand.

Benedict tossed the tail of his tuque around his neck and over his shoulder and looked about him. "I'm going to miss it here. What is it?"

Armand was regarding him in a way that made Benedict uncomfortable.

Isabelle stared at her laptop.

Her husband had returned, and the kids had come in from playing, and all around was pandemonium.

But she was sitting at the kitchen table in her own little bubble.

313

Where all was deadly quiet. There were just the two of them. Isabelle Lacoste and Katie Burke.

"So that's who you are," whispered Lacoste. And reached for the phone. While the kids chased each other and the dog barked and her husband called to them to wash up for dinner.

Jean-Guy Beauvoir had his feet crossed on the desk. A file on his lap. The information Madame Ogilvy had had her assistant give him on the Kinderoths, and Bernard Shaeffer, and Anthony Baumgartner.

He slowly lowered the file and stared at his own reflection in the window. Then, dropping his legs off the desk with a thud, he muttered, "Gotcha," as he reached for the phone.

Benedict picked up the keys to his truck from Madame Gamache and thanked her profusely and sincerely for their hospitality.

"I don't know what I'd have done," he said. "Without you."

"You're welcome back anytime, right, Armand?"

"Let me walk you to your truck," said Gamache.

As the door closed, he could hear the phone ringing.

"I don't know how I can ever thank you, sir."

"You promised me a driving lesson." Gamache looked around. There was a good four inches of snow on the road. Billy Williams would be by soon to clear it, but right now it was accumulating. "You can thank me by giving me that lesson."

"Now?"

"Is there a better time?"

"Well, it's dark, and you must be tired."

"It's six thirty. I'm not quite that old."

"I . . . I didn't mean that," stammered Benedict.

"Get in," said Gamache, walking around to the passenger side and climbing up. "Let's drive a few kilometers out of the village. I have a spot in mind."

He was quiet as they drove, and then Gamache asked, "Who's Katie Burke?"

"Who?"

Gamache was silent, staring at the snow swirling in the headlights. "She's my girlfriend."

The truck was speeding up, exceeding the limit now.

"My ex."

They were gathering speed.

"Your ex? Are you sure?"

"Yes."

"How long ago did you break up?"

"Two months."

"About the time Bertha Baumgartner died?"

The engine growled as Benedict pressed harder on the gas.

"I guess. I don't know."

"Did she know Madame Baumgartner?"

"Of course not."

"Are you sure? Be more careful with your answers."

"Maybe you should be more careful with your questions. Leave Katie out of this. You wanted a lesson? Here goes."

He put his foot to the floor just as they crested a hill.

"Benedict—" Gamache began, but got no further.

Benedict hit the brakes, and the truck spun, veering out of control.

Gamache was thrown against the door, hitting his head on the window. He heard Benedict grunt as he was tossed sideways.

"Let go of the brake," Gamache shouted.

But Benedict's foot was jammed onto the pedal as he yanked the steering wheel first one way, then the other. Fighting for control. The snowbank approached, then the truck caught and fishtailed in the other direction. Toward the other bank. And the drop-off.

Gamache released his seat belt and forced himself forward. Grabbing the wheel, he tried to steer into the spin, but Benedict's grip was too tight, and it was now almost impossible to tell which way was forward. And which would send them into the trees.

Benedict was bucking against Gamache's body, which was pinning him to the seat. Partly to try to force his foot from the brake and partly to help protect the young man against what now seemed the inevitable crash.

Gamache grabbed Benedict's pant leg, pulling it as hard as he could. Trying to yank his foot off the brake.

It finally lifted, and Gamache could feel the truck catch and slow, but he knew it was too late. In the headlights he saw the snowbank approaching and, beyond it, the trees.

He closed his eyes and braced himself.

The truck shuddered and then slowed.

Gamache opened his eyes and turned to look out the windshield. And saw not the woods but the road.

He shoved the gear into neutral, and the truck glided to a stop, pointing straight ahead.

Both men stared straight ahead, gathering themselves.

Gamache took a deep breath and exhaled while, beside him, Benedict was hyperventilating. His breaths coming out in short puffs.

"Katie Burke," said Gamache. "Tell—"

"Leave her out of this."

"Are you really prepared to kill us both? To protect her?"

"Leave her alone," said Benedict.

"Was it her idea or yours?"

"Enough."

"Or what? You'll run us off a cliff? More death? Does it get easier, Benedict, the more you do? I'm giving you a chance to tell me yourself."

Benedict was staring at him, wild-eyed, desperate.

"No?" said Gamache. "Then I'll tell you. Katie knew Madame Baumgartner. She was her first contact in the nursing home. That's how you got onto the will, isn't it?"

Benedict continued to glare at Gamache, but now with more surprise than hostility.

"Murder, Benedict. Is that what you wanted? Was it planned?"

But Benedict seemed too stunned to answer.

"Tell me. The truth now."

As soon as they walked back into the house, Reine-Marie said, "Both Jean-Guy and Isabelle have been calling. They'd like a callback."

It sounded to Armand that they would more than just "like" a call.

"You're back," said Reine-Marie to Benedict. "Everything okay? You look pale."

"He's just going to rest for a bit," said Armand, making for the study. "We've been testing the tires. We gave each other little lessons on driving in dangerous conditions."

Benedict collapsed into an armchair facing the fire.

"What did you do to him, Armand?" Reine-Marie whispered at the door to the study.

"Taught him a lesson," said her husband. "If he tries to leave, let me know. But I don't think he will."

Armand held up the keys to the truck.

Then, picking up the phone to return the calls, he noticed there was a message. A soft, now-familiar voice told him that she'd found the girl. And Armand could come get her anytime. She'd be safe.

Now it was Armand's turn to sit, almost collapse, into a chair. He closed his eyes briefly, and exhaled, whispering, *"Merci."*

Then he called Jean-Guy, who was in his car. "On my way down, *patron*. I'll be there in a few minutes."

"Great, but why?"

He explained. Then Gamache called Isabelle.

When he left the study, he found Benedict still in the armchair, a mug of hot chocolate, untouched, on the table beside him.

He was staring blankly into the cheerful fire. Reine-Marie had just put a fresh log on, and Henri was lying in front of it, while Gracie slept on the sofa. It was, to all appearances, a tranquil domestic scene.

But, as he'd just heard from Isabelle and Jean-Guy, there was delusion at work. And a certain madness.

After he'd hung up, he called Myrna and asked her to come over. She had to hear this.

"Would you like me to leave, Armand?" Reine-Marie asked. She recognized his manner and knew this was no longer a social occasion.

"*Non*, stay if you'd like."

Just then Myrna arrived, shaking snow from her tuque and kicking off her boots. "This'd better be good. I left a bowl of soup and a glass of wine to come here."

But, taking a seat by the fire, Myrna could see that whatever was happening, it wasn't good. It was bad.

"What is it?" she asked, looking at Benedict, who seemed almost comatose. "What's happened?"

"In a moment," said Armand as he went to the window. He'd seen headlights flash by.

A minute later Jean-Guy walked in.

"This," said Beauvoir as he stepped aside, "is Katie Burke."

"Katie?" said Benedict, getting up.

CHAPTER 33

⁓

"Are you fucking with me?" Amelia shouted after the boy, who stopped and turned.

They'd been wandering the back alleys for an hour. Marc was beginning to tremble, not from the cold, or fear, but from withdrawal. His mumbles had become a plaintive whine.

"I need something. Anything."

He'd already taken a tab of acid, but he was used to stronger. Needed stronger. And was getting weaker and weaker.

They all were.

The junkies and trannies and whores who straggled along after Amelia as she followed the boy from alley to tenement to empty lot. Some had broken off, desperate now for a hit. Preferring to go it alone.

Those who had stayed, the junkies and trannies and whores, were too far gone to make a decision. They just trudged after her, afraid of being left behind. Again.

"No, no, he was here an hour ago," said the kid, looking around. "He told me to come find you. It's ready."

"What is?"

"Dinner. He's made dinner for you. What the fuck do you think I mean? The shit's ready."

"Then why does he need me?" asked Amelia, feeling a surge of adrenaline.

"How should I know?"

Amelia looked over at Marc. Wanting to ask him, to ask anyone, for advice. She was tingling and wasn't sure if it was excitement or a warning. This wasn't right. Every instinct told her she was being set up. That she should stop. Turn around. Go back. Go home.

But she had no home. There was no "back" back there. Only forward.

The stud in her tongue knocked against her teeth as she considered her options.

The kid was on the move again, slipping and sliding through the slush in his running shoes.

"He must've left," he was muttering, looking this way and that. But it was night, and hardly any light from the street penetrated down these back lanes. David could've been standing feet away and they wouldn't see him.

Making up her mind, Amelia grabbed Marc's hand and dragged him, staggering, forward.

Click. Click. Click.

The sound of her stud joined the chattering of his teeth.

Katie and Benedict sat side by side on the sofa in front of the fireplace.

A platter of roast beef, chicken, and peanut-butter-and-honey sandwiches had been put out on the coffee table, along with drinks.

Katie wore a long boiled-wool skirt over bright pink jeans and a sweater made up of what looked like meatballs but were actually brown pom-poms. They hoped.

Henri was looking at her in a way that demanded monitoring.

She had the same haircut as Benedict. Almost shaved on top, and from just above the ears down it was long.

They held hands and looked very young as Katie stared at the adults surrounding them and Benedict stared at the sandwiches. And Armand stared at Henri. In warning.

Once again Armand noticed a resemblance between the shepherd and the carpenter.

"I hope you know," he began, lifting his eyes to the young couple, "that it's far too late for lies. And there've been far too many already."

While his words were firm, his voice was gentle. Encouraging. Like coaxing fawns from the forest.

Katie nodded, and Benedict's eyes met Armand's.

"How did this begin?" Gamache asked. There was no doubt that the question was aimed at Katie.

"Well, I guess it started before I was born—"

"Maybe the more recent events," said Armand. "How did Benedict get onto Madame Baumgartner's will?"

"She knows?" asked Myrna.

"And she knows why you're on too," said Beauvoir. "Don't you?"

Katie nodded again. She might look like a lunatic, but her eyes were sharp and bright and glowed with intelligence.

She was, Gamache suspected, a remarkable young woman. Certainly a one-off.

"I met Madame Baumgartner in the seniors' home," said Katie Burke. "I don't know if you know, but there aren't all that many Anglo homes around."

"Why would it matter?" asked Jean-Guy.

Katie looked at him with a weary patience, as though she were the adult and he was very, very young.

"What language would you choose to die in? It matters. We were lucky to get my grandfather into this one. I was visiting him and noticed that this one old woman hardly ever had visitors. Her family came when they could, and they seemed to care, but the days are long when you're sitting all alone. She always smiled at me and had the nicest face. A little eccentric, you know?"

The adults, as one, nodded. They could see that this young woman would be drawn to the eccentric.

"So one day I took her a tin of homemade cookies."

"Those cookies with a hole on the top filled with jam," said Benedict. "Except Katie's holes are different shapes—"

Katie patted his hand, and he stopped talking.

"Thank you," she said.

Far from being a way to shut him up, it was said with great kindness.

Affection, thought Armand. He was not only listening closely, he was watching them closely as well. Studying the dynamic. Often what seemed obvious was not a fact, or even the truth.

"We got to talking," Katie continued the story, "and she asked me to call her 'Baroness.' Well, I thought that was strange."

"Who wouldn't?" said Myrna.

"No, I mean I found it strange because I called my grandfather 'Baron.'"

"Why?" asked Myrna, her voice wary.

"It was just what he liked to be called. He was Baron, and my grandmother was Baroness. I didn't think anyone else did that. Madame Baumgartner reminded me of my grandmother, who I adored, so I'd sit with her in the home and we'd talk. Then one day I suggested they should meet. The Baron and this new Baroness. My grandmother had died the year before, and I know he was lonely."

"Did you know who she was?" asked Armand.

"By then, yes."

"And, knowing who she was, you still suggested they meet?"

Armand was leaning forward. His voice was friendly, as though this were a pleasant gathering of friends and murder wasn't hovering in the background.

"Yes."

"Did he know?" he asked.

Katie smiled for the first time. It was, they both knew, the vital question.

"He did. The Baroness Baumgartner."

Armand sat back on the sofa, not bothering to hide his amazement. "Did she know who he was?"

"No. I was afraid she'd refuse to see him. It wasn't until I introduced him that she found out."

"Who was he?" asked Myrna.

"The Baron Kinderoth," said Jean-Guy. "Katie here is a Kinderoth."

He'd discovered that when he'd been going over the file on the Kinderoths from Taylor and Ogilvy. In it were notes on the estate and who got the small amount of money in the investment account. The Kinderoths had two daughters. One had married a Burke and moved to Ontario. And had a daughter named Katherine. Katie Burke.

While Jean-Guy had started with the Kinderoths and ended up with Katie, Isabelle Lacoste had started with Katie and ended up with the Kinderoths.

She too had called Gamache and told him her findings, confirming what Beauvoir had just told him.

Different roads, but the same destination. Here. Now.

Myrna stared at Jean-Guy, taking this in. Then turned to Katie. "You're a Kinderoth?"

The young woman nodded.

"And you knew the history between the Kinderoths and the Baumgartners?" asked Myrna.

"Yes. I was raised on the story. That my great-great-grandfather was the eldest son. And the money, the title, the estates were ours. But the Baumgartners—filthy, greedy, cheating, and lying Baumgartners—had been trying to steal it for more than a hundred years."

"A hundred and thirty-two," said Benedict.

"What happened when they met?" asked Myrna.

"I introduced my grandfather. The Baron Kinderoth. He was in a wheelchair but managed to get up. He offered her the flowers he'd asked me to buy for him. Edelweiss. Then he bowed and called her Baroness."

The only sound in the room now was the muttering and crackling of logs in the fireplace. Shadows from the fire threw macabre, distorted shadows against the walls.

"And Madame Baumgartner?" asked Armand.

"She stared for a long time. It seemed forever," said Katie.

"A hundred and thirty-two years," said Benedict.

"Then she got up too. I went to help, but she refused. She stood straight, staring at the Baron. I thought she was going to say, or do, something awful. Then she reached out and took the flowers. *'Danke schön,'* she said." Katie smiled. "'Baron Kinderoth.'"

They sat in silence. Imagining the moment.

Then, very softly, as though from far away, Myrna heard humming. *Edelweiss. Edelweiss.*

She looked at Benedict. *Edelweiss*, he hummed.

"What happened then?" Myrna asked.

"I wish I could say all was forgiven on both sides, but it wasn't," said Katie. "Each time I visited, I'd take my grandfather into the solarium to have tea with the Baroness. They'd sit in silence. Then, one week, they were already there. Talking quietly together. I just left the cookies in their rooms and went home."

"They became friends?" asked Reine-Marie.

"It took a while," said Katie. "But yes."

"So how'd they get over all that history?" asked Myrna.

She'd known clients of hers when she was a practicing psychologist who never got over much less deep-seated resentments.

"Loneliness," said Katie. "They needed each other. They understood each other in ways no one else could."

"Ahhh," said Myrna. There was nothing like the pain of the present to cure the pain of the past.

"After a month or so, they were almost inseparable. Eating every meal together. She got him out into the garden, and he got her playing cribbage."

"Did they tell their families?" Armand asked.

If they had, the Baumgartner siblings had chosen not to mention it.

"They were planning to," said Katie. "But they were worried that too much damage had been done. They knew the judgment in Vienna was coming soon, and both worried that when it was announced, which-ever family won wouldn't want to share. And the family that lost would have their bitterness cemented in place. But they had a solution."

"They'd get married," said Benedict. And, not for the first time, he saw a group of people staring at him as though he were mad.

"Married?" asked Myrna. "Because of the money?"

"Because they loved each other," said Katie. "I think he loved her even more than he loved my grandmother. She made him laugh. He'd had a hard life, and it'd hardened him. But with her he could just be himself. A taxi-driver baron."

"And she could be a cleaning-woman baroness," said Reine-Marie.

"Yes. They thought if they made that sort of commitment to each other, not just in words but in action, the rest of the family would have to accept it and drop the feud."

"And share the fortune?" said Myrna. "No matter who won?"

"Yes. The plan was to leave everything to each other, with the pro-viso it be split equally among both families, when the last one died. But of course they wanted their children to not just accept grudgingly but wholeheartedly. As they had."

"But—" said Myrna.

"But my grandfather died before they could get married."

"Oh," said Reine-Marie as though she'd suffered a physical blow. "It must've been awful for the Baroness."

"It was. She hadn't told her children, and by then it was too late.

His death sent her into a tailspin. Partly physical, but mostly mental. She became confused. She called the notary in, with the intention of changing her will, as she and the Baron had discussed. Leaving everything, in the event she won the case in Vienna, split equally between the families."

"But the notary wouldn't do it," said Benedict.

"He saw the state she was in," said Katie, "and said he couldn't in all conscience allow her to change her will. He thought her mind wasn't sound. He knew the family history, the court challenges, and felt she must've been coerced somehow. He believed that the Baroness, who'd been so embittered about it all her life, would never willingly share with a Kinderoth."

"Just what the Baron and Baroness had feared from their families," said Reine-Marie.

"Yes," said Katie. "It confirmed her fears. If the notary thought she was nuts, her family sure would. But he did allow her to change one thing."

"The liquidators?" asked Myrna. "Is that when she put us on the will?"

"Yes."

"But why?" asked Armand.

"So that you could execute not just the will but her real desires. She knew that her children never would. There was too much history there. But with new liquidators there'd be none of that. The notary was right, of course. She was confused. But one thing was clear to her. The plan she had with the Baron to share the fortune had to be followed through. It became an idée fixe. A kind of obsession. It wasn't about the money, it was about letting go of all the bitterness. They could see the damage they'd done in passing it along to their children. Freeing them of it would be their real inheritance."

"But if it was that important to her," asked Reine-Marie, "why not just write her own will and sign it? Isn't that legal?"

"A holographic will," said Armand. "As long as it's written in longhand and signed by witnesses, yes, it's legal in Québec. But the notary had already seen her and decided she wasn't of sound mind."

"Exactly," said Katie. When she nodded, as now, her entire meatball sweater bobbed up and down.

It was amusing, disconcerting, and slightly nauseating. A cross between performance art and dinner.

Henri sat up and started drooling.

Armand motioned with his hand for the shepherd to lie back down, which he did, reluctantly.

"So," said Myrna, "the only thing the Baroness could do was change the liquidators."

"Yes. She took her three children off and put you on."

"But again," said Myrna. "Why us? We didn't even know her."

"Exactly. That's why. We needed someone who had no idea of the history."

"We?" asked Armand.

"I meant she."

"Of course," said Armand. "So that's why she changed liquidators, but why us specifically? Madame Landers and me?"

"The Baroness had heard that the head of the Sûreté had moved into the nearby village. She was enough of a snob to like the idea that someone so prominent would be executing her will. She also figured you'd keep her family in line. To be honest, her next choices were the queen, followed by the pope. But when she heard about you"—Katie turned to Myrna—"she immediately agreed you'd be perfect."

"A senior police officer and a respected psychologist," said Myrna, nodding. "Makes sense."

"You're a psychologist?" said Katie. "No, apparently Madame Zardo told the Baroness you were a cleaning woman. That's why she wanted you. Someone who'd understand."

Myrna's eyes narrowed in a glare, daring anyone to laugh.

The only one not smiling was Armand.

"How did the Baroness know to ask about changing the liquidators?" he asked.

"Like I said, the notary wouldn't let her change the actual will—"

"Yes, I heard. But does anyone else here know that it might be possible to change the liquidators?"

He looked around, and they all, to a person, shook their heads. Including Benedict. Who, after a sharp squeeze of his hand, stopped.

"So let me ask again," said Armand. "How did an elderly and admittedly confused person know to even ask about the liquidators?"

There was a pause before Katie answered. "It was my idea. I looked it up and suggested it to her. The Baroness agreed it was worth a try."

"And the choice of liquidators?" asked Armand.

"Was hers."

That sat there, taking in the odor of a lie. Armand let the pause stretch on. And the stench sink in. Before he finally spoke again.

"Including Benedict?"

Reine-Marie was watching this closely. Not Katie but Armand. Watching him take away, with a civility that was almost frightening, the props for her story. Until it collapsed.

"That was my idea," Katie admitted. "The Baroness actually wanted me as the third, but I said that wouldn't work. If they found out my mother's maiden name was Kinderoth, her family would accuse me of influencing her."

Jean-Guy raised his brows but chose not to say what everyone else in the room was also thinking.

"So it was agreed that my boyfriend, Benedict, would be a liquidator in my place," said Katie. "I could vouch for him. That he's honest and kind and will do what's right."

Do what she tells him, thought Jean-Guy.

"But you broke up," said Reine-Marie. "Benedict told us."

"That was planned," she said. "There couldn't be any connection. Not even the notary knew."

"So you didn't actually break up," Jean-Guy said to Benedict. "You appeared to but didn't. That was another lie."

Layer upon layer. Lie upon lie. Covering up some rotting truth. That they still hadn't reached.

"Didn't you think we'd find out?" asked Armand.

"I didn't think anyone would really ask," said Katie.

"We didn't think we were doing anything wrong," said Benedict.

Armand turned to him. "As a good rule of thumb, if you have to lie, you might be doing something wrong."

"You told me you liked my hat, sir," said Benedict, staring at Gamache. "Was that a lie?"

The question, and unmistakable challenge, sat there while Gamache stared back. Assessing and reassessing the young man.

"That was opinion," said Gamache. "Not fact. If you're lying about the facts, there's something wrong. And the two of you have been doing a lot of lying. Can you really be so surprised when we doubt you?"

"That was a great deal of effort to help an elderly woman," said Myrna.

Gamache, still watching Benedict, agreed. Though the word that came to his mind wasn't "effort" but "premeditation."

"I wasn't just helping her," said Katie. "I'd seen what this whole feud had done to my mother, my aunt, my grandparents. Myself. Spending our whole lives believing our lives could be, should be, better? Thinking we'd been screwed by the Baumgartners. Waiting for some judgment a continent away? To make us happy. It was awful." She placed a hand over her stomach, as though feeling ill. Benedict put his hand on her knee. "I agreed with the Baron and Baroness," she said. "It had to end."

"And, conveniently, make sure that whatever the judgment in Vienna was, you'd inherit?" asked Armand.

There was, Reine-Marie noticed, considerably less civility in that question. But this was not, after all, a party. The idea was not to be friendly but to get to the heart of a murder.

"We both know, monsieur, that there's nothing to inherit," said Katie. "Not after all this time. The cost of the lawsuits alone would be ruinous, never mind what the Nazis did to any Jewish property. All I'd inherit would be outrage. I don't want that. For me or my family."

Armand looked at this young woman and wondered if she really was that immune to the family plague. The creeping disease of hatred. The bindweed in the garden.

Benedict caressed Katie's hand in a way that was supportive and intimate.

"But still," said Armand, "it doesn't explain everything. As liquidators we're charged with honoring the provisions of the will. Not doing what we think is fair."

"That's why she wrote the letter," said Katie.

"What letter?" asked Armand.

"The Baroness wrote a letter, to be given to her eldest son, after the reading of the will. In it she explains everything."

"Why give it to him and not us?" asked Myrna.

"She didn't want her children to hear it from strangers," said Katie. "And she thought he'd understand."

"Understand about sharing the fortune?" asked Jean-Guy.

"About ending the fight."

"Why would she think Anthony would understand, more than the others?" asked Myrna.

"Something to do with a painting," said Katie. "Of a crazy old woman who wasn't really crazy, or something like that. Apparently the others hated it, but he wanted it. I didn't really understand what she was saying. She was rambling by then. I think she was getting confused between the painting and herself. But for some reason the painting was important to her. And to him, I guess. Anyway, she decided her eldest son was the one to get the letter."

"Did he?" Myrna asked.

Armand and Jean-Guy exchanged glances.

"We didn't find anything like that among his papers," said Jean-Guy.

Armand got up. "Will you come with me, please?" he asked Jean-Guy and Myrna.

They went to his study, and, closing the door, he made a call.

CHAPTER 34

—

"Do you know what time it is?" came Lucien's voice.

Gamache looked at his watch.

"Ten past eight," he said.

"At night."

"*Oui.* I'm sorry for calling after hours. Myrna Landers is with me, as well as Chief Inspector Beauvoir. We have you on speaker. We have some questions."

"Can't it wait?"

"If it could, do you think we'd be calling?" asked Jean-Guy.

"Did Madame Baumgartner leave a letter to be given to her son Anthony?" Gamache asked.

The television in the background was put on mute.

"Yes, she did. I found it in my father's file attached to the will."

"Why didn't you tell us about it?" asked Myrna.

"Why should I? Your job is to liquidate the will. This wasn't part of that."

"But still," said Myrna, "you could've mentioned it."

"And after Baumgartner was killed?" asked Beauvoir. "When it was clear it was murder? Didn't you think to mention it then?"

"A house fell on him," said Lucien. "The letter didn't kill him."

"How do you know?" asked Gamache. "Did you read it?"

"No."

"The truth, Maître Mercier," said Gamache.

"I did not. Why would I care what was in the letter?"

That at least had the ring of truth to it.

Unless the letter was about himself, which clearly it was not, Lucien Mercier would not be interested.

"When did you give it to him?" Beauvoir asked.

"Right after the reading of the will. After the rest of you left."

"It was just the two of you?"

"No, I think Caroline and Hugo Baumgartner were still there."

"Actually, Caroline left with us," said Myrna.

"Did he read the letter while you were there?" asked Armand.

"No. I just handed it to him and left. I have no idea when, or even if, he read it. Why does it matter?"

"It matters," said Beauvoir, "because her son has been murdered. And you gave him a letter just hours before it happened. A letter that might've led him to contact someone. Meet someone. That might explain why he went to the farmhouse and who he met there. Do you have any idea why he might've gone there that night?"

"No, none."

"Do you know what was in the letter, Maître Mercier?" Gamache asked. Again.

"No."

The three in the study exchanged glances. Not at all sure whether to believe him.

Though they could not think why he would lie.

"Lucien Mercier, the notary, confirmed that when the reading of the will was over and we'd left, he gave Anthony Baumgartner a letter from his mother," said Armand when they'd returned to the living room.

"Does he know what was in it?" Reine-Marie asked.

"He says he doesn't," said Jean-Guy, sitting back down.

"So no one knows what was in the letter?" asked Reine-Marie.

"I think one of us does."

Armand turned to Katie.

She looked at Benedict, who nodded.

"You're right," she said. "I was there when she wrote it. In the letter she explained about meeting the Baron. About hearing his side of it. About seeing he wasn't a greedy monster at all, just an old man carrying on an even older fight. She said something about a horizon. I don't know what that was about. But she did say in the letter that if Anthony loved her, as she knew he did, he'd do one last thing for her. If they won the court case, he'd share the inheritance with the Kinderoths."

"A beautiful letter," said Reine-Marie.

"And very clear," said Armand, who continued to watch Katie.

"I wonder if he read it," said Myrna. "And how he felt about it."

"And if he told his siblings," said Jean-Guy. "Pretty good motive. Without Anthony and the letter, the money was theirs. With him, they'd have to share. People are killed for twenty bucks. We're talking millions."

"That don't exist," Myrna pointed out.

"But how do we know?" asked Jean-Guy. "How do they know? We don't and they don't. Not until the court case is decided. And it doesn't really matter if it exists, just that they believe it does, or hope it does."

Myrna nodded. People were capable of believing almost anything. And hope was even more sweeping and powerful.

Reine-Marie was listening to this but watching Armand as he got up and threw another log on the fire, poking it and sending embers up the chimney. Then he turned around, the poker still in his hand.

"Who wrote the letter?" he asked.

"The Baroness," said Katie. "I told you."

But the meatballs on her sweater were trembling.

Her heart, Gamache knew. Beating so ferociously it was setting them off. Still, she was looking at him apparently calmly. Apparently coolly.

She has courage, Gamache thought. But he also thought it was a shame she needed it. So much courage demanded to look him in the eye and tell him such a lie.

"An elderly woman, declining mentally and physically, picked up a pen and wrote a letter?" he asked. "Setting it all out so clearly?"

Instead of being harsh, accusing, his voice was reasonable. Soft. Inviting her, once again, to come out of the woods.

"Yes. I watched."

Benedict took her hand and held it. "Katie," he said, and nothing else. Just the one word.

Katie.

She dropped her eyes to the rug. To the dog staring at her and drooling.

"She dictated it, but I wrote it for her."

"*Merci*," said Armand, replacing the poker and sitting back down. "You know what that means, of course."

"It means even if you find the letter, it's in my handwriting. There's no proof they were her words."

"*Oui*," said Armand.

What he didn't say, but that was clear to him and, he suspected, to Beauvoir, was that there was no proof of any of this. This could all be lies.

The reconciliation. The desire to marry. Wanting to share the inheritance.

It could all be a lie.

Anyone who could confirm the story was dead. The Baron. The Baroness. And now Anthony Baumgartner.

The other thing that was clear was that Benedict wasn't the passive boy toy he appeared to be. Dressed, styled, molded, and manipulated by Katie Burke.

He had, with one word, gotten her to speak the truth. Not, Gamache suspected, because Benedict believed in telling the truth. But because he could see that lying was no longer working.

"There was one more thing in the letter," said Katie.

"Let me tell them," said Benedict.

He looked at Gamache. "The Baroness wanted the farmhouse torn down."

"Why?"

"Because she wanted them to make a clean break. Start their own lives, fresh. She knew they'd never move on as long as that house was standing. It was where she'd brought them up. Where she'd told them all those stories about the inheritance. She wanted it gone."

"Is that why you went there?" asked Armand.

"Yes," said Benedict. "I wanted to go at night, when I knew the Baumgartners wouldn't be there. I needed to see how hard it would be to take it down. I know you said you'd have it condemned, sir, but suppose that took a while, or what if it wasn't? I felt it was up to me to make sure it was done."

"I asked him to do it," said Katie.

"I found the support beam in the kitchen and gave it a couple of good whacks with a sledgehammer. Just to test it."

"It failed the test?" asked Myrna.

"Well, yes. The place fell down. That wasn't planned."

Katie held his hand tightly as he looked across at Myrna, Jean-Guy, Armand.

"You came and found me," said Benedict. "Thank you."

"Thank you," said Katie.

Reine-Marie saw a young man.

Jean-Guy saw the cloud of concrete and plaster and snow. And heard the roar.

And the shouting. Screaming. His own. As he fought to free himself from those who held him back.

Myrna saw the huge beams and slabs coming down all around. She felt the rubble crushing in around her and the overwhelming terror, and disbelief, as she realized she was about to die. And she felt Billy Williams holding her hand.

Armand looked at Benedict in front of the cheerful fire and felt the young body on top of his, trying to shield him, as the house of Baumgartner fell and the world came to an end.

And then he saw Benedict's dust-covered face, with the blood. And beyond it the hand, thrust up through the rubble.

Anthony Baumgartner.

Amelia was beginning to shiver almost uncontrollably.

They'd been at it for hours now. Amelia recognized what this was. They were being deliberately worn down. Led by the nose through the freezing streets until they had no will, no fight left.

Her feet were soaked through, and beside her, Marc was weeping. Begging. She didn't know what for. He was just begging.

Probably for this to stop. For them to stop.

But Amelia couldn't afford to. Even as she recognized the manipulation, she had to see it through.

Up ahead the boy turned and gestured.

"I found him."

CHAPTER 35

⌐

Murder was essentially simple, Beauvoir was thinking as he walked with his father-in-law into the kitchen.

The motives, even the method, might look complicated, until you figured it out. And they were figuring this one out.

Armand closed the door into the kitchen.

"What do you think?"

"I think it's all bullshit. I think there was no friendship between the Baron and the Baroness, never mind love. Katie Burke's story's almost laughable. It sounds like a fairy tale."

"Most fairy tales are pretty dark," said Armand, taking the tarte Tatin out of the fridge and handing it to Jean-Guy. "Have you read any to Honoré? Rumpelstiltskin? It starts with a lie and ends with a death."

"I'll keep my eyes peeled for an elf," said Jean-Guy.

"An imp," said Armand. He plugged the kettle in and turned to watch Jean-Guy cutting the caramelized apple tart.

They were there, ostensibly, to get dessert, but when Reine-Marie came in to help them, she saw the look on her husband's face and went back out.

"I think she's pregnant," said Armand. "Katie, I mean."

"What makes you say that? Did the elf tell you?"

"Imp, and no. It was the way she put her hand over her abdomen when she talked about ending the family legacy of hate. And then he touched her in a way that was very tender. The way I saw you reach out for Annie when she was pregnant with Honoré. He loves her."

"They love each other," said Jean-Guy, licking his fingers and thinking. "If she is pregnant, it could be even more of a motive."

"But for what?" asked Armand. "To end the feud or to keep it going? One keeps them happy but in poverty, the other comes with a fortune but at a price. What do they want for their child? Money or peace?"

"Money," said Jean-Guy. "Always money. Peace is for people with a bank account. Look at them. He's a so-called carpenter but really a janitor, and she's a . . . what? Wannabe designer? She's never gonna make money, unless it's designing clown suits. And neither is he. And now they're looking at a baby coming? No, their only hope, their last hope, is the judgment in Vienna."

"She said she didn't believe there was any money."

"What's she gonna say? Sure, maybe her more sane self tells her there isn't a fortune left. But she's been raised on a pretty dark fairy tale. Of huge wealth coming their way. Who doesn't dream of that? No, you can't tell me that Katie Burke doesn't believe, deep down, that there's a fortune. And it belongs to them."

Delusion and madness, thought Jean-Guy. Like most fairy tales.

"Trust me," he said. "Those two are in it up to their necks."

Armand told him about what had happened in the truck.

"Do you think he was trying to crash?" asked Jean-Guy, shocked by what he heard.

"No, I think he felt cornered and was overcome with anger when I questioned him about Katie."

Though they both knew that at the root of anger was fear. And fear was what propelled most murders.

"You think they killed Anthony Baumgartner?" Armand asked.

"I do. I think there was something in that letter that sent Baumgartner to the farmhouse. Benedict met him there and killed him."

"Why kill him?" asked Armand. "If the letter is telling Baumgartner to share the fortune, why would they need to kill him?"

"Because the letter didn't say that. Katie was lying. We have no idea what was in the letter. The Baroness might've dictated one thing, like Anthony should share, but Katie wrote down something else. Like Anthony should go to the old farmhouse alone the night the will was read. Which he did. Thinking it was his mother's wish."

"We don't know that."

"No, that's my point. We have no idea what was in that letter. Katie might even be telling the truth."

Though Beauvoir clearly did not believe that.

"All we know is that Baumgartner read it, then went to the farmhouse."

"You make it sound like cause and effect," said Gamache. "Something else might've happened to send him there."

"That's true."

"It's interesting that Katie knew about the painting of Ruth. The only way she could know about it was if the Baroness told her."

"But that doesn't mean it was in the letter."

"No, no it doesn't," said Gamache. "So, to recap, we have two theories. One, that Katie wrote down exactly what the Baroness dictated. Two, that she did not."

Beauvoir was nodding. "We don't seem to be much closer."

Though that was often the odd thing about a murder investigation. They could appear to be getting further from the truth, lost in the dust thrown up by all sorts of contradictory statements. Evidence. Lies.

But then something was said, or seen, and everything that had seemed contradictory fell into place.

"That damned painting keeps coming up," said Jean-Guy. "Bernard Shaeffer even mentioned it today when I spoke with him."

He told Gamache about that interview.

"So he was there when Baumgartner hung it in his study," said Gamache. "Then he helped get the laptop up and running."

"That was supposedly why he was there," said Beauvoir. "But then it turned into something else."

"Shaeffer told you that Baumgartner was trying to think of a new password? Did he find one?"

"If he did, he was smart enough not to tell Shaeffer."

"According to Shaeffer," said Gamache.

"True. We're still trying to crack it. We've searched the home, of course. I even looked behind that damned painting, but all I saw there was the print number."

Gamache nodded, and then his brows drew together. "What did you see there?"

"It's a numbered print. They write the number on it, so buyers know what—"

"Yes, yes," said Gamache. "I know. We have some here, including one of Clara's."

He walked over to the wall by the long pine table. Beauvoir had seen the picture many times, including the original in Clara's studio, when she'd first painted it.

Now he and his father-in-law stood in front of it.

Clara called it *The Three Graces*. But instead of showing three beautiful young women, naked and intertwined in a more than slightly erotic way, she'd painted three fully clothed elderly women from the village. Including the woman, Emilie, who used to own the Gamaches' home.

They were wrinkled, sagging, frail. They held on to each other. Not because they were afraid or feeble. Just the opposite. These women were roaring with laughter. The work radiated joy. Friendship. Companionship. Power.

"The number of the print," he said, reaching out to take the large painting off the wall, "is written on the back."

"Actually—" Armand began, but it was too late. Jean-Guy had it off and had turned it around.

Something was indeed written there. But it was in Gamache's familiar hand.

"For Reine-Marie, my Grace. With love forever, Armand."

Jean-Guy colored, and, after quickly putting it back on the wall, he turned to look at Armand, who was watching him and smiling.

"Not exactly a secret," said Armand. "Or a code. What I wanted to show you is that."

Gamache pointed to the front of the painting. On the lower right corner were Clara's signature and the numbers 7/12.

"I've seen that," said Jean-Guy. "But I always thought that was the date it was finished."

"No. It's the number of the print. Seven of twelve."

"She only printed twelve?"

"It was before she became successful," said Armand. "She didn't think she could even sell twelve."

"So this must be worth—"

But he stopped and stared at *The Three Graces*. At the number. And grunted. "Huh. So what's with the number on the back of Baumgartner's painting?"

Gamache raised his brows, as did Jean-Guy. Who then walked quickly over to the phone in the kitchen and placed a call.

"Cloutier? The painting in Baumgartner's study. Yes, the crazy old woman. There's a number on the back. Did you make a note of it? Can you go over to the house and see? Better yet, bring the painting in. No, I'm not kidding. No, I don't want it in my office. Keep it by your desk. Okay then, turn it to face the wall. I don't care. Just get that number and try it on his laptop. I'll be there in an hour."

Beauvoir hung up and turned to Gamache.

"We'll know soon. I don't know what we'll find on that computer, but I'm still betting those two out there"—he jerked his head toward the living room—"are in it over their ridiculous haircuts. I think Anthony Baumgartner was greedy. Scheming. Criminal. I don't think he had any intention of sharing the wealth."

"And you think that's why he was killed?"

"I do. Don't you?"

Gamache glanced toward the closed door, and Jean-Guy, who knew him well, could guess his thoughts.

"Look, *patron*, I know you don't want Benedict to be the one. You like him. I like him. He saved your life. But—"

"You think that's why I don't believe it was Benedict?" asked Armand. "Because he did a nice thing?"

"It was a pretty nice thing," said Beauvoir.

"True, but we've arrested too many nice killers to be fooled. I just don't see any proof. That they've lied, yes, but if everyone who lied to us was a killer, there'd be slaughter in the streets. I just don't believe it."

"You don't want to believe it."

"Show me the proof and I will."

"You talked about separating facts from all the lies in this case. Well, here's a fact for you. Benedict was in the farmhouse when Baumgartner was there. He had opportunity and motive. I'm betting under all that rubble we'll find the sledgehammer, or whatever weapon he used. And then their story will collapse, like the building. With them in it."

The two men were used to arguing over cases. Challenging each other. Challenging theories, questioning evidence. This was nothing new. Though there was a slight edge to it, and Armand knew why.

Was he refusing to see what was so clear to Beauvoir? What would be so clear to him if he didn't keep feeling the trembling body on top of him and hearing the crying. Of a young man terrified of dying but instinctively protecting another. A veritable stranger.

Could such a man, just hours earlier, have taken a life?

But Armand knew the answer to that. Yes. One was instinctive. The other well thought out. Premeditated. And maybe also, at a profound level, instinctive.

A parent would do a lot to provide for his child. And if that meant killing a—what had Katie called him?—filthy, greedy, cheating, and lying Baumgartner, then so be it.

Yes, Armand had to admit. It could have been Benedict.

They returned to the living room, and Jean-Guy said his goodbyes, explaining that he had to get back to Montréal.

Myrna got up. "I'll be leaving too. Those brownies won't eat themselves."

"I thought you said it was soup you left behind," said Reine-Marie, walking her to the door.

"You must've misheard," said Myrna.

"What about us?" asked Katie.

"You're free to go," said Beauvoir.

"Me too?" asked Benedict.

Beauvoir hesitated for a moment, then nodded.

They thanked the Gamaches for their hospitality.

"And the tires," said Benedict, with a smile that a day earlier Gamache might have found disarming but now struck him as possibly calculated. "I won't forget."

"And neither will I," said Armand, shaking the young man's hand. Then he turned to Katie. "I really do like the hat, you know."

Beauvoir watched them leave, then said to Gamache, "Next time I see them, it'll be with an arrest warrant."

Gamache put on his boots and coat and hat.

"Taking the dogs for a walk?" asked Beauvoir, pulling on his mittens.

"*Non.* I'm going in to Montréal too."

"Good," said Beauvoir. "I'll drive you. You can stay over with us, if you like."

"*Non, merci.* I'll drive myself. I'll be coming back out."

"Your eyes okay?"

"They're just fine."

Beauvoir paused, studying his father-in-law. "Are you sure?"

"You're not accusing me of being blind again, are you?"

"Only to evidence so obvious your infant grandson could see it," said Beauvoir. "But I think you're okay to drive."

Gamache laughed and said good night to his son-in-law, then went and explained to Reine-Marie that he had to go into the city but would be back later.

"Would you like me to come?" she asked.

"*Non, mon coeur*—"

Just then the phone rang.

"I'll get it," he said, and went into his study.

When he reached for the phone, he paused. The number lit up on the handset was one he recognized.

He glanced out into the living room, then, with his foot, swung the door closed.

"*Oui, allô,*" he said.

His voice sounded strange in his own ears. Oddly calm, while his heart pounded.

"Monsieur Gamache?" asked the man at the other end. "Arnold Gamache?"

"Armand. *Oui.*"

"My name is Dr. Harper. I'm one of the coroners in Montréal. I'm afraid I have some bad news for you."

Gamache felt light-headed. Physically sick.

Annie? He thought. Honoré? Had there been an accident?

He stood straight but put out his hand to steady himself against the desk. Preparing for the blow.

"Go on."

"We found your name and phone number on a body that was just brought in. There was no other identification."

"Go on," said Armand. He felt his extremities going cold and tingling. He wondered if he might pass out.

"Male. Over six feet. Slender. Emaciated, really. Dressed in women's clothing."

Armand sat down and closed his eyes, lifting a trembling hand to his forehead. He exhaled.

Not Annie. Not Honoré.

"Seems to be a pre-op transsexual," the coroner was saying. "He had your name on a piece of paper in his pocket."

"She," said Gamache, sighing.

"Sorry?"

"She. Does she have on a pink coat? Frilly?"

"Not anymore. No coat. No boots, no gloves. He—"

"She."

"She was almost stripped. Do you know her?"

"Was she the only one?" asked Gamache, realizing what this might mean. "Was there anyone else with her when she was found?"

"Another body, you mean?"

"A little girl. About six years old."

"I don't know, I was only given this body."

"Well, check," said Gamache, fighting to keep from snapping at the coroner. "Please."

Normally the coroner, new to the job, wouldn't have taken orders from a stranger on the phone, but this man spoke with such authority he found himself saying, "Just a moment."

And going to check.

Gamache was put on hold. He got to his feet and paced as he waited. And waited. Finally Dr. Harper came back on.

"No. No little girl. Not in the morgue at least. Are you that Gamache? Head of the Sûreté?"

"I am."

"Do you know who this body is?"

"I think I do, but I'd have to see her. What did she die of?"

"Looks like an overdose. We're running tests."

"I'll be there in an hour."

"Yessir."

Armand headed for the door but changed his mind, and, returning to his study, he grabbed some syringes from the locked drawer in his desk.

Then he left.

Gamache stood beside the metal autopsy table, looking over at the clothing, tagged and piled on a side table. Bright purple nylon blouse, bought because it resembled silk, he suspected. Faux-leather miniskirt. Torn fishnet stockings.

Then he turned his attention to the thin body and saw the care she'd taken, for people who wouldn't care. Her bouffant blond wig was askew. The thick makeup, now smeared, had, that morning, been skillfully applied. Though nothing could cover the scabs and sores on her face.

In that wretched place, she'd made a stab at beauty.

He looked down at the body and felt overwhelming sadness.

The coroner and the technician, on hearing the head of the Sûreté muttering what sounded like the last rites, stepped away.

More from embarrassment than respect for privacy.

Gamache crossed himself and turned to them.

"Her name's Anita Facial," he said. When there was the beginning of a guffaw from the technician, he stifled it with a stern look. "Not, of course, her birth name. I don't know what that is. If you need help finding her next of kin, let me know. I'll do what I can."

Gamache noticed the mottled skin, the blue veins. The terror in the eyes, red from burst blood vessels. This was not a blissful death. Anita hadn't drifted away on a cloud of ecstasy. She had been torn from this life.

"It's carfentanil," he said.

"What?" asked the coroner.

"It's an analogue of fentanyl. An opioid."

"He's right, sir," said the technician, who'd gone to the computer. "We just got the blood work back. He has—"

"She," said the coroner.

"She has carfentanil in her system. Though not much."

"Doesn't take much," said Gamache.

"Never heard of it," said Dr. Harper. "You know it? A new opioid?"

"Newish," said Gamache. "New to the streets."

The coroner gave a deep sigh and muttered, "Goddamned drugs."

"May I?" Gamache reached out, then asked permission before touching Anita's arm.

Her body was marked with what looked like homemade tattoos. Hearts. Butterflies. On the back of one hand was *Esprit*.

Spirit.

And on the other, *Espoir*.

Hope.

Esprit. Espoir.

But it was her left forearm that interested him. More writing, in a different, though familiar, hand.

Not a tattoo, it was written in Magic Marker.

David.

And after the name there was a number: 2.

Dr. Harper went over to the computer and said something to the technician, who tapped on a few keys.

"Holy shit," he said, and turned to the coroner, who studied the screen, then turned to Gamache.

"There've been six deaths here in Montréal in the last three days. Four since this morning. All homeless. All junkies. All the same drug. What is this stuff?"

But Gamache didn't answer. It was rhetorical anyway. The coroner knew exactly what it was. A nightmare.

Gamache felt his chest tighten.

He was too late. It was being released. Six deaths already. He looked over at Anita. Seven.

But still, he hadn't heard from the undercover cops. Amelia hadn't found any. So maybe this was the forerunner, a sort of foretaste.

The main body of the drug would be on the streets soon. Perhaps within hours. But not quite yet.

"Can you bring up the autopsy pictures?" Gamache asked, stepping over to the terminal.

They did.

"Zoom in on the left forearms."

First one, then another. Then another.

"Shit," said the technician. "We missed that."

Gamache didn't respond. He was staring at the images on the screen. They had several things in common.

All junkies. All dead by carfentanil.

All with David written carefully on each left forearm. Though the numbers were, for the most part, different.

"What does it mean?" asked the coroner.

"I have no idea what this means," said Gamache, still studying the screen.

"So if a kid overdoses on this carfentanil," the coroner asked, "is there an antagonist? A rescue medication?"

"Naloxone," said Gamache. "The Sûreté and local forces are being given it. But—"

But if all the carfentanil was released onto the streets, there wouldn't be nearly enough rescue drug out there. And not enough time to administer it. Carfentanil killed too fast for much hope of rescue, unless you got there immediately.

Gamache returned to the body of Anita Facial. And heard her soft voice on the message she'd left for him that afternoon.

She'd found the little girl. She'd keep her safe until he came to get her. But he hadn't. And she hadn't. And now the girl was still out there. Alone.

In the midnight and the snow!

"'Christ save us all from a death like this,'" he muttered under his breath as he left the mortuary and returned to his car.

But he knew Christ wasn't responsible. He was. And prayer, no matter how fervent, wouldn't stop it.

Once in the privacy of his car, he placed a call.

"What the fuck is it?" came the gravelly voice.

"It's Gamache."

"Oh, shit, sorry sir," the young man whispered. "I shouldn't be talking."

"Have you seen any sign of the carfentanil? Any sign at all that it's hit the streets?"

"No, none. But there's lots of anticipation."

"There's a little girl," Gamache said. "Red tuque. Five, six years old. I want you to find her."

"I can't."

347

"This isn't a request, it's an order."

"But, sir, Choquet's on the move. I think this's it. I think she's found him."

"David?"

"Yes. I can't talk. If anyone sees . . ."

Gamache knew it was a terrible risk, calling. No homeless man should be shuffling along and talking on a phone. But now he faced a choice.

The girl or the drug.

But there really was no choice to be made.

"Stay with her," he said. "We'll be tracking you. You have the naloxone?"

"*Oui.*"

"Good luck," said Gamache.

He called his counterpart at the Montréal police and alerted him.

"We have the cell signal," said the assault-team commander. "We're ready to move as soon as we get the word."

"You'll need masks."

"Got them. You're there now?"

"Close."

"God, let's hope this's it."

The commander hung up, and Gamache drove toward the rotten core of the city he loved.

Agent Cloutier was still at her desk past midnight when Beauvoir arrived at Sûreté headquarters.

Ruth, leaning against the wall and clutching the thin, torn blue material at her throat, glared at him as he walked into the homicide department.

"Sorry," he said to Ruth, and turned her around.

"I have it here," said Cloutier, of the number he saw written there. "But waited for you to come before putting it in."

"Thanks for waiting," said Beauvoir as he pulled up a chair and nodded to her.

"Where is he?" asked Amelia, looking around.

This was an alley off an alley off a back lane. Impossible to find, except by those who were lost. She was pretty sure it wouldn't be on any map.

But once found it was never forgotten. And probably never left.

All her senses were alert, her eyes sharp, her hearing acute.

"Who?"

The voice was deep. Calm. Amused.

Not the kid anymore but someone else, speaking from a doorway.

Amelia turned and saw a figure. Arms crossed. Legs apart. Watching her.

He was young, she could tell. There was about him something that was missing from everyone else in the alley.

Except her.

Meat on his bones. And life in his voice. This man was fully alive. And, like her, fully alert.

"David," she said.

"Yes, I'd heard you were looking for him."

"Are you David?"

He laughed and stepped from the doorway. But the alley was dark, and she couldn't see him clearly. He tossed a small packet at the kid, who grabbed it and melted away.

"No," he said. "I'm not David. You already know him. Quite well."

Amelia's mind was racing. What had she missed?

"Show her," he said, and the junkies and dealers, who'd been leaning against the wall of urine frozen to the bricks, pushed up their sleeves.

All had "David" written on their forearms.

Then the man shoved up his sleeve. Even from a number of feet away, Amelia could see the tattoos. But not the name.

What did it mean? Her mind flickered this way and that, looking for the answer. It meant something.

Everyone else had "David" written on their arms. Including herself. Everyone except him.

He must have lied. He must be David. He wouldn't need to write his own name on his own forearm. Would he?

But she knew, quickly, instinctively, that he hadn't lied. He didn't need to. He was in control.

If he said she'd met this David before, then she had. But who? When? When he'd written his name on her arm, of course. But she couldn't remember anything about that. It was a complete blank. She'd passed out, far too stoned to remember anything.

She'd woken up hours later with the indelible ink on her arm.

David. Then the numbers 1 4. But actually it was 1/4.

Why was this man going around writing his name on junkies?

"Oh Christ," she whispered.

David wasn't a man. David wasn't even human.

David was the drug.

CHAPTER 36

"Damn," said Beauvoir.

He sat back in the chair and stared at the screen.

It hadn't worked. The number on the back of Clara's painting wasn't the code.

He'd been so sure of it. Had had Agent Cloutier reenter it. Two more times.

Nothing.

"Sorry, *patron*. It was a good idea," she said, and Beauvoir couldn't help but think that things were pretty desperate when Cloutier was patronizing him.

"We'll get it eventually," she said, not making him feel better. "But I do have some news. Bernard Shaeffer's handed over the information and access to the offshore money. It's a numbered account in Lebanon. Let me show you."

She brought it up, and there, very clearly, was the name Anthony Baumgartner and the amount. Just over seven million.

Beauvoir raised his brows. "A lot, but not actually as much as I expected."

"Me too," she said. "The numbers don't tally. According to the statements, the clients, all told, gave Baumgartner several hundred million. So where's the rest?"

"In another account," said Beauvoir, thinking. "With another person."

"Shaeffer?" asked Agent Cloutier.

Chief Inspector Beauvoir was nodding. Thinking.

Another reason for murder. Suppose Baumgartner realized his former lover wasn't quite as stupid, not quite as intimidated as he thought? Suppose he found out Shaeffer was stealing from him?

He'd confront Shaeffer. And Shaeffer would have killed him. Would have to, if he wanted to be free of Baumgartner and keep the fortune.

Beauvoir looked at the painting, then turned it back around so that Ruth was again scowling at him.

"A code can be symbols as well as numbers and letters, right?"

"Yes. It's even better, more secure, if some symbols are used. Why?"

"There's a symbol for you. And numbers."

He pointed to the lower right corner.

Gamache drove slowly down rue Ste.-Catherine, scanning the street.

Then, finding a parking spot, he pulled in and got out. His cell phone was connected to the agents tracking Amelia as she closed in on the back-street factory.

But right now Gamache had someone else he had to find.

"A little girl," he said to a prostitute. "She's five or six. Red Canadiens hat."

"You don't want a little girl," she said. "You want a big girl."

She grabbed her breasts.

"I don't mean for that," he said, his voice so stern the woman lowered her hands and stopped the act.

"You her father?" asked the prostitute. "Grandfather?"

"I'm a friend. Have you seen her?"

"Yeah, with Anita this afternoon."

"Anita's dead."

"Oh, not Anita too." She looked up and down the street. "I can't help you. I'm just trying to stay alive."

"You want to stay alive?" he said, handing her a fifty. "Get off the streets."

"And go where, honey? Your place? You and your nice wife gonna help me? Get out of the way and let me do my job."

"I'm serious," he said. "There's a new drug that's killing people. It killed Anita. Stay away from it."

"You look like a nice man. Let me give you some advice. Stay away from here."

But, of course, he couldn't leave. As the prostitute watched, he walked up one side of the street, then down the other.

His face grew numb in the bitter cold. He had to turn his back now and then against the wind, to catch his breath. But he kept on.

Talking to near-frozen junkies and trannies and whores.

But while most knew who he was talking about, none knew where the little girl was.

And then he saw. A bit of red. Down an alley. Disappearing into a doorway.

He followed, quickly. Once at the door, he yanked it open and saw a man holding the girl by the hand. Leading her down the corridor and into a room.

Gamache shouted, and the man, looking back and seeing him, shoved the girl into the room and slammed the door.

Breaking into a run, Gamache got to the door. It was locked. He pounded on it.

"Open up."

When there was no response, he threw himself against it. Again. And again.

Finally he broke through and stumbled into the room.

A man stood there. Middle-aged, or at least aged. Disheveled. Eyes sunken and red.

He held the girl in front of him, his large hand around her small throat.

"Give her to me," said Gamache, advancing into the room.

"I found her." His hand tightened around her throat. "She's mine."

"You need to let her go."

"I won't."

Gamache knelt down and looked into the little girl's eyes. But they were unfocused. Staring blankly ahead. Her mouth was open, and she was breathing rapidly. The Canadiens tuque had fallen off, and Gamache could see her hair, blond, filthy, matted.

"Can you close your eyes?" he asked her gently. She just continued to stare. "It's going to be all right. No one will hurt you."

But he suspected she'd heard that before. Just before she'd been hurt. Maybe beyond repair.

"I'm here to help," he said. "I know you might not believe it, but I am."

Then he stood back up.

"I won't hurt her," he said to the man. "But I will hurt you unless you let her go, right now."

"Fuck o—" was as far as he got.

Gamache took a long, rapid stride forward and hit the man so hard in the face that his nose broke. He dropped to the floor, bleeding, as Gamache grabbed the girl and lifted her into his arms.

"It's all right," he whispered, holding her tight and averting her fixed gaze from the broken man on the floor. "It's all right. You're safe."

Behind him he heard the man screaming. But the sound got fainter and fainter as Gamache and the girl went down the corridor and out into the cold night.

He got her buckled into his car and gave her a chocolate bar from his glove compartment. Jean-Guy thought he didn't know about the stash, but he did.

The girl just held it in front of her. Like a celebrant holding the cross.

"My name's Armand," he said, swinging the car back onto Ste.-Catherine. His voice was calm. Intentionally authoritative. "I'm with the police. You're safe now. I promise. I have a granddaughter your age. She lives in Paris. Her name's Florence. We call her Florie. She has a younger sister named Zora. What's your name?"

But she remained mute. Frozen in place. Barely even blinking.

Just then the cell phone burst into life.

"We've got it," said the agent. "The factory's in an abandoned building down a side street just off St.-André, north of Ste.-Catherine. She's gone inside. Should we go in?"

Gamache pulled over and hit his phone, about to say no, but the Montréal commander got there first.

"No" came the crisp voice. "Wait for us. We're five minutes away. Chief Superintendent, I have you even closer."

Gamache knew exactly the area the agents were talking about. And he was close.

He looked at the little girl. He couldn't leave her alone in the car. But neither could he take her with him.

He scanned the street and saw the answer.

"Chief Superintendent Gamache?" came the voice of the Montréal tactical commander.

"I'll be there in two minutes," he said, and then, stopping the car in the middle of the street, he bundled the girl in his arms, whispering calmly, gently, "Everything's fine. You're safe."

But he wondered, even as he spoke, if that was the biggest lie so far.

Pushing open the door into the diner, he looked around, then walked up to the waitress who'd served him two days earlier.

"My name's Gamache, I'm with the Sûreté. I have to go. Please look after her until either I return or someone from the Sûreté comes to get her."

"Are you kidding me?"

"You must." He placed the girl in one of the booths and turned to the worn waitress. "Please."

She held his eyes for a moment, then gave a curt nod.

"*Merci.*" Gamache brought out his wallet and gave her all he had. Then he knelt down and held the girl's dirty face between his large hands. Bringing out his handkerchief, he wiped her face and said quietly, "It'll be all right. This nice woman will bring you a hot chocolate and something to eat. No one will hurt you."

He stood up and looked at the waitress. "That's right, isn't it?"

She frowned and looked unhappy about all this. But he could see it was an act.

The girl would be safe.

He left, running across the street, dodging traffic, then up St.-André. He'd pulled out his phone and called Jean-Guy.

It rang and rang as he ran.

"*Patron—*"

"They've found the factory. It's off St.-André, north of Ste.-Catherine. You can track using my signal. And, Jean-Guy, there's a little girl in that diner we were in, on Ste.-Catherine. Have Lacoste come and get her. Hurry."

Without waiting for a reply, he clicked back to the map and the pulsing blue dot. And the white dot. On the horizon. Getting closer.

Beauvoir stood up and instinctively put his hand to his hip. And felt his gun there.

"I need to go."

"But we just broke the code. We're in."

By then Cloutier was talking only to Ruth, who continued to scowl. Though she did seem to be seeing something, very far away.

"What do you mean, you're going out?" demanded Lacoste's husband.

"And so are you. You need to . . . drive me."

While their neighbor looked after the kids, they drove into downtown Montréal.

"I'm not sure this's safe," said Isabelle's husband, glancing around.

"It could be worse," said Isabelle, staring out the window and wondering about the others.

Amelia was warm. Finally.

The cold that had gotten into her core and gripped her bones was letting go. Thawing.

She felt the heat slowly spreading, radiating out along her arteries and veins.

And she felt her muscles relax. Go limp. It felt . . . wonderful.

She'd bucked and fought, but they'd pinned her down. Here. In the factory she'd worked so hard to find.

She'd followed the man into the basement of the building and found something she'd only ever seen in class, at the academy. In training footage of raids on labs.

Hundreds of people were working at long tables. They wore protective gear. Masks. Rubber gloves. Smocks. In front of each was a scale, sensitive enough to show micrograms.

"Better stay back," the man said. "Did you know that the Russians used carfentanil in that hostage taking a few years ago? They pumped it into the air supply, to knock everyone out. But they had no idea what they were dealing with," he said with a laugh. "Killed most of the hostage takers and hundreds of hostages."

"All I know is that it's an elephant tranquilizer," said Amelia, standing as far back as she could from the long tables and the mounds of white powder.

"It was, but this"—he gestured toward the tables—"is another generation. Evolution. It's a wonderful thing but can also be a bit confusing. For instance, when this shit fell into our hands a few months ago, we knew what we had but didn't know how much to put in each hit."

He spoke matter-of-factly, as though talking about a soup recipe.

"So we experimented. As the release got closer, we began giving it to different people to see what happened."

Amelia looked down at her arm. Then at him.

"That's what this means. You wrote it on everyone you experimented on."

"Yes. The name of the drug, David, and the dosage. You got a quarter gram. Others weren't so lucky. But now we know the best hit. We don't want to kill too many of our customers. Of course, if they're stupid enough to take more than one dose at a time . . . well. Too dumb to live, I guess. Evolution."

"You fucker. You gave it to me?"

"You brought it on. Showing up out of nowhere. Asking questions. Beating up my dealers. You didn't think you could just arrive on the streets and take over? You really thought I'd allow it?" He laughed again, then grew serious. "I know who you really are. Not the one-eyed man. You're as blind and stupid as the rest of them, Amelia Choquet. Cadet in the Sûreté Academy."

"Former. I was kicked out."

"Mmm, yes. Trafficking. And yet instead of arresting you, they just threw you out? Now, why was that?"

"Why do you think? Oh, wait a minute. You think this's a setup? Yes, that makes sense, you dumb turd. That way I could get kicked out, move into a shithole with a junkie, and freeze my ass off. I'm living the dream. You think you're so clever. But we both know that this"—she nodded toward the long tables—"fell into your lap. And you're going to need help keeping it. Once this hits the streets, every dirty cop, every mob boss, every gang member, every wannabe cartel chief will be after you. You're right. I'm not the one-eyed man. I have two good eyes, and what I see is you gutted in some alley. You need me."

He was nodding. And then he looked past her and raised his brows.

Hands gripped her shoulders, and she was dragged backward onto the floor.

She fought, at one point thinking she'd broken free, but then a blow knocked her down and almost out. Dazed, she was turned onto her back, so that she was staring into his eyes.

"I don't think so," the man whispered, kneeling over her. "You're too dangerous. You betray everyone and everything, and eventually you'd betray me."

He stood up and nodded to someone. "Do it. Then toss her out."

Amelia bucked and fought and shouted. And felt the needle go in.

Then felt the warmth. Then it got hotter and hotter. Until it began to burn. Until her blood felt like it had turned to lava.

She opened her mouth to scream, but her eyes just rolled to the back of her head. Then turned red.

Gamache found the agents, their weapons drawn.

They gestured toward a door where two well-armed guards stood.

Then the agents pointed up. More guards stood on a fire escape and on the roofs of surrounding buildings.

Gamache gave a curt nod, then carefully backed down the alley. He turned, only to find the tactical commander and his assault team.

"Two out front," Gamache whispered. "Two on the fire escape opposite and three on the roofs."

He gestured, and the commander nodded.

"Got it." He handed Gamache a mask. "Do you have a weapon?"

"No," said Gamache.

"I might get shit for doing this, but—"

He pressed an automatic into Gamache's hand.

"*Merci.*"

"Let us go in first."

"Of course."

The commander signaled behind him. Weapons were raised, and with a few rapid silenced shots the guards dropped.

Gamache was about to move forward, right behind the commander, when he felt a hand on his shoulder.

It was Beauvoir, his own gun drawn.

"*Patron*," Jean-Guy whispered.

"Lacoste?"

"On her way to the girl."

As he spoke, his sharp eyes were on the door, with the tactical team pouring through.

He started to move forward, but Gamache stopped him. "Amelia Choquet's in there."

"So she did lead you to the stuff," said Beauvoir. "Fucking junkie. What did I—"

"She's with us. She's following my orders. We have to find her. Here." He handed Jean-Guy the mask. "Put this on."

The fight was brutal.

The tactical team arrived in force and didn't hesitate to use that force, firing on the armed guards with precision.

They moved swiftly through the lab, the first wave targeting those with weapons, the next wave of armed officers shoving workers away from the tables. Pushing them against the wall. Frisking those who complied. Subduing those who did not.

Beauvoir, gas mask on, went through ahead of Gamache and almost fell over the body.

He gestured to Gamache to back out, and, grabbing the collar of Amelia's coat, he dragged her back through the door. Away from any drug that might be floating in the air. Kicked up by the attack.

Once out the door, Beauvoir ripped off his mask and knelt by Gamache, who was on his knees beside Amelia.

Beauvoir kept his gun trained on the open door as automatic fire burst out. Ignoring it, Gamache wasted no time feeling for a pulse. He pulled the syringe from his pocket and plunged it into Amelia.

Her eyes were open. Glassy. Red. As though possessed.

Only then did he feel for a pulse as Beauvoir, still focused on the open door, called for medics.

"How is she?"

"No pulse."

Gamache tore open her coat as bullets hit the bricks above them. Beauvoir ducked, instinctively, but Gamache kept on with the compressions. Counting. Under his breath, his face fixed, his focus complete. Ignoring the gunshots all around.

"Three. Four. Five."

Beauvoir sensed movement through the door into the lab at the same moment he heard a click. Turning quickly, he saw the gun rising. Pointing at them.

A young guy held the weapon like an expert.

But Beauvoir was more expert. He fired. Three quick shots. Boom, boom, boom. And the man dropped.

When the ringing from the shots stopped bouncing off the walls, he heard Gamache beside him, still counting. Not losing a beat.

"Twenty-nine. Thirty."

The medics arrived.

Gamache bent lower and gave Amelia two breaths.

"Carfentanil," he said, continuing the compressions while Beauvoir watched the door into the lab and counted for him.

"Seven. Eight. Nine."

"I gave her the antagonist," said Gamache as he rocked back and forth, keeping the rhythm of the compressions.

"Which one?" asked the medic, kneeling beside him and preparing the defibrillator.

"Naloxone. Less than a minute ago."

"Okay," said the medic. "Step aside."

Gamache did, watching as the medics worked on Amelia. And other medics moved forward into the factory. To care for the wounded. Even as the shots continued. And more wounded were made.

Gamache looked over at Jean-Guy, who was now kneeling beside the young man he'd shot. And killed.

CHAPTER 37

⌒

"You look awful," said Isabelle's husband with a sympathetic smile. "Here."

He handed Gamache a scotch and offered Beauvoir a coffee.

"*Merci*," said Armand, accepting the drink but putting it down. "Where is she?"

It was well past midnight, and he felt like he'd been hit by a truck, but the evening wasn't over yet.

"In our daughter's room," said Isabelle. "Would you like to see?"

"Please. Do you know her name?"

"No. She hasn't spoken."

"Social services?"

"I thought I'd wait 'til morning."

"Good."

Gamache and Jean-Guy followed Isabelle down the hall.

Her husband stayed behind in the living room, watching the three of them go. Recognizing that while he and the children would always be the most important parts of Isabelle's life, these three also formed a family.

The door was open, and a night-light was on. In one bed lay Sophia, Isabelle's daughter. Fast asleep.

In the other was the little girl. On her side, curled into a tight ball under the comforter. Eyes staring. Her hands clutching the pillow at her head.

Armand walked in quietly and knelt down.

When last he'd seen the girl, her hair was matted and caked with filth. Now it was clean and brushed. She'd had a bath and smelled very faintly of lavender.

"It's Armand," he spoke softly. "We met earlier. I'm the police officer."

She cringed away, her eyes widening.

"It's all right. I won't hurt you. No one will. You're safe." He was careful not to approach further. Not to touch her. "You can go to sleep now."

He smiled in a way that, he hoped and prayed, didn't betray how his heart ached for her.

But she continued to stare at him, in terror.

"May I?" he asked, turning to Isabelle and indicating a book on the bedside table.

Isabelle nodded.

Armand brought over a chair and opened the book.

"'. . . in which we are introduced to Winnie-the-Pooh and some bees,'" he read, his voice deep and soft and tranquil. He looked up then, into her wide eyes. "'And the stories begin.'"

"Amelia?" Isabelle asked Jean-Guy.

They'd left the Chief Superintendent reading to the girl and had returned to the living room.

"We just came from the hospital," said Jean-Guy, dropping into an armchair. "They got her heart going, and she's breathing on her own."

"Brain damage?" asked Isabelle.

"They're doing tests, but we won't know until she wakes up. We're going back there right after we leave here."

She nodded. "If there's anything I can do."

"There may be. Thank you. I'll let you know."

"So she was working with the Chief all along? Did . . . anyone know?"

"No."

"Not even you?"

"No. I knew he'd expelled Amelia in hopes she'd lead him to the carfentanil, but I had no idea she was in on it."

Isabelle looked at Jean-Guy closely. "Are you okay with that? With not being told?"

He lifted his fingers off the arms of the chair, then dropped them. What could he say? What could he do? It was, he knew, the nature of the job.

Secrecy. Secrets.

Lacoste had them. All senior officers had things they kept close to the chest.

God knows, he himself had his secrets. One in particular.

He knew he'd have to tell his father-in-law soon. And this one hit closer to home and was far more personal than the secret Gamache had kept from him.

"The carfentanil?" asked Isabelle.

"Looks like we got it all, except for what was used in the experiments."

"What experiments?" Isabelle's husband asked.

"This particular opioid's so new that no one really knows the safe dose. And, of course, that also depends on weight, body type. Health. So many addicts have weak hearts, and very little will push them over the edge. This guy—"

Boom, boom, boom. Beauvoir saw, in a flash, the man drop. Dead.

Something he would never unsee. Another ghost for his longhouse.

"—experimented on junkies. Giving out different doses and writing on their arms the amount. A milligram. Two. To see who survived and who died."

Isabelle shook her head, and then her brow furrowed. "Why did he call it David?"

"It's his father's name."

Isabelle took that in. Not sure what it meant. Was it meant as a tribute or an attack, an accusation? Was it meant to thank or to hurt?

She suspected the latter.

"You okay?" she asked Jean-Guy. She could guess what he was thinking.

That he'd just killed a young man. Troubled. Criminal. A killer. It was self-defense. But he was still dead. And one day soon, Jean-Guy would have to face the boy's father. David.

"I'm tired," said Jean-Guy, and she could see that it would take much more than a shower and a good night's sleep for him to recover.

"The sound of maple logs in an open fire," she said quietly. "A hot dog at a Canadiens game. Honoré's hand . . . holding yours."

"These things I've loved," Jean-Guy whispered. *"Merci."*

She glanced down the hall to where the children were sleeping. A delicate, almost reedy sound was coming from there.

Jean-Guy and Isabelle went quietly down and looked in.

Armand had closed the book and was leaning toward the child, his elbows on the torn and filthy knees of his slacks.

He was humming. While, in the bed, the little girl's eyes were closed. *Edelweiss. Edelweiss.*

Hours later Amelia Choquet opened her eyes, squinting into the bright light.

She felt a hand on her shoulder and startled.

"It's all right, you're in the hospital. My name's Dr. Boudreau. I'll be looking after you."

He spoke slowly. Clearly.

"Can you tell me your name?"

There was a pause.

"Amelia . . . Choquet."

"That's right. And do you know who this is?"

Dr. Boudreau looked at the man standing beside him.

"Shit. Head," she mumbled.

"Wha—" the doctor began, but Gamache gave a gruff laugh.

"She got that right too," he said, and looked across the bed to Jean-Guy, who was smiling with relief.

"I'm sorry, Amelia," said Gamache. "For this."

"Did you—"

"Yes, we got it all."

She closed her eyes, and Gamache thought she'd drifted off. But she spoke again, her eyes still closed.

"Girl."

"We have her. She's safe," said Jean-Guy. "Your friend Marc is here in the hospital too. They're looking after him."

Amelia nodded, then went silent.

Gamache took the doctor aside. "Will she be all right?"

"I think so. She's healthy, and you got the rescue med to her in time. She's lucky."

"Yeah, well," said Jean-Guy, "I can hardly wait to hear her version of that when she's fully awake."

Before he left, Armand took the worn little book from his pocket and pressed it into her hands.

"Erasmus," he whispered, though he wasn't sure she could hear him. "For company."

They left the hospital, but there was one more stop they had to make before the day, or night, was over.

Agent Cloutier was asleep in her chair but awoke quickly and stood up at her desk when she saw the Chief Superintendent come in with Chief Inspector Beauvoir.

Both men looked exhausted. Unshaved and disheveled.

She'd heard what had happened and had begun toward them when she stopped. And smiled. Broadly. On seeing who walked slowly in behind them.

"Chief Inspector," said Cloutier, going over to Lacoste and hugging her.

"Is that how we greeted each other, *patron*, when you were head of homicide?" asked Jean-Guy.

"Only in private."

Beauvoir laughed and pulled over two chairs to join the two already in front of the laptop on Cloutier's desk.

Isabelle sat and took a moment to look at Ruth glaring back at her.

"Amazing," she said. "I keep expecting her to say 'numbnuts.'"

"Why would the Virgin Mary say that?" asked Cloutier.

"Not important," said Beauvoir. "Show us what you have."

As Agent Cloutier walked them through the files they'd found on Anthony Baumgartner's computer, a pattern emerged.

The three of them stared at the screen. Then at each other. Then at Agent Cloutier.

Beauvoir had known some of this when he'd been called away. But most of it Cloutier had uncovered on her own.

"It's genius," Cloutier said in admiration. "Almost too simple to believe, and that made it hard to find." She shook her head. "Incredible."

The other three were leaning forward. Examining the details.

"It's suggestive," said Gamache.

"It's more than that, sir," she said. "It says it all."

"No. It says one thing, but there's no proof this is what actually happened," said Gamache.

"We need proof, Agent Cloutier," said Jean-Guy. "But this at least tells us where to look."

"I have proof," she said. "Follow the money."

She smiled and started tapping rapidly on the keys. Different pages popped up and disappeared from the screen.

"This is," she said as she typed, "the same route Anthony Baumgartner took. Circuitous, but then it would have to be."

There, finally, on the screen was the home page of a corporation in the British Virgin Islands.

"Is that where Baumgartner hid the rest of the money?" asked Beauvoir.

"With Shaeffer's help. But it's a launch point, not the final stop," said Cloutier. "People who want to hide money set up a corporation in a tax haven like BVI, then funnel it to a numbered account. Switzerland used to be the country of choice. But then came the crackdown. This"— she hit another page—"took over."

A bank in Singapore came up.

"How do you know this's where Baumgartner hid his money?" asked Beauvoir.

"Because I found the account."

"How?" he asked.

Agent Cloutier glanced over at Ruth. "A little help from the crazy lady."

Lacoste and Gamache looked puzzled, but Beauvoir's brows cleared.

"The number on the back of the painting," said Beauvoir.

"Yes. It wasn't his password, it was the account number. He wrote it there so he wouldn't forget it."

She put in the numbers, and up popped the account. Under the name Baumgartner.

"Three hundred and seventy-seven million dollars," Lacoste read off the screen.

"A motive for murder," said Beauvoir. He stood up and placed a call. Ordering agents to arrest Bernard Shaeffer.

The sun was up and flooding into the offices of Horowitz Investments when Beauvoir arrived. He'd had time to shower and change and had asked Hugo and Caroline Baumgartner to meet him in Hugo's office.

The office was as impressive as Hugo Baumgartner was unimpressive. Floor-to-ceiling windows looked out over the city. It spoke of success but didn't drip wealth. It was restrained, while saying all it needed to say.

Jean-Guy took note. Wondering if he could make over his office like this.

The siblings sat side by side, like a princess and a toad. Caroline self-contained and elegant. Hugo squat and disheveled. No tailor could ever make him look tailored. But his bulging eyes were warm and encouraging, and he rested his hand on his sister's.

"You have news, you said?"

"We do," said Beauvoir.

He'd brought Agent Cloutier with him. He'd invited Gamache as well, but having also showered and changed, he had another meeting to go to. With the Premier Ministre du Québec.

The review board had come down with its recommendations.

Just before entering the meeting with the Baumgartners, Beauvoir had received a call from Gamache.

"I've had a message from Kontrollinspektor Gund in Vienna. There's been a decision on the will."

Beauvoir listened, and then, after wishing Gamache good luck, he hung up and entered his own meeting.

"You know who killed Anthony?" asked Caroline.

"Yes. Early this morning we arrested Bernard Shaeffer."

She closed her eyes and exhaled. "Oh, poor Anthony."

"But why would Shaeffer kill him?" asked Hugo. "Revenge for being fired? That was a couple of years ago."

"You'd be surprised how long people can hold on to things."

"Were they still seeing each other?" Caroline asked.

"Not that we can tell," said Beauvoir. "Not as lovers anyway. But there's evidence that your brother got him a job after he was fired. He's working at the Caisse Populaire."

"At a bank?" asked Hugo. "Why would Tony do that? It doesn't make sense."

"It does if you need to set up false accounts and hide money."

Hugo opened his mouth to speak, then shut it and stared at the Chief Inspector.

"You have proof?"

Beauvoir nodded. "Shaeffer admitted he'd set up a shell company and a numbered account in Lebanon in your brother's name, in exchange for the job and his silence. We found millions."

Caroline looked at Hugo. "What does this mean? Anthony really was stealing?"

"It looks like it. Are you sure it was him, Chief Inspector? Maybe Shaeffer set up an account in Tony's name but used the money himself. Tony found out, confronted him, and Shaeffer killed him."

"We considered that possibility," said Beauvoir. "That your brother actually knew nothing about it. There was also the strange issue of the amount in the account. Slightly over seven million."

"Sounds like a lot to me," said Caroline.

But Hugo understood. He was watching Beauvoir, his ugly face expressive. "According to the statements you showed me, he'd taken hundreds of millions. So where's the rest?"

"Exactly."

Beauvoir nodded to Agent Cloutier, who put Anthony Baumgartner's laptop on the table and set it up.

"It took us a while, but we finally got into your brother's computer." Beauvoir looked at them. "I hope this won't upset you."

They looked at each other, and Caroline gave a curt nod. "Best we know. I expect it'll all be made public soon enough."

"The interesting thing about your brother," said Beauvoir as Cloutier brought up the files, "is that almost without exception he was described as decent, brilliant. A great mentor and a man of integrity, who when he discovered wrongdoing, turned the person in, knowing he'd get some of the blame."

"That was the Tony we knew," said Hugo.

"But his actions told a different story. A man who was brilliant, yes, but deceitful. Embezzling not just tens of millions but hundreds of millions. Who betrayed a young co-conspirator and turned him in when it looked like they'd be caught. It's a familiar story for those of us in homicide. People lead double lives. They appear to be one thing while actually being not just something else but something totally opposite to what people think."

"How else do they get away with it?" said Hugo.

Beauvoir was nodding. "Except most don't. Let me show you what we found on his laptop."

The Premier stood at his desk, and Gamache rose also.

He'd been in the Premier's Montréal office less than ten minutes.

These things didn't take long.

"I'm sorry, Armand," said the Premier, looking down at the unopened envelope on his desk. "If there was any other course possible, I'd have taken it."

"I appreciate your telling me yourself, and in person. I knew what would probably happen when I made those decisions. It could've been worse. You could be arresting me."

"You've made some enemies, Armand, but you have a lot more friends. I hope you know I'm one of them."

"I do."

"And you got the drugs back, that's what matters. I've been reading the preliminary report on what happened. You do know that if you hadn't already been suspended, you'd have been suspended for what you just did." He looked at Gamache closely. "And no one else knew you'd had a cadet thrown out of the academy and that she was working with you?"

"No one."

"Not even Beauvoir?"

"Not even him. Just Cadet Choquet and me."

The Premier nodded slowly. But decided not to question it further. The less he knew . . . He walked forward, to show Gamache the door.

"How is she?"

"Recovering. She'll be running the Sûreté one day."

"Yeah, well, the job's open. Apparently you have to be half crazed to accept it, so that bodes well for her. I just hope I'm long retired by the time there's a Chief Superintendent Choquet."

Gamache smiled, then paused at the threshold. "There is something you can help me with."

"Name it."

"There's a little girl. . . ."

Gamache called Reine-Marie and told her what happened, then drove across town to the low-rise apartment building and pressed the button for the caretaker's apartment.

Benedict let him in, and a few minutes later Gamache was sitting on a worn sofa in the tiny basement apartment. Katie and Benedict were across from him, sitting on boxes.

"Have you figured out who killed Monsieur Baumgartner?" Benedict asked. "You know, I thought for a minute yesterday, at your place, that you suspected us."

"More than a minute," said Katie.

"No, I haven't come about that. Chief Inspector Beauvoir will be by later this morning to talk with you."

They exchanged glances, then Katie asked, "Why have you come?"

"There's a decision in the court case in Vienna. It came down this morning."

Benedict took Katie's hand, and they waited.

"They ruled in favor of the Baumgartners."

The couple sat still for a moment, then Benedict put his arm around Katie and she nodded.

"It's what we expected," said Katie. "And without that letter the Baron and Baroness's wishes won't be followed. They'll keep it for themselves."

"It's theirs to keep," Benedict said. "You did your best. We'll be fine."

He hugged her closer.

"The sins I was told were mine from birth / And the Guilt of an old inheritance," thought Gamache as he left them and headed over the Champlain Bridge toward Reine-Marie and home.

Maybe it stops now, with their child.

Hugo Baumgartner was staring at the laptop, his lower lip thrust out in concentration.

"Are you following?" asked Agent Cloutier.

"Yes, thank you," he said with a patient smile. And returned to the screen. After a few minutes, he sighed. "So Tony and Shaeffer were working together after all. I was wrong. I'm sorry. I really didn't think Tony had it in him."

"I'm afraid that's what it looks like," said Beauvoir. He scrolled down as he spoke.

Hugo was studying the screen, nodding. "They've taken the usual routes to hide money."

"You know a lot about it?" asked Beauvoir.

"More than some," he admitted. "But less than most. Mr. Horowitz asked me to head a committee investigating offshore accounts."

"To set them up?" asked Beauvoir.

Hugo gave him an amused look. "To make sure we weren't inadvertently helping clients hide money. Partly moral, but also practical. Mr. Horowitz is wealthy enough, he doesn't need that money, and he sure doesn't need the trouble if the regulators and the media find out."

"Did you find any?" asked Beauvoir.

"More than we expected, Chief Inspector. The wealthy have a way of justifying things. They live in distorted reality. If everyone at the club's doing it, it must be okay."

"'They'?" asked Beauvoir. "You don't consider yourself one of them?"

"Wealthy? No," he laughed. "I'm very well off, rich by most standards, but these people have hundreds of millions. I'm not in that club, nor do I wish to be. I'm happy where I am."

Hugo returned to the screen. "One thing I do know is that we'll need to find the number of the account in Singapore. Has Shaeffer given it to you?"

"He says he doesn't have it. In fact, he seemed surprised about this second account."

"He must be lying," said Hugo. "Unfortunately, the bank in Singapore won't tell you, and they can't be compelled to give out the information. But Tony must've written it down somewhere."

"Well," said Beauvoir. "You're right about that. It was written down."

"You found it?" asked Hugo.

"Behind the painting," said Agent Cloutier.

"Which painting?" asked Caroline.

"The one in his study," said Beauvoir. "Above the fireplace."

"Of the crazy old lady?" said Caroline. "That's where Anthony hid it?" She thought for a moment, then said, "Smart, actually. It'd be pretty safe there. I can tell you that no one goes near it. God knows what the Baroness saw in that thing. Miserable piece of so-called art. You thought the same thing, didn't you?"

Hugo nodded.

"Poor Anthony ended up with it," she said. "Told her he liked it. Something about a white dot in the distance. He was just being polite, and look where it got him. She gave it to him, and he had to hang it up. No matter what you say he did, there was a lot of kindness in him."

"I haven't said he did anything," said Beauvoir. "At least not anything illegal."

"What do you mean?" She pointed to the laptop. "Isn't that the proof?"

Beauvoir nodded to Cloutier, who started putting the numbers in.

"After all our high-tech hunting, it was writing on the back of a painting that finally gave us the proof we needed."

Cloutier hit enter, and up came the account.

Caroline's eyes widened.

"Three hundred and seventy-seven million," she whispered.

Then her expression changed, to confusion.

"But I don't understand. That says Hugo Baumgartner." She turned to her brother. "Was Anthony trying to make it look like it was you?" And then she understood.

Jean-Guy Beauvoir stood, and Agent Cloutier experienced another first.

Her first arrest for murder.

CHAPTER 38

"So." Ruth's voice, querulous, stalked in from the living room to the kitchen, where Armand and Reine-Marie were preparing warm hors d'oeuvres. "The idea is to run around the village green at minus twenty, in our bathing suits, wearing snowshoes?"

"Yes," said Gabri. "It was Myrna's idea."

"Was not."

"Was too."

"I think it's brilliant," said Ruth. "Count me in."

"We're doing this at night, right?" Clara whispered to Gabri.

"Now we are."

"Have you heard from Justin Trudeau yet?" Myrna asked. "Is he coming?"

"Oddly, the Baroness Bertha Baumgartner here has not yet heard back from the Prime Minister's office," said Olivier.

"You used her name?" asked Ruth.

"It was Myrna's idea," said Gabri.

"Was not."

"Was too."

"That's . . . that's . . ." Ruth struggled to find the right word. "Brilliant too. She'd have liked that. But I can't believe Justin Trudeau isn't keen to strip down and race around a tiny village. He's taken his shirt off for less. He once did it for a bag of Cheetos. I think."

"We still have time," said Gabri. "He'll reply. The winter carnival isn't until the weekend."

"If there was a ribbon for faint hope, he'd win," said Olivier with pride.

"Okay, here's a question," said Ruth. "One that philosophers have been asking for centuries. Which would you rather have? A numb skull or a numb nut?"

"Dear God," whispered Reine-Marie, peering around the corner of the kitchen at their assembled guests. "What've we done?"

"Ahh, the age-old question," said Stephen Horowitz, sitting beside Ruth on the sofa. "I believe Socrates asked his students the same thing."

"It was Plato," said Ruth.

"Was not."

"Was too."

"I think," Armand said to Reine-Marie, "we should keep an eye out for two more Horsemen."

"Well, he's your godfather," she said. "And it was your idea to invite him down to meet Ruth."

"I kind of thought they might cancel each other out."

"More like Godzilla meets Mothra," said Gabri, walking into the kitchen and taking a grilled parmesan on baguette off the tray they were preparing. "Tokyo is not safe. We, by the way, are Tokyo."

"There you are, Armand," said Stephen when they returned to the living room. "I have some questions for you."

"Numb skull," said Armand.

"No, not that. Though that is the right answer." The elderly man looked at the hors d'oeuvre platter and asked, "Caviar?"

"They're provincial," said Ruth. "Come over to my place later. I have a little jar and a chilled bottle of Dom Perignon."

"Taken from us on New Year's Eve," muttered Olivier, still fuming.

"The jar of caviar was open," said Clara. "By now it'll probably kill her."

"That's the one you took," said Myrna. "We ate it the next day, with chopped egg on toast."

"Oh right. Never mind."

Stephen held out his glass, and Armand refreshed it. "You know what I'm going to ask."

"I'll let Jean-Guy explain," said Armand, correctly guessing what was on Stephen Horowitz's mind. "He's the head of homicide. He figured it out."

Jean-Guy looked uncomfortable, and not just because Rosa was

374

sitting on his lap. Beside him, in the crook of his arm, Honoré was staring at Rosa, transfixed by the duck, who was muttering, "Fuck, fuck, fuck."

Then Jean-Guy heard another voice repeating the same word.

His eyes widened, and he looked at Annie, who was staring at their son.

His first word.

Not "Mama." Not "Papa."

"Shhh," said Jean-Guy, but by now others had noticed the odd echo coming from the armchair.

"I think," said Annie, going over and scooping up their son, "it's time for a bath."

And that's when Honoré let loose. One great, long "Fuuuuck!"

Even Rosa looked startled, but then ducks often did.

"Ahh," said Reine-Marie and looked at the fire, while Armand raised his eyes to the ceiling, suddenly finding the plaster fascinating.

Ruth hooted with delight, and Stephen said, "Attaboy, Ray-Ray. You tell 'em."

Armand dropped his eyes and looked at his godfather. "Nice. *Merci.*"

"Only you, my dear boy, could have a grandson whose greatest influence is a mallard."

"Is she a mallard?" Clara asked Ruth, who shrugged and took a long swig of Stephen's drink.

"Okay, off we go," said Annie while Honoré, in her arms and noticing the reaction his first word got, wailed it all the way down the hall.

"Good God," sighed Reine-Marie.

"Good lungs," said Stephen.

Beauvoir tried not to notice the tightly pressed lips of Clara, Myrna, Gabri, and Olivier. Even Armand and Reine-Marie looked amused.

"You have some questions, sir?" Jean-Guy asked Stephen.

It had been a day since the arrests of Bernard Shaeffer and Hugo Baumgartner. One for embezzlement, one for murder.

"Hugo. What happened? I can follow the scheme," said Stephen. "But I don't know the details. He wasn't just my employee. A senior vice president. I trusted him. I must be getting old."

"You're already there," said Ruth.

"I can tell you most of what happened," said Jean-Guy.

Everyone leaned forward.

Even Myrna, who already knew. Armand had told her. And she, in confidence, had told Clara. Who had told Gabri in confidence, who immediately told Olivier, swearing him to secrecy. Who then spilled it to Ruth in exchange for the crystal water jug she'd also lifted on New Year's Eve.

"Yes," said Clara. "Please, tell us."

"The idea started when Anthony turned Shaeffer in. Shaeffer was fired, and Anthony Baumgartner had his license to trade taken away," said Jean-Guy.

"The original embezzlement," said Stephen.

"Yes. Hugo knew Anthony wasn't to blame, but he also knew his reputation had been damaged. The street, as you call it, believed Anthony Baumgartner was also in on it and that only his senior position in the firm had saved him. They believed he was as dirty as Shaeffer. Hugo saw his opportunity. He approached Bernard Shaeffer, who was clearly a crook, and offered to get him a job in the Caisse Populaire, in exchange for certain favors."

"Hugo was the one who wrote the letter of recommendation to the Caisse," said Myrna. "Not his brother."

"And what were the favors?" asked Olivier. They knew the broad outlines of the crime, but not the details.

"Shaeffer would use the facilities and connections of the bank to set up an account in Anthony's name."

"Don't you mean Hugo's name?" asked Clara.

"No, that was the brilliance of what Hugo did. He was setting Anthony up. If anyone clued in to what was happening, they'd only find Anthony's name, on a numbered account in Lebanon."

"They put seven million into it," said Stephen. He was listening closely. So far this wasn't anything he didn't already know.

"*Merde*," said Olivier. "Wish he'd incriminated me."

"That was nothing," said Beauvoir. "The real money was going into a numbered account in Singapore. Not even Shaeffer knew about that. He had no idea of the scope of the embezzlement."

He looked at Gamache, inviting him to join in. Armand leaned forward, his glass of scotch between his hands.

"It worked well for a few years," said Armand. "As with most things, it started small. A little money from one or two. But when Hugo realized they weren't questioning, as long as they got their dividend checks, he increased the amounts and the number of clients."

"He got greedy," said Clara.

"Greed, yes. But I've seen this sort of thing before," said Stephen. "It becomes a game. A thrill. A sort of addiction. They have to keep increasing the hit. No one needs three hundred million. He could've stopped at fifty and been safe and comfortable for the rest of his life. No, there was something else at work. And I didn't see it."

He looked not just upset but drained.

Despite her kidding, Reine-Marie knew perfectly well why Armand had invited his godfather out for a few days. And introduced him to Ruth.

It was so he wouldn't be alone with his thoughts. With his wounds.

Things were pretty dire when Ruth was the healing agent.

"So what went wrong?" asked Gabri.

"Anthony ran into one of the so-called clients on the street last summer," said Beauvoir. "The man thanked Anthony for the great job he was doing. Baumgartner didn't think much of it until he started going through his client list and realized this fellow wasn't on it. He contacted the man and asked for the financial statement."

"So he knew someone was stealing, and using his name," said Stephen. "I got that. But how did he figure out it was his brother?"

Ruth, sitting between Gabri and Stephen, had fallen asleep and was snoring softly. Her head lolling on Stephen's shoulder. A bit of spittle landing on his cashmere sweater.

But he didn't push her away.

"He didn't. Not at first," said Beauvoir. "When we got into his laptop and uncovered his search history, we found that he seemed to be searching for something. At first we assumed he was looking around for places to put the money, but then we checked the timelines and realized it wasn't that."

"He was trying to retrace someone's steps," said Armand. "To figure out who was responsible."

"He started with his own company," said Jean-Guy. "With Madame Ogilvy, in fact. Then spread it out. When all else failed, he began looking further afield."

"Or closer to home, really," said Armand. And not, he thought, in a field but in a garden. Apparently healthy but actually choked with bindweed.

He tried to imagine Anthony Baumgartner's shock when he realized who was stealing. And setting him up.

Matthew 10:36.

Armand sometimes wished he'd never paused on that piece of Scripture. And he certainly wished he didn't know the truth it contained.

"What I don't understand is how Anthony Baumgartner even found that trail," said Stephen. "Hugo would've hidden it well."

"Let me ask you this," said Armand. "If you were going to embezzle, would you use your own computer?"

Stephen's face opened, and he gave a small grunt. "No. I'd use someone else's and take the opportunity to implicate them while I'm at it, in case it's ever caught. Smart Hugo."

"Smart Hugo," said Beauvoir. "He and Anthony got together once a week for meals. While Tony cooked, Hugo used his brother's laptop, supposedly to get caught up on the markets."

"But actually to transfer money," said Stephen.

"But wouldn't it be obvious?" asked Olivier. "I do our accounting online, and it's all right there."

"Not hard to bury it," said Beauvoir. "Especially if you want to. And Hugo wanted to. But not too deep. He also wanted people to be able to find it, if need be. And we eventually did. And yes, it made it look like Anthony was the one doing it. Why wouldn't it? Without the password for the numbered account in Singapore, there'd be no proof it was anyone other than Anthony."

"But Anthony found it?" said Clara.

"*Oui*," Beauvoir continued. "We found Anthony's searches. He'd made no attempt to hide those. They were more and more frantic, it seems. And then, in September of last year, they stopped."

"He had what he was looking for," said Armand.

"He knew then, months ago, that Hugo was stealing?" said Stephen. "Why didn't he stop it then? Why wait until now to say something? Denial?"

"Maybe," said Armand. "But I think it might've been something else."

"His mother," said Clara. "He waited until his mother died."

"Yes," said Armand.

"I can see why Hugo would need someone else to blame, but why not use Shaeffer for that too?" asked Olivier. "Why drag his own brother into it?"

"Hard to tell," said Jean-Guy. "There was the convenience of the laptop and the fact Anthony was already tarred by the street. Hugo isn't admitting anything."

"I think there was something else," said Myrna. "Jealousy. And can you blame him?"

"For killing his brother?" asked Clara. "I think I can."

"No, I mean for being jealous. Resentful. One tall, handsome, respected, decent. Married with children. The other squat, physically unattractive, even slightly repulsive. Imagine growing up together?"

"But lots do," said Gabri. "I have a younger brother who's not nearly as attractive as me. It hasn't led to murder."

"Early days," said Olivier.

"But there was more," said Myrna. "Who was the Baroness's favorite? Who understood Clara's painting? Hugo might've looked like his mother, but Anthony was more like her in every way that mattered. That's why Hugo dragged Anthony's name into it."

"'The sins I was told were mine from birth,'" said Stephen, looking down at the woman drooling on his sweater, "'and the Guilt of an old inheritance.'"

Ruth woke up with a snort. "Guilt? Sin?"

"You were singing her song," said Gabri.

"Wait a minute," said Stephen. "I know about these numbered accounts. You got the number for the one in Lebanon from that Shaeffer fellow, but what about the other?"

"We found it behind Clara's painting," said Beauvoir.

"Yes, yes, but how did Anthony Baumgartner find it and put it there? These codes are closely guarded. The bank only sends them out over secure, encrypted emails. There's no way Anthony could've just stumbled on it and then written it behind that painting. By the way," he said to Clara. "I'd like to see the original. Is it for sale?"

"Ten bucks and she's yours," said Gabri, pointing to Ruth.

"We can talk," said Clara.

"You're right," said Jean-Guy. "Anthony could never find the code.

It's the one thing that Hugo knew would incriminate him. The only place where he needed his real name. On the account in Singapore that had three hundred seventy-seven million in it."

Olivier groaned.

"So how did Anthony find it and get into the account?" asked Stephen.

"He didn't."

They stared at Jean-Guy.

Armand crossed his legs and sat back. Marveling at Jean-Guy. His protégé, who now no longer needed any protection. He was soaring on his own.

"Anthony Baumgartner didn't write the access code there," said Jean-Guy. "Hugo did."

"And Anthony found it?" asked Myrna.

"No. He didn't. When he confronted Hugo that night at their old farmhouse, he didn't have the final proof. I think he must've begged Hugo to explain, but when Hugo couldn't, Anthony told him he'd have to turn him in."

"And that's why Hugo killed him," said Ruth.

"*Oui.*"

"Do you think Hugo meant to kill him?" asked Gabri.

"How should I know?" asked Ruth.

"I was asking the head of homicide," said Gabri. "Not the demented poet."

"Oh," she said. "Well, go on, numbnuts."

"Hard to tell," said Jean-Guy. "He was a man who planned. He must've had some sort of exit strategy, in case the embezzlement was found out. But I doubt his plan was to kill his brother."

"He was cornered," said Armand. "And when Anthony refused to turn a blind eye, he lashed out."

"You see what comes of integrity, Armand?" said Stephen. "Of decency?"

"Some godfather," said Myrna.

"Decency didn't kill him," said Armand. "Indecency did. Jealousy. Greed. Resentment."

"We were looking at one feud when it was another that did the damage," said Myrna.

They were quiet for a moment, until Gabri broke the silence.

"Is it rude to say I'm hungry?"

"So'm I," said Stephen. "What's for dinner? Lobster?"

"Stew," said Olivier.

"Eh," said Stephen. "Let's call it boeuf bourguignon."

"I see you're reading the book I gave you," Ruth said to Jean-Guy as they got up. She pointed to the coffee table.

"You gave him *The Gashlycrumb Tinies*?" asked Stephen. "By Edward Gorey? Oh, I think I really do love you," he said to Ruth.

While Stephen read the book out loud, Jean-Guy took Myrna aside.

"We found the letter," he said.

"In the wreck of the farmhouse?"

"Yes. Torn and dirty. It was exactly what Katie Burke described. Written in her hand, though the envelope looked like it was written by the Baroness. In it she asked Anthony to share the fortune should it come their way. Which it did."

"Thank you for telling me," said Myrna.

Annie caught her husband's eye. Jean-Guy took a deep breath, and then, excusing himself from Myrna, he approached his father-in-law.

"I'm going to say good night to Honoré. Want to come? Gets us out of preparing dinner."

"After dinner to avoid the dishes would be better," said Armand, but he followed Jean-Guy to their room.

As he left, he noticed Annie taking Reine-Marie into the study and closing the door.

"Why didn't you accept the job you were offered?" asked Jean-Guy, once in the bedroom with the door closed.

After calling Reine-Marie the day before, about his meeting with the Premier and the decision of the disciplinary committee, he'd called Jean-Guy. And told him he'd been asked to resign as Chief Superintendent.

Which he'd done. He'd had the letter prepared and in his breast pocket.

"You told me about resigning," said Jean-Guy in a whisper so as not to wake up his son. "But you didn't tell me you were offered your old job back. As head of homicide."

"True," said Gamache. "It was academic. I was never going to accept."

"Because of Lacoste?"

"*Non.* I made it a condition of my resignation that Isabelle was offered the post of Superintendent in charge of Serious Crimes. It'll be held for her until she's ready. Did you know they've started the paperwork to foster the little girl?"

"No, I hadn't heard. That's terrific."

Beauvoir sat on the side of the bed and looked at the crib where Honoré was sound asleep. He gave a deep sigh.

"I hope she accepts," said Armand, joining him. "The Sûreté needs her."

"It needs you, *patron.* So if not because of Isabelle, then why turn down Chief Inspector of Homicide? Ego?"

Gamache laughed and tapped Beauvoir's knee. "You know me better than that, old son."

"Then why?"

"You know why. It's your job. Your department. You're more than ready. You're Chief Inspector Beauvoir, the head of Homicide for the Sûreté. And I couldn't be more pleased." His smile faded, and he looked serious. "Or proud."

"Take the job."

"Why?" asked Armand, his eyes narrowing slightly as he studied Jean-Guy.

"Because I'm leaving."

He saw his signature, scribbled quickly before he could change his mind, on the papers that had been pushed across the polished desk.

"I've accepted a position with GHS Engineering. As their Head of Strategic Planning."

There was a long silence finally broken by "I see."

"I'm sorry. I wanted to tell you sooner but couldn't find the right time."

"No, no. I understand. I really do, Jean-Guy. You have a family, and it comes first."

"It's more than that. These last few years have been brutal, *patron.* And then to be suspended and investigated by our own people? It was just too much. I love my job, but I'm tired. I'm tired of death. Of killing."

They sat quietly, looking at the sleeping child. Hearing his soft breathing. Inhaling the scent of Honoré.

"Time to live," said Armand. "You've done more than anyone could ever ask. More than I could ever ask or expect. You're doing the right thing. Look at me."

Jean-Guy dragged his eyes from the crib to look at Armand. And he saw a smile that started at his mouth and coursed along the laugh lines. Up to the deep brown eyes.

"I'm happy for you. This is wonderful news."

And Jean-Guy could see there was genuine happiness there. "One more thing," he said.

"*Oui?*"

"The job's in Paris."

"Ahhh," said Armand.

"So that's the famous picture," said Stephen, taking a seat beside Ruth and gesturing toward Clara's painting.

"No, that's of the Three Graces," said Ruth. "The one the Baroness had is of me."

"The Virgin Mary," said Clara.

"The Virgin Mary as me," said Ruth.

"Other way around," said Clara.

"There you are," said Gabri as Jean-Guy returned. "Our little boy learned any new words? '*Merde*'? '*Tabernac*'?"

"No, he's sleeping. Papa's just tucking him in," said Jean-Guy, serving a portion of stew and creamy mashed potatoes and handing it to Annie.

"And Mama's gone to help," said Annie, taking it and catching his eye.

"You okay?" Armand asked Reine-Marie.

She'd closed the door behind her and put a hand on Armand's back as he held the sleeping infant.

It was a good thing, thought Armand, putting his face close to the child's head and inhaling, that the scent was uniquely Honoré. If he ever came across it unexpectedly—on a walk, in a restaurant, from a passing infant—he'd be overwhelmed with the grief he felt now.

And yet there was happiness there too.

It was wonderful and terrible. Joyous and devastating.

And there was relief.

Jean-Guy was out. He was safe. And so were Annie and Honoré. Safe and far away.

He handed Honoré to his grandmother, then put his arms around them both, smelling again the scent of the child mixing with the subtle perfume of old garden roses. He closed his eyes and thought, *Croissants. The first log fire in autumn. The scent of fresh-cut grass. Croissants.*

But it would take a very long list of things he loved to overcome this.

Reine-Marie held her grandson and breathed in the scent of Honoré and sandalwood. And felt Armand's embrace and the very slight tremble of his right hand.

She never thought Paris would break their hearts.

After dinner Stephen took Armand aside.

"I have some news for you."

"But first I want to thank you. Jean-Guy's accepted the job," said Armand. "And he'll be good at it. Strategic planning's what he's been doing for years at the Sûreté."

"Only now no one will be shooting at him," said Stephen.

"Exactly. But he must never know it came from you or me."

"I'm a cipher."

"You didn't tell me the job was in Paris."

"Would it have mattered?"

Armand considered for a moment before answering. "*Non.* It just would've been nice to have had warning."

"*Désolé.* I should have told you."

"What's your news?"

"Remember I told you that I had an idea and would do some digging around about that will thing?"

"I do remember, but you don't need to anymore. It's been decided in favor of the Baumgartners."

"Yes, I heard. I asked colleagues in Vienna to look into it. That

Shlomo Kinderoth was a piece of work. He must've known the trouble it would cause, leaving the estate to both sons."

"Maybe he just couldn't decide," said Armand.

"Or maybe he was a numbskull. A hundred and thirty years of acrimony. My people tell me there's no money left. What didn't go in legal fees was stolen by the Nazis."

Armand shook his head. "Not a surprise, but tragic."

"Yes, well, there's more. Besides the money, the Baroness left a large building in the center of Vienna."

"Yes."

"But, unlike the money, that building is real. It's still there and actually did once belong to the family. She wasn't totally delusional. It's now the head office of an international bank."

Armand nodded, but Stephen kept looking at him. Waiting for more.

"What is it?" Armand asked.

"The Nazis. There's reparation, Armand. The Austrian government is paying billions to families who can prove that the Nazis took their property. There's clear title."

"What're you saying?"

"That building's worth tens of millions. Maybe more. If the Baumgartners and Kinderoths can get together and file a joint claim, the money will be theirs."

"My God," said Armand. He was silent for a moment, thinking of the young couple in the basement apartment. "My God."

After dinner Ruth invited Stephen back to her place.

"To look at her prints," said Stephen with a gleam in his eye and a duck under his arm.

"Don't be late," said Armand. "I'll be waiting up."

"Don't," said Ruth.

Myrna had left with Clara.

"Nightcap?" asked Clara at the door to the bistro.

"No, I can't."

Clara was about to ask why not when she saw why not.

Billy Williams, all scrubbed and shaved and in nice clothes, was sitting by the fire. Two glasses of red wine and a pink tulip on the table in front of him.

"I see," said Clara.

After giving her friend a hug, she walked back to her home. Smiling and humming.

Pausing at the door, Myrna tilted her head back and looked up into the night sky. At all the dots of light shining down on her.

Then Myrna stepped forward.

ACKNOWLEDGMENTS

A funny thing happened on my way to not writing this book.

I started writing.

The truth is, I've known since I began writing *Still Life* that if Michael died, I couldn't continue with the series. Not simply because he was the inspiration for Gamache, and it would be too painful, but because he's imbued every aspect of the books. The writing, the promotion, the conferences, the travel, the tours. He was the first to read a new book, and the last to criticize. Always telling me it was great, even when the first draft was quite clearly *merde*.

We were truly partners.

How could I go on when half of me was missing? I could barely get out of bed.

I told my agent and publishers that I was taking a year off. That might have been a lie. In my heart I knew I could never write Gamache again. (And, sadly, would have to give back the next advance.)

But then, a few months later, I found myself sitting at the long pine dining table, where I always wrote. Laptop open.

And I wrote two words: Armand Gamache

Then the next day I wrote: slowed his car to a crawl

And the next day: then stopped on the snow-covered secondary road. *Kingdom of the Blind* was begun. Not with sadness. Not because I had to, but with joy. Because I wanted to.

My heart was light. Even as I wrote about some very dark themes, it was with gladness. With relief. That I get to keep doing this.

Far from leaving Michael behind, he became even more infused in the books. All the things we had together came together, in Three Pines. Love, companionship, friendship. His integrity. His courage. Laughter.

I realized, too, that the books are far more than Michael. Far more than Gamache. They're the common yearning for community. For belonging. They're about kindness, acceptance. Gratitude. They're not so much about death, as life. And the consequences of the choices we make.

Now, the publishers, wonderful people, had no idea I was writing. It wasn't until six months later that I told them. But even then, I warned them the book might not be ready in time.

My wonderful agent, Teresa Chris, and Andy Martin, my U.S. publisher with Minotaur Books, were magnificent. Telling me not to worry. To take whatever time I needed. Stop writing, if I needed.

And that was all I needed, to keep going.

And so *Kingdom of the Blind* was born. It is the child that was never going to be. But happened. My love child.

I want to thank a number of people for their patience and kindness.

My assistant, Lise, my great friend, who held my heart when it was too heavy for me.

Andy Martin, the head of Minotaur Books in the U.S. My editor, Hope Dellon, to whom this book is dedicated. Paul Hochman and Sarah Melnyk. Sally Richardson and Don Weisberg. All so much more than colleagues.

Thank you to Kelley Ragland, for leaping in where needed.

To Teresa Chris, my long-suffering and passionate agent and friend.

To Ed Wood, Kirsteen Astor, David Shelley, and all the team at Little, Brown UK.

Thank you to Louise Loiselle at Flammarion Québec, for placing the books in the hands of so many French Canadians.

Thank you, Linda Lyall in Scotland, for the great social media design, and for answering so many of the emails.

I want to thank Kirk Lawrence and Walter Marinelli, for their unwavering friendship and support. And Danny and Lucy at Brome Lake Books.

Thank you to Rocky and Steve Gottlieb for their courage in allowing me to use a story from their own lives.

Thank you to Stephen Jarislowsky, a great character himself, for being, with good humor, the inspiration for a new character.

To Troy McEachren, who helped me with a legal plot point. Where there's a will . . .

And my family. Rob and Audi. Doug and Mary. My nieces and nephews. For enveloping me in their lives. I promise not to make too much of a mess.

As I sit here, at the long pine table, writing to you, I see forests and hear birds. I see a bench inscribed with *Surprised by Joy*. Just down that path through the trees is a café, and the bookstore.

I choose to live in the beautiful little Québec village of Knowlton. For the simple reason that this is home.

I want to thank my neighbors, for their patience and kindness. For saving a place at the table for both Michael and me.

And I want to thank you. For your company.

We are very fortunate, aren't we? To have found each other in Three Pines.

1. Snow is a virtual character in this book, "both beautiful and alarming." In chapter 4, we are told, "In the countryside, winter was a gorgeous, glorious, luminous killer." What other passages about snow are particularly striking, and how does the weather affect the story?

2. There are different kinds of families in the novel, from the Baumgartners to the Gamaches to the bonds between Benedict and Katie ("Benedict wondered if he tried, really, really tried, if he could build a relationship that solid"), to the team of Armand, Jean-Guy, and Isabelle: "Her husband stayed behind in the living room, watching the three of them go. Recognizing that while he and the children would always be the most important parts of Isabelle's life, these three also formed a family." There is even the drug dealer who names the new opioid "David" after his father. What are the strengths and weaknesses of these families?

3. In what ways does Louise misdirect the reader about the actions of various characters, including Benedict, Amelia, and the Baumgartner siblings, as well as Beauvoir and his possible "betrayal" of Gamache? How does she obscure Gamache's own intentions?

4. What were your worst fears for the characters, and how satisfying did you find the resolutions of their stories?

5. A number of the characters in the story are outliers in outward appearance and/or manner, including Benedict, Katie, the notary, Hugo, Billy Williams, Gracie, and arguably Ruth. How do first impressions

line up with final ones? What conclusions, if any, can you draw about the importance of looks and behavior?

6. What are the roles of the various women in *Kingdom of the Blind*? In what ways do they meet or defy conventional expectations?

7. "You do know that the earth is round," Gamache says to his godfather at lunch, to which Stephen Horowitz replies, "The earth might be, but human nature isn't. It has caverns and abysses and all sorts of traps." What aspects of human nature do we see throughout the novel?

8. When Beauvoir visits Taylor and Ogilvy, he notes that it seems like "a play. A set. Something that looked like one thing but was actually another," with "fake originals." What kinds of authenticity are important in this story?

9. The Montréal underworld could not seem more different from the sanctuary of Three Pines, yet Amelia finds herself in "an alley off an alley off a back lane. Impossible to find, except by those who were lost. She was pretty sure it wouldn't be on any map. But once found, it was never forgotten. And probably never left." This echoes language that is customarily used to describe Three Pines. Why do you think Louise describes the two places in such similar ways?

10. "How do you do it?" Isabelle asks Gamache in chapter 11, as she struggles to recover from being shot in the head. When he responds, "Remember?" she answers, "Forget." What do you make of Gamache's story about the longhouse, where nothing can ever be expelled or hidden away?

11. Gamache also tells Isabelle, "I made mental lists and followed the things I love, the people I love, back to sanity. I still do." How does this compare with the description of Ruth's approach in chapter 9: "Ruth remembered everything. Every meal, every drink, every sight, every slight, real and imagined and manufactured. Every compliment. Every word spoken and unspoken. She retained it all, and rendered those memories into feelings and the feelings into poetry"?

12. What new relationships are forming in this book, and what do you think of them?

13. There are numerous instances in which characters are literally or figuratively blinded—by snow, by the debris from the house, by perspective (for example, consider Annie's comment in chapter 3, "Dad had no choice. But they might not see it that way," and Beauvoir's reply, "Then they're blind"). How do these relate to the book's title and the original passage from Erasmus?

14. Why does Amelia Choquet call herself "the one-eyed man"? What do you think of this "stoned former prostitute junkie who's dealing opioids in the academy" at various points in the story?

15. At the end of the novel, Myrna looks "up into the night sky. At all the dots of light shining down on her." How does this connect to "Ruth and a dot of light" in Clara's most famous painting, and what does that dot mean to you?

Jean-François Bérubé

Louise Penny is the author of #1 *New York Times* and *Globe and Mail* bestselling series of Chief Inspector Armand Gamache novels. She has won numerous awards, including a CWA Dagger and the Agatha Award (six times), and was a finalist for the Edgar Award for Best Novel. In 2017 she received the Order of Canada for her contributions to Canadian culture. Louise lives in a small village south of Montréal.

READ THE ENTIRE
CHIEF INSPECTOR GAMACHE
SERIES

AUGUST 2019

EXCLUSIVE CONTENT
FOR LOUISE PENNY'S

~

KINGDOM
OF THE
BLIND

The World of Three Pines

Rivière Bella Bella

Du Moulin

Old Stage D

Du Moulin

HADLEY MILL

LS DAVIES

When I started writing about Three Pines, and creating the characters that would populate my Armand Gamache novels, I often turned to the world around me here in the Eastern Townships of Québec. It quickly became clear to me that the setting was also a character. Three Pines came alive, not just because of the villagers but because of the places where Armand, Clara, Olivier, Gabri, Ruth, and foulmouthed Rosa and company could be found. I wish I could say I invented those places, but the truth is, they were inspired by where I live. By where I shop. Two of them, La Rumeur Affamée in the village of Sutton and Brome Lake Books in Knowlton, became the inspiration for specific shops in Three Pines—Sarah's Boulangerie and Myrna's New and Used Bookstore. One provides food for the body, the other for the mind. Both vital. Just as we love introducing friends to each other, so I want to introduce you to these places that mean so much to me. I asked their owners to tell us about them, and this is what they wrote. I hope this visit to the boulangerie and the bookshop gives you a glimpse into the world that has inspired the Gamache books.

−LOUISE PENNY, NOVEMBER 2018

LA RUMEUR AFFAMÉE

*"More people go to Sarah's Boulangerie than ever show up at
church," snapped Ruth. "They buy pastry with an instrument
of torture on it. I know you think I'm crazy, but maybe I'm the
only sane one here."*

        —*from* The Cruelest Month, *chapter one*

Nestled in the picturesque Eastern Townships of Québec lies the en-
chanting hamlet of Sutton and its acclaimed ski hill, "Mont Sutton."
La Rumeur Affamée General Store is located in the center of the village and is the meeting place for local residents, including Louise, and
tourists alike.

 Entering La Rumeur Affamée is a sensory experience. After taking
in the eye-appealing décor, our well-trained professional team members welcome you with friendly *"Bonjours"* and smiles from behind the
bread and cheese counters, but the truly exceptional greeting is from

the enticing smell of freshly baked breads, croissants, brownies, and our signature *Tarte au Sirop d'érable* (maple syrup pie).

You are immediately drawn to the original handcrafted, all-wood counters and display cases, well-used hardwood floors, and high ceilings from the 1860s that instantly make you feel like you have entered an era of times gone by.

Sutton was settled by Loyalists following the American Revolution. The Town Hall was built in 1859, and in 1861, George Henry Boright, a settler from New Hampshire, built the brick building that housed his general store, post office, and stage coach depot which La Rumeur has now occupied since 1999. It is truly the heart of the community.

In the early days, the main economy of Sutton was driven by farming, and in 1960, the Mont Sutton ski resort opened and the village has since become reliant on tourism. The town has become a popular year-round destination for its vineyards, art galleries, mountain biking, road biking, hiking, and, of course, skiing, snowboarding, and cross-country skiing.

Sutton is populated by the highest proportion of artists in Canada, hosting annual festivals such as Le Tour des Arts, the International Sculpture Symposium, and many art galleries. Sutton has historically been an English enclave in a predominantly French province. The ratio now sits at approximately 40 percent English to 60 percent French.

La Rumeur Affamée roughly translates to "The Famished Rumor." Kelly Shanahan, co-owner of La Rumeur Affamée, certainly knows how to quash that rumor by providing a vast selection of irresistible baked goods, local and international cheeses, charcuteries, sausages, locally raised duck products, delectable ready-made meals, tantalizing sandwiches, aromatic coffees, extra virgin olive oils, vinegars, mouth-watering chocolates and desserts, Québec craft beer, wine, and non-gluten and certified organic products.

Kelly has an impressive background as a foodie, having owned and operated L'Aperitif—a fine food shop in the neighboring town of Knowlton—managed a massive cheese department at Central Market in Dallas, Texas, and worked at David Woods Fine Foods' signature store in Toronto, as well as having offered cooking classes and working many years in the restaurant world.

Being a former executive in the chain restaurant business, I recognized the value of supporting my wife of thirty years in her culinary endeavors in a small-town environment. A native of Québec City, I worked in the fast-paced cities of Toronto, Vancouver, Montréal, and Dallas before accepting Kelly's challenge of a simpler life.

The Great Wall of Bread at La Rumeur awaits you with freshly baked baguettes and artisanal loaves of spelt, kamut, quinoa, flax, rye, nut, olive, and cheese. Our nongluten and nonlactose breads include quinoa, rye, raisin, and nut bread. Our chocolate orange muffins are to die for as is the selection of croissants, chocolatines, and *vienoiseries*.

Kelly says, "Although it's hard to beat the mind-boggling aroma of fresh bread, our signature maple syrup pies are the hands-down winner with our regular patrons." Fresh daily fruit pies, cookies, squares, cakes, and *sucre à la crème* round out the alluring selection of baked goods.

The fact that the town has a population of less than 4,000 defies the general store's ability to maintain a massive selection of almost 200 cheeses from around the world, including over half from Québec.

"Our 1608 cheese was crafted in 2008 in the Charlevoix region to celebrate the 400th anniversary of Québec City, the oldest city in Canada. Using raw milk from Ancien Canadien cows, of which there are less than 1,000 head left in the world, this semi-firm award-winning cheese is a huge seller," says Kelly.

Seeing the wide-eyed reaction of first-time customers as they take in the old-world charm and enticing odors of our 1860s-style general store is reward enough for the lovingly hard work we put in daily.

It is easy to see why Louise Penny drew inspiration from this jewel in the Eastern Townships for the local boulangerie in her best-selling novels. The joie de vivre is alive and well at La Rumeur and chances are you might spot L'inspecteur Gamache sampling one of our many Québec craft beers, remarking *c'est si bon* the next time you drop in.

—WAYNE SHANAHAN, CO-OWNER, LA RUMEUR AFFAMÉE

Sutton is located six miles north of Vermont, one hour southeast of Montréal, four hours northwest of Boston, and six hours north of New York City. La Rumeur Affamée, 15 Principal North, contact: 450-538-5516 or find us on Facebook.

BROME LAKE BOOKS

"You feel you're letting down a friend," said Reine-Marie.
   "Partly, but I run a bookstore," said Myrna, *looking at the
row upon row of books, lining the walls and creating corridors in
the open space.*

— *from* The Nature of the Beast, *chapter four*

*So often, a visit to a bookshop has cheered me, and reminded me
that there are good things in the world.*

—Vincent van Gogh

Founded in 1998, Brome Lake Books is a little village bookstore with
a lovingly curated collection of new titles and old favorites for the discerning booklover. Local authors and books on the area are featured

in their own sections. Wooden shelves made by a local craftsman line the walls. Lower units in the middle of the room are fitted with casters for smooth movement along the wide plank pine floors (you do have to be prepared for those impromptu dance parties). The high tin ceiling and a large wall of Victorian windows overlook the park and the mill pond in the heart of the Loyalist village of Knowlton.

Originally a farming area, the natural beauty of the townships soon attracted wealthy families escaping the city heat who came to build lavish summer homes along the shores of Lac Brome. More recently the area has become a hub for visual artists who have set up home studios and art circuits. Wineries and local breweries have sprung up and the bookstore reflects this diverse and eclectic community. Classic story books for the grandchildren visiting for the summer, *New York Times* bestsellers for the young professionals, edgy crime thrillers for the brooding artists, and lots of beautiful photographic books to spark the imagination of them all.

A reading area is dedicated to Louise Penny with a little woodstove and three pine tree–shaped shelves to display Louise's books, Three Pines café-au-lait mugs, F.I.N.E. T-shirts, and a decanter of licorice pipes. On the wall is a framed copy of the Three Pines inspirational map. A braided rug made by a friend's mother along with two cozy armchairs and a little coffee table complete the area. Lining the top of the bookshelves are samples of Louise Penny's books in various languages.

On most days my wife, Lucy Hoblyn, and I may be found puttering around the store. We walk in to work early with our Portuguese sheepdog, Watson, or the "big hairy carpet," as he is often called. Watson is the official greeter at Brome Lake Books and he has many friends that stop by for a friendly wag. Our three boys, Angus, Adam, and Benjamin, have all grown up with the bookstore and have inherited a love of reading—the very best gift a parent can give.

In May of this year, Brome Lake Books moved into a building across the street and we were overwhelmed by all the generous help that we received. Thirty-five friends, neighbors, and customers turned up to carry boxes and boxes of books and heavy shelves. A local book club prepared a sumptuous picnic lunch for all of us to share. One of

the happy helpers was none other than Louise Penny herself. Everyone was smiling and jovial and then someone starting singing their A-B-C's as it helped put the books in alphabetical order. It was a very Three Pines day.

One of the great pleasures at Brome Lake Books is having the chance to meet and correspond with the many fans of Louise Penny. Whether it be Arleen from Texas, Diana from Nova Scotia, or Andrea from Australia, Louise always has the best fans. Louise inspires us to be kind, caring, and thoughtful people. Her books are more about love and community than murder, more about art, poetry, and food than crime. More about living than dying. *Vive Gamache, vive Louise!*

–DANNY MCAULEY, CO-OWNER, BROME LAKE BOOKS